Love Be Mine

ALSO BY
SHIRLEE BUSBEE

Lovers Forever

A Heart for the Taking

Love Be Mine

Shirlee Busbee

WARNER BOOKS

A Time Warner Company

Cover photo by Franco Accornero
Hand lettering by David Gatti

Warner Books, Inc.
1271 Avenue of the Americas
New York, NY 10020

Visit our Web site at
http://warnerbooks.com

 A Time Warner Company

Printed in the United States of America

ISBN: 0-7394-0054-1

To more dear friends and fine companions.

PHELPS and PATTY DEWEY, who gave us a succinct explanation of the "jerk" factor in the publishing business and especially, dear, *dear* Patty, who always strokes my ego!

AND

JEFF and LINDA CARTER, long-lost relatives, the kind that you are delighted and pleased to discover and are *really* happy to claim.

And, my one and only, HOWARD.

Chapter One

"Merci! What do you mean, he is moving *here*? Surely you have misread the letter, *Maman*?"

Lisette Dupree sent her daughter a reproving look. "I assure you, *petite*, that I did not make a mistake. Hugh Lancaster states quite clearly that he is moving to the New Orleans area just as soon as he is able to put his business affairs in Natchez in order. Here, read the letter yourself."

Somewhat gingerly, almost as if she expected it to bite her, Micaela Dupree took the letter from her mother. She sighed heavily as she read the offending document. "It is true," she said gloomily. "He is moving here."

The two women were seated side by side on a delicate settee covered in a worn blue velvet in a small room at the rear of the Dupree town house in New Orleans. It was midmorning on a cool, wet Monday in late February of 1804 and the two ladies had been enjoying a cup of chicory-laden coffee when the letter from Hugh Lancaster had been delivered.

The arrival of a letter had been unusual enough to add some excitement to a dull day, but the news it brought had totally destroyed their pleasant mood as they sipped their coffee and chatted comfortably with each other.

Micaela's lovely dark eyes were troubled as she looked at her mother. "François," she said slowly, referring to her brother, a year younger than she, "is going to be most disturbed by this news."

Lisette nodded. "And your *oncle* Jean, too."

The two women sighed almost simultaneously. Their resemblance to each other was obvious. Only a few weeks away from her twenty-first birthday, Micaela was in the full power of her undeniable beauty, while Lisette, having turned thirty-eight just the previous month, was a fetchingly mature version of her only daughter. They did not look precisely alike; Micaela's nose was longer than her mother's charmingly retroussé affair, her brows thicker and more noticeably arched, and her mouth was more lavishly formed, with a decidedly saucy curve to it. Both women were small-boned, although Micaela, much to her chagrin, stood three inches taller than her petite mother. The shapes under their simple muslin gowns were curvaceous, with full bosoms, narrow waists, and generously rounded hips. The celebrated creamy matte complexion which each possessed contrasted enchantingly with their gleaming blue-black hair and long-lashed midnight black eyes. With lips as red as cherries, pale lovely skin, and flashing ebony glances, their proud Creole blood was very evident.

"What are we going to do?" Micaela asked as she handed the letter back to Lisette.

Lisette shrugged. "There is nothing that we *can* do— the *Américain* is coming to live in New Orleans— whether we like it or not."

Micaela stood up and took several agitated steps around the pleasantly shabby little room. Stopping to look out the window at the rain-splattered courtyard, she said moodily, "If only that arrogant creature Napoléon had not seen fit to sell us to the *Américains* like a shipload of fish! I still cannot believe that it is done—that we are now to call ourselves *Américains*. Unthinkable! We are French! Creoles!"

Though it had been over seven months since the inhabitants of New Orleans had heard of the sale of the entire Louisiana Territory to the fledgling United States, the actual exchange had taken place barely two months before in the waning days of 1803.

It was not fair, Micaela thought unhappily, to be sold to those rude, overbearing Americans on the whim of an upstart Corsican general who now had the gall to name himself Emperor of the French!

The local population almost unanimously resented the presence of the new owners of the Territory, many unwilling to even speak to one of those cursed *Américains*, their wives often refusing to have them in their homes. Of course, the Americans reciprocated the feeling in full measure, convinced that the Creoles were lazy, vain, and frivolous. Each faction regarded the other with loathing, suspicion, and mistrust.

Micaela's mouth twisted. And Hugh Lancaster, one of those despised *Américains*, was going to make the Dupree family painfully aware of just how much had changed since the Territory had become American. Her brother and her uncle were going to be livid.

"I wonder," Micaela said softly, "why *Monsieur* Lancaster wrote to you and not *Oncle* Jean? Should not *mon oncle* have been notified first?"

Lisette looked uncomfortable. "Your *oncle* has not been very—ah—pleasant to *Monsieur* Lancaster those times when he has come to the city on business. I assume he thought that I would view his intentions more kindly."

Micaela glanced at her mother. "Do you?"

Lisette became extremely interested in the fabric of her gown. "Not exactly . . ." A rosy hue blooming in her cheeks, she murmured, "I-I-I have never held the Americans in quite the aversion that everyone else does." Meeting her daughter's astonished gaze, she added firmly, "I actually liked young Hugh the few times I have met him—he-he seems a personable young man."

"But *Maman*! He will ruin us! You know that he believes that someone is stealing from the company. You know that the last time he was here, he almost as good as accused *mon oncle* of outright thievery—François, too—do not forget that!"

"I have not forgotten—and he did not accuse Jean—Jean took offense and merely interpreted his questions that way. I think that Hugh is mistaken, however, in his belief that someone in the company is cleverly stealing from it, but I do not blame him for being concerned. Something is obviously amiss. The profits of Galland, Lancaster and Dupree have been falling for the past eighteen months, alarmingly so in recent months, and the report that we received in September, when Hugh was last here, makes it clear that *something* must be done—and soon! In all the years that we have been in partnership with Hugh's stepfather, John, we have never suffered a decline in profits like we have recently."

"You mean since *Papa* and *grand-père* died and Jean and François have been overseeing the family import-export business, do you not?" Micaela demanded.

"Your grandfather died over two years ago," Lisette gently reminded Micaela. "Your father has been dead for five, and Jean has been handling Renault's share of the business for you and François since that time. Do you suspect your *oncle* of doing something to harm his own fortune, as well as yours and François's?" She arched a brow and then went on calmly, "As for your brother . . ." An indulgent smile crossed her face. "I know he is young, just turned twenty, and he is spoiled, I will not deny it. But he will grow up into a fine man—he only needs time. Do you really think that François would do anything to harm the firm his own father and grandfather founded? Do you truly think that he would steal from himself?"

Micaela made a face, trying to think of a tactful way to tell her mother that François was more than just spoiled. He was, Micaela thought unhappily, *extremely* spoiled. His father's only son and heir, and presently his uncle's heir, too, from birth François had been pampered and doted upon by everyone. Her charming, handsome brother was not selfish by nature, Micaela admitted fairly—he could be quite generous and thoughtful— when the whim struck him. She sighed. Perhaps *Maman* was right—he was simply young and in time would be more responsible than he appeared to be now.

As if her thoughts had conjured him up, François strolled into the room with a merry smile upon his delicately handsome features. He was a slim, elegant young man, not more than an inch taller than his sister, and was fashionably garbed in a form-fitting jacket of Spanish Blue cloth with a striped Marseilles waistcoat above his nankeen breeches and boots. His black hair gleamed in the light of the candles, which had been lit because of the gray day, and his dark eyes were warm as they fell upon the two women. Approaching Lisette with his quick light stride, he bent down and exuberantly kissed her on both cheeks. "Ah, *Maman!* You grow lovelier every day. I am a fortunate son, to have such a beautiful and charming *maman!*"

Lisette smiled and caressed his cheek. "Such gallantry, so early in the morning, *mon amour!* I suspect that there is a fine new horse that you simply *must* have—or is it a new carriage?" The fondness of her expression took any sting out of the words.

François laughed without embarrassment. "Ah. *Maman*—you know me too well! Which does not mean that I do not truly think you beautiful and charming."

Glancing across to Micaela, he said, "*Bonjour*, Caela, you are also looking extremely becoming today."

Micaela cocked a brow at his fulsome manner and wasn't the least surprised at the hint of color which leaped into his cheeks at her expression. Turning hurriedly back to Lisette, he sat down gracefully beside her and took one of her hands in his. He said in a coaxing voice, "*Maman*, there *is* a horse . . . a most handsome animal I assure you, and the cost will not be too dear."

Involuntarily Micaela made a vexed sound. "Have you run through your allowance already—gambled it away?" she asked quietly.

"It is none of your affair," he said haughtily. Then he spoiled the effect by demanding, "What difference is it to you? I am a man now, and my money is mine to spend as I see fit."

"Perhaps if you would spend it more wisely, you would not have to come begging to *Maman* to buy you a new horse!" Micaela snapped before she could stop herself.

A scowl marred François's handsome features, and a hot retort hovered on his lips.

"Children!" Lisette said hastily. "That is enough! The

day is unpleasant enough without the two of you squabbling."

Micaela made a face and turned away to stare out the window once more. It was senseless to try to convince François that the Duprees were not as wealthy as they once had been. They were not poor. *Merci, non!* But they no longer commanded a fortune that was so large that it seemed endless. Her father's and her grandfather's gambling habits had seen to that.

Because of Christophe's gaming losses, a pair of outsiders, Jasper De Marco and Alain Husson, now possessed an interest in the family firm, although quite small, a mere three percent and two percent respectively. Unfortunately it appeared that François had inherited the fatal trait. It did not help that François hung on Husson's every word and deed and tried to emulate his much-admired older friend. Husson might be a family acquaintance of long standing, but there was no denying that he was also a reckless, inveterate gambler, with a handsome fortune to finance his vices.

Regrettably, François could not seem to be brought to understand that, unlike his friend, he could not game away a small fortune night after night and still be able to live in the grand manner in which they had in the past. And *Maman*, she thought, half-annoyed, half-tenderly, cannot seem to understand that it is doing François no good for her to continue to buy him whatever strikes his fancy as had been done since he was a child! Another horse! Why there must be a half dozen or so eating their heads off in the Dupree stables at this very moment—and those were only the horses in the city!

Closing her ears to François's wheedling voice, Micaela stared unseeing down at the wet courtyard. She already knew how this little tête-à-tête was going to end—François would get his horse. A rueful smile suddenly curved her mouth. She did not know why she resented François's actions so very much—*Maman* would do the same for her if she expressed a yearning for a new gown, or even a new horse, no matter how outrageously expensive.

Telling herself that there was nothing she could do about François's spendthrift habits, she turned her thoughts to the disturbing letter announcing Hugh Lancaster's imminent arrival in the city. Lisette had met him a few times previously, but Micaela had not—not until this past September, when Jean had reluctantly invited Lancaster to dine and stay the night at Riverbend, the family plantation, which was some miles below New Orleans. Even now, several months later, she could still feel the powerful jolt of awareness that had gone through her when Hugh Lancaster, a tall, powerfully built man of thirty, had politely bent over her hand and brushed his lips across her suddenly sensitized flesh, his cool, gray-eyed glance moving quickly past her.

Micaela, though unmarried at an age when most Creole daughters were already wives and mothers of many years, was not used to personable, handsome men looking at her in a dismissing manner. Almost without fail, there was a glint of admiration in their eyes when they met her, and, without being vain, she had expected no less from Hugh Lancaster. That he had seemed utterly indifferent to her had been something of a shock, especially when she saw the charming manner with which he had greeted and conversed with Lisette. Of course, Lisette had been clearly pleased to see him, while the remainder of the family, including Micaela, had been stiff and icily polite.

Micaela had told herself repeatedly that it did not matter that Hugh Lancaster did not hold her in high esteem—after all, he was an *Américain*. What did she care for his opinion of her?

Only to herself would she admit that the tall, broad-shouldered *Américain* had, despite her will to the contrary, piqued her interest. He was very different from the Creole gentlemen whom she had known all her life, although, with his black hair and olive complexion, he had the look of the Creole—especially those of Spanish blood. Whether it was his commanding height, for at six feet he towered over all of the Duprees, or the startling impact of those thickly lashed gray eyes in that dark face, or the cool, precise way he talked compared to the excited volubility of her relatives, she couldn't tell. But something about him awoke an odd feeling within her—a feeling that none of her many Creole suitors had ever aroused—and it frightened her. She scowled, suddenly angry at herself. *Zut!* She did *not* want to think about Hugh Lancaster!

Micaela had not been paying attention to the conversation between Lisette and François, but the moment she heard him exclaim, "*Mon Dieu*! You are not serious!" she knew *Maman* had told him of Hugh's plan to move to New Orleans.

Micaela swung around and watched his face as he finished reading the letter, all signs of his merry smile and light mood vanished. His face pale with outrage, he glanced toward Lisette. "Why did he write to you? Does the swine have no manners? It is to *mon oncle* that he should have imparted this news."

Seeing that her mother was groping for a tactful way to explain the probable reasons for Hugh's actions, Micaela said swiftly, "It does not matter to whom he has written—

all that matters is that he is determined to move to New Orleans within the next few months.

François jumped up from the settee. "I will not have that overbearing *Américain* snooping in our business! From the very beginning the Duprees and our grandfather Galland have always controlled this end of the partnership—without interference from the Lancasters. I will not have it! *Sacrebleu!* To have him looking over our shoulders all the time, prying and questioning everything we do. It is insupportable!"

Micaela said nothing, merely watching as her brother raged about the room, his handsome features tight with anger. She did not blame him—there was a certain amount of truth in what he said.

In the very early 1780's when Christophe Galland, John Lancaster, and Renault and Jean Dupree had formed the import-export firm of Galland, Lancaster and Dupree, it had been decided, as François had said, that the Galland and Dupree partners would handle all the affairs in New Orleans. This had been agreed upon simply because they were residents and could deal with the local officials, the overtly suspicious Spaniards—something that John Lancaster, as an American, could not.

John Lancaster might have originally owned fifty-five percent of the new partnership, but without Christophe Galland and the Dupree brothers he would not have been able to do business freely in New Orleans, and so he had wisely given the Creole partners carte blanche there. But it was Lancaster, headquartered upriver in Natchez, who procured the majority of the raw products which were barged down the Mississippi River to New Orleans and which were loaded onto the ships for export. It was Lancaster, too, who dispersed most of the goods the firm imported from Europe to eager American buyers. For nearly twenty years, it had been a *very* profitable partnership and it had worked exceedingly well, because Lancaster astutely stayed in Natchez and, with scant interference, let the Creole faction run the New Orleans end. But apparently that was about to change.

Three years ago John Lancaster, thinking to retire, had sold Hugh a forty-five percent interest in the partnership, retaining only a ten percent interest for himself. Hugh had acted as his stepfather's agent for a number of years prior to the sale and already had a keen understanding of the business—at least the Natchez end of things. But since then, with increasing frequency, he had been asking many pointed questions about the affairs of the New Orleans portion of the business. Considering that Hugh was now the largest single shareholder, his deepening interest was justified, but both Micaela's grandfather and uncle had been highly affronted by his actions. And while she had listened to them rail against what they claimed to be Hugh's unwarranted intervention in affairs none of his business, she had privately thought his visits and queries not exactly *un*reasonable—annoying and irritating, perhaps, but not totally without justification.

Her grandfather's death, however, seemed to have engendered in Hugh Lancaster an acute concern about the future of the partnership. Micaela suspected that it was because of the ill-disguised hostility which existed between Hugh and Jean. Christophe Galland had acted as a buffer between the two younger men, but his death had forced the pair of them to deal directly with each other.

As his only child, Lisette had inherited Christophe's remaining shares. Not inclined toward business herself, she had asked her brother-in-law to handle her shares, just as he did his brother's for François and Micaela. John Lancaster preferred to let Hugh run things these days.

Since the shares owned by De Marco and Husson were nominal, and their dabbling in the business was perfunctory, Hugh and Jean, as the two active principals, were almost continually at odds. The situation between Hugh and Jean, however, was a most uncomfortable state of affairs—especially when coupled with the general animosity shared by most Creoles for Americans. An animosity that was now further exacerbated by the sale of the Louisiana Territory to those same despised Americans.

Growing weary of François's tiresome tirade against the American, she glanced at him and commented, "François, you are beginning to repeat yourself. I think that you have made your feelings about *Monsieur* Lancaster quite clear to both *Maman* and me. Obviously, you are not happy at the prospect of *Monsieur* Lancaster living in the area, but there is nothing that *Maman* and I can do about it—I suggest that you take your views to *Monsieur* Lancaster."

"Bah! What good would that do? He will look down that long nose of his and ignore me! I tell you, *Maman*, there will be trouble once he starts his snooping and prying."

The two women exchanged glances, a faint frown marring Lisette's forehead.

François looked from one woman to the other. He drew himself up stiffly. "You think that I would challenge Hugh Lancaster to a duel, *oui*?" Fierce pride glittering in his dark eyes, he spat, "You have nothing to fear—I would not sully my hands fighting with an *Américain*!"

"That is very high-minded of you," Lisette said gently, "but if you do not wish to provoke a quarrel with him inadvertently, I would suggest that you, if not graciously, at least politely, accept the fact that he *is* moving to New Orleans."

François grimaced. Sending a sheepish grin to both women, he muttered, "I have been acting rather a fool, have I not?"

Micaela smiled warmly back at him. François's mercurial moods were one of his charms. A teasing gleam in her eyes, she said lightly, "Since I do not intend to risk another display such as we have just seen, I shall not answer that question."

François laughed, and, bowing to first one and then the other, he said, "Forgive me! I let my vile temper rule me."

"There is nothing to forgive, *mon fils*," Lisette said fondly. "It is understandable that you would be upset by the news, but we must accept the fact that Hugh Lancaster will be living in the city and that he will, no doubt, be taking an even more active interest in the business."

François sat down once more by his mother. Shaking his head, he said wryly, "Well, if you think that I took the news badly, *mon Dieu*! I do not even want to consider how *mon oncle* will take it. We should be grateful that he is out of the city until tomorrow. At least we will not have to face his rage today."

It happened that the family had more of a respite than twenty-four hours before having to face Jean's expected displeasure at their news. He had been due back from Riverbend the next day, but that very afternoon a servant appeared with a note from him, informing François that it would be three days hence, on Thursday, before he returned. By tacit agreement no one sent a return message to him revealing Hugh Lancaster's intentions.

On Friday morning, they were still at breakfast, seated around a small table, considering how to break the news of Hugh's unsettling plans to Jean, when the door to the pleasant room was suddenly flung open. His dark eyes blazing, his normally even features twisted with outrage, Jean Dupree burst into the room. "Do you know," he demanded in savage accents, "who just walked up to me on Chartres Street? *Hugh Lancaster!*"

Chapter Two

Stripping off his gloves, Jean tossed them onto a mahogany sideboard and continued in angry tones, "He apparently just stepped off a barge from Natchez this
morning, and he informed me with that arrogant smile of
his, damn his eyes! that this is to be no mere visit—he intends to take up residence here!"

Slinging his high-crowned hat onto a nearby chair, he
ran agitated fingers through his abundant black hair.
"*Mon Dieu*! We will never be rid of him—he will hover
unceasingly over our shoulders like a harbinger of doom,
asking endless questions, insisting on answers I do not
have! I am only glad that Renault and Christophe did not
live to see this day!"

Micaela caught her breath. "He is here *already*? But
his letter telling *Maman* of this news only arrived a few
days ago. He wrote that it would be months before he
came to New Orleans. How can he be here today?"

"Letter? What letter?" Jean inquired sharply, his black
eyes flashing as he glanced at Lisette. "And why was I
not told of it?"

"You were out of the city," François said, "and we did

not wish to spoil your trip with this unfortunate business."

"Spoil my trip?" Jean gave an ugly laugh. "Our *lives* are spoiled!"

Lisette motioned him to take a seat near her, and murmured, "Oh come, now, Jean, it is not that bad. You are putting too dramatic a face, as you usually do, on something which will not affect us all that much. Here now, have some coffee, and I shall ring Antoine to bring you some freshly fried beignets from the kitchen."

Jean grimaced but did as his sister-in-law requested. They had known each other a long time and they were of an age—Jean had turned thirty-seven this past December. It was natural that they were used to each other's moods.

Unlike the punctilious politeness he showed Lisette, Jean had always been fondly indulgent and generous to both Micaela and François—often more so than Renault. After their father had died, Jean had deftly stepped into Renault's shoes. Since he had not yet married and set up his own home, he had always lived with them at Riverbend, which was half his anyway, although he did have his own comfortable quarters a mile downriver from the big house. In town, on Bienville Street, he also kept his own suite of rooms, but he had run tame through their various households ever since Micaela could remember. The polite restraint between Lisette and Jean vaguely troubled Micaela although she knew that her mother relied upon Jean and trusted him—otherwise, she would not have left her affairs in his hands.

Antoine, their mulatto house servant, answered Lisette's ring almost immediately. "Some more of Marie's beignets for *Monsieur* Jean, *s'il vous plaît*, Antoine. Oh, and we shall need some more hot milk and fresh chocolate and coffee."

As soon as the door shut behind Antoine, Jean looked at Lisette, and said sourly, "So, *soeurette*, tell me of this letter."

Lisette made a face. "On Monday, I received a letter from *Monsieur* Hugh, telling me that he planned on moving here."

"Why did he write to you?" Jean demanded moodily. "He should have written to me—not involved the women of my family."

With an edge to her voice, Lisette said, "It was a very polite letter, and since you usually look like you are suffering from a stomach ache whenever you are in his presence, I am not surprised that he wrote to me. I am at least pleasant to him!"

Jean's lip lifted in a sneer. "Pleasant? I think softheaded would be more like it—as usual, in the presence of a wealthy Américain!"

François sprang to his feet, his hand instinctively going to the place where he would normally be wearing a small sword cane. "*Sacrebleu!* How dare you insult *Maman* so!" he declared hotly, his features flushed with quick anger.

Jean rolled his eyes. Settling back more comfortably in his chair, he said wearily, "Oh, sit down, you young fool—I have no intention of meeting my own nephew on the field of honor, and I meant no insult to your *maman*. I am merely furious and out of sorts at this unexpected turn of events." Sending Lisette an apologetic smile, he asked, "Having vented most of my spleen, may I now, please, see the letter?"

Lisette nodded. "When Antoine returns with your beignets, I shall send him to my rooms for it."

There was desultory conversation among the four of them until Antoine arrived with a tray heaped high with sugary beignets, steaming milk, and a pot each of fresh chocolate and coffee. Hearing Lisette's request, he bowed and departed, returning shortly with Hugh's letter.

Sipping his coffee, Jean read the letter in silence. Laying it down near his untouched beignets, he muttered, "*Mon Dieu*! It is really true! He really is here—and means to stay."

"What are we going to do about it?" François demanded, leaning forward, the light of battle in his expressive eyes.

Jean shrugged. "There is nothing that we can do, *mon fils*. The territory is now *Américain*, we cannot prevent him from moving here."

Uncertainly, Micaela asked, "But will it really be so very bad? He *is* one of the partners, and you have dealt with him for years. His living here in the city should not change things very much."

François curled a scornful lip. "It is easy for you to say—you do not have to meet him or even speak to him, but we"—he nodded toward Jean—"do not share that same happy state of affairs. We will have to face his arrogant ways almost every day."

Rising gracefully to her feet, Lisette said calmly, "I think that all of you are making far too much of this development. As Micaela said, you have been dealing with Hugh Lancaster for years; he is one of the partners, the partner with the largest share in the business, I might add, and his living here should not change a thing. Why do you not try working with him for once, instead of immediately assuming that he is trying to discredit you or destroy the company?"

"Because he *is* trying to do just that," Jean said gloomily. "He is blaming us for the drop in profits, accusing me of not paying close enough attention to what is going on. He does not hesitate to tell me that I am a careless and inept businessman. *Mon Dieu*! The overweening conceit of the man!"

Lisette sent him a cynical glance, and Jean moved restively under her look. Like most wealthy Creoles, the Duprees did not actually soil their hands in the day-to-day running of Galland, Lancaster and Dupree—they employed others to do that tiresome task. Instead, they mostly just cast an intelligent, if erratic, eye over the firm which bore their names and it was no wonder that Lisette looked at him so.

She said nothing to Jean, however, merely glanced at Micaela and murmured, "Come, *petite*, I had thought that since it is a fairly pleasant day we should visit the dressmaker and see if she has some new materials which might interest us."

A little silence fell after the two women left the room. Jean finished his cup of coffee before saying glumly, "That damned *Américain*! I do not want him here! I wish to God that we had never formed this cursed partnership with John Lancaster!"

"But it is not John Lancaster who is causing us so much trouble," François said fairly. "It is his stepson."

"Do not remind me," Jean muttered. "To think that we shall be tripping over Hugh Lancaster everywhere we go in the city. It is enough to make me bilious! And as for having him constantly underfoot at our place of business, always asking questions and demanding to know why such and such is done a certain way . . ." Jean shook his head, unable to complete the terrible thought.

Well aware of how Jean Dupree felt about him, Hugh Lancaster, with a rueful smile, had watched him stalk away down Chartres Street after their unexpected meeting. He had not intended to arrive in New Orleans so soon after his letter announcing his plans, but having made up his mind to move to the area, it had seemed useless to wait. By May, early June, most of Creole society would have departed the city for their plantations and when summer arrived, and with it the fever season, New Orleans would be deserted except for those poor souls who had to remain within the city. Consequently, after a brief consultation with his stepfather, and another determined attempt to convince the older man to join him, Hugh had wasted little time. Not three days after he had sent his letter to Lisette Dupree, he was stepping on a barge sailing for New Orleans. Beyond personal effects, Hugh had brought little with him—once he reached his destination and had found suitable quarters he planned to buy any furnishings or household items he might need.

Strolling down the street in the direction opposite that taken by Jean, Hugh decided that he wasn't sorry at the unexpected meeting. The Duprees had to learn of his presence in the city soon enough, and getting it out of the way in this fashion saved him from making a formal call on the family. A twinge of regret nudged him. He would have, he admitted with amusement, enjoyed watching Micaela Dupree's magnificent dark eyes sparkle with disdain when she learned who was actually in her home, but it seemed that pleasure was to be denied him. Ah well, there were bound to be other opportunities to bring that delightful expression of smelling offal to her pretty face.

Chuckling to himself, he walked into a coffee shop and looked around for a familiar face. The place was full of Creole gentlemen sitting around several tables leisurely drinking coffee and smoking long black cheroots, their canes and gloves lying on the polished tops of the tables. The rhythmic sounds of the French tongue came to his ears, as did the intoxicating odor of freshly brewed coffee mingled with the scent of fine tobacco.

There was, he decided pleasurably, no place like a coffeehouse in New Orleans. Spotting a lively profile he knew very well, Hugh made his way in that direction, aware of the slight cessation in noise as he sauntered across the room and aware, too, that every eye was on him.

Hugh did not make it completely to his destination before his target, a tall elegant gentleman about his own age, glanced over to see what had caused the fluctuation in the various conversations and, spying him, sprang to his feet with a wide smile and a glad cry. "*Mon ami!*" Jasper De Marco exclaimed gaily. "You have arrived so soon! I did not expect you for months, yet. Tell me, all is well with your step-*papa*? It is not bad news that brings you to our fair city so early?"

Giving Hugh no chance to reply, Jasper grasped his shoulders and kissed him exuberantly on both cheeks. Well used to the affectionate French greeting, Hugh returned it and said with a twinkle in his gray eyes, "*Bonjour, mon ami.* I see that you are, as usual, wasting away the time when you could be helping me toward our mutual goal."

Jasper managed to look mournful, despite the teasing gleam in his dark eyes. "Ah, *mon ami*, I must take you in hand and teach you that there is much more to life than work, work, work. You Americans, business is all you think about."

Allowing Jasper to urge him toward a seat, Hugh murmured, "And you Creoles, all you think about is pleasure!"

"*Oui!* And which one of us enjoys life more? Hmm?" Jasper retorted with a grin.

Hugh laughed and shook his head. "You will not catch me arguing with you on that one."

Hugh and Jasper had known each other for nearly ten years—ever since Hugh's first visit to New Orleans. They had gotten into a hot disagreement about the charms of a certain lovely quadroon and had immediately proceeded to retire, with their less-than-sober seconds, to the dueling field beneath the oaks. Fortunately, the two principals were both more than a little drunk themselves and were both equally expert with the sword. Despite the heat of the moment and the Madeira fumes in their brains, they were impressed with each other's skill and instead of killing each other, as they had sworn vehemently to do, they had left the field of honor as brothers under the skin and had ended the night in Jasper's town house. Even in the morning, when the Madeira fumes had faded, each discovered that he had not been mistaken in his estimation of the other, and their friendship was sealed that very morning over several cups of hot coffee.

Few Creoles would even acknowledge an American, much less befriend one, but Jasper De Marco, the only son of a great French heiress and a major Spanish official, cared nothing for a man's nationality. Hugh had proven himself to Jasper's satisfaction to be an honorable man. Besides, as he told his friends and family with a teasing sparkle in his dark eyes, he did not want to be enemies with a man who was nearly as good as he with a sword!

Once Hugh had been served his coffee and Jasper's cup had been refilled, the two men talked idly for a few minutes. Replying fluently in French to Jasper's questions, not for the first time, Hugh silently thanked his stepfather for insisting he learn the language. From the moment Hugh had first expressed an interest in joining Galland, Lancaster and Dupree when he had been a youth of sixteen, John had been adamant that he learn French—otherwise, his stepfather explained, he would be always at a disadvantage when dealing with the partners in New Orleans. And thinking of the many sharp exchanges he'd had with Jean Dupree, Hugh had to agree fervently with his stepfather.

"Now what, *mon ami*, brings that look to your face?" Jasper asked suddenly.

Hugh grimaced. "I was merely thinking of our good friend, Jean Dupree."

"Ah, yes, our esteemed partner. I wonder how he is going to take the news that you are moving to New Orleans."

"Badly," Hugh said with a grin. "I met him on my way here and informed him that I intended to become a permanent resident. He was *not* pleased."

Jasper laughed. "If only I could have been there!"

The two men were vastly different in temperament; Hugh, normally thoughtful and carefully controlled; Jasper, hotheaded and reckless, but together they made an effective team. Less than a year in age separated them: Hugh would turn thirty-one in April, while Jasper had turned thirty-one the previous August. They both had black hair and were dark-complected, but any similarity ended there. Hugh was built like a powerful oak to Jasper's graceful beech, although their heights were nearly identical. Both had compelling eyes—Hugh's being a pale, striking gray; Jasper's a gleaming black with a sleepy cast to them which, like Hugh's deceptively lazy glances, masked an agile brain. They were a very handsome pair, but again very different; Hugh's features were far more craggy, his black brows heavier, his nose bolder, and his jaw more stubborn than Jasper's more chiseled profile. But if they were very different in looks and personality, there were some things that they shared; each had lost his parents at a young age and had been raised by another relative—in Hugh's case, his stepfather, and in Jasper's, an uncle—it was a bond between them. They were both wealthy and used to arranging events to suit themselves, and they took great delight in testing their wits against each other.

Pushing aside his coffee, Hugh asked abruptly, "Have you been able to discover anything?"

"No, *mon ami*, I have not," Jasper replied disgustedly. "Though I have wasted much time and charm in ingratiating myself with one of the bookkeepers, a young man by the name of Etienne Gras, it has done me little good." He grimaced. "The three percent that I won from old Christophe Galland just before he died does not give me much power—and Jean has given orders that while everyone is to be polite and helpful to me, they are not to answer my questions—*he* will answer them. The Duprees tend to think of the business as solely theirs. They conveniently forget it is only *partly* owned by them."

Hugh smiled grimly. "It will be interesting to see if *Monsieur* Jean will try to keep *me* from getting answers to my questions."

"Now that is one confrontation that I must insist you put off until I can be there to see the expression on his face."

"I shall try my best," Hugh replied lightly. "But tell me, since I have arrived long before you expected me, can you recommend a place for me to stay until I can find permanent quarters?"

"You will, of course, stay with me," Jasper answered promptly. "Until you find a place that you wish to buy, it is nonsense for you to reside anywhere else—my home is yours, you know that, *mon ami*."

Hugh dipped his head in acknowledgment. "If you are certain it will not be an inconvenience, I will gladly accept your invitation."

"Inconvenient? I shall be happy of company—my home was built for a large family and there are only myself and my servants rattling around in it."

"So when, my friend, are you going to do your duty and find a wife and start producing the next generation of De Marcos to fill up your empty house?" Hugh asked with a teasing glint in his eyes.

"Ah, I am waiting for you to sample the waters first! I wish to see how you survive domestication before I attempt it."

Hugh looked thoughtful. "Then you should start counting your days of freedom."

"What! Do not tell me that you are getting married!" Jasper exclaimed, clearly dismayed.

Hugh shrugged. "I am thinking seriously of it. As my stepfather reminded me, I am his only heir, and he is not a young man any longer—he would like to see me settled and with children of my own before he dies."

"I do not believe my ears! Surely you are jesting?"

"No, unfortunately, I am not. I believe that it is time for me to find a wife and, God willing, beget some heirs for my stepfather."

With great trepidation, Jasper asked, "And have you decided upon your choice of a bride?"

The image of Micaela Dupree flashed unexpectedly across Hugh's brain, but he shook himself irritably and murmured, "There is a young American woman, Miss Alice Summerfield—I knew her and her family in Natchez, but she has recently moved to New Orleans. Her father is on Governor Claiborne's staff, and I think she would do well enough."

Jasper looked offended. "Do well enough!" he spat the words out. "Listen to yourself, *mon ami*! Do well enough. *Non. Non!*"

"Now why are you so upset?" Hugh asked with lazy amusement. "Do not you Creoles have arranged marriages? Is it not true that, in most cases, bride and groom have not laid eyes on each other a half a dozen times before they are wed? Do not tell me you expect to marry for love?"

"My parents had just such an arranged marriage of which you speak," Jasper admitted bitterly. "And they fought like a cat and a dog tied together in a sack. I was almost relieved when they died of the fever—at least I did not have to listen to their battles anymore."

"I am sorry," Hugh said quietly. "I had forgotten—I did not mean to make light of the situation."

Jasper flashed his ready smile. "It happened a long time ago, *mon ami*, but I would not like to see you married to this cold-blooded American girl."

"Now how do you know she is cold-blooded?" Hugh asked, slightly nettled.

"She is American, is she not?" Jasper asked dulcetly. At Hugh's wary nod, he said, "Then what more do you need to know? I am sure that she is very prim and proper, perhaps even lovely, but I would wager you my new stallion that ice water runs in her veins."

Thinking of Alice's cool, slim blond beauty and her politely aloof manner, Hugh decided not to take up Jasper's wager. Instead with an edge to his voice, he demanded, "Then what do you suggest I do? marry one of your Creole beauties?"

Jasper beamed at him. "But of course, *mon ami*! You would have a charming and loyal companion, a loving mother for your children, and a soft, warm, yielding armful for your bed. What more could a man ask for in a wife?"

Hugh snorted. "Since I have not committed myself to Miss Summerfield, I shall take your suggestion under advisement—but I make no promises to you. In the meantime, I think I should get my things settled in your house. And after that, I think we should pay a visit to Galland, Lancaster and Dupree."

The two men made a commanding pair as they left the coffeehouse, and Hugh was again aware that there were many eyes upon him and that most were not friendly. Stepping outside onto the banquettes, he asked with a sigh, "Do you think your countrymen will ever get used to being American? Or to Americans?"

"Perhaps. In time. Many are still very resentful at the trick Napoléon played upon us."

The two men chatted amiably as they walked along the wooden banquettes, enjoying the unexpectedly fine weather. The morning was almost warm, and gentle golden sunlight danced on the uneven rooftops of the buildings, and dappled the wrought-iron grillwork adorning the galleries for which New Orleans was famous. Jasper's town house was on Dumaine Street, and they were about to leave Chartres and turn up Dumaine when Hugh spied a pair of feminine figures, discreetly followed by a black manservant, not a half block in front of him.

Despite the shawls covering their heads and partially obscuring their features, he recognized at once the spirited tilt of the younger woman's head. As they drew nearer, he was aware of a sudden leap in his pulse when Micaela Dupree's dark, startled eyes met his. Sweeping his hat from his head, Hugh bowed to the women.

"*Bonjour, Madame* Dupree, *Mademoiselle* Dupree," he said politely, his words and actions echoed by Jasper.

Micaela thought her heart would stop beating when she glanced up and saw that it was Hugh Lancaster standing in front of her. She had hoped that when they next met she would not find him so troublingly attractive, but looking into that dark face, snared by those too-knowing gray eyes, she realized that her hopes had come to naught. Wearing a dark blue coat which expertly fit his splendid physique and a pair of pale gray breeches which shamelessly clung to his long, muscled legs, he was, Micaela realized, appallingly attractive. Angry and ashamed of herself, she kept her gaze half-averted, as if by not looking at him she could convince herself that he was *not* quite the most fascinating man she had ever met.

There was a flurry of greetings and polite exchanges. Hugh's lips quirked in a faint sardonic smile at the air of reserve which quickly overcame Micaela once she had recovered her surprise. Her nose was not exactly tilted as if she smelled something offensive, but very near. Unlike her mother, who was plainly pleased to see him.

Hugh was so busy covertly studying Micaela's charming profile that he was barely aware of the conversation going on between Lisette and Jasper. It wasn't until Lisette said with amusement, "So, *Monsieur* Lancaster, you and *Monsieur* De Marco will join us for dinner tomorrow night, *oui*?" that he was recalled to himself.

Recovering himself quickly, he murmured, "Dinner? Tomorrow night? It shall be my pleasure."

"*Bon!*" Lisette said with a twinkle in her dark eyes. "We shall expect you at seven o'clock tomorrow evening."

Hugh and Jasper bowed again. "Indeed you shall,"

Hugh said easily. "But for now, may we escort you to your destination?"

Micaela, whose pulse had been acting erratically ever since she had first glanced up and met Hugh's glinting gray-eyed glance, said stiffly, "That will not be necessary, *monsieur*—we are almost there."

"Ah, but I would be gravely remiss if I did not see you safely to where you are going. Just consider, *mademoiselle*—you might be accosted by someone—ah—objectionable." Hugh drawled, clearly enjoying the vexed flush which stained Micaela's cheek.

Micaela's bosom swelled with indignation. *Dieu!* The *Américain* was arrogant! A *Creole* would have graciously accepted the dismissal and would never have continued to insinuate himself where he was plainly not wanted. Smiling sweetly, she murmured, "But *monsieur*, you forget, this is still a city of Creoles, and *Maman* and I are not worried about being confronted by someone who would be so rude and overbearing as to force himself upon us." Her eyes sparkling with the light of battle, she added in dulcet tones, "New Orleans is not like your rough *américain* cities—our Creole gentlemen know how to take care of their own."

Hugh grinned. "Well, that certainly put me in my place, did it not?"

Micaela's eyes dropped, and she replied demurely, "One hopes so, *monsieur*, one sincerely hopes so."

"Micaela!" Lisette burst out, a thread of laughter in her voice. "Do not be rude!"

Micaela's gaze met Hugh's dancing gray eyes. "Oh," she asked, all innocence, "was I rude?"

Hugh slowly shook his head, the expression in his eyes suddenly making Micaela breathless. "Rude?" he murmured as he caught her hand in his and dropped a chaste kiss on the soft skin. "Oh, no, never rude . . . provoking, perhaps?"

Her skin prickling as if she had grabbed a nettle, Micaela snatched her hand away and decided that the *Américain* was utterly detestable. Her emotions in a turmoil, she was relieved to hear Lisette say, "We thank you for your offer of an escort, *messieurs*, but our destination is just a few more doors down the street. Good day to you both."

Conscious of the tall *Américain*'s amused look, Micaela was inordinately grateful when she and Lisette swept past the two gentlemen and continued on their way. It didn't help her frame of mind that it took until they reached *Madame* Hubert's shop for her heart to return to its normal beat. Unable to help herself, just as she was to enter the shop, she risked a glance over her shoulder in Hugh's direction. To her chagrin (and delight?) he was still staring at her. A flush stained her cheeks when he smiled knowingly and tipped his hat at her. Muttering under her breath, her nose went up in the air, and she sailed haughtily into the shop. *Merci*! But he was arrogant!

Jasper had watched the exchange with interest, and as he and Hugh resumed their journey, he said slyly, "Now if you were to marry a Creole . . . perhaps, even Micaela Dupree, it would be a good business decision, *oui*?"

Hugh looked at him as if he'd gone mad. "Micaela Dupree? What utter nonsense! I think you have stood in the sun too long, my friend, and it has fried your brains!"

"Hmm, you think so? I do not, *mon ami*." Jasper went on imperturbably. "Think of it. She is lovely, unmarried . . . and she will control ten percent of the business when she marries, and will gain another five percent when the sad day comes and her charming mother has passed on. When she marries, her shares will no doubt be managed by her husband . . . what if she were to marry that lout Husson, hmm? Marriage to Micaela Dupree wold be a great coup for you—you would personally control fifty-five percent of Galland, Lancaster and Dupree. No one could gainsay you."

"You forget," Hugh said softly, "that with my stepfather's remaining ten percent I *already* control the firm."

"Ah, yes, this is true . . . but suppose your wise step-*papa* were to remarry? He is not an old man, despite his protestations to the contrary—not yet fifty, did you not say? He could marry and leave his shares to a new wife—or even father a child."

Hugh shrugged. "The shares belong to him—what he does with them is his business."

"*Oui*, but if you were to marry *Mademoiselle* Dupree . . . it would not matter *what* your esteemed step-*papa* did with his shares, would it?"

Annoyed with this conversation, Hugh sent his friend a dark look. "I may or may not marry Miss Summerfield, but I can practically guarantee you that the *last* woman I would be likely to marry is Micaela Dupree! And her shares be damned!"

Chapter Three

The offices of Galland, Lancaster and Dupree were on Decatur Street, the warehouses on Tchoupitoulas Street at the riverfront. That afternoon, having seen his few belongings delivered and settled in at Jasper's town house, Hugh made his way to Decatur Street alone.

Jasper had wanted to accompany him, but Hugh had politely declined his company. "It will be better if I go by myself," he had said, as they had risen from the table. "For the time being it might be better if you do not champion my cause quite so obviously."

"As you wish, *mon ami*." A sheepish grin had crossed Jasper's face. "It is just as well—I promised some friends that I would attend a cockfight with them this afternoon if the weather was pleasant."

Hugh had shaken his head in mock dismay. "And the business, what about it?"

Jasper had smiled sunnily back at him. "But you are here now—you shall see to it."

Laughing, Hugh had departed, wondering how anything was ever accomplished in New Orleans, considering the Creole preoccupation with pleasurable pursuits.

As he reached his destination, the sun was still shining, but its luster had dimmed, and there was a faint chill in the air.

The offices of Galland, Lancaster and Dupree were housed in one of the few buildings which had escaped the periodic fires which swept through the city, and retained much of the early French construction. The handsome pale yellow stucco structure was built long and low. Stepping through the stout wooden double doors, Hugh was pleased to see the place busy, various clerks and accountants bent industriously over their ledgers and papers.

The head accountant, a fussy little Frenchman by the name of Pierre Brisson, glanced up, and his eyes widened as he caught sight of Hugh. Springing to his feet, he laid down his quill and hurried over to greet Hugh.

"*Monsieur* Lancaster! This *is* a pleasant surprise. No one mentioned that you were expected in the city and would pay us a visit. Please, please allow me to escort you to the owners' offices."

Hugh waved him away with a smile. "That shan't be necessary, Brisson. I would like to look around on my own, if you do not mind." Raising his voice, he said, "You shall see a great deal of me from now on, I am afraid. I am moving to New Orleans and intend to be here most days."

Hugh was aware of the startled murmur as his news was assimilated, but no one seemed particularly alarmed by it. Which was rather what he expected, he mused sardonically. Whoever was stealing from Galland, Lancaster and Dupree, and he was very certain that someone in the firm was, was being clever about it. He hadn't expected that his announcement would flush his quarry. He had hoped, however, that someone might betray a little dismay at his announcement and give him some direction in which to search. No one had.

He moved easily along the wide, desk-lined aisles, halting to talk to first one man, then another, introducing himself to any new faces that had not been there during his last trip to New Orleans in September. Brisson tended to hover around him, but since he hadn't expected to find out anything today, Hugh put up with the fellow's nervous fawning.

Approaching a fresh-faced young man near the rear of the room, Hugh's gaze ran thoughtfully over him when he learned that his name was Etienne Gras. So this was the young man Jasper was attempting to befriend. He was surprised to learn that Etienne had worked for the company for nearly three years . . . yet they had never met. Odd.

Almost as if he guessed Hugh's thought, Etienne smiled, and said, "I have long wanted the honor of meeting you, *Monsieur* Lancaster, but each time you have visited here I was at one of the warehouses, inventorying and recording the latest shipments."

Hugh nodded. "And that is your job? Inventorying the goods upon arrival?"

"Among others," Etienne answered earnestly.

Hugh stood talking to the young man and several others for a few moments before he finally allowed Brisson to escort him to the private offices. Looking around the spacious room, Hugh snorted. The room looked like a leisured gentleman's study—*not* an office!

Faint sunlight from a window at the rear of the room brought out the shades of russet and green of the fine carpet which lay upon the floor. Several comfortable brown leather chairs and small tables were scattered about, various newspapers and leaflets strewn across them. Idly

lifting one of the leaflets, Hugh's lips twisted cynically—
as he expected, the leaflet announced a cockfight. God
forbid that the Duprees should read anything that per-
tained to business!

Continuing his appraisal of the office, he noted a mahogany sideboard sitting against one wall, the top littered
with crystal bottles holding a variety of spirits. A gilt-
framed mirror hung above the sideboard, and several
hunting prints adorned the remaining walls. A pair of
doors opposite each other gave entrance, Hugh remembered, to twin private offices. It was a pleasant enough
room, and Hugh did not object to working in pleasing
surroundings, but from the bare, gleaming expanse of the
impressive desk which was situated at the far end of the
room, it was clear that Jean and François seldom used it,
and then certainly not for *work*!

Hugh said nothing for several seconds, then he turned
and said, "Those doors lead to the other offices, am I correct?"

"Oh, *oui, monsieur*," Pierre said quickly. "There is one
on either side of this room. When they were here, this
was *Monsieur* Galland's office, and the Duprees were on
either side of him." He coughed slightly. "Of late *Monsieur* Jean and *Monsieur* François have been using this
office exclusively."

"Well, not any longer," Hugh said decisively. "Have a
locksmith in—I want all the locks changed, and I am to
have the only keys." He smiled down at Brisson's worried features. "Do not worry, I shall inform the other
owners of the change."

Timidly Brisson asked, "Does this mean that you shall
be here regularly, *monsieur*?"

"Every day," Hugh said with relish.

A smile lit Brisson's sallow features. "Ah, *bon, mon-*

sieur! I have often wished that the other . . ." He stopped, not wishing to appear disloyal, and added hastily, "It will be, er, convenient to have one of the owners regularly on the premises."

Satisfied with his afternoon's visit, Hugh was whistling softly to himself as he strolled back toward Jasper's house. Once there, he made himself at home in Jasper's study, writing notes to various American acquaintances in the city, advising them of his presence. One of those polite notes went to Alice Summerfield's father, and as he sealed the letter, Hugh looked at it thoughtfully, Jasper's words about a cold-blooded American coming back to haunt him. Was he being unwise to court Alice? He had always found her a charming companion, politely reserved yes, but then one did not want a forward hoyden for a wife. Admittedly, with her pale blond hair, soft blue eyes, and tall, slender build, she was a lovely woman, but he was aware that she aroused little passion in him. Of course, he reminded himself, he was of an age when he should not be consumed with a youth's wild, indiscriminate lust. He was fond of Alice. He admired her. She was well connected, came from a good family, and had a little money of her own—he did not have to fear that it was solely his fortune that attracted her.

Alice would be an asset to him, he admitted candidly. She would see that his household ran smoothly; she would preside graciously over his table and, in time, God willing, would present him with the heirs which would please his stepfather. Surely those were all legitimate reasons for marrying her? Then why did he feel uneasy about it?

Jasper's words slid slyly through his mind, followed swiftly by Micaela Dupree's image, her dark eyes flashing, her saucy mouth tempting and beckoning. Hugh instantly felt his body tighten with a powerful surge of desire. Damn Jasper! These unseemly thoughts of Micaela Dupree were all his fault! He would be courting Alice Summerfield, *not* that haughty piece of work, Micaela Dupree!

If Jasper found his friend short-tempered and out of sorts that evening, he put it down to Hugh's preoccupation with work and proceeded to bedevil him unmercifully about it, which, of course, did nothing to improve Hugh's mood. It was with relief that Hugh finally sought out his bed, and as he lay there, his thoughts of his best friend were uncharitable—at best.

By morning Hugh had recovered most of his usual good spirits. He spent several hours arranging things to suit himself at the offices of Galland, Lancaster and Dupree. He had also taken time to pay the warehouses on Tchoupitoulas Street a visit and, having made his plans for remaining in the city and taking a firmer hand in the business known to the dockworkers, was feeling rather satisfied with himself. Whoever was stealing from the company was not going to find it as easy as he had in the past—he would see to that!

As he bathed and dressed that evening for dinner at the Duprees, Hugh was conscious of a feeling of anticipation, an almost boyish eagerness that he had not felt in a long time. Checking his cravat one last time in the cheval glass in his room, he told himself firmly that his light mood had absolutely nothing to do with the fact that he would be seeing Micaela Dupree shortly. He was merely pleased with his day's work.

Micaela could not say that she was looking forward to the coming evening. Yet she could not deny that she took especial care with her dress that evening and that there was a sparkle in her eyes that a mere dinner with friends and family should not have put there. Her dark, gleaming locks, piled high on her head, were held in place with pearl-and-ebony combs and her pale pink silk gown lent a rosy glow to her alabaster skin and intensified the cherry hue of her lips. A fringed shawl in delicate shades of cream and green was around her shoulders, and as she descended the stairs to join her mother in the second-best parlor, she was conscious of a flutter of excitement—and annoyed by it.

The dinner party had grown somewhat since Lisette had invited Hugh and Jasper. Alain Husson, his sister and Micaela's best friend, Cecile, had also been invited, as well as their widowed mother, *Madame* Husson. *Madame* Husson's sister-in-law, *Madame* Marie Husson, had been included in the invitation, as much because she was related to the Duprees—Renault and Jean's father had been her brother—as the fact that being a widow herself, she lived with the rest of the Hussons. And, of course, Jean and François would be there—resentfully. Both men had been extremely put out when they had learned who was to be their dinner guest that Saturday night, but Lisette had merely arched a brow at their protestations and wafted serenely from the room. It was, as she had informed them, *her* dinner party. They could attend or not.

Despite the slight undercurrent of tension, the evening went surprisingly well—everyone was, after all, on their very best behavior. It was true that *Madame* Husson and *Tante* Marie, as she was known to Micaela and François, as well as Alain and Cecile, were coolly polite to the *Américain* in their midst, but Jasper, ably assisted by Lisette, was quick to smooth over any awkward moments. Jean kept a civil tongue in his mouth, and François followed his uncle's lead. Micaela studiously ignored

Hugh, allowing herself only the occasional surreptitious glance in his direction; Cecile, not yet eighteen, was plainly awed by the tall, handsome *Américain*, and Alain, who was Micaela's most persistent suitor, chose to pretend that Hugh was not present and lavished the majority of his conversation and longing looks on Micaela.

Hugh had met Alain Husson only once previously, and he held no particular opinion about the man. He knew that, like Jasper, Alain had gained a small share in Galland, Lancaster and Dupree two and a half years ago because of Christophe's penchant for reckless gaming. The wager, if he remembered correctly, had had something to do with how far a frog would leap. Hugh grimaced. The Creole love of gambling and their willingness to wager large sums on the most ridiculous events completely mystified him.

Alain was about Hugh's age. He was not tall, but he was built like a bull, solid, with powerful shoulders and strong, muscular thighs. He was rather handsome, his features attractively sculpted and his smile most charming, but watching him bend his dark head attentively next to Micaela's, Hugh decided abruptly that he didn't much care for the man.

When the ladies rose from the table, leaving the gentlemen to their tobacco and wine, there was a moment of silence. Then Jasper said gaily as he looked across the table at Hugh, "This is most fortunate, *mon ami*—it so happens, that with the exception of your step-*papa*, *Madame* Dupree has assembled all the partners in Galland, Lancaster and Dupree in her dining room tonight. Now would be an excellent opportunity for you to explain what you have been doing since your arrival and what your plans are for the company, *oui*?"

In the act of lighting a slim, black cheroot, Hugh

glanced wryly at Jasper's mocking face. Trust Jasper to put the cat amongst the pigeons.

Taking in an appreciative drag of his cheroot, Hugh watched the thin stream of blue smoke rise toward the ceiling. "I had thought to call a meeting tomorrow, but if you gentlemen . . . ?"

Jean nodded curtly; the others concurred.

Taking a sip of his Madeira, Hugh said mildly, "I expect that most of what I plan to do will affect you little. I will warn you, however, that I intend to take an extremely active part in the running of the business. By that I mean, except for certain times of the year, most notably the fever season, that I shall be at our offices every day and that little will be done without my having first overseen it." He shot Jean a sardonic look. "I do not, of course, expect you to change your habits. I assume that you will continue as you have in the past."

His face resentful, Jean's lip curled. "You would become a '*chaca*,' a tradesman?"

"I *am* a tradesman," Hugh said levelly, not rising to the challenge. "And I think you forget that it is 'trade' which is our business."

Jean sniffed. "Very well. You will be at the office every day and nothing will be done without your permission. What else?"

"Why nothing," Hugh said dulcetly. He stared carefully at the burning tip of his cheroot before adding softly, "There is one thing more, though—I have taken over Christophe's old office for my own private and personal use. I hope that you will not mind. For the amount of time the rest of you spend there, I am sure that you can comfortably manage your affairs in one of the other two private offices."

"You are throwing us out of my *grand-père*'s office?"

François demanded angrily. "What right do you have to do such a thing?"

Hugh smiled grimly. "The right of someone who intends to get a great deal of work done in that office . . . and my right as owner of the major shares of the business."

There was a sullen silence, but neither of the Duprees offered further challenge. Hugh waited a moment, then said quietly, "I know that the next few months are going to be trying for all of us—I shall try not to step on too many toes, or offend your sensibilities if I can help it, but I intend to find out precisely why we seem to be losing so much money. You can either help me . . . or . . ."

"But of course, we will help you," Jasper exclaimed. He looked around at the others. "It is to our advantage, *oui*?"

Grudgingly the other three nodded, François going so far as to say, "Perhaps this will be a good thing."

Alain shot him a look, and François suddenly became very interested in his wineglass.

Throwing down his napkin and rising to his feet, Jean said abruptly, "Since there is nothing else to discuss, I suggest we join the ladies."

It was clear to Micaela that something had happened in the dining room to upset her brother and uncle the instant they entered the room, and she felt a faint stab of anxiety. What had the *Américain* said to them to make both men look so grim?

As the gentlemen began to gravitate toward Lisette, who was pouring coffee near the cheery fire, Micaela plucked at François's sleeve. He glanced at her, and she tipped her head, indicating a small alcove near one end of the large room.

Discreetly, brother and sister retired in that direction,

and Micaela asked in a low voice, "What is wrong, *mon cher*? What did the *Américain* say to you?"

François's jaw hardened, and his hands clenched into fists. "The arrogance of the creature! Not here two days, and already he has commandeered *Grand-père*'s office and loftily informed the rest of us that it is to be his alone!" His dark eyes burned as he added dramatically. "We shall be nothing more than lowly clerks if he has his way!"

Micaela looked shocked. "He is going to make you work as a clerk? But you are one of the owners! Can he do this?"

Resentfully, François said, "Apparently, he thinks he can do anything he pleases and that we must obey him."

"But we are *owners*, too!"

"Tell that to him!"

Furious for her brother, Micaela's delicate lips thinned. How dare this, this, *usurper* dictate to her family! Why he wasn't even one of the original partners. How dare he!

Sipping his coffee near the fire, over the rim of his cup Hugh had observed the interplay between brother and sister, and, from the expressions on their faces, he had a very good idea what had been said. If the angry cast to her mouth was any indication, it was obvious that Micaela was firmly committed to her brother's camp. He sighed. He might have been a little high-handed in his manner, but, dammit, things had been allowed to slide for too long, and he didn't have the patience or the inclination to tread carefully around the excitable sensibilities of the Duprees. It was better, he told himself wearily, that he establish his position right from the start. In time, perhaps, he could use a bit more finesse in dealing with them. But not now.

Returning to join the group clustered around the fire,

Micaela's sense of injustice grew as she watched Cecile hang on every word that passed Hugh's lips. Cecile was clearly entranced, and Micaela found herself holding Hugh's easy charm against him. Her chin lifted. No doubt he was merely amusing himself at Cecile's expense. How sad that her friend was being taken in by such a black-guard.

Accepting a cup of coffee from her mother, a militant light in her fine eyes, Micaela wandered over to where Hugh, Cecile, and Jasper were standing. She stood listening to their banter for a few moments, then asked Hugh, "So, *Monsieur* Lancaster, have you found a place to stay in our fair city?"

Hugh's brow lifted. The proud little *mademoiselle* was deigning to speak to him? He sent her a lazy smile. "Indeed I have, *Mademoiselle* Dupree—Jasper has kindly offered me the hospitality of his home for as long as I wish."

Micaela cocked her head. Taking a sip of her coffee, then slowly turning away, she said softly over her shoulder, "How strange . . . I would have thought that you would have made your quarters at the offices of the company. But then, it *is* possible, I suppose, for the premises to survive without your presence during the night."

Cecile smothered a gasp, and Jasper laughed aloud. Hugh merely smiled, although there was a glint in his gray eyes which made Micaela strangely breathless. He bowed low, acknowledging her barb, but instead of feeling victorious, Micaela stalked away with a sense of having survived a dangerous escape.

Alain instantly appeared at her shoulder, and she spent several moments conversing with him and recovering her composure. She liked Alain and was flattered by his attention—he was considered a very eligible *parti*, and there were several other young ladies who would have been ecstatic to have him dancing attendance on them. But Micaela could not bring herself to accept his attentions seriously. François and Jean both had been vigorously pushing his suit for several months now. Was that why she could not bring herself to say yes and become betrothed to Alain? Because they wanted it so desperately?

She hoped she wasn't that disobliging, but she had to admit that she had no good reason for refusing to accept an offer from Alain. He and François were close friends, although Alain was nearly a decade older than her brother. They had all grown up together—the Husson plantation was not far from the Duprees'. The Hussons were respectable and wealthy. There was even an indirect tie of blood—*Tante* Marie. It would be an eminently suitable match, so why was she dithering?

Unaccountably her gaze slid to the tall *Américain* near the fire. He was laughing at something her mother had said, his handsome face full of amusement. Across the room Hugh's eyes suddenly met hers, and Micaela felt her heart leap in her breast. Blushing furiously at the gleam which sprang into his gaze, she glanced hastily away.

Merci! Merci! What was wrong with her? Pasting a smile on her lips, she forced herself to concentrate on what Alain was saying, determined not to spare one more glance at the *Américain* for the rest of the evening. She managed to do just that until Hugh and Jasper were taking their leave. The Husson family had departed a few minutes previously, and the remaining members of the party were gathered in the entryway bidding each other good night.

Micaela was standing next to her mother, François and

Jean nearby. Jasper had already said his good-byes and was waiting at the door. Hugh bent over Lisette's hand and warmly thanked her for the evening.

A glinting smile on his lips, he added, "Perhaps you will allow me to return the favor? I would very much like to have you and your family as my guests at one of the hotels for dinner. Will you allow me to arrange it?"

To her intense dismay, Micaela's pulse quickened at his words. François and Jean were quick to offer polite protests, but Lisette, paying them no heed, beamed at Hugh. "Why, *monsieur*, that would be most famous. I am sure that we should enjoy it."

The door had barely closed behind Hugh and Jasper before François burst out, "*Maman*! How could you? Tonight was bad enough, but must you encourage the man? He is our enemy. And he has treated Jean and me most cavalierly. Let me tell you what he has done to us."

As François proceeded vociferously to lay out Hugh's many crimes to his mother, Micaela drifted away, eager for the solace of her bedchamber. Jean's touch on her arm stopped her, and she looked inquiringly at him.

"A word with you, *petite*?"

Mystified, Micaela followed him into one of the smaller rooms. "What is it?"

Jean took a turn around the room, then, his hands behind his back, he said quietly, "I wondered if you had made a decision about Alain Husson. He spoke to me earlier this evening before the others arrived. He indicated again how very much he wants to marry you."

Micaela bit her lip, her eyes on the floor in front of her. "I-I-I h-h-had not thought about it very much."

"Not thought about it very much!" Jean repeated, dismayed. "How can you *not* have thought about it? Alain Husson is a very suitable match. He is young, handsome, and comes from a good family. What more do you want in a husband?"

Micaela couldn't answer that question, but realizing that she also could not expect Alain to wait endlessly for her answer, she took a deep breath. Meeting Jean's gaze, she said softly, "I have been most unfair—I should have told you weeks ago that I do not wish to marry him."

"Perhaps you should consider someone else besides yourself before you make a final decision," Jean said quietly. "I know that you are aware that our business affairs have not gone so well of late, but are you aware of the fact that Alain holds a rather large vowel signed by your brother? A debt that is difficult for François to pay?" Jean looked uncomfortable. "Alain has, in the most discreet fashion imaginable, made it clear that the day your betrothal is announced, he will happily destroy the note—as a sign of good faith toward his soon-to-be-brother-in-law."

Dismay filled Micaela. "A gambling debt?"

Jean nodded unhappily. "François is young—he has not yet learned not to be foolish with his money. It is fortunate for us that it is Alain who holds the note."

When Micaela remained silent, Jean crossed to her. Taking one of her hands in his, he said earnestly, "I do not like to put this burden on your shoulders, *ma chère*, but it is important that you understand that this is a troubling time for all of us right now. Alain is most desperate to marry you—he has even mentioned that a great dowry is not important to him." Steadily holding her gaze, he added softly, "Besides saving your brother from an embarrassing situation, there is much to recommend this match, *petite*. In fact I cannot think of one reason against it. Do not forget, too, that if you marry Alain Husson, you will, in effect, be keeping the shares of the business in the family. With this *Américain* underfoot, it is important that as a family we all stick together."

Her eyes painfully searching his, Micaela said miserably, "You have given me much to think about, *oncle* . . . but I must be truthful with you and tell you that I do not want to marry Alain Husson."

"Not even to save your family?" he demanded swiftly.

"I do not know," she admitted huskily. "I shall have to think on it. You ask a great deal of me."

Her heart heavy in her breast, Micaela bade her uncle good night and swiftly left the room.

After Micaela had departed, Jean wandered moodily about, his thoughts most unpleasant. He had been so certain that she would accept Husson's offer. Something must be done to make her see sense.

François entered, a question in his eyes. Jean shook his head. "She does not want to marry him."

François's face fell. "I do not understand her! Why is she being so stubborn? Does she want to die a spinster? There are dozens of girls who would swoon with delight if Alain wanted to marry them."

"Unfortunately, your sister is not one of them," Jean replied dryly.

"What are we to do? Alain is pressing me for the money—or Micaela's hand."

Jean took a deep breath. "I think that we shall have to make up her mind for her."

"What do you mean?"

"I mean that we shall have to arrange a . . . situation. A situation which will make it impossible for her to refuse to marry Alain."

François's eyes widened. "You mean . . . ?"

Jean slowly nodded. "*Oui*," he said heavily. "I find this entire situation distasteful, but I see no other way out. If

your father were alive, he would no doubt simply order
her to marry the man of his choice, but we cannot. And so
we must stoop to an unpleasant subterfuge." Uncomfortably, Jean continued, "With Alain's help, and I do not
doubt that he will be most willing to play his part, we
must see to it that your sister is thoroughly compromised
and that she has no choice but to accept marriage to Alain
Husson."

Chapter Four

The next weeks passed swiftly as Hugh settled into life in New Orleans. He spent long hours at the firm's offices, and by the end of March he was thoroughly familiar with all aspects of the workings of Galland, Lancaster and Dupree. Jean and François remained touchy about the situation, but he had to give them credit for not interfering any more than they did. He also had to admit that Jean had assembled a competent and hardworking staff. Jean Dupree, he conceded grudgingly, was not a complete fool. In fact, the man had a good business head—when he used it.

His dinner party at the hotel for the Duprees had not yet come about, primarily because the week following his invitation, the ladies and Jean had departed New Orleans for Riverbend. It was sugar-cane planting time, and Jean needed to be there to oversee the setting out of the young crop. François had remained in the city, and Jean had made periodic trips into New Orleans to keep a no-doubt-jealous eye on events at Galland, Lancaster and Dupree.

Hugh had been surprised at the wave of disappointment which had swept through him when he had learned that the Dupree ladies had left the city for the country. He told himself that it was because he would miss Lisette Dupree's leavening presence in dealing with François and Jean, but there was a part of him that knew he was blatantly lying to himself. To prove to himself that it *really* was Lisette's presence he missed, he spent time in the company of Alice Summerfield and her family—much to Jasper's obvious disapproval.

Meeting Hugh as he was on his way out the door to dine at the Summerfield home that evening, Jasper made a face. "The icy Miss Summerfield again, *mon ami?*" When Hugh nodded, he waved an admonishing finger under Hugh's nose. "I would be careful, if I were you—you may find yourself leg-shackled before you realize what has happened. You have been seen much in her company of late and tongues are beginning to wag—even amongst the Creoles."

Hugh smiled. "I told you I was looking for a wife."

"But amongst the wrong females! What about the so-sweet Cecile Husson? She appeared to be quite taken with you. You could not find a better-connected or wealthier match in the city."

"Too young for my taste," Hugh muttered, and hastily departed. He had hoped that Jasper's promotion of a Creole bride had been a momentary aberration, but such had not been the case. At every opportunity, Jasper shamelessly touted the charms of every eligible Creole female within a twenty-mile radius of New Orleans. One name, Hugh had been irritatingly aware, had been noticeably absent. Which, of course, meant nothing to him. It was Alice Summerfield who currently held his attention, he told himself firmly.

Hugh was startled to find François among the guests at the Summerfields' home, but then he shrugged. It was perhaps a sign of things to come—Creole and American conversing amiably together. Dismissing François's presence, Hugh enjoyed himself that evening at the elegant house of Alice's parents. Alice's father was a genial man who had been a friend of John Lancaster's in Natchez, and his wife was a lavish hostess. Hugh was also acquainted with several of the other American guests, and he discovered that he was oddly relieved that it was not to be an intimate family dinner. Aware of several arch looks when he went up and engaged Alice in conversation after dinner, he wondered if perhaps Jasper wasn't right. Mayhap he should be a bit more circumspect for the time being.

Noticing the sudden frown which marred his handsome face, Alice asked, "Is something amiss? You look very fierce."

Hugh's features softened as he gazed down at her appreciatively. She was a sight to gladden any man's heart, in a blue-satin gown which matched her lovely eyes and displayed to advantage her tall, slim, elegant figure. Her blond hair was arranged in ringlets around her chiseled features; her blue eye were large and limpid, but even as he looked with sincere admiration at Alice, he was conscious that her cool beauty left him unmoved . . . even bored.

Rousing himself, he smiled at her. "Do I? I assure you that I do not mean to—not with such a charming sight as yourself before me."

"That was a very pretty compliment," she replied sedately, her gaze moving serenely over the other guests. She was supremely confident that it was only a matter of time before Hugh asked her father for permission to solicit her hand in marriage. She would, she had decided calmly, say yes when Hugh asked her to marry him.

Fixing her lovely blue eyes on Hugh's, she said, "Father mentioned that you have bought a new pair of horses, matched chestnuts, I believe he said."

"Indeed I have—as sweet a pair of goers it has been my pleasure ever to drive." He smiled ruefully. "Though until the ground dries out, I doubt I will be able to drive them very much."

Alice gave a delicate shudder. "I know—aren't the roads simply terrible? More like quagmires."

"Well, the rainy season will not last much longer, and then we shall all be complaining about the dust," Hugh replied cheerfully.

Catching sight of François talking animatedly with a fellow Creole, Bernard Marigny, who was a member of General Wilkinson's staff, Hugh nodded in that direction. "I was surprised to see François Dupree here tonight. I did not know that your father was acquainted with him."

"I believe that Mr. Marigny introduced us to him." She glanced slyly at Hugh. "He has come several times to call, and my mother is quite taken with his Gallic charms . . . I must confess that I, too, have found his company delightful. His command of English is very good—it is my understanding that his grandfather insisted that he and his sister learn not only English but Spanish as well."

François's fluency in English and Spanish came as no surprise to Hugh—old Christophe Galland had been no fool, and it made sense for anyone living in New Orleans to have at least a working vocabulary of the three languages heard most often. It was François's visits to the Summerfield home that surprised him. Why, Hugh wondered, is François making himself so agreeable to the Summerfield family? His gaze slid consideringly to the young woman at his side. Alice? François had no doubt heard the same gossip as Jasper. Was the younger man merely seeing for himself the woman whose name had been linked to his, or was François putting himself forward as a rival? It was an interesting thought.

Catching Hugh's eyes on him, François smiled sunnily and walked over to where Hugh and Alice were standing. After bowing profusely over Alice's hand and exclaiming his enjoyment of the evening, François looked at Hugh and said, "My uncle has returned to the city. He arrived not a half hour before I had to leave to attend this evening's so-delightful entertainment." This last was said with another profuse bow to Alice.

"What a pity," Alice said. "If only we had known that he was going to be in the city, we certainly would have been happy to invite him to accompany you tonight."

François made a polite noise. "Do not distress yourself, *mademoiselle*. There will, no doubt, be other times. Besides, it was planned for our friend, Alain Husson, to come by this evening and visit with him. They have—ah—business to discuss."

Hugh flicked a brow upward. "Business? Galland, Lancaster and Dupree business, perhaps?"

"*Non*! Why, we would not dare to do such a thing without first asking your permission, *monsieur*," François said mockingly, a challenging gleam sparkling in his dark eyes.

Amused by François's thinly disguised hostility, Hugh merely smiled.

When Hugh did not rise to his baiting, François went on smoothly, "Actually, I think that my uncle does wish to discuss some business with you—he will no doubt see you tomorrow at the company offices."

Deciding that she had been ignored long enough, Alice asked, "Does your uncle plan to stay in the city long?"

"Ah, *non*. Not more than a day or two—this is a very busy time for him. There is much for him to oversee at the plantation this time of year."

Alice and François began to talk about the plantation, and, only half-listening to their conversation, Hugh stared meditatively at François. Now why does Jean want to meet with me? he wondered. The open resentment and displeasure of the Duprees at his arrival and active presence in the firm seemed to have faded, and Hugh had been growing hopeful that the worst was behind him. Was he wrong?

That question was answered at eleven o'clock the next morning, when Jean, with François at his heels, breezed into Hugh's office. Hugh was seated behind his desk, going over some of the invoices from the previous year when the Duprees arrived, and he glanced up when they entered without knocking.

A quizzical expression on his face, he looked up at them. "Good morning, gentlemen," he said politely. "What may I do for you?"

Nattily attired in a gray-striped jacket and an elegant waistcoat above his long, dark gray pantaloons, Jean seated himself in one of the chairs before Hugh's desk. Crossing one booted foot over the other, he said amiably, "I trust that you will forgive the intrusion, but I, we, have a proposal to place before you."

Laying aside the invoice, Hugh leaned back in his chair. His features carefully bland, he regarded the two men in front of him, his brain racing. What the devil were they planning?

Calmly he asked, "Yes? What is this proposal?"

"We have had a family meeting," Jean said bluntly, "and we would like to buy half of your shares in the business."

"Thereby gaining a controlling interest," Hugh replied slowly, his sleepy gray eyes unrevealing.

"*Oui*!" François said. "This current situation is intolerable, and we have decided that this is the only way to resolve it."

"And if I do not want to sell? Suppose I would prefer to buy *your* shares?" Hugh asked levelly.

Jean's face tightened. "We do not wish to sell, *monsieur*."

"Even if I do not want to sell either?"

"*Mon Dieu*!" François burst out angrily. "Why are you being so difficult? We are willing to pay you a good sum for your interest." His lips lifted in a sneer. "A good sum to get rid of your interference in a business begun by my father and grandfather."

"And my stepfather," Hugh said softly, his eyes on François's turbulent features.

François made a disgusted sound and sprang to his feet. "You talk to him," he muttered to Jean. "I cannot." Spinning on his heels, François stalked from the office, slamming the door behind him.

"He is very young," Jean said slowly, his gaze meeting Hugh's. "He loses his temper easily."

"I have noticed it is a trait you seem to share."

Jean smiled ruefully. "You are correct—you must put it down to the excitability of the Creole temperament. We do not have the measured, placid nature of you *Américains*. And this is why we would like to buy a controlling interest in the business. We think that it will be much better for all of us, if you sell to us and . . ." Jean grimaced. "There is no polite way to say it—and remove yourself from New Orleans." Jean leaned forward, his expression intent. "Let us tend to our own affairs. We have done so for over twenty years, with little interference from your step-*papa*—we would like to continue to do so."

Hugh rubbed his chin thoughtfully. He had never considered selling part of his interest, and, in fact, his own sense of honor would not have let him. His stepfather had been very generous to him, and he would not make any bargain with the Duprees without first writing to John Lancaster. When John had sold him a controlling interest, he had known that the business would be safe in Hugh's hands. He sighed. Something that could not be said about the Duprees, although he would admit that Jean was not entirely without a business head. But there was another reason which made him hesitate—he knew himself too well, and he was grimly aware that he would never be able simply to step aside and give the Duprees full rein—not as long as he owned even one percent of the business.

This offer of the Duprees made one thing clear—they were far more unhappy with him at the helm than he had thought, and it was obvious that the past few weeks had been merely a temporary truce. If the Duprees were desperate enough to make this offer, perhaps he should accept it . . . with one slight change. . . .

His mind suddenly made up, Hugh said, "I will not sell part of my interest—you may buy all of it—provided my stepfather approves. It is possible that John will even sell you his shares." A cynical smile crossed his face. "Then you will be completely rid of us."

There was a stunned silence. "All of it?" Jean asked at last.

Hugh nodded. "Pending John Lancaster's approval."

Jean made a face. "It is generous of you, but we cannot. I will be honest with you—to buy only half of your shares will very nearly bring us to the brink of bankruptcy. There is simply no way that we would be able to buy it all."

"Then I am afraid that we are at an impasse."

"You will not consider selling us half?"

Hugh shook his head. "You have been honest with me—I shall be so with you . . . I fear that if Galland, Lancaster and Dupree is left in your hands, in less than two years, there will *be* no business."

"I beg your pardon?" Jean said stiffly, his features congealing into an expression of haughty anger.

Hugh sighed. So much for their moment of honesty with each other. "For the past twenty-two months we have taken severe losses, and during that time you have continued to authorize expenditures at the same rate you have in the past. We cannot keep dipping into our capital in this manner."

"I told Micaela that it was useless to try to talk to you," Jean snarled, springing to his feet.

"This was *Micaela's* idea?" Hugh asked, startled.

Jean nodded curtly. "She knew that her brother and I were upset with the situation, and she suggested that we try to buy a controlling interest. She was even willing to risk every cent of her own small fortune which came to her from her *grand-père*." An ugly smile curved his mouth. "She agreed to do anything that would get rid of *you*! My niece is very loyal to her family—she is willing to do whatever is necessary for her family's sake."

"I see," Hugh replied, with an odd sensation of disappointment knifing through him. It was ridiculous of course. Micaela Dupree's opinion meant nothing to him.

Rising to his own feet, Hugh said softly, "It seems that we have nothing else to say to each other."

"You think so," Jean snapped. "You are mistaken, *monsieur*, if you think that we shall give in so easily."

Jean left in the same manner as François's earlier departure from the room, even slamming the door. Shaking his head, Hugh slowly sat down. Unwilling to let himself dwell on the unpleasant scene which had just taken place, even less willing to examine his emotions concerning Micaela's part in it, he quickly buried himself in work.

It was several hours later that he noticed something odd. Starting shortly after Christophe's death, there were, interspersed throughout, invoices that were different. Close examination convinced him that there was nothing *on* the paper to arouse his curiosity, everything was there that should be, there were no suspicious smudges or indecipherable writing, nothing appeared to be altered, but there was something. It wasn't until he was idly rubbing his thumb across one of pages that it dawned on him—the quality of the paper was just slightly different . . . crisper, smoother . . .

His interest piqued, he quickly found the other invoices which had troubled him and discovered the same thing. Buried in the middle of each extensive invoice were, sometimes just one, upon occasion two or three, pages whose quality *felt* different from all the rest.

Leaning back in his chair, Hugh stared at the dozen or so invoices before him. There *could* be a logical explanation for the substitution of paper. But it was interesting, he decided grimly, that these odd pages started showing up about the time the company started losing money and that only very large invoices, consisting of several pages, had the different paper. Another thing—the questionable pages were always in the middle . . . almost as if someone had buried them there knowing that normally they would never be noticed. . . . As a matter of fact, it had taken *him* several weeks of searching to discover the differences.

His discovery didn't prove anything, but it certainly gave him food for thought. He picked up one of the suspect invoices and leafed through it. There were a lot of reasonable explanations for the differences in the quality of paper, including manufacturer defects, but somehow he didn't think that was the answer. No. A pattern of blatant, outright thievery was revealing itself to him, and it was as simple as it was ingenious.

Rapidly the possible scenario played itself in his brain. A shipment, he mused slowly, would arrive from Europe and follow the usual routine of unloading and storage in the warehouses . . . but at some point after that, the thief or thieves, would help themselves to what they wanted from the warehouse. The invoice which accompanied the shipment would be altered, not individual amounts, but an entire counterfeit page would be substituted for the original. Clever. And it smacked of the culprit or culprits being closely aligned with the company.

Galland, Lancaster and Dupree had obviously been paying for goods which they had indeed received, but a portion of which simply disappeared and, with it, their profit. Hugh rubbed his chin. The only way he could prove it was either secretly to institute a system of double record keeping here in New Orleans and wait for the thief to strike, or write and privately request that an original copy of one of the suspicious invoices be sent directly to him. He grimaced. If he wrote that day and the letter sailed with the next ship, it would be three months or more before he received his requested copy from Europe. Three long months before he would be able to compare it with the one in the office. All of which, he admitted glumly, would only confirm the *way* the thievery was happening, *not* who!

He sighed heavily. Well, he had plenty of time—he'd

moved to New Orleans, hadn't he? And he couldn't say that he was displeased with what he had discovered. At least now, he had some idea how the profits were disappearing. All he had to do was to find the thief—or thieves.

A rude growl from his stomach reminded him that it was late afternoon and that he had not eaten since early morning. Gathering up the invoices which interested him, he locked them in the bottom drawer of his desk and, after shrugging into his dark blue coat and putting on his curly-brimmed beaver hat, left his office, carefully locking it behind him.

Telling Brisson that he was leaving for the day, Hugh stepped out into the soft sunlight. Heading toward Jasper's house, he hoped that he would find his host at home; no doubt, he thought with a grin, resting between amusements.

Hugh had almost reached Dumaine Street when he spied a trim form in front of him that he recognized immediately. Micaela Dupree. But what, he wondered, was she doing in the city?

Deciding to find out, he stopped and waited for her to approach him. Micaela appeared to be alone, except for a young maid and a black male servant.

Micaela had spotted him coming toward her almost at the same instant, and if she hadn't been raised to be a proper young lady, she would have stamped her foot and spun around and walked swiftly in the opposite direction. But she had been raised to be gracious, even, she told herself fiercely, to *américain* gentlemen with mocking eyes and arrogant smiles.

Forcing a polite, albeit cool, expression on her face, she acknowledged Hugh's broad presence on the wooden banquette in front of her. "*Monsieur* Lancaster.

How . . . nice to see you. Are you enjoying this fine weather we have had the past few days?"

Sweeping aside his hat, he took her hand and dropped a kiss on the soft skin. "Indeed I am, *mademoiselle*. It gives one hope that the rainy season will truly end soon, does it not?"

To her annoyance, Micaela felt the touch of his warm lips on her hand all the way down to her toes. With more haste than grace, she jerked her hand from his light grasp. "*Oui*," she said stiffly, wishing she had taken another street.

The amusement lurking in his gray eyes did nothing to quell her annoyance, but before she could think of a polite way to end this meeting, Hugh said, "But what brings you to the city? I saw your uncle and brother this morning, and they did not mention that you were in the city. I assume that your mother came with you?"

Micaela gave a curt nod and began to edge away from him. "*Oui*, I accompanied *Maman* to the city. She was bored at the plantation and wanted to come in for a day or two to visit with some friends. We arrived last night with my uncle and plan to return to the plantation before the end of the week."

To her dismay, Hugh fell in step beside her.

He smiled down at her, seemingly oblivious to the fact that she wished the ground would open up and swallow him whole. Which naturally made him all the more determined to attach himself to her side.

A thread of laughter in his voice, he asked, "And you? Were you bored in the country?"

Glad of the presence of her maid and manservant following discreetly behind them, Micaela replied honestly, "Oh, *non!*" An impish smile suddenly lit her taking features, that elusive and utterly charming dimple of hers coming into view. "I adore the country. If I had my way, I would stay there year-round."

Hugh's brow flew up. "Indeed?" he said with surprise. "I would have thought you more, er, at ease, in the city."

Reminding herself that she did not like him, Micaela's smile faded, and she said coolly, "But then you do not know me very well, do you, *monsieur*?"

"You have me there . . . but that fact can be easily remedied," he replied in a low, oddly intimate tone. With rapt interest, he watched the delightful flush which stained her cheeks and the wary look which entered the wide dark eyes. "Perhaps," he went on softly, "if you knew me better, you would not be so willing to let your uncle use your fortune to try to buy a controlling interest in the firm from me, hmm?"

"H-h-he told you?"

Placing her hand on his arm, Hugh smiled down at her. "Yes, he did. Just one of the things he mentioned during his visit to me this morning."

Micaela bit her lip, not certain what to say. It was clear that he was waiting for an answer. But she couldn't very well tell him that the reason she had agreed to let Jean and François use her fortune from her grandfather had been because of a guilty conscience—a fact which had nothing to do with him. Both her uncle and brother were unhappy with her because of her continued determination not to marry Alain Husson. Knowing, too, how Hugh's interference galled them, in desperation, she had offered them her own tidy little fortune to use to buy out the *Américain*, thinking that if they were able to buy enough shares to give them a majority, they might be happier— and less inclined to berate her for her selfishness in refusing to marry Husson. She hadn't thought that either

Jean or François would mention that it was her money which had enabled them to make the offer.

Taking the bold approach, her head swung up proudly, and she demanded, "And did you sell him what he wanted?"

"No, and I do not intend to. Unless, he wishes to buy *all* my shares."

Micaela's eyes opened very wide. "A-a-all your shares? You would do this?"

They stopped walking and suddenly, inexplicably, oblivious to the servants behind them and the horses and carriages driving by only a few feet away, they stared intently into each other's faces. Hugh was instantly lost in the deep, mysterious pools of her liquid black eyes, and he was aware of his heart thumping wildly in his chest, of his blood quickening, his body suddenly hard and aching. Micaela was conscious of nothing but the tall, dark-haired man looming before her, his icy gray eyes, not icy at all, but gleaming with a sudden heat that made her feel giddy and not at all like herself.

"Yes," he said dazedly, as if an astounding idea had just occurred to him. "Yes, I might be very willing indeed . . . if the price were right. . . ." Almost against his will, he reached up and gently caressed her silken cheek. "If the price were right, I would be willing to do just about anything."

Micaela's throat felt tight and she was unbearably aware of how close he was standing to her, painfully aware of a shimmer of excitement racing through her. "And what p-p-price would that be, *monsieur*?"

. Hugh smiled enigmatically, and, bending over, he lifted her hand once more to his lips. His eyes on her soft mouth, he pressed a warm, lingering kiss into her sensitive palm, and murmured. "Oh, I think you could guess, sweetheart. I think you could guess exactly what I would demand."

It took several moments after Hugh had departed for Micaela's heart to stop pounding so fiercely. A thrill, a curious mixture of elation and shock, had coursed through her at his words, and, despite telling herself sternly that he couldn't have meant what she thought he had meant, she couldn't forget the look in his eyes or the seductive quality of his voice. Ah bah! she thought disgustedly. She was acting no better than that silly goose Cecile! The American had been toying with her, teasing her like one would a naive child.

Satisfied that she had explained his behavior, Micaela continued on her errands—buying some thread for *Maman*, some tooth powder for herself; going to see if the modiste whom they patronized had received any new pattern books from France. It was nearly an hour later when she returned home, two newly arrived pattern books tucked securely under her arm. She and her mother could spend a cozy evening perusing the books, and they could place an order for any garment which caught their fancy before they left for Riverbend at the end of the week.

There was no sign of Jean or François at dinner that night, and the evening progressed just as Micaela had foreseen. The pattern books were full of sketches, of tempting gowns with high waists which Josephine, Napoléon's wife and soon-to-be-Empress, had brought into style. They were very flattering, and normally Micaela would have been excited at the prospect of a new gown. But as she slowly turned the pages later that evening, she found her thoughts straying back to the disturbing meeting with Hugh Lancaster.

A dreamy look in her eyes, Micaela stared blindly at a

charming gown in apple green silk, Brussels lace at the low neckline and at the edges of the puffed sleeves. *Had he meant what he had implied?* Would he truly give up his shares in Galland, Lancaster and Dupree for *her*?

A queer feeling trembled deep within her as she considered the possibility that she had not mistaken his meaning at all. Had he meant marriage? Or had he been slyly insulting her, hinting at a less honorable situation? And if he had been, what difference did it make to her? she reminded herself sharply. Either would be equally unacceptable! Why, she'd be more likely to become his mistress than marry him—and becoming any man's kept woman was simply unthinkable! She was angry at herself for not being able to put his words out of her mind. Impatiently she flipped the page of the pattern book.

"Oh, did you not like that gown?" Lisette asked. She was sitting on the sofa beside Micaela, leafing through the other pattern book with the occasional glance over at her unusually quiet daughter. "I thought," she added lightly, "it was particularly attractive and would look lovely on you, *chérie*."

Micaela started. Jerking her thoughts away from Hugh, she turned the page back. "It is a pretty gown," she admitted, really seeing it for the first time. Then she shrugged. "But I have an armoire full of gowns, I do not need another."

Lisette looked at her for a long moment. "I suppose that you are right," she said, a twinkle in her eyes, "but I thought that you might like something new to wear when we dine with Hugh Lancaster. . . ."

"For him," Micaela muttered savagely, "I shall wear the *oldest*, shabbiest garment I own!"

A little smile quivered at the corners of Lisette's mouth. "Ah, I see," she murmured.

"What do you mean by that?" Micaela demanded, a fierce look on her pretty face.

Innocently Lisette asked, "What, *chérie*?"

Realizing that she was venting her own bad temper on her mother, Micaela glared at the apple green gown. "Never mind. It was not important." It *was* a lovely gown, however . . . and there was that dinner . . . Airily, she added, "But if you think I should have it made up, I shall be guided by your wishes."

Lisette smiled at her. She bent and kissed Micaela's cheek. "Do what you want, *petite*."

But that was the problem, Micaela thought unhappily. I do not know what I want! Not anymore. . . .

Chapter Five

*F*eeling rather pleased with himself for having clearly left Micaela speechless, Hugh continued his stroll home. The stunned expression on her pretty face crossed his mind several times that afternoon and evening. As a matter of fact, thoughts of Micaela nearly cost him his life.

He had gone to a gaming establishment with Jasper that evening. The Dupree men were there as was Alain Husson, and Hugh was not surprised that the three of them greeted him coolly. It was obvious that Alain had learned of his refusal to sell and was firmly in the Dupree camp.

Some hours later, increasingly restless, Hugh had finally left Jasper at the faro table and begun to walk home. It was several blocks to Jasper's house. Despite the light from the oil lamps which hung from chains at every street corner, there were deep pockets of blackness, and as he approached one of these danger struck. His thoughts dwelling pleasurably on the meeting with Micaela this afternoon, he was not aware of the peril which stalked him until, out of the corner of his eye, he caught the vicious movement of a cudgel.

Hugh whirled away, the cudgel barely missing his head as his hand went instantly to the sword cane he carried at his side—as did most fashionable gentlemen in New Orleans. The small sword sang free and with grim features, he swung back to face his attacker.

There were three of them; each carried a cudgel, and as they fanned out around him in the shadowy darkness, like wolves circling their prey, Hugh's confidence wavered. One or two he could defeat, but three?

Despite their strength, they did not seem eager to join battle, contenting themselves with threatening gestures and the occasional, almost halfhearted feint. But as the seconds passed they grew bolder, pressing closer, staying just out of the range of his sword.

The middle one, apparently the leader, spat on the ground and muttered, "*Allons, mes amis*! We do not get paid unless we beat him soundly. At him!"

As one, the three surged toward Hugh; desperately he thrust with his sword. Dancing deftly backward from their approach, he slashed at first one and then another, hearing with fierce satisfaction the man on his left cry out with pain. But Hugh paid for it as one of the cudgels struck his shoulder with terrible power.

Hugh groaned, his sword arm feeling as if it were numb, but he recovered almost immediately, lunging violently after his attacker. He took another blow, a glancing one on the head, which left his ears ringing. Outnumbered, he retreated until he felt the wall of one of the buildings which lined the dark, narrow street against his back.

With labored breathing he faced his attackers, waiting for their next advance. Fortunately, it did not come.

There was the sound of footsteps on the wooden banquette and a second later, in the murky light, Hugh recognized Jasper. "*A l'aide!*" Hugh shouted as he fended off a brutal blow from one of his tormentors. "*Au secours!*"

It took Jasper but an instant to read the situation, and his sword was in view almost immediately. There was a violent oath from one of the men and then, almost as one, they took to their heels, disappearing into the darkness.

Jasper hurried to Hugh's side. "Are you hurt, *mon ami?*" He took a deep breath. "*Diantre!* But those were bold robbers."

Hugh shook his head and winced. "Perhaps a trifle." His eyes met Jasper's. "But they were no robbers—they were hired to attack me."

"*Mon Dieu!* But this is beyond belief. Are you certain?"

Hugh nodded gingerly. "Yes. In rallying the others, one said as much."

The remainder of the journey to the house was made in grim silence by the two men. Only after he had assured himself that Hugh had not been badly injured did Jasper's tense features relax. Handing Hugh a glass of port as they made themselves comfortable in his study, Jasper observed, "You are very fortunate—it could have been much worse."

"I know—if you had not happened along . . ." Hugh smiled crookedly and raised his glass. "To you, my friend. You may have saved my life. Certainly you saved me from a vicious beating."

Jasper shrugged. "It was nothing—I am your friend— you would have done the same for me."

Hugh nodded. A dangerous gleam suddenly lit his gray eyes. "But," he said softly, "someone else is very definitely *not* my friend. And I intend to find out who."

*   *   *

Hugh found himself tossing sleeplessly in his bed that night, thoughts of Micaela drifting tantalizingly through his mind—when he was not considering the implications of the attack on him earlier this evening. Staring thoughtfully up at the canopy over his head, he finally admitted that events were not following any path he had ever considered.

When he had left Natchez such a short time ago, he'd had his entire future mapped out. He would settle in New Orleans, resolve the trouble at Galland, Lancaster and Dupree and, after a suitable courtship, marry Alice Summerfield and set up his nursery. He would be a loving father and a kind husband, and he would settle sedately into the life he had chosen for himself. It was a future that he had looked forward to and had been confident would be his.

But now after seeing Micaela this afternoon and realizing with the suddenness of a lightning bolt that he would gladly, no eagerly, give up a great deal to possess her, he felt badly shaken. And the knowledge that someone hated him or feared him enough to arrange what would have no doubt been a brutal beating infuriated him as much as it mystified him. Was it simply the Duprees venting their spleen at his refusal to sell out to them? Or something more sinister that he had not yet considered?

Sleep was impossible. Swearing in two languages, he got out of bed and yanked on a black-silk robe. Entering the adjoining sitting room, he walked over to the sideboard and from a crystal decanter of brandy poured himself a half snifter of the amber-colored liquor.

His features grim, he wandered about the dark sitting room, absently swirling his untasted brandy. Since he was in no mood just yet to dwell on the attack, he let his thoughts drift to Micaela—as if he could stop them.

Perhaps, he thought reluctantly, even if he forgot about the wild notion of trading his shares for her hand in marriage, marrying Micaela Dupree was not quite the insane idea it had first appeared. There would be, he admitted wryly, several advantages. He would have aligned himself with one of the most respected and aristocratic families in New Orleans. Jasper would certainly be ecstatic, he conceded ruefully. But looking at it pragmatically, it would keep the business totally within the control of the current partners . . . and allow him to have Micaela in his bed—a notion which had crept with increasing frequency through his dreams of late.

On the other hand, he reminded himself coolly, it would create a whole host of new problems—especially if his suspicions proved correct and it turned out to be either Jean or François, or both, who were stealing from the company. With Micaela as his wife, he would find it rather awkward to accuse her brother or her uncle of thievery—or of hiring someone to beat him soundly. Certainly prosecuting them would be out of the question. A tempting vision of Micaela suddenly floated before him. But there would be, he admitted to himself as he took a sip of his brandy, advantages. . . .

Hugh shook his head disgustedly. He wasn't seriously considering marrying Micaela Dupree, was he? She made her opinion of him clear, and he wasn't fool enough to marry a woman who disliked him. Such a union would bring nothing but trouble, and he wasn't one who willingly went looking for trouble.

He would concede, however, that Micaela aroused some elemental emotion within him. A night or two, he thought wryly, spent in the arms of a clever courtesan would no doubt cure him of his damnable preoccupation with *Mademoiselle* Dupree! In a few weeks, a month, he would look back on this time and wonder how he had allowed himself to be so befuddled by her. She was undeniably a seductive armful, and if she had been of a certain class of woman, he would not have hesitated a moment before setting her up as his mistress. But wife? He shook his head. Ridiculous!

And as for whoever had set those ruffians on him . . . Hugh smiled like a lazy tiger. He was going to enjoy exposing his enemy—and teaching him a lesson, a lesson that would not soon be forgotten.

Feeling considerably better about the situation, Hugh finished his brandy and, a short while later, returned to his bed. To sleep. And to dream of flashing dark eyes and soft, tempting cherry red lips.

Certain that he had been suffering from a momentary aberration, during the following days Hugh firmly banished any thoughts of Micaela from his mind and concentrated on affairs at Galland, Lancaster and Dupree. There were no further attacks on him, and he wondered if he had been mistaken in what he had overheard. Perhaps.

March faded into April, and Hugh was still no closer to discovering his thief—or his attackers—or their reasons. On the twenty-ninth of March, he had written to the firm which handled their affairs in Europe and had requested a *complete* copy of several of the suspicious invoices. He had offered no reasons, but he had asked that they be sent privately to him at Jasper's town residence. There was no point in alarming anyone at Galland, Lancaster and Dupree . . . yet.

He had also delved more deeply into the tasks of each person employed by the firm. There were only so many people who had access to the invoices, and he was painstakingly eliminating them from his list of suspects. He had considered that the order for the attack on him could have originated from someone in the company other than the Duprees, but he had found nothing to support that theory. And as for the person who might have altered the invoices—originally he had been suspicious of everyone, but as the weeks had passed he had narrowed down his list to four men—aside from Jean, François, and Alain Husson.

Hugh had not been inclined to consider Husson on his list of suspects in the beginning, but the more he learned of the man and his connection to François, the more he wondered. The losses had not really started until after Husson had won his shares from Christophe. Of course, the same could be said of Jasper, but the notion of Jasper stealing from the firm was absurd. Husson was a different story though.

The Creole was certainly wealthy, but Hugh had learned through discreet inquiry that Husson was also a great gambler. As was François, Hugh thought grimly. However, Husson seemed to win more than he lost, and there were rumors that a wise man did not often wager against him. Husson was, according to several American friends, nearly unbeatable. More interesting to Hugh, however, was the information that while Husson graciously accepted any man's vowels, only a fool did not repay the debt . . . promptly. A whisper here and there had come to Hugh's ears that men unwise enough not to redeem their vowels, were not only dishonored, but *things* happened to them . . . decidedly unpleasant things. Noses and legs were broken. Houses and crops burned. Loans were denied. Livestock disappeared. All of which made Hugh wonder if Husson could have been behind the attack on him. It didn't seem likely, but it certainly had been the sort of thing often connected with Husson's name.

It was clear that Alain Husson was not a man to be trifled with. And François, Hugh had discovered, owed Husson a *very* large debt It was murmured that the debt had been growing for some time and that Husson had finally demanded his money but François was having trouble meeting that demand. It was possible, Hugh considered uneasily, that Husson had put pressure on François to repay his gambling debts and François had been compelled to do so the only way he could—steal from his own company. Then again, Hugh thought dryly, Husson and François could be in collusion with each other and whether the idea to steal from Galland, Lancaster and Dupree had come from François or Husson made little difference. They also could have conspired to have him beaten, thinking to drive him out.

Because he had nothing definite to go on, Hugh was forced into a waiting game. Until the next large shipment arrived from Europe, or the copies of the invoices he had sent for were finally in his hands, he could do nothing.

At a standstill in his quest to find the thief or the person who had ordered the attack on him, and strangely reluctant to proceed with his courtship of Alice Summerfield, Hugh found himself irritated and frustrated. With an eye toward purchase, he had looked at several prospective town houses and had even seen a few larger estates in the country. He would need both eventually, but viewing the various houses and lands did not give him the pleasure he had thought it would. Some spark, he acknowledged uncomfortably, was missing.

As April melted into May and the days lengthened and grew warmer and more humid, he found himself oddly restless and unsettled, nothing holding his attention for very long. Even Jasper's lively company did not soothe the impatient, ceaseless stirrings within him, and his temper grew short.

The invitation to stay several days at Riverbend came as a total surprise, and Hugh was doubly irritated by the flush of anticipation and pleasure which had rushed through him when he had read Lisette's note. His bad temper vanished, and for the first time in weeks he found himself looking forward to an event with eager expectancy. It was, he told himself firmly, the prospect of getting away from the city and seeing more of the lush Louisiana countryside that had raised his spirits. It had *nothing* to do with the fact that he would see Micaela. Nothing.

Some of Hugh's anticipation lessened when he learned that it was a large house party that he had been invited to attend. He was pleased and not surprised that Jasper had been invited, but the news that Alice Summerfield and her parents had also received an invitation brought a faint frown to his face. The connection had to be François, but what in Hades was that young puppy trying to do? Cut him out? Hugh snorted. The way he felt right now, François had his blessing!

The Husson family had also been invited, but would not be staying at Riverbend. Like the other neighbors who would be attending the various entertainments scheduled for the Dupree guests, they would be riding and driving over each day and returning to their own home afterward. Why this pleased Hugh when Jasper mentioned it, he did *not* care to speculate.

Micaela had been startled when Jean first proposed the house party to Lisette one evening at dinner. She had stared at his unreadable features and had wondered what was behind this sudden decision. The news that Jean intended for Hugh Lancaster to be amongst the invited guests made her eyes widen. *Ma foi*! Had her *oncle* had a change of heart about the *Américains*? It seemed so, especially when Jean went on to mention that he also intended for the Summerfield family to attend the house party.

Micaela looked across the table at François's suspiciously bland face. It had been François, she recalled, who had introduced her and Lisette to the Summerfields when they had come into the city in March, and she had wondered then what had prompted her brother's interest in the *Américains*. Of course, *Mademoiselle* Summerfield was very lovely, but surely François was not . . .

Her gaze narrowed as she studied her brother. Was he thinking of marriage? To an *Américain*? Bah! That was unlikely . . . as unlikely as her becoming Hugh's mistress! Or her marrying Alain Husson!

Later that evening as she prepared for bed, Micaela frowned when she thought of Alain Husson. He had paid several visits to the plantation since she and Lisette had returned from their last trip to New Orleans and his determined pursuit of her had become so persistent and so unrelenting that she was feeling decidedly harassed. Despite her previous strong hints and increased coolness to him, Alain seemed oblivious to the fact that she was not enamored with him and that she had no intention of marrying him—if he should be so foolish as to ask her!

During the days that followed Jean's announcement of his plans for the house party, Alain's pursuit of Micaela continued and her manner toward him became increasingly sharp, sometimes almost bordering on rudeness. Her less-than-welcoming manner did not seem to faze him one bit, and there appeared no escaping his attentions—not when François was always inviting him to visit or stay for dinner.

This evening was no exception. Alain had come to dine. Once the meal was finished, Alain asked, as he usually did, if he could escort her for a brief stroll around the gardens before he departed for his own home. Micaela accepted with ill-disguised reluctance. No one else seemed inclined to join them, so they were alone as they left the dining room and stepped out into the warm night air.

Determined to make it as short a walk as possible, Micaela set off at a brisk pace down the winding path which ambled through the extensive gardens at the side of the house. They had not gone far before Alain asked, "Why are you in such a hurry, *ma coeur*? It is a beautiful night—almost as beautiful as you. . . ."

Micaela snorted and cast him an exasperated look. "And I have told you repeatedly that I do not find your compliments welcome—nor, I might add, speaking plainly, your continued pursuit. I have asked, no, pleaded with you to turn your attentions elsewhere, but you refuse to listen to me."

Alain smiled. "Ah, *ma belle*, you do not really mean that. You know that I adore you . . . that both our families are waiting in momentary expectation of our announcement that we shall be married." A complacent expression on his handsome face, he reached for her hand. "Perhaps," he purred, "I have been too discreet and sedate in my courtship . . . perhaps you have been waiting for me to show you how much I desire you."

He suddenly pulled her into his arms, his mouth crushing down on hers as he held her tightly against him. Her first reaction was astonishment, then as his hand moved boldly to her breasts, sheer fury erupted through her. She fought him, twisting and squirming violently in her efforts to escape his hot, seeking mouth and equally bold hands.

Managing finally to break free of him, her bosom heaving with temper and exertion, she glared at him in the moonlight. Without thinking, she soundly boxed his ears as he stood before her with that superior smile on his face.

"I would *never,*" she hissed in a shaken, furious tone, "consent to marry a man who acts so boorishly! How dare you force yourself upon me."

Alain's eyes glittered with an emotion that made her distinctly uneasy, and she stepped away from him. "Come one step nearer to me, and I shall scream," she warned him.

"And you think that your uncle or brother will come to help you?" Alain asked coolly. "You are a pretty little fool, *chérie*, and I wonder if it is not your hesitation to marry me which holds my interest."

"*Hesitation?*" Micaela spat. "Just so you have no illusions, let me explain my position to you—I will *not* marry you—*under any circumstances!*"

Alain almost smirked. "Will you not? Shall we make a wager on it?"

"Bah! It is useless to talk to you," she said disgustedly. "Go home, Alain. For the sake of the long friendship between our families, I will try to pretend that tonight did not happen. I hope that the next time we meet you will have recovered your senses."

His confidence not the least battered, Alain bowed and left.

Greatly disturbed by the incident, Micaela had gone immediately in search of her uncle. She found him looking over some papers in his office, which was in a separate building behind the main house.

The words tumbling out of her mouth, she poured out her story in bald detail. To her growing unease, Jean did not seem overly concerned. Deciding that he had not understood just how far Alain had gone beyond the bounds of acceptable behavior, a blush staining her cheeks, she muttered, "He kissed me, *oncle*, and t-t-touched me in a much too familiar manner."

His dark eyes shuttered, Jean merely glanced at her and remarked, "I think you make too much of his behavior. He is a young man in love. An extremely eligible young man. A young man who would make an excellent addition to our family."

Micaela flushed with anger. "I told you that I was *not* going to marry him! It is unfair of you and François to encourage his visits. And I do not appreciate having him always lurking about and . . . and pawing at me whenever we are out of sight of others."

Jean shrugged. "As I said, he is in love. A hot-blooded Creole in pursuit of his bride. You are cruel to keep him at a distance."

Micaela's eyes narrowed. "You do not intend to do anything about him, do you? You are trying to force me to marry him."

Jean looked away, unable to meet her accusing gaze. "Force you, *chérie*? I think you are becoming hysterical."

Micaela snorted. "And I think that you have become hard-of-hearing."

Jean shook his head and said quietly, "You know how important it is for the family, especially your brother, for you to marry Husson. I suggest you rethink your position." A coaxing note entered his voice. "Becoming a spinster aunt to François's children is no future for you, *petite*. You are far too lovely to remain unmarried. By re-fusing Alain, you are simply being foolish and stubborn."

Micaela's hands clenched into fists. "And you will do nothing to stop Alain from continuing to persist in his un-wanted attentions to me?"

Jean forced a smile. "As I said earlier, *petite*, I think you are making too much of his behavior. He is impetu-ous, and I will admit that perhaps he has let his desire for your hand in marriage go to his head. . . . You have been gently reared—it is perfectly natural that you should re-sist him, but I am afraid that in Alain's case, your reluc-tance only adds spice to the chase." His smile gone, a shadow on his face, he added with sudden weariness, "You might be wise to accept him, while it is still your choice."

"What do you mean?"

Jean sighed and, picking his words with great care, said, "Sometimes . . . events . . . happen which take away one's choices. You would do well to remember that the next time Alain comes to call."

Micaela was so incensed, so angry at Jean's lack of support that his words and the implied threat in them went right over her head. Her lovely face flushed with temper, her dark eyes flashing, she snapped, "And you would do well to remember that I will not be forced into a marriage I find repugnant!" Having said the last word, she stalked regally from the room.

Dissatisfied with Jean's reaction, she considered briefly talking to François. Alain was, after all, François's friend. Perhaps if she made it clear to her brother . . . ? But talking to François, she realized bitterly, would do no good—he, or at least his gambling, was the most urgent reason why the match with Alain was viewed with such favor.

Knowing there was at least one sympathetic ear into which she could pour out her troubles, Micaela stormed up the stairs, intending to tell her mother all that had transpired. *Maman* would support her. *Maman* would make the males of the family listen to reason. Halfway to Lisette's room she stopped abruptly. She was not a child any longer, she chided herself sternly, to run to *Maman* at the first sign of difficulty. She was an adult. And her situation was not so very precarious—unpleasant, perhaps, but not particularly serious. And the solution was simple—all she had to do was avoid Alain and keep saying no—vehemently! She would take great care that she did not find herself in the same position that she had tonight. A faint smile curved her mouth. Eventually even the most ardent suitor would lose heart if he was continually met with an icy shoulder and a frozen stare.

The date of the house party approached swiftly. To Micaela's relief there were no further incidents with Alain, and she wondered if Jean had, after all, had a word with him. Perhaps Alain had finally realized that she was serious about her refusal to marry him? Whatever the reason for Alain's absence, Micaela was grateful for it.

Sitting alone on Tuesday morning in the gazebo which overlooked the river, she snatched a few minutes respite from the frantic preparations which had consumed the household in preparation of the party.

The house would be full of guests in a few hours and several pleasurable activities had been planned for their amusements. Tomorrow there would be a tour of the plantation and dinner al fresco in the gardens; Thursday afternoon, a riverboat trip had been arranged; on Friday they were all going for an extended ride in the country; a midday interlude had been arranged. At a favorite family stopping point, a pleasant area littered with moss-draped live oaks and with a commanding view of the Mississippi River, a luncheon would be served by the servants, who would have ridden ahead to have everything all ready to serve the riders when they arrived. On Saturday night, Lisette had planned a grand ball to which everyone for miles around had been invited. Other amusements were planned and, of course, the gentlemen would be able to hunt and ride as the mood took them; the ladies would be able to explore the extensive and beautiful gardens and grounds adjacent to the house.

Knowing that Hugh Lancaster had been invited, Micaela was both looking forward to and dreading the coming party. She could not understand her decidedly antagonistic attitude toward him—even if he was an *Américain*! She had, she admitted uneasily, met several *Américains*, the Summerfield family for instance, and not once had she been prompted to make a hostile comment while in their company. Normally a warm, congenial person, she was secretly appalled at the aggravating things that came out of her mouth whenever she was around Hugh Lancaster. It was embarrassing and, she confessed with guilty pleasure, *very* exciting. Every stinging barb she aimed at him filled her with that odd mixture of guilt and excitement. Rather, she thought ruefully as she rose and began to walk toward the house, like pulling the whiskers of a sleek, sleeping tiger.

Hugh's appearance that afternoon when he arrived at the Dupree plantation was as far from the description of a *sleeping* tiger as one could get. After he had swung off his horse, a big, restive bay, she greeted him as she stood beside her mother and Jean on the wide steps of the plantation house. Micaela confessed to herself that she had never before in her life met such a virile and exciting man. One lazy glance from his surprisingly long-lashed gray eyes and she was burningly aware of herself in a way she had never experienced. She felt . . . *female*, and something inside of her responded irresistibly to his very maleness. It was unsettling. So when it was her turn to welcome him, she said coolly, "*Monsieur* Lancaster, how . . . ah, nice that you could bring yourself to leave behind the pressing affairs of Galland, Lancaster and Dupree and accept my uncle's humble invitation to join us for a few days."

Still holding her hand in his, Hugh grinned. Little vixen! If they were alone, he'd teach her to watch that impudent tongue. In fact, he thought with a sudden, sweet stab in his loins, he'd enjoy teaching her some extremely pleasurable uses for that sharp little tongue.

A glitter in his gray eyes, Hugh murmured, "But *mademoiselle*, surely you know that the promise of your charming company holds far more allure for me than mere business."

Micaela blinked at the unexpected compliment, and she suddenly looked very young and vulnerable. Adorably so, Hugh thought.

Flustered, she managed to stammer, "H-h-how, very g-g-gallant, *monsieur*."

Jean's gaze narrowed. The interplay made him uneasy, and he was frowning as he watched Hugh, escorted by the two women, disappear into the house. Between Lancaster's meddling at the firm, Husson's pressing for payment of François's debt, and Micaela's stubborn refusal to marry Husson—thereby relieving their most pressing needs—he needed no further complications at this date. Worriedly Jean played back the exchange between Micaela and Hugh. Lancaster's interest in Micaela had better not go beyond polite flirtation.

Later that afternoon, after all the guests had arrived and everyone had been shown to their various rooms and were dressing for dinner, Jean had a word with François. A troubled frown between his eyes, Jean asked François, "Have you noticed, er, anything unusual between your sister and the *Américain*?"

François, who was reclining comfortably in a chair in Jean's office, looked astonished. "Micaela and Lancaster? Are you jesting?"

Jean shrugged. "Just an idle question. When they met this afternoon, I thought that there was something."

François snorted. "You are imagining things. Lancaster's interest is well-known to lie with a certain blond, very lovely *Américaine*."

"Which is why the Summerfields were invited—and why you have been paying much attention to this same young lady, *non*?"

François laughed, his dark eyes dancing. "She *is* very lovely, even you must admit—*américaine* though she is. And if I can tweak the tiger's nose by flirting with his intended bride, why would you deny me my pleasure—you do not like him either."

"Is that all it is—tweaking Hugh's nose?"

"Of course, what other interest would I have in an *américaine* female?" François asked, surprised.

Rubbing a hand across the back of his neck, Jean muttered, "We need no complications, remember that."

It was François's turn to shrug. "But we will have none after Friday night, will we? My debt to Husson will be paid, you will have the capital you need for the plantation, and Husson will have what he wants—Micaela."

"Everything is arranged?"

François nodded. "Everything. Husson knows what he has to do, and he is most eager. With my help, it will be easy enough for him to separate her from the others—I shall be blind and deaf—except to the comfort of the rest of our guests, of course. And I shall swiftly lead them away. The fact that two of our party disappear on the ride will not be noticed until after we return home, and by then it will be dusk. Far too late to go looking for the two missing members. It will be Saturday morning before we can institute a search for them." Reluctantly, he added, "And by then, it will be much, *much* too late for Micaela. Honor will demand that she and Husson marry." François could not meet Jean's gaze, a nagging feeling of guilt rushing through him, especially when he realized that it was *his* debts that had brought them to this point—his debts and unrelenting pressure from Husson.

Unhappily, Jean muttered, "If only there were some other way." He grimaced, knowing there was not, and said bleakly, "It is unfortunate that circumstances have driven us to this dishonorable, desperate plan. We, who should protect her, are willing to sacrifice her for our own gain."

Chapter Six

It was not a huge house party, by Creole standards, but there was no denying that the spacious Dupree house was certainly full. In addition to Lancaster and the Summerfields there were two Creole families also staying at the house. Both couples were longtime friends of the Duprees', and both lived near each other, about a six-hour ride north of New Orleans. The first couple, *Monsieur* and *Madame* L'Aramy and their two sons and their youngest daughter, just turned seventeen, were particular favorites of Lisette's. They were a strikingly handsome family, tall for Creoles. The eldest son, René, at thirty years old and with his mother's striking green eyes, was considered one of the most eligible young men in New Orleans. Gaston, the second son, just twenty-five, was also much sighed over by Creole maidens, and their sister, Rachelle, with her cat green eyes and porcelain skin, was already one of the reigning belles in the area. The second family, *Monsieur* and *Madame* Charbonneau, had also brought their older children with them—the son, Bellamy, was a very handsome young man of twenty-seven; there had been a time when he had dangled after

Micaela, but it had come to naught, although he was still unattached. His so-charming sisters—Colette, eighteen, and Henrietta, seventeen—were both petite, pretty creatures with masses of dusky curls and merry laughs. With so many young and unmarried guests, the party was likely to prove to be most lively.

Since the festivities were not scheduled to begin until the next day, dinner that evening was composed only of those guests actually staying at the house and the Husson family. François had been particularly insistent that they be invited.

Dinner that evening was a boisterous affair, the antics of the younger members causing smiles and chuckles from the older contingent. And while Lisette had planned no other activities, it wasn't very long after dinner that François and Bellamy had prevailed upon her to play the piano and Jean the violin so that they all might dance. Everyone retired to the music room; chairs and tables were pushed aside, and soon one might have thought that a grand ball was being held.

Despite his easy dismissal of Jean's comment about Hugh and Micaela, François, when he was not squiring one of the young ladies about the room, found himself watching the pair of them. Noticing them standing with three or four others near the opened French doors, François unobtrusively joined the group.

Jasper made some teasing sally, and Hugh grinned. Shaking his head, Hugh said, "*Mon ami*, if I followed your advice, I would never accomplish anything and would instead become as frivolous and heedless of business affairs as you are yourself."

"Oh?" Micaela asked with a raised brow. "You find us frivolous, *monsieur*?"

"But very, very lovely," Hugh murmured, with a deep bow in her direction.

Ignoring the warm rush his comment gave her, over the top of her gaily painted silk fan, Micaela regarded him. "Are you never frivolous, *monsieur*?"

"I do not believe so, *mademoiselle*," Hugh answered gravely, a hint of laughter in his eyes. "Americans are not known for their, ah, frivolity."

Micaela gave an exaggerated sigh. Opening her eyes very wide, she murmured, "*Merci*! How utterly boring you *Américains* must be."

Hugh's shout of laughter made several heads turn in that direction, but beyond Micaela's strategic retreat to another part of the room, there was nothing to see. One might have wondered, however, at the color in her cheeks and the sparkle in her eyes.

Drifting over to a table spread with refreshments, Micaela waited while a servant poured her a glass of lemonade. Sipping it, she turned back to survey the room, sighing when Alain appeared at her side.

"What did he say to you that makes you look so pleased with yourself?" Alain inquired silkily, as he boldly took her arm and began to escort her away from the table.

Micaela accompanied him a few steps, but when she saw he was attempting to lead her outside, she stopped and said bluntly, "Let go of my arm, Alain. I am not leaving this room with you. And to answer your question—it is none of your affair. Now go find someone who may find your company more welcome that I do."

Alain smiled confidently down at her. "Ah, you are still angry with me, are you not, *ma belle*?"

Giving him a level glance, she said coolly, "No, I am not angry with you. I am simply indifferent to you. And I would appreciate it if you would do as I say and leave me alone."

"Do you know that I find your anger most exciting?" Alain murmured, his smile unabated.

Tapping him sharply on the arm with her fan, she muttered, "Oh, *go away*! You are tiresome."

Completely unmoved by her manner, Alain's smile only deepened. Kissing her hand, he said softly, "You wound me, *ma mie*, but your words are my command."

Micaela snatched her hand away and, with an ill-disguised expression of irritation on her pretty face, hastily put the width of the room between them.

Glumly François had watched the interplay, well aware that Hugh's attentions had not seemed to annoy her, while Alain's obviously had. There was no denying it—there *did* seem to be something shimmering in the air between Micaela and the *Américain*, something that made him decidedly uneasy.

It was worrisome, even though he knew that nothing could come of it—by Friday night Micaela's fate would be sealed—but the situation alarmed him. Arranging a moment alone with both Jean and Alain had not been easy. But having alerted his uncle to the need for a private word, they were able to discreetly detain Alain, who was riding his own horse, from immediately following his family as their carriage pulled away. Waiting until the other guests had gone back into the house, the three men stood near Alain's horse, talking in low tones.

"I think that it would be wise if we kept an eye on Lancaster—and my sister," François said. He glanced at Jean. "After your remark this afternoon, I paid closer attention to them tonight, and it did seem to me that there is *some*thing going on between them."

Alain's face tightened. "*Mon Dieu*! Are you saying that

having spurned *me*, that Micaela has developed a *tendre* for the *Américain*?"

"*Non. Non.* Nothing like that," François replied swiftly. "Only that . . ." He looked helplessly at Jean.

"He means," Jean said smoothly, "that we should be extremely careful on Friday. *If* Lancaster is—er—attracted to Micaela, he would naturally be aware of her whereabouts at all times—which might make her abduction from the group more difficult for you."

Alain snorted. Mounting his horse, he said, "Perhaps, it should be arranged that Lancaster is"—he paused—"oh, shall we say, unavoidably absent from Friday's pleasures?"

Despite feeling that there was some ulterior purpose behind Jean's invitation, Hugh found that he was enjoying himself immensely. The house and grounds were magnificent; Lisette was as warm and welcoming as always; his increasing fascination with Micaela refused to abate, and the growing notion of tasting that ripe, tempting mouth of hers filled him with a feeling of fierce anticipation. Jean treated him cordially and François seemed undecided whether to scorn him or charm him— much to Hugh's amusement. His status as a guest of the Dupree family and the fact that he spoke flawless French thawed the icy manner of many of the Creoles and allowed him to participate fully in the many enjoyments offered.

It was much the same for the Summerfield family. Their French might not equal Hugh's, but six months in New Orleans had enabled them to gain a smattering of the Gallic tongue. Summerfield's position on the governor's staff helped, too. The Creoles might not like being forced to accept American possession, but they were not fools either!

The riverboat ride on Wednesday and the tour of the plantation, specifically its sugar-cane operation, proved to be engrossing for Hugh, but despite his best efforts, a part of him was braced for Jean's reasons for inviting him to surface. With every passing hour, he knew that the likelihood of Jean revealing his motives became more certain, and Hugh was aware of a growing tenseness which gradually overshadowed his enjoyment.

On Thursday afternoon, while several of the others were resting up for the evening's entertainment, Jean asked Hugh for a moment in private. Hugh agreed politely and followed Jean to the other man's office in the small building behind the main house.

Once they were seated, Jean said bluntly, "I am sure that you have guessed that I had a specific reason for inviting you to attend the party?"

Hugh nodded curtly.

Jean smiled crookedly. "You have had time to think about what we proposed last month. I hope that further reflection on your part has perhaps allowed you to see the wisdom of selling out to us." Jean looked sheepish. "And as for your invitation here—I thought that perhaps in more, er, pleasant and relaxed surroundings we could more amiably discuss our proposition."

"We can discuss it," Hugh said equitably, "all you want, anywhere you want, but it will not change anything. My position remains the same—pending my stepfather's approval, I will sell you all my shares or none."

"You stubborn, stubborn *Américain*!" Jean cried angrily. "Why are you being so unreasonable? We are willing to pay you a fair price! I have explained to you that we can*not* afford to buy all your shares. There is only enough money to buy half."

"Then, as I said the last time we had this conversation—we are at an impasse," Hugh said quietly. He hesitated then added, "Unless you wish to sell me your shares?"

Jean could not have looked more affronted if Hugh had spit in his face. "*Sacrebleu*! Sell you the entire Dupree interest in the firm? You insult me, *monsieur*! It is *our* company!"

Hugh sighed knowing there was no arguing with the other man. Jean was conveniently forgetting that from the very beginning John Lancaster had held the largest share of the business—fifty-five percent—and that the remainder had been split up between Christophe, Renault, and Jean. Originally, Christophe had owned twenty-five percent and Renault and Jean each ten percent. The Duprees in fact had owned the smallest share in the business when it began and upon Renault's death, his original ten percent and the additional ten percent he had received from Christophe when he had married Lisette was now split between Micaela and François, giving his two children each ten percent. Christophe's remaining share had been further reduced when he had lost two percent to Husson and three percent to Jasper; upon his death Christophe only retained ten percent—which was now owned by Lisette. It was all very confusing, but the fact remained that with Hugh owning forty-five percent and John ten percent, the Americans still controlled the largest block and the Creole faction the smallest. And there seemed no way out of the dilemma.

Unless, Hugh mused distractedly, he was insane enough to offer his shares for Micaela's hand. Shaken by how very appealing he found that idea, he said in a harsher tone than he intended, "As I said, we seem to be at an impasse."

An ugly look on his face, Jean muttered, "I hope, *monsieur*, that you do not regret your stubbornness."

"Are you threatening me?" Hugh asked idly.

Jean smiled tightly. "*Non*. Warning you, perhaps. You are, after all, my guest and it would be," Jean said cynically, "the height of incivility for me to threaten you while you are under my roof."

Hugh stared steadily at him. "Would you like for me to leave?"

His quick temper ebbing, Jean shook his head ruefully. "*Non, monsieur*. You are my guest, and if you were not quite so hardheaded and stubborn, I might even learn to like you."

Hugh smiled, "And I, you."

In something resembling cordiality, the two men left Jean's office, going their separate ways upon reaching the house. Hugh went in search of Jasper, who was also staying at the Dupree house. A brief inquiry to Lisette elicited the information that Jasper was at the stables taking another look at a mare which Jean was thinking of selling. The stables had been included in the tour, so Hugh knew exactly which direction to take. The path to the stable was a pleasant one, winding along a bluff which overlooked the river, skirting a small white gazebo before dropping down and curving through a small woodland which concealed the stable area from the house and its grounds.

Hugh was concentrating so deeply on the conversation with Jean and trying to find a workable solution to their mutual problem that he was upon the gazebo before he realized it. His approach had been silent, and it was clear the two occupants of the gazebo were unaware of his presence. He would have continued on his way, or at least

let the two people inside know that he was there, if he
hadn't heard something that stopped him in his tracks.

"—but I do not want to marry him! And how you can
persist in believing that he would even consider a match
with me after the way I have treated him? . . ." She muttered something under her breath and added tightly,
"François, I insult him, or attempt to, nearly every time I
am in his company. Didn't you notice my manner with
him last evening? I know that he seems impervious to my
remarks, even amused by them, but you are foolish to
think that marriage will eventually result."

"Whether you want to marry him or not is not the
point," François said swiftly. "If you cannot bring yourself to care for him, then you must view your union as a
business liaison—if you married him, your shares of the
business, added to his, would increase his authority."

"He does not *need* my shares—he is wealthy enough
without them!" Micaela exclaimed exasperatedly. Her
voice softened as she said, "I would do just about anything for you—you know that. You are my brother and I
love you, but, François, you are being utterly selfish to
expect me to throw away my life simply because it will
be convenient for you—or good business!"

Bitterly François replied, "But Caela, you are not fair!
I am not asking you to mary some decrepit, ugly old
man—I am pleading with you to marry a man who is
young and handsome and who will be one of the wealthiest, most influential citizens in New Orleans before
many more years pass. What is so selfish about that?"

"Have you not heard a word I have said? *I do not want
to marry him!* I do not even like him very much."

"But Caela, think of it! If you were to marry him, it
would solve all of our problems." A wheedling note entered his voice. "And would it be so very bad? You would

have your own home, servants to command, a handsome, doting husband. I have seen the way he looks at you—despite the way you treat him." There was a taut silence, then François added, "Are you very sure that his fortune does not tempt you?"

"*Oui!*" Micaela spat. "Do you really expect me to marry a man I do not like simply because you wish it—for his *fortune?*"

"But it is *not* just for me," he muttered stubbornly. "It is for Jean and *Maman* as well. Have you thought of them? You know that our finances are troubled at the moment, and that your refusal to marry him affects all of us, even *Maman.*"

"Unfair! You know that I would do *any*thing for *Maman!*"

"Then think of *her,*" François said urgently. "Think of her before you throw away an opportunity to enrich us all."

"Oh, leave me be!" Micaela cried, her distress carrying clearly to where Hugh stood listening.

"But you will think about it?"

"I will think about it," she answered dully.

Deciding that he didn't want to be discovered shamelessly eavesdropping on what was an extremely intimate conversation, Hugh silently drifted away. His pleasant mood had been totally destroyed by what he had just overheard. And while he was not a vain man, he was certain that he could guess the identity of the man who had been the subject of the conversation between Micaela and François. It could be, he thought with a black scowl, none other than himself. He seriously doubted that anyone else, other than himself, had been the object of Micaela's pointed little barbs. And her comments *had* always amused him . . . until now.

It never occurred to Hugh that the two younger Duprees might be talking about somebody else. Who else did she insult at every turn? Last night's exchange went through his head. And to think he had thought her enchanting! His lips thinned. Of course they had to have been talking about him. Aside from her manner toward him, who else could so easily solve all their problems? And as for the connection to the business . . . Hugh snorted. She had been right about that—he sure as hell didn't need her shares!

Despite having considered marriage with Micaela, the knowledge that she obviously did *not* want to marry him sat ill with him. In her conversation with her brother, she had made it plain that his wealth and position could not compensate for having to have him as a husband, and it rankled a great deal. It was one thing to think about marrying a woman who seemed to enjoy their stinging repartee and another to wed a female who had clearly expressed her obvious repugnance at the idea of marriage to him. *Mademoiselle* Dupree did not have to worry about any more advances on his part! The lady had made her position painfully clear, and he bloody well was not going to pine after a woman who disliked him.

Telling himself that he had escaped a near disaster, and that he would be on his guard for the rest of his stay, Hugh forced himself to smile at Jasper when he spied the other man coming toward him. And if Jasper noticed that his friend seemed unusually preoccupied, he kept that knowledge to himself.

As planned, dinner that evening was held al fresco in the gardens adjacent to the house. Tables had been set up outside near the house, brimstone was burned to keep the insects at bay and servants bustled about waiting on guests. The stately trees surrounding the area were strung with lanterns, and the soft light cast a charming glow over the gently meandering paths of the gardens, which were lined with wonderfully scented flowers. But Hugh had no eye for the bucolic loveliness when, after dinner, he and Jasper joined several other guests and began to stroll through the lantern-strewn gardens.

An unaccustomed feeling of betrayal and resentment had been raging in his breast during the hours since he had overheard that damning conversation at the gazebo, and the passing time had not lessened it. But aside from his resentment, he was also angry with himself for letting a pretty face blind him to the reality of the situation. Actually, he was furious that he had allowed Micaela to invade his dreams and thoroughly disgusted with himself that he had considered, even for one moment, marriage with her.

And, of course, he reminded himself viciously as he stared blindly at gardenias awash with white blooms at the edge of the oyster-shell path, it wasn't as if the lady had given him any encouragement! She had made her dislike of him plain. Fool that he was, he had chosen to be amused, chosen to believe that there was something other than mere dislike which prompted her actions. Grimly he admitted that he had allowed himself to be captivated by her tart sallies and flashing eyes, instead of shearing off and going in search of more welcoming company. Fool!

One good thing had come from his eavesdropping. At least now he was forewarned that Micaela might try to sink her objections to him and begin to encourage his pursuit. His lip curled. To be married for her family's sake and his fortune held absolutely no allure at all for him. If the lady gave in to her brother's appeals and threw any lures his way, he'd be ready for them. A nasty smile suddenly crossed his face. He was almost looking forward to rebuffing her advances. Almost.

"And what," Jasper asked idly, "brings that sort of smile to your face, *mon ami*?"

Shaken from his unpleasant thoughts, Hugh almost visibly started, but, recovering himself swiftly, he smiled, and murmured, "Nothing that you would want to know about, believe me."

Jasper cocked a brow. "Hmm. I wonder. You have been very quiet this evening . . . are you certain there is nothing wrong?"

They came upon a small group admiring the golden swirl of tiny fish in a large pond, and the moment for private conversation was lost. Hugh stiffened when he spied Micaela standing next to Cecile Husson. Lisette and *Mesdames* L'Aramy and Charbonneau comprised the remainder of the group.

It was not surprising that the ladies had stopped to watch the fish. It was a very pretty spot, the walkway around the pond bordered with bright blooming scarlet and pink azaleas and beyond them several huge magnolia trees ringed the pond. The pond itself was eye-catching with its raised, rippled edge and striking tilework. Blue and pink water lilies floated serenely on the surface of the pool, the light from lanterns glinting like stars on the water.

Micaela's heart leaped when she caught sight of Hugh's tall form. No one had ever made her feel the way he did. All it took was one look from his heavily lidded gray eyes or that crooked smile of his, and she was filled with giddiness and left oddly breathless. And if he were to touch her, to hold her as Alain had done . . . Micaela swallowed with difficulty, stunned by the shocking heat which bloomed low in her abdomen.

Watching him beneath her lashes as he and Jasper greeted the ladies, Micaela finally admitted to herself something she had known all along: Hugh Lancaster was dangerous to her. Dangerous, because she very much feared that no matter how hard she tried to act cool and indifferent around him, her reckless heart had very different ideas.

Made miserable by the earlier conversation with François, Micaela's thoughts had been chasing themselves around in her brain like rats in a trap all afternoon. She would do much to save her brother, but she balked at ruining her own life for him. But Lisette . . . François had used the one weapon that could strike a fatal blow—her mother. For Lisette, she thought wretchedly, she would sacrifice herself. And while Lisette had not even once hinted that marriage to Husson was desirable, Micaela knew that there was only one way out of her quandary. She would, the next time he pressed his suit, accept Alain's offer. It was a painful decision that brought her no joy, and seeing Hugh Lancaster, realizing that the emotions he aroused within her breast were stronger, more powerful, more exciting than anything she had ever felt before in her life, only made the knowledge that she was going to force herself to marry Alain Husson all the more wrenching.

She managed to hide her unhappiness all evening, smiling and laughing as if she hadn't a care in the world as she mingled with their many guests, but the sight of Hugh's lean, handsome features and the realization that whatever silly, girlish notions she might have about him were finished caused her mask to slip slightly. When he approached her after greeting the older ladies, and bent politely over her hand, she was unaware of the softening of her gaze, the naked vulnerability in her dark eyes as their glances met.

To her astonishment, Hugh's manner was rather coolly abrupt with her. Leaving her perplexed by his coldness, she watched as he turned to smile warmly at Cecile. Have I offended him? she wondered. It was true that she had made some deliberately provocative statements in his presence and that some imp always prompted her to behave just this side of outright rudeness, but he had never seemed to mind. In fact, she thought with growing puzzlement, he had seemed to like the thrust and parry of their conversation, lazy amusement gleaming in his eyes those times when she had been particularly outrageous. And she could not deny that she had looked forward to their verbal tussles. What had changed?

Jean, François, and Alain Husson came up to them just then, and the groups merged, each gentleman offering an arm to the ladies. Despite Alain's determined push to her side, it was Hugh's arm that lay beneath Micaela's slender hand as the enlarged party began to walk slowly down the garden path. Hugh and Micaela brought up the rear, Jasper and Cecile walking sedately in front of them.

The expression in Micaela's usually laughing eyes when they had met had not gone unnoticed by Hugh and while just the day before, it would have caused his pulse to pound, this evening it only added fuel to his fury. Convinced by her languishing glance that she had given in to François's pleas and was now attempting to lure him into her web, his anger hardened. The lady it would appear, he thought wrathfully, has made her decision. Little fool! Does she honestly believe that all it will take is a limpid glance from those lovely eyes of hers to melt *my* heart! She will find, he vowed grimly, before she is much older that she is very much mistaken!

It was that vow which prompted him to make certain that he was Micaela's escort as they strolled through the garden. Determined to make his position clear—as much because he preferred plain speaking as the unacknowledged worry that he might, even knowing that her emotions were not involved, succumb to her wiles, he maneuvered events so that they were at the end of the line of couples.

They had not walked far when he halted and let the others increase their distance between them. Micaela's glance was startled as she looked up at him.

"What is it, *monsieur*? Why do we stop?" she asked softly.

Steeling his emotions against the lovely picture she made in the lanternlight, her dark hair piled elegantly on her small head, her eyes full of mystery and her tempting mouth only inches from his, he said bluntly, "I think I should tell you that while I find your company delightful, I have no intention of allowing myself to be trapped in any snare set by you or your family. You are, I will admit, a tempting baggage, but I will not marry you under any circumstances, so I suggest that you put any ideas of that sort out of your head."

Micaela blinked, hardly believing what she was hearing. As the full import of his words sank in, she stiffened. Full of Creole pride, her quick temper soared. She stepped away from him, glaring, and spat, "How *dare* you!" Ignoring the stab of pain in her heart, nearly choking with righteous indignation, she sputtered, "You are mad! And vain and conceited if you think that I would lower myself to marry such as you!" Her straight little nose went up in the air, her dark eyes flashing as she regarded him across the small distance which separated them. "You need not bother to escort me further," she said with icy disdain. "Fortunately this is my home, and I can find my way alone. I certainly do not need or *want* the company of someone like you—you boorish, ill-bred *Américain!*"

"Since we understand each other and I have nothing now to lose," Hugh said darkly, a peculiar look on his handsome face, "I might as well confirm your opinion of me and satisfy myself. . . ."

His hands suddenly gripped her shoulders, and, before she could react, his mouth came down urgently on hers. Micaela's lips stung from the barely leashed hunger of his mouth, the heat from his kiss, burning her, making her dizzy, making her pulse race and her heart pound like thunder in her chest. But there was an almost unbearable sweetness in his embrace, too, and for one brief, fleeting moment she let herself melt against him, let her lips soften.

His muffled groan and the realization of what she was doing suddenly brought Micaela hurtling back to reality. With a gasp, part shame, part fury, she tore herself from his arms, which, to her amazement, had somehow closed around her and had been holding her cradled next to him. Her eyes wide with shock and anger, her hand connected to his cheek before she had time to think. The sharp sound echoed through the night.

Tears of rage and hurt sparkling on her lashes, Micaela spun on her heels, intent upon putting as much distance as possible between herself and the infuriating creature behind her. She froze, and her breath caught in her throat as her gaze fell upon Alain Husson; François was standing just behind him.

"What is going on here?" Alain asked tightly, his hands clenched into fists at his side. "What have you done to her?"

"*Oui,*" François chimed in immediately. "What have you done to my sister to distress her so?"

It was obvious that they had not heard or seen all of the exchange, perhaps none of it, but it was also clear that they had picked up on the tension between Micaela and Hugh. The air was suddenly thick and full of dangerous currents, and Micaela's heart began to pound with fear. Recognizing that Alain was spoiling for a fight and that she must act swiftly to prevent a tragedy, Micaela forced a smile onto her stiff features. "*Ma foi!*" she said lightly. "It is nothing. I have the headache and am going to the house." Stopping in front of Alain's rigid body, she touched the lapel of his jacket. Softly, she added, "Truly, Alain, *Monsieur* Lancaster has done nothing to make you look at him in that manner. Come, you may escort me to the house."

Alain paid her no heed, his gaze locked on Hugh's taut features. Almost absently he put Micaela away from him, and, stalking up to Hugh's silent figure, he said, "Well, *monsieur*, what do you have to say for yourself?"

One of Hugh's brows rose. "I do not," he said levelly, "feel that I owe you an explanation."

"Do you not," Alain said with relish, an ugly expression glittering in his dark eyes. "I am afraid that I must take a different view, *monsieur.*"

"I repeat, it is not any of your business," Hugh said slowly, aware that he was treading on extremely treacherous ground.

Her eyes wide with alarm, Micaela grasped François's arm. "Do something!" she hissed. "Stop them before this goes any further."

"I think," François said gently, "that you should leave. You have done your part."

She stared at him as if she had never seen him before

in her life. "You want this to happen," she breathed weakly. "You want them to duel."

François tore his gaze away from the two principals. "You are mistaken. I did not arrange this situation—you did! And now you must live with the consequences of your own folly. Go away, Caela, there is nothing that you can do."

With a stricken look at Hugh's hard face, she picked up her skirts and fled. Racing down the pathway, she frantically searched for Jasper De Marco. Hugh would need him.

Alain had gasped at Hugh's cool reply, his face twisting with fury. "I find you insulting, *monsieur*," he finally choked out.

Hugh shrugged. He was aware that he might have been able to defuse this situation if he had wanted, but he discovered that he had no intention of turning away from the dangerous predicament in which he found himself. In fact, he thought with fierce satisfaction, facing Husson on the dueling field had definite allure.

"It is unfortunate that you feel that way," Hugh murmured, aware that Alain was trying to incite a challenge from him, "but I think that it is your problem. Not mine."

"*Mon Dieu*! Are you stupid, *Monsieur* Lancaster?" When Hugh merely smiled, Alain's tenuous hold on his temper was lost, and, reaching across the space which separated them, he furiously slapped Hugh on the cheek. "I challenge you, *monsieur*, to the duel! Name your seconds!"

A breathless Jasper, having been found by Micaela, who had frantically whispered the dangerousness of the situation into his ear, suddenly ran up. He was closely followed by René and Bellamy. Arriving to hear Alain's words, Jasper winced. Coolly he said, "Of course, I shall act as *Monsieur* Lancaster's second."

"And I shall be honored to be Husson's second," muttered François. René joined Jasper as Hugh's second and Bellamy found himself aligned with Alain and François.

The most immediate formalities out of the way, François asked Jasper, "When do you want to meet to discuss the conditions?"

Hugh spoke up. "There is no need for such refinements." His eyes fixed on Alain's angry face, he said slowly, "I believe that choice of weapons and place are mine." At Alain's curt nod and despite Jasper's protestations, Hugh said grimly, "Then there is no need of further discussion. Pistols at thirty paces, at dawn tomorrow." He bowed to Alain. "You may have the choosing of the site."

It was only when Hugh, Jasper, and René were in Hugh's room that Jasper let his agitation show. "*Mon Dieu*! Are you deliberately trying to get yourself killed?"

Worriedly René added, "Alain is reputed to be very good with the pistol."

Hugh shrugged. "I am not exactly a novice myself."

"That is not the point!" Jasper bit out. "The point is that in a matter of hours, you are going to be standing and facing a man who will be aiming a pistol at you. And firing that pistol right at your breast, hoping to kill you!"

Hugh smiled lazily. "You are forgetting something."

"What?" Jasper snapped.

Hugh's smile deepened. "I get to fire back."

Chapter Seven

*F*ull of fear as she had raced away from Alain and Hugh, Micaela had nearly wept with joy when she almost immediately found Jasper talking to René and Bellamy on the pathway. Everyone else had gone inside and Jasper had joined the other two men. One look at Micaela's features had warned him of trouble, and her urgently whispered account of the situation confirmed it.

Indecisively Micaela had watched the three men disappear down the path. Every instinct urged her to follow them, but she knew that such action would accomplish little. The gentlemen would only close ranks in front of her, and she would learn nothing from them. She considered going in search of her uncle, but quickly discounted that idea. If, as she suspected, Alain was determined to demand satisfaction from Hugh on the dueling field, Jasper would be able to handle the situation as well as Jean. She could only pray that Jasper would arrive in time to prevent the fatal words from being spoken. And if he didn't . . . Her heart squeezed painfully.

Hugh Lancaster was undoubtedly the most infuriating, overbearing, utterly conceited man she had ever met in her life—but she didn't want him to die in a duel. Especially a duel that she had inadvertently caused.

It didn't matter that it had been Hugh's own words and that unforgettable kiss that had made her react as she had, or that it had been simply bad luck that Alain and François had come upon them before she'd had a chance to compose herself. All that mattered was that Hugh not be harmed. It was enormously important to her that nothing happen to Hugh, and she didn't care to speculate about why she was so concerned about his well-being. He had certainly, she thought with a brief flare of anger, made his contempt of her obvious. And as for that kiss! How dare he!

But she was too worried to sustain much anger for very long. Tense and unhappy, she paced back and forth along the pathway, waiting anxiously for the return of the men. She knew Alain's reputation—he was a ruthless duelist, and whenever she pictured Alain and Hugh facing each other on the dueling field, the pain in the region of her heart was nearly unbearable.

It seemed to Micaela that she had walked back and forth along this same strip of pathway for hours before François came strolling into view, but it probably hadn't been for very long. She flew to her brother, and, hands clutching his arm, she demanded, "What happened? Is everything all right?"

François lifted his brows. "Of course, everything is all right. Why should it not be?"

Urgently she searched his features, trying desperately to ascertain if he was telling the truth. "Alain did not challenge *Monsieur* Lancaster?"

"Should he have?" François shot back.

Micaela stamped her foot in vexation. "Naturally not! But Alain looked so . . . so *angry* that I feared . . ."

"There was nothing to fear. Alain *was* angry. He wants to marry you, after all, and he was not pleased to find you looking so distressed and alone with a man he does not like." His gaze sharpened. "What really did happen between the two of you?"

"Nothing! I tell you nothing."

François shrugged. "And I am telling you that you have nothing to worry about—the matter is settled."

Instead of calming Micaela, François's words deepened her anxiety. Was he lying? Men did. Particularly about duels.

Despite her best efforts to discover more, François proved irritatingly unresponsive to her queries, and Micaela was finally forced to retire to her bed, knowing little more than she did already. She wanted to believe her brother, but she didn't quite trust him. François could be a little beast when he wanted!

But even if she didn't have the possibility of a duel to worry over, Hugh's wounding statements, not to mention his kiss, would have kept her sleepless most of the night. Tossing restlessly on her bed, she stared up at the netting overhead.

Nothing had *ever* hurt her—or enraged her as much as his words. How dare he, she thought again with anger. Who did he think he was, speaking like that to her? And where, she wondered with growing resentment, had he gotten the ridiculous idea that she wanted to marry him? And as for trapping him! She was a Dupree—they did not have to *trap* their spouses! Bah! He was a vain fool, and she would rather marry *any*one other than Hugh Lancaster! By concentrating on his words and telling herself what an overbearing beast he was, Micaela was able to keep the searing memory of his kiss from her thoughts, but not the very real fear that Hugh might be facing Alain on the dueling field.

The spot Alain had selected for the duel was a small, secluded meadow in sight of the river a few miles from the Dupree plantation. Dismounting from his horse in the murky half-light of predawn, Hugh marveled at his actions. He had fought several duels as a youth—in fact, it was how he had met Jasper—but as he had grown older, dueling was not a sport that found favor with him any longer. Duels could be deadly and were more often than not fought for ridiculous reasons, especially amongst the quick-tempered Creoles. An imagined slight. An ill-judged comment. Even the accidental stepping on the gown of one's partner at a ball could be reason enough for a member of the woman's family to call out the erring gentleman. Duels, in Hugh's opinion, were, for the most part, the province of young hotheaded fools! Something he was no longer. And yet, he thought wryly, he had purposefully allowed himself to be embroiled in one. A smile crooked his mouth. The kiss was worth it.

There was little talking as the six men set about arranging the site to their satisfaction. It was Jasper who had conveniently supplied the pistols—and Jasper, too, who had rounded up a physician to be in attendance. The physician, a rotund little man, *Monsieur* Tessier, rode up just a few minutes later, his small black satchel clutched tightly in his hand. As the others laid out the course and went over the terms, *Monsieur* Tessier stood on the sidelines.

All was in readiness. Misty tendrils of fog drifted ghostlike through the area; the gray-green Spanish moss seemed to float mysteriously from the massive oaks scattered here and there and added to the eerie atmosphere.

The sun had barely turned the sky pink and gold above the swirling mist when Alain and Hugh finally faced each other. Both were garbed in drab clothing; neither wore anything that would give the other a target at which to aim—no shiny buttons, nothing white at the throat.

Hugh had little doubt that Alain meant to kill him. Alain's reputation alone warned him of that fact, as did the cold glitter in the other man's eyes. Hugh did not expect to die this morning, but he would have been foolhardy indeed if he had not considered the possibility. In his room at the Dupree house, he had left a letter for his stepfather and had enclosed instructions for the dispersal of his estate if the worst were to happen. It was a letter that Hugh was hopeful John would never receive.

Observing the formalities of the duel took longer than the actual act. It was several minutes later before the two men were ready to fire. The seconds and the physician hovered nearby. Jasper called out the paces. A second later, the sharp crack of pistol fire rent the air, and the scent of black powder assailed the nostrils. Blue smoke floated lazily upward to mingle with the rising fog.

"*Mon Dieu!*" exclaimed François in horrified accents. "The *Américain* has shot Alain!"

Alain lay crumpled on the field, clutching his shoulder, his face contorted with pain; Hugh was standing calmly thirty feet away from him, apparently unharmed. The physician and Alain's seconds rushed toward the stricken man.

Releasing his pent-up breath, Jasper, with René following him, strolled more leisurely toward Hugh. "Very pretty shooting, *mon ami*," Jasper drawled, just as if he had never wasted a moment's worry on the outcome.

"Indeed," added René, "you are very expert with the pistol, *monsieur*. Alain has fought several duels, usually killing his man. To my knowledge this is the first time he has ever suffered any harm, and did not hit his mark."

Casually taking a handkerchief from an inside pocket of his jacket, Hugh gingerly dabbed his temple. "Oh, he did not miss his mark—he merely misjudged it!"

Seeing the smear of blood on the handkerchief, Jasper's eyes widened. "You are hurt! He *did* hit you."

Hugh nodded. "It is only a grazed temple and I suspect that I will have a headache for a few hours, but I am thankful indeed that his aim was a trifle off this morning."

Examining the faint bloody furrow along the side of Hugh's head, Jasper nodded. "You are very lucky, *mon ami*. Just a bit more to the left . . ."

Coolly putting away his bloodied handkerchief, Hugh murmured, "Yes. I am fortunate, and I am certain our friend over there intended for me to be lying dead on the ground." He glanced over at the men assembled around Alain. "Shall we see how bad he is?"

A twinkle in his dark eyes, Jasper said softly, "First you must tell us, how badly hit *you* think he is."

"Well, unless I miss my guess," Hugh said lightly, "I suspect that *Monsieur* Husson has a broken shoulder, in addition to his wound." Hugh made a face. "I meant merely to nick him, but I think my aim was also off."

Jasper snorted. "At least a broken shoulder will keep him out from under our feet for a while. But be aware, *mon ami*, that you have made a dangerous enemy in him this morning."

René nodded, his green eyes grave. "Alain does not like to lose, and he seldom does."

Hugh nodded again and winced as a stab of pain went through his head. "I am not likely to forget," he muttered.

Hugh's assessment of the situation was correct; his

bullet had indeed broken Alain's shoulder. The wound was not critical; *Monsieur* Tessier deftly removed the bullet just as Hugh and his seconds arrived.

His face twisted with pain, Alain glared up at Hugh. "This is not over, *monsieur*. We will meet again."

Hugh bowed. "Whatever pleases you, *Monsieur* Husson. But for now, shall we cry quits?"

Monsieur Tessier began to set the broken shoulder, and it was some minutes later, his shoulder in place and competently bound, before Alain could speak. François and Bellamy had gently helped him to his feet, and Alain's face was white and drawn from his ordeal. With black eyes full of venom, he stared at Hugh. "For now," he said tightly. "For now."

Hugh and his seconds bowed again, then turned and walked back to their horses. François and Bellamy would see that Alain arrived safely home.

Hugh's head was aching by the time they reached Riverbend, and he was grateful to seek out the solace of his own room. The cross-country ride was not scheduled to begin for a few hours yet, and he looked forward to some quiet and rest. A grim smile crossed his face as he gently laid his head on the pillow. At least *he* would be able to attend the ride. Alain Husson would be riding nowhere for several weeks.

That fact had occurred to François the instant he had discovered the extent of Alain's wound. Alain could not have been more seriously wounded, as far as François was concerned, than if Hugh had killed him! It was obvious that even if he had been foolhardy enough to do so, Alain was certainly not going to be in any condition to participate in the ride which was scheduled for today. And as for their plans for Micaela . . . François sighed, half-relieved. Those would have to be postponed.

Alain was also grimly aware of that aspect, and he was fairly smoldering with rage by the time the Husson plantation came into view. Fortunately, the ladies of the household had not yet risen and François and Bellamy, along with the help of Alain's valet, were able to get him settled in his rooms with no one the wiser as to what had happened. There was no chance for private conversation with Bellamy in attendance. So Alain had been forced to swallow his fury—difficult for him to do when all he wanted to do was to roar his rage and smash everything in sight. Defeat tasted most bitter on his tongue.

His face set in petulant lines, he bade his erstwhile seconds *adieu* and, leaning back against the pile of pillows, began to plot ways in which to make *Monsieur* Lancaster most, *most* unhappy.

Jean Dupree took the news of the duel and the postponement of their plans for Micaela with unexpected resignation. Hearing of the disaster which had overtaken them, he merely shook his head and muttered, "*Eh bien*! So it is. We shall simply have to think of something else."

"Is that all you have to say?" François muttered. "Are you not worried that Alain will change his mind?"

"That is a chance which we will have to take, but I think you dwell too much upon it—Alain clearly means to marry your sister. I do not believe that a setback such as this will deter him from his ultimate goal."

"Easy enough for you to say! It is not *your* vowels which he holds!"

Jean shrugged. "I warned you about him. Husson nearly always wins, and you were a fool to think that you could best him." He sent his nephew a thoughtful look. "You want so very much to prove yourself a man that you take risks which only prove how very young you are."

Furious with Jean's attitude, François slammed out of his uncle's office. But by the time the hour for the ride had come, François had, with one of his mercurial turnabouts, recovered his usual merry spirits. Not a sign of his earlier black mood was in evidence as he moved easily amongst the guests, his warm smile flashing as he effortlessly charmed both the older ladies as well as the younger ones.

The horses for the guests staying at the house were all saddled and ready, and as more and more riders from outlying plantations began to arrive, it was apparent that the ride was going to be one of the high points of the festivities. Once the ladies of the household were all helped onto their mounts, the gentlemen sought out their own horses.

Hugh was startled when François suddenly appeared before him leading a magnificent blood bay gelding. His expression rueful, François thrust the reins at Hugh. "I have not," he said with attractive contriteness, "been a very good host to you these past few days. Please, I would like you to ride one of my favorite mounts. He is named Coquin." François smiled at Hugh's wary expression. "This is not a trick, *monsieur*, I assure you, and despite his name, Coquin is not a rascal. I think that you will like him very much and find him a spirited but trustworthy mount."

Deciding not to probe for ulterior reasons, Hugh politely accepted François's offer at its face value. The boy was young and spoiled, but apparently not without some redeeming qualities.

The horse proved to be everything François had claimed, and by the time the party stopped for a lavish picnic at a stunning spot overlooking the Mississippi River, Hugh was quite in charity with his younger host.

In fact, despite the nagging headache from his wound, Hugh had been enjoying himself so much that he was feeling rather charitably toward everyone . . . except for one, small, raven-haired vixen, whose haughty aloofness irritatingly reminded him of last night's confrontation.

Despite his best intentions to avoid her, Hugh found himself often in the crowd of riders around Micaela. To his annoyance, even knowing her for what she was—a clever, conniving little baggage—he could not seem to stay away from her, or forget her soft, trembling lips beneath his. His eyes unwillingly fixed on her, he admitted grudgingly that she was certainly eye-catching in a rusty orange riding habit as she elegantly sat sidesaddle on a small, fiery chestnut mare named Lampyre. Micaela's masses of gleaming black hair were caught under a frivolous hat in the same shade as the habit; an impudently curved feather in shades of brown and green adorned the hat and brushed against her smooth cheek, and Hugh was suddenly aware of an elemental urge to brush his own fingers against that same soft skin. Cursing under his breath, he stifled the urge. But he was still held enthralled. The sight of that arrogant little nose lifted in disdain whenever their eyes met and the saucy toss of her head when she immediately turned away from him, made his lips twitch in appreciation.

Determined to forget about Micaela Dupree, Hugh attached himself to Alice Summerfield and proceeded to flirt lazily with her. Glancing across at her as they rode side by side, he murmured, "You are looking particularly fetching this morning, Miss Summerfield."

Alice smiled complacently. "Why, thank you," she said demurely. "Mama commented just the other day that this shade of pale blue is very complimentary to someone of my delicate coloring."

Since he had been about to say something of that nature, Hugh was momentarily at a loss. Swiftly regrouping, he remarked. "Your mama has excellent taste."

"Yes, she does, does she not?"

At a standstill, Hugh simply smiled.

Alice did look rather fetching in the pale blue riding habit, her golden curls gleaming from beneath her deeper blue hat. She rode her dainty black mare with an easy expertise, her slim, gloved hands light and sure on the reins, her seat confident and elegant.

A faint rosy flush stained her cheeks, and her eyes were serene pools of china blue as she looked over at Hugh. "It has been an interesting visit so far, has it not? Although I have trouble following the language some of the time. They speak so swiftly and with such excitability, do they not?"

"Er, yes," Hugh muttered, Alice's faintly condescending tone grating on him.

"Mama says that we shall just have to get used to their way of talking. . . ." She shot him an admiring look. "You speak the language very well. Perhaps you could help me improve my skills?"

"Ah, I am afraid that I am going to be rather busy during the next few months, but I am sure that I can recommend someone to teach you French if you like," Hugh said hastily. They continued to converse for several more minutes, but growing bored with Alice's sedate company, he eventually pulled his horse up and fell back to ride with Jasper.

It was gorgeous country through which they rode. Untamed and primordial, green and lush. Bayous, their murky waters slow and sinuous in movement, interspersed the area. Palmettos and Spanish dagger, reeds and swamp grasses grew rampant. In the wetter areas, huge, soaring cypress trees showed their knobby knees; water locusts thrived along the damp shores, and in the drier places oaks, magnolias, and pecan trees thrust their limbs upward, their branches clawing toward the brilliant blue sky and the golden glow of the sun. It was breathtaking.

Used to the area from childhood, Micaela did not find the sights so riveting, but it was a pleasant day, and though she tried to deny it, the fact that Hugh Lancaster was not lying dead somewhere added a special sheen to the ride. Naturally, the gentlemen had not breathed a word about the duel, but word of it and the outcome had managed to reach the ears of the ladies. And, as was the custom, everyone pretended that nothing out of the ordinary had occurred. Regret that the Husson family had been unavoidably detained and would not be joining them today had been expressed, and that was the end of it.

Micaela couldn't help feeling guilty over her part in the resulting duel, though it really hadn't been her fault. And while she was thankful that Hugh was unharmed, she was still furious with him. Her pride smarted from his words last night, and a flush of excitement rioted through her whenever the memory of his kiss flashed through her mind. Through discreetly lowered lashes, she watched him flirt with Alice Summerfield. Ah, bah! she finally told herself with a fierce scowl, the arrogant creature's dalliance with another woman meant absolutely nothing to her! The *Américaine mademoiselle* was welcome to him!

There were easily fifty riders in the party, and there was much movement up and down the ranks as different riders slowed down to join another group and others galloped ahead to merge with a different knot of riders. The horses were strung out over nearly a mile around four o'clock that afternoon when the signal was given and they finally began the homeward trek.

No one paid any particular attention to the whereabouts of anyone else amidst the laughing group—the assumption being that the missing rider was either somewhere ahead or behind. Which had been one of the reasons that Alain, Jean, and François had decided that the ride would give them perfect cover for Micaela's kidnapping by Alain. The forest was all around them, the verdant green foliage pressing close toward the riders, and the plotters had been counting on the relaxed, easy atmosphere of the ride and the fact that the various riders were often out of sight of one another for several minutes at a time for the success of their scheme.

Never guessing for a second the near escape she'd had, Micaela was glad when they finally started homeward. The passing time and the fact that they were still several miles from home had begun to worry her. She'd been keeping a wary eye on the gradually darkening sky for some time now and had mentioned it to François almost an hour earlier. The event had been most successful so far, and there was no reason to end it on a wet and stormy note—which could very well happen if she read the sky right. François had shrugged and told her not to worry. The clouds probably meant nothing.

Hiding her annoyance, Micaela had dropped back to ride beside Rachelle for a while. Rachelle was enjoying herself enormously, and, listening to her excited chatter, Micaela told herself that François was no doubt right. Except that by the time he finally motioned for them to ride in the direction of the plantation, the sky was ominously black, and there was the scent of rain in the charged air.

And as Micaela had expected, a few minutes later, it began to sprinkle.

Then the rain began in earnest, and what had been a pleasant outing soon turned into a nightmare. They no longer rode at a leisurely pace. First one and then another began to spur their horses to greater speed. The party spread out, the more intrepid riders dashing ahead, the more timid falling behind.

At first there was some attempt to keep everyone together, but the rain fell in such torrents and the black sky was torn again and again by the jagged bolts of lightning that all efforts of an orderly retreat were soon given up. The lightning and the booming thunder spooked many of the animals, and there was much snorting and rearing of horses as well as the occasional runaway. Chaos reigned.

Because she was familiar with the area and because it had obviously not occurred to either François or Jean, Micaela instinctively fell back, searching through the deepening gloom and pouring rain for any stragglers. Rider after rider passed her, their heads bent low, their horses racing through the storm.

Eventually Micaela halted her dancing horse, peering intently through the rain for sign of anyone else coming up the rear. After several minutes, she was convinced that she was alone and that everyone was ahead of her. Soaked to the skin and suddenly feeling at one with the storm, she gave herself up to the fury of the storm, and gaily tossed aside her dainty riding hat, shaking her hair free. Lifting her face to the warm rain, she let the water wash away all the hurt and tension of the past few days, and she forgot about everything but the sheer delight of being one with the elements. The rain pelted down, clumping her lashes and running into her mouth, and she laughed aloud, feeling alive and energized by the storm.

Her hair tumbled in wet disorder around her shoulders, and, looking like a wild, black-haired Valkyrie, she finally kicked her horse into a reckless gallop and through the lightning-streaked darkness began to race toward home.

Several minutes later, she spied a lone rider ahead of her. She recognized the horse first, Coquin, and almost instantly realized that the big, broad-shouldered man in front of her was Hugh Lancaster. She made a face and immediately halted Lampyre. Absolutely the *last* thing she wanted was a tête-à-tête with that conceited oaf!

Frightened by the storm, Coquin was behaving badly, and, as Micaela watched, the horse danced and half reared as a bolt of lighting struck a tree nearby. Hugh managed the plunging horse easily, and Micaela was forced to admire his gentle strength with the obviously terrified animal. Hugh had just gotten Coquin under control when the heavens sent another spear of lightning hurtling downward, the bolt striking a tree perilously close to the horse and rider.

As the tree exploded into a fiery shower of hot sparks, there was no restraining Coquin this time. The gelding reared straight up in the air and, before Micaela's horrified gaze, fell over backward, taking his rider with him. Hugh barely had time to kick free of the stirrups before the horse crashed down on him. Heedless of anything but Hugh's safety, her heart in her mouth, she spurred Lampyre forward.

Hugh was lying motionless on the ground, one hand still unconsciously clinging to the reins, when Micaela flung herself from the saddle and raced to his side. Coquin immediately struggled to his feet and was standing trembling beside him. Soothing Coquin, she swiftly tied both horses safely away from the motionless figure lying in the rain and flew once more to his side.

Her anxious, probing fingers found no outward sign of injury, but she knew well enough that his chest could be cracked or even crushed and that there could be lethal internal damage. Few men survived having a horse fall over backward with them—it was one of the most dangerous of all accidents.

Biting her lip, she glanced around. The rain and resulting darkness made it hard to see much, but she knew where she was, and if she remembered correctly, there was a small hunting shack not a quarter of a mile away. Her eyes slid back to Hugh. The question was, did she dare try to move him? And if she did, could she get him as far as the hunting shack?

Hugh moaned and lifted one hand to his head. His eyes opened, and he blinked up at Micaela. "What in thunder!" he muttered. "Where am I? And what the devil are you doing here?"

"You fell off your horse, *monsieur*," Micaela answered stiffly. "I was coming up behind you and saw it all."

Hugh started to nod, then winced. His head felt as if it would explode, and lying on the wet ground and being pounded by rain was not his idea of a pleasant situation. Ignoring Micaela's pleas to the contrary, he managed to stagger to his feet.

"I am not injured," he said testily. "The breath was knocked from me, and I am a bit dizzy, but I am fine. Do not fuss so."

Biting back a rude comment, Micaela said grimly, "For which you should thank *le bon Dieu*. It was no easy tumble you took."

"Thank you for your concern *Mademoiselle* Dupree.

Now if you do not mind, I think we should mount our horses and find the others."

Her back ramrod straight, Micaela marched to her horse and leaped nimbly into her saddle. As proud as any queen, she looked down her nose at him and said, "Follow me. I know of a place where we can shelter until the worst of the storm is over."

His face hard, Hugh carefully swung up onto his own horse. "I am sure you do," he said sarcastically. "But I am afraid that I would rather take my chances with the elements. I do not want your male relatives rushing in on us and demanding that I do the honorable thing and marry you." His lip lifted in a sneer. "I told you I would not be caught by your snares."

Choking back the furious torrent that threatened to burst from her, Micaela sent him a look full of loathing and regally kicked her mare into motion. Vile *canaille*! She hoped that he had broken his handsome head!

They had not traveled far before it became obvious that Hugh was not going to make it to the plantation. He was swaying dangerously in the saddle, and Micaela's reluctant inquiries into his state of health brought only a low groan from him.

Taking matters into her own hands, she quietly took Coquin's reins and with Hugh half-dazed and unaware of their progress, swiftly guided them to the hunting shack. Her heart sank when she glimpsed the ramshackle little building through the shadowy rainfall, but there was no other choice.

The roof looked sound, and it should give them some surcease from the inclement weather until her brother and uncle could find them. After dismounting, Micaela securely tied both horses to a tree and, leaving Hugh slumped in the saddle, cautiously approached the hunting shack.

To her delight, the interior was far more inviting than the outside. There were no leaks, and it seemed relatively clean. No unpleasant critters had found their way inside, and, more importantly, in the dim light, she could barely make out the outline of some wood laid near the small hearth. A quick search of the rough mantel revealed some flint and a small lamp with some bear grease in it.

Buoyed up by their luck, she had a fire going in seconds and the lamp lit. There was no food, but a sturdy-looking cot was against one wall, a worn, vermin-free blanket thrown carelessly across it.

Ten minutes later, nearly staggering under his much greater weight, Micaela helped Hugh to the cot. In the firelight his face was pale, his brows and lashes shockingly black against the whiteness of his skin.

Knowing that it might be hours before they were found, Micaela removed his soaking jacket and waist-coat, as well as his jabot and boots, and set them near the fire to dry. Her own boots and jacket joined them as well.

Gingerly seating herself before the fire, she rested her chin on her knees and stared at the leaping flames. Soon, she told herself firmly, François and the others would come looking for them. Just as soon as it was discovered that they were missing. The storm would let up and a few hours from now she would be at home soaking in a tub of steaming hot water.

She cast a worried eye at Hugh's still form. And he will be fine, she thought staunchly. In no time at all he would be up and walking about and acting as arrogant and impossible as ever—the conceited swine!

Chapter Eight

*H*ugh woke with a groan, his hand going to his head. Blearily he glanced around, trying to remember where he was. A lamp spluttered on the mantel of the tiny room; the only other light came from the glowing coals on the hearth. The sound of rain and the occasional clap of thunder rent the air.

He shook his head trying to clear his thoughts and groaned again as pain shafted through him. Dimly he remembered the storm and the fall from his horse . . . and Micaela looking like a lovely young witch.

Despite his aching head, he sat up and noticed the slim figure lying asleep on the floor in the shadows. *Micaela!*

Realizing instantly what must have happened, Hugh surged to his feet. They could not remain here! Not if he didn't want to find himself tied to a vixen with the devil's own tongue.

The fact that it could already be too late occurred unpleasantly to him. He had no idea what time it was, nor how many hours they had already spent confined alone together in this little room. One thing was certain—if he didn't want to find himself facing her angry relatives demanding satisfaction, *Mademoiselle* Dupree and he had better get on their horses and ride like hell for Riverbend. His aching head and the storm raging outside be damned!

Stepping nearer to Micaela's slumbering form, Hugh stared down at her fine features, the golden glow of the coals gilding her sculpted little nose and caressing her cheeks and sweetly curved mouth. Her hair tumbled in wild disarray around her face, and the gentle rise and fall of her bosom beneath the delicate lawn blouse she wore fascinated him. Hugh swallowed. She was lovely. And he was appalled at how much, how *very* much, he wanted to sink down on the floor beside her and pull her into his arms and kiss her awake.

Cursing his own stupidity, he nudged her ungently with his toe. "Micaela! Wake up! We have to leave—now!"

Micaela stirred. Not quite awake, she gave a shriek of fright at the sight of the tall, menacing figure looming above her. She scrambled frantically to her feet, one hand held out protectively in front of her. "Do not touch me!" she commanded in a shaken voice.

"I have no intention of touching you," Hugh bit out, "except, perhaps, to strangle you!"

Fully awake now, she stared at him with widened eyes. "But why?" she demanded. "What have I done *now* to enrage you so?"

His hands on his hips, Hugh smiled nastily. "Very prettily done, my dear, but it does not fool me! And I did not think that even you would stoop so low as to try this sort of trick."

Was the man mad? thought Micaela incredulously. Her temper rising, she snapped, "I do not know what you are talking about! I do not play *tricks*!"

They were both flushed with anger and so intent on

each other that the sudden opening of the door made them both start. Hugh swung around, half-pushing Micaela behind him in an instinctive attempt to shield her from whatever danger they might face.

Jean and François stepped into the dimly lit room, looking grim and unhappy. Only they knew what a bitter moment this was for them. It should have been Alain who was with Micaela, and it would have been if not for the disastrous duel this morning. It was ironic that the concept of their original plan had certainly borne fruit, but it had gone terribly awry. Micaela was indeed compromised—but by the wrong man!

Something in their expressions made Micaela's heart feel as if it had dropped right down to her toes. Stepping from behind Hugh, heedless of her dishevelment, she asked, "What? What is it? Why do you look so?" Fear etched her features. "*Maman*? Nothing has happened to her? She arrived home safely?"

Jean took a deep breath. "It is not your *Maman* who is in trouble, *ma fille*, but you!"

Utter confusion on her face, Micaela stared back at them, not fully understanding. "What do you mean?"

Wearily François answered her. "Do you not know what time it is? Do you not know that we, nearly everyone, has been searching and searching for the pair of you since it was discovered that you were missing. *Maman* is frantic! She is certain that we will find you with your neck broken or drowned in the swamp. And I almost wish we had—anything would be better than *this*!"

Micaela looked miserably at her brother, one part of her dimly aware that her life had just changed forever, the other unwilling to accept it.

"Micaela!" François said in anguished accents, "It is well past midnight! You have been alone, alone and *un-*

chaperoned, with the *Américain* for hours." He looked away from her suddenly white features. Dully he added, "We tried to be discreet, but most of our neighbors and friends had to be told that you were missing in order to help in the search. There is no way we can conceal your dishonor, and there is only one way in which our honor can be restored and your reputation repaired."

The sound of clapping shattered the bleak silence which met his words. "Excellent!" Hugh exclaimed. "I do not think I have seen so realistic a performance in my entire life."

Jean's brow drew together. "Explain yourself, *monsieur!*"

"I have no intention of doing so," Hugh said curtly. "Suffice to say that I will play my part in this charade and marry your niece."

"*Non!*" Micaela said desperately. "I will not marry this *canaille!*"

The three men looked at her, and what she read in their faces made her grit her teeth in frustration. "We have done nothing!" she cried angrily. "It was the storm and *Monsieur* Lancaster's fall from Coquin which brought us here." When the three men remained unmoved by her words, she grasped the front of François's cloak and said urgently, "He has been asleep the entire time—he never touched me! Please, please, you must believe me! There is no need for this to go any further."

Jean sadly shook his head. "You are wrong, *petite*. Whether you and *Monsieur* Lancaster acted improperly or not does not matter—simply by being alone with him, here in this private place for several hours, you have thoroughly ruined yourself and brought dishonor upon the Dupree name."

She glanced across to Hugh, the amused contempt on

his handsome face telling her clearer than words that she would find no help from him. Glaring at him, she said accusingly, "You do not want to marry me—you said so!"

"What?" demanded Jean, his brow darkening. "You are refusing to do what is right and honorable, *monsieur*?"

Hugh smiled grimly. "Of course not. If you will recall, not a moment ago I offered to marry her."

Sneeringly François said, "I am sure that you did, *monsieur*. After all, it is no doubt what you planned."

"And what," Hugh asked in a dangerous tone, "do you mean by that?"

"Why only that marriage to my sister is a clever way in which to get your hands on the shares that she controls." Ignoring Micaela's gasp and Jean's startled exclamation, François continued hotly, "I do not believe that it was any *accident* what happened. You saw a chance to compromise my sister and you took it. We would not sell you our shares and so you found another way in which to get your greedy hands on some of them." He glared at Hugh and added tightly, "I wonder what other schemes you have concocted to wrest the remainder of our shares from us."

Hugh regarded him icily. "You are a damn young fool! But because of the unfortunate situation already facing us, I will not give you the response your ridiculous accusation deserves."

François only curled his lip and looked superior.

There was quick suspicion in Micaela's gaze as François's ugly words sank in and she wondered sickly if she hadn't misread Hugh's predicament entirely and instead of helping him had herself been cleverly maneuvered into an inalterable position.

Jean looked thoughtful. Had the American fooled them all? And yet even if he had, there was nothing to be done.

To save them from scandal, the marriage must take place. Grimly, he said, "Whatever the reason, do I have your word as a gentleman that you will marry Micaela?"

Hugh nodded. Bitterly he said, "You have nothing to worry about—on my honor, I swear that I will marry your blasted niece just as soon as it can be arranged."

Jean nodded coolly. "François and I had already decided that if our worst fears were confirmed, your betrothal can be announced at tomorrow's ball." He smiled tightly. "We shall let it be known that, with the family's blessing, there was already an understanding between the pair of you and that the entire purpose of the ball was for the express purpose of formally making the announcement of your coming nuptials."

"I do not want to marry this beastly creature!" Micaela suddenly burst out furiously, appalled at how easily they were disposing of her entire future. "I refuse to marry him! You cannot force me!"

Walking over to where Micaela stood glaring at them, Hugh said grimly, "You have won, Micaela. Cease this playacting and accept your victory. I have."

"Do you know," Micaela spat, her eyes glittering with fury, "that I think it is you, *monsieur*, who has won, and I absolutely *loathe* you for it!"

"Ah, well, I shall have to see what I can do about changing your mind." He smiled crookedly. "Come now! Enough of this! Our fate is sealed, and there is nothing that you can do about it."

Micaela knew that Hugh spoke the truth, but all during the long, miserable journey back to Riverbend, she tried desperately to find a way out of the trap in which she found herself. It was all the more galling to realize that by doing an act of simple kindness for a fellow creature she had brought this on herself. I should have, she thought viciously, left him lying there in the rain. *Zut!* He is far too arrogant to have come to any real harm!

It was a somber foursome which rode through the falling rain, no one pleased at the outcome. Hugh was, however, feeling rather resigned to his fate. It had never occurred to him *not* to marry Micaela. He was, after all, an honorable man. Yet he had the uncomfortable suspicion that there was a part of him that was actually a little *too* resigned to his fate. He would have preferred a more traditional courtship, but he was not exactly dissatisfied by what had transpired. All of his previous reasons for considering a union between them came flooding back. Nothing had really changed—it was still a good business decision and he would get what he wanted—Micaela in his bed. His mouth hardened. At least now he knew her for what she was, a scheming, greedy little minx.

Lisette gave a choked cry when she was reunited with her daughter. Micaela's features were white and strained, and Lisette immediately enfolded her into a warm, maternal embrace, scolding and petting at the same time. They were all gathered in the library, the other guests having gone to bed.

Having satisfied herself that her daughter had suffered no lasting damage, Lisette glanced at the three gentlemen, a question in her fine eyes. Hugh bowed, and said quietly, "Your daughter has done me the honor of agreeing to marry me. I hope this meets with your approval, *madame*."

Into her mother's shoulder, Micaela hissed, "I do not want to marry him, *Maman*! I did nothing wrong!"

Lisette sighed and rumpled Micaela's dark tousled hair. "Shh, *petite*. I know you did nothing wrong, but the circumstances are such . . ." She dropped a kiss on Micaela's cheek. "Too many people know what happened, *bébé*. There is no way that we can hide the fact that you were alone with a man not a member of your family for so many hours. You have to marry him."

Micaela realized that further talk was useless. Gently disengaging Lisette's arms, she stood up. Sending her husband-to-be a most *un*loving glance, she muttered, "Since I seem to have no say in the matter, I shall leave you all to plan my future."

Ignoring Lisette's exclamation of protest, she stalked out of the room. In a daze she walked up the stairs to her room and numbly stripped out of her wet and ruined riding habit, any thoughts of a long, hot bath completely vanished. Too much had happened and her brain felt fuzzy—she could not seem to think at all. Creeping between the sheets of her bed, she welcomed the blessed darkness which swept over her.

It was sometime later that Hugh was finally able to seek out his own bed, and he was aware of an odd sense of satisfaction as he entered his room and began to undress. Everything was settled. The betrothal would be announced at the ball tomorrow. The wedding would take place in three weeks, just long enough away to give an air of respectability to the whole affair. If he had any regrets about the hastiness of his wedding, it was that his stepfather would not be able to attend. Getting a message upriver to John Lancaster could take several weeks, and everyone was agreed that the sooner the marriage took place and people had other things to talk about, the better.

There had been a long silence after Hugh departed from the library, leaving each of the three Duprees busy with their own thoughts. It was Lisette who broke it, saying with forced cheerfulness, "*Eh, bien!* It may not be so very bad. He has agreed to marry her—and tonight's ball will be a most appropriate time to make the announcement."

"How can you accept it so easily, *Maman*?" demanded François. "She is marrying an *Américain*!"

Lisette shrugged eloquently.

Jean gave a hard laugh. "Your *Maman* has always had a soft spot for the *Américains*. Is that not so, *ma soeurette*?"

Lisette flushed. Rising to her feet, and despite her pink cheeks, she said calmly, "If you will excuse me, I think that I, too, shall go to bed. *Bonne nuit!*"

A frown on his face, François glanced at his uncle. "What did you mean by that?"

Jean made a face. "Put it from your mind—it was unimportant. And since we will have a busy day in front of us, I suggest that we try to get a few hours of sleep ourselves before we have to face our guests."

François's frown grew blacker. "*Mon Dieu*, but you seem to be taking all of this rather well," he said hotly. "What about Alain? And my vouchers?" An expression of unease crossed his face. "How will we face him with this news?" He swallowed. "He is going to be utterly furious!"

"I would not worry," Jean said. "Remember that whatever the reasons behind it, your sister is going to marry a *very* rich man, wealthier even than Alain Husson. Console yourself with the knowledge that in less than a month, your sister will be able to dip freely into a purse which is rumored to be nearly boundless!"

Much struck by this observation, François's features cleared magically. "Do you know," he said confidingly as the two men walked from the library, "this marriage to the *Américain* may not be such a bad thing!"

*   *   *

All during those swiftly passing hours before the formal announcement of the betrothal that Saturday evening, Micaela vehemently protested her innocence. But to no avail; her betrothal to the *Américain* was going to be announced as planned that night—the family was adamant. Jean and François had obviously had further conversation with Hugh, because her brother, somewhat amazed, told her that Hugh had coolly refused a dowry. But, he reminded her just before they descended the stairs that night, Hugh's act wasn't as generous as it appeared— she *did* own ten percent in Galland, Lancaster and Dupree. In François's stated opinion, the American had gotten what he wanted.

The evening was a nightmare for Micaela. She kept hoping desperately that something would change the outcome. It wasn't until Jean began to tap a crystal goblet for attention and she found Hugh suddenly at her side, that she accepted that her fate was sealed. Numbly she let Hugh escort her to where Jean stood, Lisette and François flanking him.

Hugh's hand was warm around hers as they joined the others in the center of the room and oddly enough the feel of that strong clasp gave her a sort of comfort. Uncertainly she gazed up at his unrevealing profile, wondering what he was thinking. Was he pleased at the outcome? Did he have any doubts about what he had done?

Jean played his part superbly. A smile on his lips, a faint twinkle in his dark eyes, he said gaily, "*Mes amis*, it has been a secret these past few days, but tonight it gives me great joy to tell you that my dear niece and the *Américain*, Hugh Lancaster, will be married. They are impatient, these two, and the wedding will take place in three weeks."

'There was a collective gasp—Jean's words clearly having caught everyone by surprise. Then an excited babble arose, congratulations, exclamations of astonishment permeating the air. There were some disapproving faces in the crowd, a few of the older Creoles obviously aghast at the match, but overall, most of the guests seemed to accept readily the idea of the marriage. That the Duprees were apparently happy with the match stilled even the most outspoken critic.

Micaela did not even have time to blink before she and Hugh were engulfed by the guests. The Creoles, voluble and excited as ever, rushed forward to press kisses and wishes for good fortune upon them. It all passed before her in a frenzy of motion and noise, Hugh's hand the only real thing in a sea of confusion.

She was vaguely aware of Alice Summerfield and her parents eventually coming forward to offer their felicitations. If they seemed a bit stiff and cool after all the warmth and spontaneity of the other guests, Micaela put it down to their disappointment at Hugh's choice of a bride—she *had* heard the rumors about his marked attentions to the *Américaine* young woman. Not by so much as a flicker of an eyelash did the older Summerfields give any clue to what they were feeling. Shaking Hugh's hand, Alice's father said politely, "John is going to be very pleased, my boy. Very pleased. Congratulations." Alice's mother added her own brief words, then it was Alice's turn.

Her face frozen, Alice murmured, "My congratulations to you both." Only the glimpse of rage and hurt in her eyes before she swiftly lowered her gaze from Hugh's face revealed her chagrin and disappointment.

Then as the others looked on, Micaela was stunned when Hugh gallantly presented her with a ring, a delicately wrought thing of gold and pearls. Brushing a kiss against her pale cheek, he murmured, "Did you think I would forget the most important symbol of our betrothal, sweetheart?"

"*N-n-non*. But when did you . . . ?"

He bent near her ear and whispered, "I rose at dawn and rode to New Orleans. I returned with just enough time to bathe and dress." He sent her an enigmatic glance. "I did not want my betrothed to find me wanting."

Wordlessly she stared up at him, a part of her deeply touched by his consideration, another suspicious of his motives. He was a stranger. Not only a stranger, but a man whose culture and ways were vastly different from her own. And she was to marry him. . . . She sighed and decided with a streak of good Creole practicability that for the sake of her future happiness her wisest course was to view his actions in the best light possible.

A muted smile touched her lips, and she said quietly, "Thank you. It was very kind and thoughtful of you."

Hugh cocked a brow. "What, no barbed reply? Now that we are betrothed does this mean that I will no longer be the target of that sharp tongue of yours?"

Before Micaela could reply, Jasper came up to them, and, slapping Hugh on the back, he cried, "*Mon ami*, I am so happy! Did I not tell you that only a Creole bride would do for you? I am elated that, for once, you actually followed my advice!"

Green eyes sparkling with pleasure, Jasper extravagantly kissed Micaela on both cheeks. "You have me," he told her gaily, "Jasper De Marco, to thank for your good fortune, *chérie*." He winked, adding outrageously, "And I expect for you to name your firstborn son after me! I tell you now, I will be devastated if you do not name me godfather to him also."

Micaela blushed, and Hugh grinned. "And what if our children are all girls, my friend? What then?"

"Ah, *non*! Me, I am certain that before many years pass, there will be an entire *litter* of Lancaster sons to bedevil all our Creole maidens."

It was several minutes before Micaela could decently escape from the crowd, and at the first chance, she sidled outside to snatch a moment alone. In the pale moonlight she stared down dazedly at the ring on her finger. She was betrothed! It seemed incredible, part dream, part nightmare.

"You think that you have been rather clever, do you not?" Alice Summerfield said accusingly from behind her.

Micaela whirled to stare at the other woman. Alice's face was pinched and hard, her mouth held in a thin, tight line and her blue eyes blazed with sheer dislike.

"*Mademoiselle*, I am sorry," Micaela began softly, "that you feel this way."

"Sorry!" Alice hissed. "I do not need *your* sympathy." Her hands opened and closed convulsively. "I do not know what sort of trick you used to force an offer from him, but I tell you—it is you who will be sorry." She gave an angry titter. "He loves me! We planned to marry—and you stole him from me!" Fury glittering in her eyes, she said bitterly, "You think you have won, but I do not envy you becoming the wife of a man who is only marrying you because he was forced into it."

A horrible suspicion took root in Micaela's mind. Had Hugh told Alice the circumstances surrounding their betrothal? Her voice tight, she asked, "And how do you know he was forced into it, *mademoiselle*?"

An expression of confusion crossed Alice's face, as if she could not conceive of any other reason for their betrothal. "Because he was going to marry me," she said stubbornly. She gave Micaela a scornful look. "And the only way you could have gotten a proposal out of him was if you tricked him."

The relief which swept through Micaela was nearly palpable—Hugh had not revealed the truth. But Alice's certainty that Hugh would have married her, that he loved her, sent a pang through Micaela, and an odd ache bloomed in her chest. Quietly she said, "Again, *mademoiselle*, I am sorry that you feel the way you do, but I can do nothing about it."

Behind Alice's fury, it was apparent that she was suffering, that the announcement of Hugh's betrothal had hurt. Micaela felt a stirring of pity. Her life was not the only one to have been changed so painfully. Impulsively she reached for Alice's hand, and said softly, "I am sorry for your pain. You must think of your future. You are young and very beautiful—someday there will be another who will touch your heart."

Alice jerked her hand away. "I do not want another man! I want Hugh!" she almost wailed, as if her wishes were the only ones that mattered.

Becoming annoyed. Micaela snapped, "*Zut!* Hush, you foolish creature. Believe me, *mademoiselle*, if I could give him to you, I would!"

Alice's eyes went round. "You do not want him? How can you not? He is so handsome and very, very rich."

Wishing she had kept her tongue still, and conscious that with a few ill-chosen words she was in danger of exposing the careful facade erected by her family, Micaela muttered, "Of course I want him. As you said, he is rich and handsome."

But Alice's suspicions were roused. Speculatively she eyed Micaela. "I know he does not love you . . . and you apparently do not love him. . . ." She gasped as enlightenment dawned. "You are only marrying him because of the business!"

Micaela was not about to get into her reasons for marrying Hugh. Feeling that she had spent enough time with Miss Alice Summerfield, she said frostily, "You may believe what you like, *mademoiselle*. I do not wish to be rude, but I think that it is time we rejoined the party."

Uncaring if the other woman followed her or not, Micaela fled inside. Alice's words pierced her confused emotions like hot needles. She already knew that Hugh did not love her, but Alice's confirmation of that fact hurt in ways she had never expected. And the hurt did not abate one bit when she looked up a few minutes later and noticed that Alice had indeed followed her inside, but was now smiling enchantingly up at Hugh. Micaela's fingers bit into the flesh of her hand. I am not jealous, she told herself fiercely. I am *not*!

Jealousy would have been the least of her emotions if she had been privy to the conversation that was taking place between Alice and Hugh. And she would have been astonished at Alice's broad interpretation of their brief conversation.

Looking seductively at Hugh over the rim of her wine goblet, Alice said, "She is not in love with you, you know."

His expression shuttered, Hugh glanced at her. His first instinct was to ignore her, but that devil curiosity prompted him to ask, "Oh, and how do you know that?"

"Because I just had a very interesting conversation with her. And she told me so."

Hugh's eyes narrowed. "She told you so?"

"Ummhmm. That and the fact that your marriage will be purely a business arrangement. She was very honest about it." She shot him a considering look. Driven by the need to strike back, she added, "It is only because you own the largest single share of Galland, Lancaster and Dupree that she consented to the match. Your marriage will be a very good thing for her family." Alice smiled deprecatingly. "You know these Creoles—they will do anything, even sacrifice themselves, for their family. Such a pity you fell into her clutches."

Hugh's gaze found Micaela standing across the room from him. Intently he stared at her vivid features as she suddenly smiled at something her brother said. "Perhaps," he said slowly, "I did not fall . . . perhaps, I went quite, quite willingly. Did you ever think of that?"

"You are not serious! What about us?" Alice demanded, color burning in her cheeks.

"What about us?" Hugh asked quietly, tearing his gaze away from Micaela.

Under her breath, Alice muttered, "Well, I thought, that is, your attentions led me to believe that—"

"I am a very good friend to you and your family," Hugh gently interspersed. "None of you knew anyone in New Orleans when you first arrived, and I did what I could to make things easier for you."

Their eyes met for a long time. "And that is all it was?" she asked painfully.

Hugh lifted her hand and pressed a kiss to the back of it. "That and my sincere admiration for your beauty."

Her lip trembled, and she looked away, blinking her eyes furiously. There was a small silence, and then she tossed her head and gave a tight little laugh, "Oh my, there is young *Monsieur* L'Aramy. I seem to remember that I promised him the next dance."

A moment later she was gone, having amply fertilized,

watered, and added a few of her own to the seeds of doubt which already lay between Hugh and Micaela.

As if in a nightmare, Micaela drifted through the days before the wedding. On the surface, she was furious at the trick fate, or perhaps the very man she was marrying, had played on her. Yet deep within herself, buried so deeply that she was hardly aware of it, was a tiny spark of excitement, a thrilling, insistent eagerness to begin her new life as Hugh's wife. She did not admit her emotions to herself, instead, she pushed them determinedly from her mind just as she did the memory of all those times a mere glance from Hugh's gray eyes would set her heart beating so fast she feared it would leap from her breast. She pretended to forget the way that gleaming smile of his had made her feel vibrantly alive. She definitely did not dwell on the memory his kiss. Bah! She would not remember those times. Rather she would remember his hateful words the night he had sworn not to marry her and Alice's assertions that she was the one he loved as well as François's opinion that Hugh's only reason for marrying her were cold-blooded, mercenary ones.

Their wedding was set for Monday, the twenty-first of May. They would be married in New Orleans, and as was custom, at the St. Louis Cathedral at four o'clock in the afternoon. And despite her fervent wish to the contrary, at the appointed hour, Micaela found herself standing at the *Américain's* side before the priest, her family and friends seated solemnly in the pews behind them. Wearing a gown of rose silk decorated with pearls, her great-grandmother's wedding veil crowned with orange blossoms resting on her head, a bouquet of orange blossoms held in her hands, she heard herself exchange the vows which would make her Hugh Lancaster's wife. She watched numbly as he slipped on the two interlaced bands of gold which had been inscribed with both their initials and the date of their marriage. It was over. She was married.

The faces of the guests passed fuzzily before her, most were smiling and happy, but there were a few dour expressions amongst them—some of the most rigid Creoles, still not quite accepting the unpleasant fact that a member of one of their finest families had aligned herself with a mongrel *Américain*. Alain Husson was definitely among the latter.

His arm still in a sling, Alain had forced himself to attend the wedding, as much to still any speculation about the state of his emotions as a penance for having not managed to kill the *Américain*. The rage, fury, and chagrin burning in his chest when Hugh slipped the rings on Micaela's finger were indescribable. Somehow he managed to keep his features composed, while every instinct was urging him to surge to his feet, take his sword, and run the *Américain* through. Thinking of Hugh lying dead on the steps of the altar brought a genuine smile to his face. Anyone who saw it marveled at his apparent generosity toward the man who had married the woman believed to be his own future bride.

As Hugh's best man, Jasper had stood proudly at the *Américain's* side, his features fairly beaming. When the newlyweds left the church, Jasper was the first to congratulate them and remind them again of his desire to be named godfather to their firstborn son.

Following the wedding there was a grand banquet held at the Dupree town house, the atmosphere, the wine, the food, and the music superb enough to satisfy even the most exacting European taste. The meal passed in a blur for Micaela, and she hardly tasted any of the spicy gumbo, delicate turtle soup, roast veal, baked ham, and golden brown pastries which were served to her.

When the dancing began, Lisette and *Tante* Marie, acting as a surrogate *grand-mère*, discreetly hustled her away upstairs to the suite of rooms that she would share with her new husband. The older women gently helped her undress and put on a charming nightgown of finest lawn, lavishly trimmed with lace and emerald green ribbons. In minutes she was settled beneath the bedclothes.

Micaela had spoken little. With a faint frown on her face, Lisette murmured, "It will not be so very bad, *ma petite*. Hugh seems a nice young man." She bit her lip. Creole brides were notoriously innocent about the physical side of marriage, and Lisette was uncertain how to approach the subject. It was her duty as a loving mother to give her daughter some warning of what was to come. What happened in the marriage bed was not something they had ever discussed, and though, unlike many of her contemporaries, Micaela was much older, she was still very innocent. Lisette cleared her throat and muttered, "You know that you will share this bed with your husband?"

Micaela glanced at her and nodded, a quiver, half fright, half excitement going through her.

Heightened color in her cheeks, Lisette asked, "Do you understand that you must allow him to do what he wants with you? He now has the right to"—her flush deepened—"touch you as he pleases and do 'things' to you." Her discomfort growing, she muttered, "No matter what your husband does to you tonight, you are not to cry out or fight him—it may be painful the first time and embarrassing, but you will grow used to it. You are to submit to him like a good Creole bride."

Tante Marie spoke up. "You must remember," she said

sternly, "to always be modest, always—even in your most intimate moments." Proudly, she added, "In forty years of marriage, my husband never saw me indecently attired and *never* without my clothes. You must remember that a husband does not want a crude, wanton creature in his bed. No matter what he does to you, you must submit quietly. Remain still, do not thrash around and cry out. Let him have his way. Accept without comment whatever he does to you. You must never, *never* do anything he might find offensive—no matter what he demands of you." She looked severe. "A Creole wife never embarrasses her husband with an outward, indecorous show of emotion." She wagged a bony finger under Micaela's nose. "You do not want to be like one Creole wife—it is said that she took such lewd and lascivious delight in her marriage bed that her husband was thoroughly disgusted and repulsed by her and sought to divorce her. You do not," she ended grimly, "want that fate, do you?"

Her cheeks red, Micaela muttered, "I will not disgrace our family. I married him to keep the family's honor intact, I will do nothing to sully our name. I will be a good Creole wife."

Relieved that the uncomfortable subject was behind them and feeling that she had done her duty as a proper surrogate *grand-mère, Tante* Marie said gently, "I know that you are unhappy, but really, there was no other choice. If you had not married him, you would have been thoroughly ruined, *ma chérie*."

Nodding to Lisette, *Tante* Marie left the room, certain she had done her best to ensure a happy marriage.

Lisette watched her go and then looked back at Micaela. "Do not take her words too seriously, *petite*, although much of what she said is true. Her views are oldfashioned, but she is right about one thing—you

would have been ruined." She sighed. "It was unfortunate
that so many people knew of your indiscretion, no matter
how innocent it was. But I think," she went on briskly,
"that we have avoided a terrible scandal, and you should
be very glad."

"*Maman*! How can you say so? I am *married* to him!"
Micaela protested. "It is easy for you to say. You do not
know what it is like to be married to a man you do not
like."

A look crossed Lisette's face, and Micaela sat up
abruptly. Her expression shocked, she whispered, "You
did not like *Papa*? But it was a love match! Everyone
said so! *Grand-père* always laughed and talked about
how romantic it was, the way the pair of you could not
wait to be married and talked him into letting you get
married before the banns could even be called."

"*Eh bien*! That was a long time ago," Lisette said
stiffly. "And we are talking about *your* marriage, not
mine." Her face softened. "Are you so very certain that
you do not like Hugh, *ma chérie*?"

Confusion evident in her dark eyes, Micaela muttered,
"I do not know. One moment I hate him and the next . . ."
An odd expression crept into her eyes.

Her cheeks suddenly stained rosy by her thoughts, Micaela's lashes dropped, and she said stoutly, "But mostly,
I think he is an arrogant, wickedly scheming beast!"

As the "arrogant, wickedly scheming beast" was entering the room just then, her remark was ill timed, and
Hugh's mouth tightened as he heard her words. Micaela's
actions and attitude had utterly baffled him these past
weeks. She had gotten what she wanted, marriage to him.
So why did she continue to act as if he was doing her a
great wrong? He was the one who had been cleverly

snared and forced to marry a young woman who found his fortune far more interesting than she did him!

Nothing, he thought grimly, would ever convince him that Micaela's "rescue" of him had not been a case of seeing an opportunity and instantly seizing upon it. She had been clever, he would grant her that. And her continued performance since their betrothal had been superb—like a great actress, she had portrayed her reluctance to perfection. If he hadn't known better, he would have believed that she was entirely innocent of any plotting. But he did know, he reminded himself, the conversation in the gazebo never far from his mind.

The women were unaware of his presence. When he politely cleared his throat, they both jumped, Lisette swinging around sharply and Micaela clutching the bedclothes to her chin. His mouth twisted. Such a delightful welcome to his marriage bed.

Lisette recovered first, and said lightly, "*Monsieur*! You startled us! We did not know you were there." Turning back to Micaela, she dropped a kiss on her cheek and swiftly exited the room, leaving the newlyweds alone together.

Even knowing that she had trapped him into this marriage, Hugh couldn't help the surge of tenderness that went through him as he stared at Micaela. She looked lovely. Her black hair flowing around her shoulders like silk, her eyes dark and mysterious, her softly curved mouth a rosy lure. She also, he admitted uneasily, looked scared to death.

His gaze softened. Did she, he wondered, know what to expect from tonight? Hugh did not doubt for a moment that he was facing a virgin bride.

At least, he thought, he and Micaela had some knowledge of each other. He was not almost a total stranger to

her as was often the case in Creole marriages, especially
if the vigilant chaperons had done their work well.
Watching with interest the fluctuation of color across Micaela's revealing face, Hugh sighed. The next few hours
were going to be critical for the future of their life together. God knew that he had never made love to a virgin
before, and he was suddenly nervous.

He knew how to please a woman—past experience had
made him confident of that—but would he be able to
please his bride? His resentful, innocent bride?

Spying several decanters sitting on the top of a long
mahogany sideboard on the other side of the room, Hugh
almost fell upon them with relief. After pouring himself a
small snifter of brandy, he turned back to look at Micaela,
wondering at his next move.

Micaela watched him, her heart thumping in her chest.
He looked very handsome in his wedding attire, the
black-silk coat expertly fitting his broad shoulders, the
starched and pristine white cravat neatly arranged at his
throat. He wore black-silk breeches and white-silk stockings, and as her gaze slid innocently along the long length
of him, admiring him, a strange emotion unfurled low in
her belly.

The silence grew more awkward by the moment, and
Hugh said abruptly, "You made a lovely bride. Orange
blossoms become you."

Feeling rather silly still clutching the bedclothes to her
chin, Micaela slowly dropped them, and replied stiltedly,
"*Merci beaucoup, monsieur*. You made a handsome
bridegroom."

Hugh laughed aloud, his uneasiness vanishing. Amusement dancing in his gray eyes, he asked, "Aren't we
being very formal with each other? Considering we are
now man and wife?"

"You forget, *monsieur*," Micaela said stiffly, "the circumstances of our marriage."

Hugh's laughter faded. "Indeed I have not," he said slowly, "but since we are married, I suggest that we start making the best of a bad bargain."

Micaela's eyes flashed. "I do not," she muttered, "like being called a 'bad bargain'!"

"My apologies, *Madame* Wife, I should have said a bargain not of my own choosing." His gaze crossed her face. "But it does not change the fact," he said softly, "that we *are* married."

Something in his tone of voice, the look in his eyes, made Micaela suddenly very aware of the fact that they were alone together, that only a thin garment covered her nakedness, and that no matter what happened, no one was going to interrupt them. He *was* her husband, and he could do with her what he wanted. The conversation with her mother flitted through her mind, and, to her horror, she found herself intensely curious about the "things" he would do to her.

Hugh took another sip of his brandy, noting the slight flush in her cheeks. His gaze dropped, traveling with sensual appreciation over the soft curves mistily revealed by the delicate nightgown. Heat flooded his loins, and desire, swift and sure, spiraled through him. Micaela might have trapped him, but there was one thing that he could never deny—he wanted her. He always had. And now, he thought with a dizzying surge of anticipation, she was his wife.

"I do not," he said quietly, "believe that further conversation will accomplish much, do you? You have gained what you wanted." A frankly carnal expression leaped to his eyes, and he muttered, "And soon I shall have what I want. . . ."

Her breathing suddenly constricted, Micaela watched as he deliberately set down his brandy snifter. His eyes on hers, he slowly undid his cravat and tossed it on a nearby chair. His jacket followed, and her mouth grew dry as she stared at the powerful muscles of his arms and chest which were revealed when he shrugged out of his linen shirt. His skin gleamed like polished bronze in the candlelight, the thick, curly black hair on his chest coming as a shock to Micaela, but she could not look away from him. Odd new sensations were flowing through her as she stared at his near nakedness. He was beautiful, tall and muscular. The thought of those strong arms closing around her caused a sharp cramp, half-painful, half-pleasurable, to form between her thighs.

Apparently undisturbed by Micaela's riveted stare, almost as if he had done it countless times previously, Hugh sat down on the edge of the bed and slipped off his footwear and silk stockings. It was only when he stood up, his hands going to the fastening of his breeches that Micaela's courage broke.

"*Monsieur!*" she cried in agitated accents.

Hugh crooked a brow at her.

Her color high, she choked out, "The candles? Could you not blow them out? Please?"

Wordlessly they looked at each other and to her great relief, a moment later, the room was in darkness. There was the rustle of clothing, then Hugh was beside her in bed. She jumped when his arms closed around her and he gently pulled her next to him. His mouth inches from her ear, he murmured, "Believe me, sweetheart, there is nothing at this moment, that I want to do more than please you."

Chapter Nine

*H*ugh's mouth settled warmly and persuasively on hers. Micaela had remembered the touch of his lips on hers, but memory could not compare to the actual act. She marveled at how something so simple could be so exciting, so very pleasurable. He kissed her a long time, many times, his mouth moving gently over her lips, her temples, her closed lids, the tingling lobe of her ear. His touch was light and languorous.

Despite the pleasure of his kisses, Micaela lay stiff and unmoving in the bed, her body half-braced as if for an attack. Hugh was, after all, very nearly a virtual stranger to her, and the circumstances surrounding their marriage were not the sort to instill confidence in a bride. She *did* resent the fact that he still believed that she had deliberately trapped him into marriage. And there was the added fact that he was an *Américain*, a foreigner, and a man the men of her own family viewed as an interloper, an arrogant usurper of their rights in the family business. Yet, Micaela had to admit to herself that there was something about Hugh Lancaster that drew her. There had always been that spark between them, and she admitted, rather shamefully, that if she had had to choose a husband between Alain or Hugh, she would have chosen the *Américain* without hesitation.

It never occurred to Micaela to attempt to stop Hugh from consummating their marriage. She was too well brought up to even envision such a shocking thing, and Lisette and *Tante* Marie's words were still ringing in her ears. But even considering all of that, there was also the undeniable fact that he aroused some powerful emotion deep within her. She was actually eager to find out what happened between a man and a woman in the marriage bed. She admitted with a guilty start that she could not imagine any man other than Hugh teaching her those mysteries—even if he was an arrogant beast!

She was also understandably nervous and uncertain about what would happen. Just the knowledge that a naked man was lying next to her in bed was astonishing. Knowing that he could touch her and kiss her at will made her mouth go dry and her heart beat rapidly. She told herself firmly that she was not afraid of what he would do despite the tiny quiver of unease that lingered at the back of her mind. But as the minutes passed and Hugh did nothing more unsettling than press those sweetly exploring kisses upon her, she began to relax, to become aware of just how enjoyable kissing could be.

Micaela had no conception of the restraint her husband was showering upon her. While pleased with her acceptance of his caresses, Hugh was also struggling with a primitive urge to ravage all the sweet loveliness before him. He had wanted her a long time, and the knowledge that she was his wife, his to do with as he wished, was a powerful aphrodisiac. His body flooded with erotic longing, his manhood hard and aching between his legs. But aware of her innocence, aware of how little she knew about what was to come, he tried to pace himself, to awaken her to the pleasure that could be found between them. A time would come when he could unleash all his hungers and lose himself in her soft body, but not now, not tonight. Tonight she needed gentleness and he was determined to give it to her if it killed him.

In spite of his displeasure and anger at the way she had tricked him into marriage, he saw no point in making their marriage bed a battleground. He wanted this first joining to be as pleasurable for her as he could make it. He knew, though he would try hard not to, that he would probably give her pain. That was inevitable, but if he could also give her some pleasurable moments, too . . . He half smiled to himself. If he gave her pleasure, might he engender a liking for the act? Arouse within her an eagerness, a delight in their marriage bed?

Just the mere idea of Micaela ardently responding to his lovemaking made the ache between his thighs more insistent. Finally unable to control the urge to taste her, his mouth found her once more, this time, his lips demanding entrance. A shocked exclamation came from Micaela, and she stiffened when his tongue suddenly surged into her mouth. Instinctively her hands came up to push him away, but he said softly, "No. You must let me, sweetheart." His voice thickened. "Let me teach you, show you. . . ."

Mindful of *Tante* Marie's warnings and her mother's words about the "things" he would do to her, when his mouth took hers again and he deepened the kiss once more, she did not push him away. Instead, to her amazement, as his tongue gently probed and explored, her breathing quickened, her nipples tingled, and hot, honeyed heat flared between her legs. He tasted of the brandy he had drunk earlier, and she found that oddly exciting, but not nearly as exciting as the sensation of his tongue brushing erotically against hers. Her whole body was reacting wildly to his intimate kisses, her nipples now burning and throbbing, the heat between her legs streaking through her entire body. As he continued to drink deeply of her, Micaela began to tremble with the force of the elemental emotions he roused within her.

She was hardly aware of her hands clenching and unclenching like a kitten's contented kneading on his shoulders, hardly conscious of the inviting arch of her body against him. But Hugh was, *very*. Her unexpected response to him was so open, so generous, so damned arousing, that only by the greatest of restraint was he able to prevent himself from jerking up her nightgown and taking what he most desperately wanted.

He knew that his hold on his own passion was tenuous, her reactions to his kisses making it even more difficult to control his own responses. He fought fiercely against the base commands of his body. Everything within him demanded that he seek satisfaction, but with a groan, half-pained, half-delighted, he ignored his coarser feelings. But her gown, he admitted determinedly, that damned concealing garment, was going to have to go.

The thought had barely flitted through his mind before his hands were already on the offending gown, his fingers tugging impatiently at the ribbons at the neck. The garment had been conceived with easy removal in mind, and before Micaela fully understood what he was doing, she was half-lifted against him and her gown jerked unceremoniously over her head. Hugh might be attempting to proceed slowly, but there were limits to what a man could endure.

"Monsieur!" Micaela exclaimed, assailed by sheer amazement at finding herself utterly naked and held

firmly against an equally naked male body. A riot of new sensations exploded through her and she trembled, half-frightened, half-exhilarated.

Wherever they touched, his flesh was hot against hers, the thick mat of black hair on his broad chest cushioning her bosom, making her nipples swell to hard, little aching buds; the disturbing heat lower in her body bursting into a pulsating wildfire, which only increased the dazed pleasure flooding her.

Hugh thought he would go mad at the feel of her nipples burning into his chest, the silky warmth of her skin beneath his hands every erotic delight he had ever imagined and more. But feeling her tremble, he brushed his lips across hers and said shakily, "Do not be frightened, my love. I will not hurt you." He bit his lips, knowing that was not precisely true. "Not more than necessary," he added gruffly. "I will try to be gentle."

Her voice full of awe, she said, "I am not frightened, *Monsieur*—it is, oh, so very exciting, *oui*?"

Hugh groaned, wondering if she realized what her words were doing to him. Unable to help himself, he pushed her down into the mattress. Half-lying on her, his chest crushed against hers, one leg nudging between her thighs, he kissed her passionately.

Micaela was aware of him in every fiber of her being, his scent was in her nostrils, his taste upon her tongue, and the feel of his naked flesh pressing intimately against her own was astoundingly sweet. Filled with giddy emotion, unabashedly eager to learn more of the "things" he would do to her, her arms closed around him. Later she would be shocked at her actions. Later she would be ashamed at her forwardness and recall *Tante* Marie's advice. Much, much later she would be embarrassed at what was happening, but not now, oh, definitely not now.

Yet when Hugh's hand actually touched her breast, cupped it, his thumb rubbing erotically across her nipple, she couldn't help crying out. "*Monsieur*! What are you doing?"

A thread of laughter lacing through the passion, Hugh murmured, "I am making love to my wife . . . and do you not think that it is time you called me by my given name?" He kissed her soundly and said, "Can you not bring yourself to call me Hugh? It would please me to hear my name upon your lips."

The sensations that were streaking through her as he continued to pull and tug at her nipple made it hard to think, but eventually she got out breathlessly, "Very well, *M-m*—H-h-hugh."

Hugh's head dipped and Micaela arched up uncontrollably as his mouth closed around her nipple. The gentle scrape of his teeth made her gasp and clutch at him. Whether she meant to push him away or pull him to her, she never knew. The sensations were so intense, so sweet, that she floated dazedly, aching and yearning for something she could not name.

To her dizzying delight, he toyed with her breasts for some time, stroking them, shaping them to his liking. The only sound in the room was their heavy breathing and the little moans she unknowingly made as Hugh lured her deeper into the sensual maze he was weaving about her, about them both. Her reactions to his caresses and kisses, the sounds which came from deep in her throat, were every bit as carnally exciting to Hugh as her actions were to him.

The gnawing hunger to take her, to finally ease his aching flesh into hers, was unbearable. In the weeks preceding their marriage, he had found himself going about half-erect, the knowledge that one night soon he would be lying abed with her never far from his mind. To be touching her finally as he was now, to feel the firm, silken weight of her breasts in his hands, to nuzzle and suckle at those same sweet breasts was an intoxicating, lingering torture, but a torture he did not want to end, even as his body demanded he find satisfaction.

Gripped by his own passion, his hand slid from her breast, down the narrow rib cage, across the silken expanse of her belly, to the patch of tight curly hair at the junction of her thighs. Unerringly his seeking fingers parted the soft folds, petting and stroking, exploring and learning her.

Micaela gasped and jerked at his touch, embarrassment and a burst of indecent pleasure inundating her. Instinctively, she clamped her thighs together and grabbed his hand. "Please. Oh, please, stop."

Hugh stilled, his mouth pressed against the wildly fluttering pulse in her throat. He muttered, "What is it? Did I hurt you?"

In a voice which shook, she said, "*Non*. It is not that! I am afraid. It is as if my body is not mine any longer. You are making me feel things—wicked things I am sure no decent woman should feel. It is too shocking and shameful what you are doing to me."

Micaela felt his lips twitch in a smile against her throat. "Sweetheart," he said gently, "what I am doing to you is the most natural thing in the world. There is nothing shocking or the least shameful about it. It is a glorious thing, what our bodies can share." His voice deepened. "What we are doing is what men have been doing to women since time began." His lips slid down to her breast and he nipped lightly. "And what women have been doing to men. . . ."

To her horror and utterly wanton pleasure, he reached

for her hand and put it on him. Carefully he wrapped her trembling fingers around the solid length of himself, and a shudder went through him at her warm clasp. Slowly he taught her the motion which pleased him, another shudder racking him at her quick skill. In an oddly breathless tone he said, "You see? When you touch me, I feel those same wicked things . . . only they are not really wicked, are they?" Deliberately, his fingers sought the warmth between her legs and stroked her. "No, not wicked," he said thickly, "but glorious and oh so sweet. . . ."

Micaela's reply was lost as his mouth crushed hers, his fingers parting her and sinking deeply within her. She twisted up against him, her own fingers clenching around him, tearing a groan, half pain, half pleasure from Hugh. "Gently," he murmured. "Gently."

Certain he had never experienced such agonizingly sweet desire, Hugh's lips found Micaela's once more and he showed her the pleasure which could be found in another's caress. But the leash upon his hunger was badly frayed, and with a muffled imprecation, he suddenly stopped her inflaming ministrations. Capturing her wrist, he dragged it above her head. "No," he gasped. "No more."

Bewildered, Micaela stared up at him in the darkness, wishing erratically that she had not had him blow out the candles. She wanted to see him. See the long, naked length of him. See what that hot length of silken steel she had been caressing really looked like. More stunningly, she wanted him to see her. . . .

The warnings from *Tante* Marie stabbed through her, and, wondering if the Devil had possessed her, Micaela felt her face flame with mortification. She was confused. Frightened and yet not frightened. To her intense embarrassment, she was oddly *un*embarrassed by what they were doing. She *liked* what they were doing. A strange, giddy excitement welled up inside her as Hugh kissed her and explored her body. She had felt bold and yet wildly thrilled when he had let her touch him. She wanted to touch him again, to feel him shudder and know that he was feeling all the same wild sensations which sang through her.

But Hugh had been pushed to his limit, and he suddenly grasped her thighs and parted them, his big body fitting snugly between them. For a moment he simply lay there, savoring the heat of her body, the scent of their passion and the press of her warm thighs against his hips. Then his mouth found hers, his hands slid beneath her, lifting her as he began to carefully push his aching staff inside of her.

Micaela's breath was lodged somewhere in her chest, her blood thundering in her veins as he slowly, sweetly made them one. There was pain, but she was so assaulted by all the new sensations and emotions exploding through her body that she paid it little heed. She was a wife! she thought with a burst of simple pride. A true wife. And then Hugh began to move on her, thrusting deeper and deeper within her, widening her, making her completely his, and she forgot everything but the rapture of this moment.

Burning within her, Hugh shuddered, the tight, clinging heat of her silken sheath giving him the most erotic bliss he had ever experienced in his life. And when he stroked deeper the leash on his control snapped and he drove into her again and again as he strained to find sweet relief from the carnal urges which assailed him. He had thought that nothing could compare to the pleasure he had first experienced as their bodies had become one, but he discovered that he had deluded himself, that the bliss only intensified, intensified so powerfully that he could not bear it a second longer. Clutching her even tighter to him, he jerked and trembled as ecstasy swept him away.

They remained locked together for several moments, Hugh able now to kiss her with lazy relish, the frantic motions of his body lessening. Regretfully, he finally slid from her soft flesh. Lying beside her, remembering that at the last he had lost all restraint, he pulled her next to him, and asked quietly, "Did I hurt you very much?"

Almost unbearably aware of him, of their nakedness and of what they had just done, Micaela said shyly, "Only a little."

Unexpectedly moved by those words, Hugh kissed her gently and muttered, "I promise you it shall never hurt again and next time . . . next time I shall try to give you more pleasure."

Feeling rather sophisticated and blasé now that the act was over, Micaela murmured, "It was very nice what we did together, *oui*?"

"*Nice!*" he replied in stunned, outraged tones, remembering vividly the scalding ecstasy that had been his. He had never experienced that sort of utter fulfillment before in his life. It was rather mortifying to realize that for all his care and restraint, for her, their joining had not even begun to approach the level of ecstasy which he had reached. Reminding himself that she had been an innocent made him feel a little better and lessened some of his outrage. Nice! he thought half-furiously, half-wryly. His bride thought his lovemaking was nice! What a dismal reflection on his skills as a lover. He supposed, he admitted acidly, that he should be pleased with the outcome. She did not fear him and had not found the act distasteful or terrifying, at least he could take comfort in *that*! A feral smile suddenly crossed his face. He could not undo tonight, but in time, he vowed with great relish, in time she would share with him that same blinding ecstasy and would never, ever, again refer to their lovemaking as *nice*!

Completely unaware of the chagrin she had aroused in her husband's breast, Micaela yawned, and asked drowsily, "Is there anything else that we have to do?"

"No," he said wryly, thinking of several other things he would show and teach her in the coming days, "there is nothing else, sweetheart. Go to sleep."

His words fell on deaf ears. Micaela was already sound asleep, the strain of the day and evening having taken its toll. But for Hugh sleep did not come easily. To his astonishment, not many minutes had passed before the novelty of having Micaela lying naked beside him began to have a decided effect upon him. Feeling his body harden, he sighed. One might have supposed that having been dismissed as merely "nice" that a certain part of his anatomy would have had the decency to, er, hide its head in shame, but, no, it was upright and eager to join sweet battle again.

Ignoring the base promptings of his body, Hugh shifted, trying to get comfortable. Under different circumstances, he would have slaked his hunger with a renewed bout of lovemaking, but his unbridled confidence in his expertness as a lover had suffered a definite dent. He shook his head ruefully. After taking such care with her, to have his efforts dismissed as nice! was a smack to his masculine pride, and he was in no mood to risk being so carelessly discarded again.

In spite of his best intentions, however, just before dawn Hugh woke, and Micaela's warmly nestled body proved to be too great a temptation. He kissed and caressed her awake and took her with an odd urgency, his body thrusting desperately into hers. She gladly accepted him, eagerly received his caresses and his almost frantic invasion of her yielding flesh. But afterward he was gallingly aware that while he had known again that same sweet delirium, she had not. He had made certain that she had been aroused, moist and ready for him when he had taken her and yet . . . It was nothing she said—she fell back asleep almost immediately—but he was expert enough to realize that she had not attained that most-longed-for peak of glorious release.

He scowled in the faint light. It was as well, he thought dryly, that she did not yet know what she was missing! She would certainly have found her new husband a disappointment! It seemed utterly incredible to him, that now when it mattered most, he could not satisfy his wife. Oh, he doubted that she was *un*satisfied. His mouth quirked. No doubt she had thought their latest joining had been nice, too!

Realizing that only time, and hopefully, his skill could change the situation, Hugh fell back asleep. When he woke again, sunlight was streaming into the pleasant room. He became instantly aware that the area beside him was empty, and he jerked upright, only to relax back against the pillows when he spied Micaela seated at a small table beneath one of the windows, sedately sipping a cup of hot chocolate. She had been looking at him and seeing that he was awake, she smiled uncertainly.

"Good morning, *M-m-mon*, er, Hugh," she said politely. "Did you sleep well?"

A sensuous smile curved his lips. "Except for one or two incidents, indeed, yes!"

Micaela blushed. Just thinking of his hands on her body made her breasts tingle and her lower body clench with excitement. Ashamed of her wanton reaction to his words, she said stiffly, "I am happy to hear it." Gesturing to the tray on the table, she asked, "Would you like some hot chocolate? There is also coffee, if you would like."

What he would like, Hugh thought frankly, was to take her back to bed and begin immediately exploring ways to have her screaming and writhing in wanton abandon beneath him. Instead, he flung aside the bedclothes and reached for the black-silk robe which had been laid on the bed for him. "Coffee will be fine."

Heedless of his nakedness, he stood up and shrugged into the robe. Crossing to the marble washstand in one corner, he made quick work of his morning ablutions. His hair damp and curling around his dark, handsome face, he finally turned and approached the table where Micaela sat.

Her fingers trembled as she poured his coffee, for the sight of that lean, magnificent body had shaken her. He was so tall, so virile and beautiful in an utterly masculine way that she could hardly believe that he was her husband and that last night she had lain in his arms. Something hot and aching unfurled in her belly. *Merci!* But this was disgraceful! She should not be thinking these indecent thoughts! The marriage bed was a necessary part of their life together, she told herself prosaically, but surely it should not intrude into her mind this way. *Tante* Marie would think her a shameless creature, and she was duly ashamed of herself—and her thoughts.

Putting on a cool smile to hide the tumult and confusion within her, she handed him the cup of coffee and murmured, "There are also some calas and fruit, if you would like them."

162   *Shirlee Busbee*

Seating himself in a chair across from her, he sipped his coffee. "Rice cakes? Are they still hot?"

Her eyes twinkled. "*Mais oui! Maman* would be insulted if we were to be served cold food!"

Biting into one of the golden brown rice cakes, Hugh closed his eyes in open enjoyment. "We shall have to make certain that our own cook fixes these often."

"Do we have a cook?" Micaela asked, startled. In the days before their marriage, her meetings with her husband had been few and then always in company of others. There had not been much discussion of household affairs. Everything had happened with such haste that such interesting affairs as living quarters had been pushed aside. It suddenly occurred to Micaela that she didn't even have any idea where they were going to live. Most of her married friends either continued to live under their parents' roof with their husbands or moved into their husband's family home. Somehow, from what little she did know of him, she did not think that Hugh was going to have them continue to live with her family. He would want, she realized slowly, his own home.

"Yes, we do have a cook—a very fine one, I am told. And a butler, several housemaids and some kitchen assistants for the cook, as well as sundry others." He glanced across at her. "I hope you do not mind, but I have been assembling a staff for us. Jasper and your *Tante* Marie helped and your *maman*, also."

Micaela smiled impishly. "And a house? Do we have one of those, too?"

Pushing aside his empty plate, Hugh grinned back at her. "Indeed we do, *Madame* Wife. Thanks to Jasper's intervention and the fact that I was marrying into a solidly respectable Creole family, I was able to purchase a fine piece of property, a few houses down from Jasper's own house. Ownership changed hands not three days ago."

She considered this news for a moment. "Old *Monsieur* Follet's house?"

"You know it?" Hugh asked, surprised.

"Yes. *Maman* has taken me there to visit many times, and since *Monsieur* Follet is the last of his family, it is the only place I could imagine that you would have been able to buy." She grinned at him, suddenly looking extremely mischievous, that kissable dimple coming into view. "You must know that Creole property is seldom for sale at any price—it usually passes from one generation to the next and few, if any, would sell to an *Américain*—but since *Monsieur* Follet is the last of his line and you have married me, *voilà*! It arranges itself, *oui*?"

"Yes, it does," Hugh replied, thinking that he liked the sparkle in her fine dark eyes and the mischievous grin on her pretty face. "You will, naturally, want to refurbish it. Since *Monsieur* Follet is planning to return to France, he left a great many pieces of furniture in the house, but it is by no means completely furnished." He smiled at her. "You may draw freely upon my purse for whatever you think we might need. And, of course, I shall be delighted to take you to our warehouses, for you to select anything there that catches your eye."

Micaela found herself both excited and intimidated at the notion of having her very own home. *Monsieur* Follet's house was very large and grand . . . Delight suddenly swelled within her. And Hugh had bought it for them. The look she bent upon him was glowing and warm. "You are very kind."

Hugh cocked a brow. "And you, sweetheart, are being very formal with your husband."

She made a face. "It is all very strange, *hein*? We hardly know each other, and yet we are married."

Micaela could have bitten her tongue off as his face suddenly closed down. He rose to his feet and walked over to a tall mahogany wardrobe where a change of clothes for him had been placed yesterday. "Not so very strange," he said coolly, "when one considers the bold scheme which brought it about."

Her fists clenched and all of the kind thoughts she had had of him vanished. "You are insulting!"

He glanced over his shoulder at her. "Am I? I feel it is more of a case of speaking bluntly." He smiled crookedly at her. "A trait you Creoles find appalling in Americans, among other things."

Her quick temper rising, she jumped up and snapped, "*Oui*, this is true. We also find you rude, overbearing, and arrogant!"

"Ah, but necessary to marry, yes?"

"Bah!" Micaela spat, her eyes flashing. Turning her back on him, she stared stonily out of one of the windows. "I will not continue this ridiculous conversation with you."

Hugh shrugged and calmly began to dress. He had brought his longtime valet, Jeffers, with him from Natchez, but this morning Hugh had dispensed with his services. In fact, at this very moment, Jeffers should be overseeing the setting up of the new household.

Having finished garbing himself, Hugh turned to stare at Micaela's rigid back. She was really being very foolish, he thought to himself. She had gotten what she wanted—a wealthy husband. What more did she want? If he could accept being married for his purse, surely she could admit her own part in bringing about their marriage?

Shaking his head at the mysterious workings of a woman's mind, he said, "Well, if you will excuse me, I shall go to the office for a few hours—there is something I wish to check on. I shall not be long."

Micaela whirled around, her expression horrified. "You are leaving me?" she gasped.

Hugh frowned. "As I said, only for a few hours."

"But you cannot!" she exclaimed in agitated accents. Crossing to stand before him, her fingers clutched the lapels of his dark blue jacket. "Do you not understand, you *cannot!*"

Puzzled, Hugh regarded her tense features. "Why not?" he asked slowly.

"It is *not* done," she said urgently. "Creole brides and grooms are expected to remain alone in their bedroom with each other for five days—or more. For one of us, or even both, to leave before that time would bring shame and disgrace on our family!"

Looking slightly stunned, Hugh stared back at her. "We are confined here for five days?"

Micaela nodded vigorously. "*Oui*—at least. Meals will be brought and left at the door, but we are not to venture forth before the five days has passed. It would be utterly scandalous to do so."

"Good Lord," Hugh muttered, "of all the damned archaic notions, that is the most . . ." He stopped, deciding hastily that his bride would not take kindly to hearing a Creole custom decried. It seemed a barbaric tradition, but realizing that most Creole brides and grooms hardly knew each other, he could see how it might have originated. His lips quirked. Being confined in a bedroom with one's spouse for several days was one way of ensuring the new couple became well acquainted with the other. Very *well* acquainted.

An extremely carnal smile on his lips, Hugh absently began to undo his just-tied cravat. His gaze boldly caressing Micaela, he asked huskily, "And precisely how do you expect us to spend these five days, hmm?"

Chapter Ten

*I*gnoring the sudden pounding of her heart, Micaela took a prudent step away from him. "We shall t-t-talk and learn to know each other better," she said primly.

Since the only knowledge which interested Hugh at the moment was the Biblical kind, he barely hesitated before he swept her into his arms and began kissing her. "We have years and years in which to talk, sweetheart. I think our time would be better spent in retiring to our marriage bed and learning all the wonderful ways in which we can pleasure each other."

"N-n-now?" she stammered in astonishment, her senses spinning from his ardent embrace. "During the day? S-s-should we not wait until evening?"

His face buried in the fragrant dark clouds of her hair, Hugh made a face. In view of everything, it would be sensible to proceed slowly with his bride.

Firmly setting her tempting body away from him, he said, "Since what we do here is important only to us, we can do what we wish, when we wish it, but perhaps you are right—perhaps it is time that we learned more about each other." Seating himself at the small table, his long legs stretched out in front him and crossed at the ankles, he slanted her a sardonic glance. "So. What do you want to talk about?"

Uncertainty evident in her gaze, she sat down across the table from him. She bit her lip, racking her brain for a topic. "We could talk about your family," she said finally. "You know about mine, but I know nothing of yours other than *Monsieur* John Lancaster is your step-*papa*."

"There is not much to tell," Hugh replied slowly, resigned to following her lead. "My father, Sidney Lancaster, died from injuries suffered when his horse bolted and took him over a bluff when I was four years old." His face softened. "He was much older than my mother, but she adored him. She always maintained that she had buried her heart with him. They had only been married five years, and she was just twenty-three years old when he died."

"Do you remember your *papa* at all?" Micaela asked, her dark eyes full of sympathy.

Hugh shook his head. "No, I was too young to have any clear memory of him. Mother claimed, however, that I was his very image."

"And *Monsieur* John Lancaster? When did your *maman* fall in love and marry him?"

A mocking expression lit his face. "They did not fall in love, sweetheart," he drawled. "Their marriage was a mutual business decision. John was a distant relative of my father's, a second or third cousin, removed a few times, I think. His property adjoined ours, and my father and John had undertaken several business ventures together prior to my father's death. Our interests were entwined and after several years, mother and John simply decided that it made good business sense for them to marry. He acquired a wife and a hostess; she got an excellent business manager and a father for her son." His mocking expression became more pronounced. "They neither one pretended it was anything other than convenient for both of them."

"I see," said Micaela, wondering sickly if he considered their marriage *convenient.* If François was right, her husband not only considered their union convenient, but expedient! But deciding not to tread on dangerous subjects, she asked, "And *Monsieur* John, was he a good step-*papa* to you?"

Hugh grinned. "The very best! Because of the situation, it has been John who has acted as my father for as far back as I can remember. I was elated when he and mother told me of their decision to marry." A reminiscent smile curved his mouth. "They were married the day after my eleventh birthday, and I felt every inch a man when I escorted my mother down the aisle and put her hand in John's. John formally adopted me a few hours later. It was a very momentous day."

"And your *maman*? You do not speak of her."

Hugh looked away. "She died," he said simply, "a little under three years after they were married. I was not yet fourteen."

"Oh, I am so sorry," Micaela said, her tender heart moved by the unspoken pain she glimpsed behind those blunt words.

"Well, at least you will have only one in-law to contend with," he said dryly, "and one you will be meeting not too many more weeks in the future."

"You think he will come to New Orleans?" Micaela asked with a little frown. "He never has in the past. *Maman* said he was here when the company was formed, but never once since—in spite of being the major owner of the company."

"Perhaps," Hugh said dryly, "he took an aversion to the place. Remember he has not been the major owner for a few years now . . . or have you forgotten? I am the one who now owns the major share."

Micaela's lips tightened. "How could I forget, when it is because of that fact that we are married?

Hugh smiled mirthlessly. "I suppose I should be flattered that you are finally being honest about your motives for having arranged this union between us."

"I did not 'arrange' a thing, and that was not what I meant at all!" she snapped, appalled at how quickly the mood between them had changed. Hanging on to her fraying temper, she muttered, "I meant that if you were not the major owner, you would not have come to New Orleans." Defiantly her gaze met his. "We would never have met and certainly would never have been forced to marry each other!" The openly mocking smile which curved his lips was her undoing. It was obvious he did not believe a word of what she had just said. Her eyes blazed, and she added furiously, "And I, for one, wish that I had never laid eyes on you!"

It was, Hugh decided sardonically as he watched her spring to her feet and stalk majestically to the far end of the room, going to be a long five days. His gaze fell upon their bed. A grin crossed his face. Then again, perhaps not.

But Hugh's prediction proved to be more accurate than not. It *was* a long five days. Not that he was bored, nor was it that Micaela denied him his conjugal rights—in fact that was the only time that there was not a faintly simmering air of suspicion behind their every word. At night, Micaela came into his arms easily enough, her

body docilely accepting his, but she was a passive participant in their lovemaking. Her soft, almost-smothered
sighs and oh-so-subtle reactions to his caresses were the
only outward signs that she did not find the entire act totally repugnant.

They did talk, and even laughed together upon occasion and inevitably grew more comfortable with each
other. It was an unspoken rule between them *not* to speak
of the reasons for their hasty marriage, or the events surrounding it, as well as the dangerous subject of the affairs
of Galland, Lancaster and Dupree.

Hugh found much pleasure in making love to his wife,
but he was increasingly frustrated that he could not seem
to give her the same scalding release he experienced in
her arms. And he would have been utterly astonished at
how *very* difficult his wife was finding it not to respond
to his skilled lovemaking with an openly wanton delight.
He'd be even more astonished to learn that by fiercely
suppressing every frantic urge to respond with delirious
vigor to his exciting caresses that she thought she was behaving in a manner which pleased him.

Micaela might not have known precisely what to expect from the marriage bed, but after Lisette's and especially *Tante* Marie's strictures, she did know that it was
her duty as a good, decent Creole wife merely to accept
her husband's lovemaking—very little was required of
her beyond passivity. It would have been unthinkable for
her to cry aloud her pleasure, or even more inconceiv-
able, boldly to touch her husband or freely caress him—
or even, horror, invite his passion. Innocent as she had
been, she had taken *Tante* Marie's words to heart, especially the part about a Creole husband who had once
wanted to divorce his bride, because he thought she had
been too exuberant in expressing her joys of the marriage

bed. Micaela and Hugh might have been forced by circumstances and convention to marry, but Micaela was determined to be a good wife to him, even if it meant submissively accepting him into her bed and body, when every nerve, every fiber of her being called out for her to greet their joinings with wanton abandon.

It was an uncomfortable situation for both of them; Hugh determined to bring her earthshaking ecstasy; Micaela equally determined not to give any indication of the wild, shuddering delight his merest touch aroused within her. Each grew to dread the marriage bed.

By the time the five days had passed, it would have been hard to guess which one of them was the most relieved. At least now they would not be forced to spend hour after agonizing hour in the sole company of their unknowing tormentor. Following custom, Micaela would still not be seen in public for another week or two, but they were not longer confined to their bedroom, and Hugh would be able to take up his normal activities. Micaela could discreetly visit their new home and begin personally overseeing its renovations.

On the sixth morning after their marriage, they joined Lisette and Jean at the breakfast table. François, they were informed, had eaten earlier and had left to visit with Alain, who was healing well and had returned to the city for the wedding. Facing her relatives, embarrassingly aware that they knew exactly what she and Hugh had been doing the past five nights, was not the ordeal that Micaela had feared it would be, and five minutes after being seated by her husband, she was smiling and talking to her mother as if she had been married for six years instead of six days.

Jean seemed to have accepted with reasonably good grace the fact that the *Américain* was now part of the family and he made a decided effort to be friendly. For perhaps the first time ever in their long relationship, Jean and Hugh held a decidedly amiable conversation; but there was no denying that the mood lightened considerably when Jean finally rose and took leave of the others.

Shortly after his departure, having finished his own meal, Hugh put down his cup of coffee, and asked Micaela, "Would you like to see the house this morning? I intend to go into the office this afternoon, but for now, my time is yours."

Micaela's eyes sparkled. "Oh, *oui*!" She glanced at Lisette. "Would you care to come with us, *Maman*?" Uncertainly, she threw a look at her husband. "That is, if you do not mind, H-h-hugh."

Hugh grinned. "I am your husband, *petite*, not an ogre." To Lisette, he said, "Would you join us, *madame*? It would please me and, of course, my wife."

Lisette happily accepted, and a few minutes later, the trio left the house and walked to old *Monsieur* Follet's house on Dumaine Street. As Hugh had mentioned, it was just a few doors down from Jasper's town house. Like most Creole houses, it was built right to the edge of the banquette. The second-story balcony, festooned with delicate iron grillwork, jutted out over the banquette.

Micaela was filled with both pride and excitement when she stepped inside the elegant house, knowing that this would be her New Orleans home. As they wandered about, investigating places and areas that had been private during their other visits to *Monsieur* Follet, Micaela and Lisette exclaimed delightedly over the many spacious rooms. The house was, not surprisingly, furnished in an old-fashioned manner, but Hugh had made it clear that his purse was open and that Micaela could dip into it freely. Her cheeks flushed with pleasure, Micaela had immediately begun to make a list of the furnishings that she intended to buy.

The servants were introduced to their new mistress and Micaela was quite pleased to recognize a few faces from home. Most were strangers to her, but she had no doubt that she would grow familiar with them in a short time.

The inspection done, Hugh escorted the ladies home. The day was growing hot and humid, and both ladies were happy to retire to a shady corner of the courtyard and sip lemonade. Hugh saw them settled and, finishing his own drink, rose to his feet.

"If I am to get any work done today, I am afraid that I must leave you ladies now."

Micaela was both disappointed and relieved that she would be spared his disturbing presence for several hours and said nothing. But Lisette made a face and said half-teasingly, half-seriously, "You *Américains*! All you think of is work—and you not married a week."

Hugh smiled faintly. "Someone in the family has to work, *madame*—I have new demands on my purse these days and must make certain that it is full enough and *stays* full enough to please my wife."

A shadow entered Micaela's eyes. "I am certain that I will not act the spendthrift with your purse, *monsieur*," Micaela said stiffly. "And I do have money of my own— I did not come to you penniless."

"I am certain that is true," Hugh said slowly, his gaze on her slightly averted features. He had said the words in jest, but it appeared his bride had taken them to heart. Hugh sighed. He had much to learn of his new wife. Gently, he said, "Do not fear, sweetheart, it is a *very* deep purse. I would prefer you spend my money for major expenditures and keep yours for any personal trifles which catch your eye. Believe me when I say that you shall have whatever your heart desires."

"Will I?" she asked with sudden intensity, oblivious to her mother's presence. "Will I?"

Hugh picked up her slender hand and dropped a kiss on it. "I swear it," he promised gravely, his gray eyes fixed on hers.

Micaela flushed and dropped her gaze, conscious of the rapid beating of her heart. How does he do this to me, she wondered miserably. A look, a word, and my emotions are not my own, and I forget the circumstances of our marriage. He smiles at me, kisses me, and I instantly forget that François might have been right. This man I married may have connived to bring about our union for monetary reasons. Despite his kindnesses, and he *has* been kind, very, his interest is only in the shares of the family business which I brought to our marriage.

Micaela's shares in Galland, Lancaster and Dupree were being discussed at that very moment in the Husson town house. Alain, François, and Jean were seated in Alain's study, which overlooked the courtyard of the house. They were scattered comfortably about the room, a cup of coffee near each man's hand.

Alain's wound was healing swiftly, but because of the broken shoulder, he was still tightly bandaged, and his arm was carried in a black-silk sling, which gave him a romantic air. It would be at least another month before he could dispense with the sling, and he was looking forward to it—and the moment he could take his revenge on the *Américain*.

He had many scores to settle with Hugh Lancaster, especially Hugh's marriage to the woman Alain considered his own. Forgetting that the duel had been of his own making, he was convinced that the *Américain* had cleverly arranged it all to get him out of the way, while boldly stealing his bride-to-be. Alain conveniently forgot that Micaela had bluntly refused his offer of marriage and that the only way he had been going to be able to marry her was by an underhanded, nefarious trick. He was utterly incensed that the *Américain* had been able to marry her by using that same method. Not given to deep thinking, the irony entirely escaped him.

It was François who brought up the subject of Micaela's shares. His voice full of gloom, he muttered, "And to think that now instead of you, our friend, commanding those shares, it is the *Américain*! I tell you, I cannot bear it!"

"Do not be such a melodramatic young fool!" Jean said forthrightly. "It is not so very bad, what has transpired." As both younger men turned disbelieving, furious eyes upon him, he said coolly, "I think you are forgetting that while he may be her husband, he does not actually own her shares. She does. Together they may own a larger share, but individually . . ."

"Are you trying to tell us that nothing has changed?" François demanded incredulously.

"*Non*," Alain said slowly, "that is not what your uncle is saying." An ugly smile suddenly crossed his face. "Ah, I begin to see . . ." His eyes narrowed. "They own their shares individually, but *they* are joined, and if *Monsieur* Lancaster were to suffer an unfortunate accident, his shares would come to his young widow, *oui*? If fate is kind, sweet Micaela could end up owning the lion's share of the business."

"*Mon Dieu!*" Jean burst out, obviously startled, "That is not what I meant at all. All I meant was that Micaela's loyalty would still be to us."

"But it is true, *hein*?" Alain asked softly. "That she would inherit his shares?"

"Well, yes, I suppose so," Jean admitted, his gaze moving thoughtfully from one young face to the other.

Alain smiled across at François. "You see, *mon ami*? It arranges itself, *oui*?"

Hugh was whistling softly to himself when he entered the offices of Galland, Lancaster and Dupree. Despite the difficulties in his marriage, he was feeling rather pleased about life in general. He was in his office not more than five minutes, however, before his good mood vanished. The report just given him by *Monsieur* Brisson was enough to ruin anybody's good mood! Hugh thought disgustedly.

Frowning, Hugh asked in a dangerous tone, "Do you mean to tell me that *Le Lys Bleu* arrived with a large shipment of goods for us three days ago and no one thought to tell me about it?"

Monsieur Brisson nearly wrung his hands in trepidation at the expression on Hugh's face. "But *monsieur*," he cried, greatly upset, "what could I do—you were just wedded!"

Hugh swore viciously under his breath. "You could have," he ground out, "sent me a note, informing me of the fact."

"But you were just wed!" *Monsieur* Brisson burst out, clearly aghast at such a notion.

"What the hell difference does that make? I told you that the *moment* a ship arrived I wanted to be notified."

Brushing past *Monsieur* Brisson, Hugh left his office. Striding to where Etienne Gras was seated at his desk, he demanded, "Do you have the original ship's inventory from *Le Lys Bleu*?"

A hasty shuffle of papers on his desk brought it to light, and wordlessly Etienne handed the bulky document to Hugh. Hugh smothered a curse at the size of it. He had no doubt that this was the shipment he had been waiting for—and no doubt his thieves had been, too. It looked, he thought grimly, as he carefully scanned the document, to have been an extensive shipment of goods—just the sort to tempt whoever was stealing from the company, and that dolt Brisson had not notified him!

Spinning away, he strode back into his office and grimly dismissed Brisson. Several minutes later, an expression, part disgust, part satisfaction upon his face, he sat back in his chair. Well, he had been right. Idly his fingers ran over the betraying pages of the invoice.

As with the other suspicious documents, concealed in the middle of the invoice were once again those pages of a subtly different quality. He stared thoughtfully at the invoice for several long moments, an unpleasant idea sliding through his mind.

The arrival dates of ships were never exact, but approximate dates were known from dispatches which were carried on ships that had sailed earlier and consequently arrived in New Orleans, days or even weeks ahead of the later-sailing ship. Information about the size and content of the expected cargo was usually included in the dispatch by their business associates. Hugh had been intently studying the various dispatches which had arrived over the weeks with an eye to spotting a shipment of the quantity carried by *Le Lys Bleu.* After the fact, he realized that nothing had crossed his desk which had even mentioned *Le Lys Bleu,* neither her expected arrival date, nor what she carried in her hold for Galland, Lancaster and Dupree. Interesting.

He leaned back in his chair and rubbed his chin. So.

Had there been no dispatch sent? Or had it simply not arrived? Or had it arrived and not reached his hands?

His lips thinned. It would be unusual for the firms they did business with abroad not to have sent advance notice of a shipment, especially one of the size carried by *Le Lys Bleu*. It was possible, he admitted grimly, that the ship carrying the dispatch had been lost at sea—but he did not recall talk of any recent disappearances. The loss of a ship was not an *un*common occurrence, it was part of the cost of doing business, but news of such a disaster was normally common knowledge. So he felt confident in dismissing that theory. As a matter of fact, he vaguely remembered that another ship from France had arrived the week before his marriage with a small shipment for the firm—but there had not been any dispatches. At least, he amended carefully, none that he had seen. But had there been one and had someone else gotten his hands on it?

Now, who in the firm would have been first to receive the newly arrived dispatch? Ah. Yes, of course. Etienne Gras normally handled that part of the business, just as young Etienne was usually the first one to inventory the newly arrived goods.

A few minutes later, in response to Hugh's request for his company, Etienne stood uncertainly before Hugh's desk. His young face pale, he swallowed several times before he was finally able to answer Hugh's question.

"A d-d-dispatch, *monsieur*? I am afraid, I do not know what you are talking about. I received nothing mentioning the approximate arrival date of the *Le Lys Bleu*." He tried a smile. "It is unusual, but it does happen occasionally that we have no advance warning of a shipment's arrival."

Hugh nodded and dismissed him, but he stared a long time at the door Etienne had shut behind him as he had departed. Now, was that young man simply nervous because he had been called before his employer? Or had there been another reason, such as guilty knowledge?

Jasper wandered in an hour later. Having first stopped by the Dupree house and learning of Hugh's whereabouts, he had immediately strolled to the office. After greetings had been exchanged, Hugh asked abruptly, "What do you know of Etienne Gras?"

Seated in a chair in front of Hugh's desk, his elegantly clad legs stretched out in front of him, Jasper looked surprised. "Young Gras?" At Hugh's nod, his expression became thoughtful. "Do you suspect him?"

Hugh made a face. "Yes and no. I just want to know more about him. His family, friends, and habits will do nicely to start."

"You do not ask much, *mon ami*," Jasper replied with a grin. His face sobered almost immediately and he said slowly, "The family is well respected. Not wealthy, you understand, not of the crème de la crème. He *is* working for you, after all. But still they are accepted everywhere, and most Creole *papas* would not be too displeased by a union with one of their daughters and a Gras son or vice versa." Jasper frowned. "As for his friends and habits, I am afraid I cannot help you there. François is more of an age with young Gras. Now that I think of it, I believe that I have seen them together about town now and then."

"Nothing else?"

Jasper leaned back in the chair, staring down at his glossy black boots, obviously racking his brain for more information. "There is something else," he said eventually. His eyes met Hugh's. "A few years ago, I remember hearing talk that he owed Husson some money. A gaming debt."

A look of intense satisfaction crossed Hugh's face.

"Husson!" he said with relish. "Is it not strange how often his name intrudes into our discussions?"

"I would not be too pleased, *mon ami*." Jasper cautioned. "New Orleans is, after all, a close-knit community. Husson is a prominent member of Creole society. His gambling connections are not unknown, and if young Gras likes to gamble, which he does as I recall, it is not surprising that he has owed Husson money from time to time. Many people have—you will end up chasing your tail if you suspect everyone who has ever owed Husson a gambling debt." He grinned. "Do not forget that even old Christophe Galland owed him, which is why we presently have Husson as a partner, *oui*?" Hugh grimaced, and Jasper laughed. "And do not forget, that I, too, won my shares from Christophe. Does that make you suspect me also?"

Hugh snorted. "If you were fleecing the firm, *mon ami*, you would have left no traces."

Jasper's eyes danced. *"Merci beaucoup*—I think."

"But I still like the connection between Husson and Gras. Could you do a little discreet snooping and see what reveals itself?"

"To please you, *oui* . . . but do not expect very much."

Business out of the way, Jasper cajoled Hugh into joining him in a visit to one of the coffeehouses—which had been the entire purpose of his visit. It was apparent, Hugh thought with amusement, that his friend was determined to woo him away from the nasty habit of actually working and was slyly trying to turn him into an indolent Creole gentleman of leisure. For today he would allow his friend to think he was succeeding.

The following week saw the removal of the newly-weds from the Dupree town house into their own home.

Overnight the Follet house had become the Lancaster house, but the changes went much deeper than merely a name change. The house had been newly repainted inside and out; new airy summer hangings now ornamented the windows; fresh grass matting covered the cypress floors; and several handsome pieces of fine mahogany furniture had been added to complement the furniture left behind by *Monsieur* Follet. It took Hugh and Micaela several days to settle fully into their new home, but by the third week of June, they were each feeling optimistic about the future and the establishment of their own home.

But they were not going to have much time to enjoy the residence they now shared—the fever season was approaching and Hugh had informed Micaela that he was removing her to the country until October or November, when the danger had subsided. They had just finished their evening meal and were enjoying a final cup of coffee in the dining room, when Hugh had mentioned leaving.

"But where are we to stay? With *Maman*?" she asked, her fine eyes wide and puzzled.

Hugh shook his head and smiled. "No—although until a week or so ago, that was a very real possibility."

"Then?"

"An excellent property, some distance north of the city, was recently brought to my attention by René L'Aramy. We looked at it last Wednesday, and the owner and I finally struck a bargain today."

"I see," Micaela said slowly. "You did not think I would care to know of this *before* you bought it? Or that I might have preferred to live nearer *Maman*?"

Hugh frowned. He was long used to arranging events to suit himself, with no one gainsaying his plans. To his credit, he had debated telling Micaela of the possible purchase, he had even considered taking her to view it. But the owner, a handsome Creole widow, *Madame* Justine, had vacillated on several points, all the while flirting outrageously with René, and Hugh had not been positive that the purchase would actually take place. His motives had been pure. He had not wanted his bride to be disappointed if the widow could not be brought to terms. In fact, he had planned the purchase as a surprise—he'd had no doubts, until this very moment, that Micaela would find the place as attractive and eminently suitable as he had. From the expression on her face, he realized uneasily, that he had very definitely put a foot wrong. Marriage, he admitted wryly, was not quite the easy affair he had assumed it to be.

"You must forgive me," he said slowly. "Having to consider another's sensibilities is new to me."

Micaela felt a mortifying blush sweep up her face. Her wretched, *wretched* tongue! Would she ever learn to control it? How shrewish she had been! How had she dared to question him? No self-respecting Creole wife would have done such a thing! Her gaze dropped, and she said huskily, "It does not matter. I am sure that I shall be satisfied with the place."

Seeing her discomfort, never guessing its cause, Hugh instantly got up from the table and stopped beside her. Gently lifting her chin with one finger, he stared down into her lovely face. "If you do not like the Justine property," he said quietly, "we shall sell it and buy another." Drowning in the dark beauty of her gaze, he was amazed to hear himself murmuring, "I want you to be happy, Micaela. We may have started out badly, but I intend to be a good husband to you, believe that, please."

Her throat constricted by the rush of emotion his simple words gave her, Micaela slowly nodded. He *was* a good husband, she thought fiercely. He was a handsome, unbearably exciting lover, as well as a generous, wealthy man who treated her with consideration and kindness. Many Creole wives would have envied her. And if there had been no love between them when they married, what did it matter? Very few Creole marriages were based on love; fortune and social ascension were behind the majority. By those standards, her own marriage was hugely successful. So why did she wish so desperately that she could forget Alice Summerfield's confident assertion that Hugh loved *her*; why could she not forget the fact that, whatever the reasons behind it, they had been *forced* to marry? And why, since love had nothing to do with their marriage, did her heart ache with such painful intensity?

Chapter Eleven

With affairs at Galland, Lancaster and Dupree unresolved, Hugh was considering remaining in the city throughout the summer, despite its attendant dangers.

It was midmorning the next day, and Hugh was seated behind his desk at the company offices. He had been moodily flipping the pages of the inventory from *Le Lys Bleu*, his mind more on his baffling, beguiling wife than the problem in front of him. He supposed that he had no room for any real complaint. On the surface, his marriage was everything he had expected it to be; he had a charming chatelaine for his home, a delightful social companion, a beautiful creature to share his bed, and he had no doubt that when children arrived Micaela would prove to be a superb mother. After all, he had known from the beginning that she did not care a jot for him. Their marriage, he admitted bleakly, was little more than a business arrangement. And like any good business associate, Micaela was willing to do her part to ensure a successful union between them.

She was nearly always courteous; seldom out of sorts; she saw to it that his household ran smoothly and allowed him the use of her body. What more did he want? His frown deepened. *Allowed* him to make love to her—that was the rub, the ugly canker that was eating away at him. Despite his best efforts to change things between them, Micaela remained a sweetly passive participant in their lovemaking, and it was driving him wild. He could not complain that she denied him his conjugal rights, for she did not. Nor could he complain that she lay stiff and unyielding in his arms, because she did not—she was always soft and accommodating.

He pushed the inventory away from him with a muttered curse. What the hell did he want from her? It rankled, and he could not deny it, that he had been forced into this marriage. But he admitted that if he had not been willing to have Micaela for his wife, he would never have allowed himself to be coerced into marrying her.

From their very first meeting he had found Micaela to be a tempting, tantalizing little baggage. He had enjoyed her barbs, the lively intelligence in those dark eyes of hers and that dazzling, flashing smile of hers. And as for the rest . . . He sighed. Oh, very well, he would admit it— he had wanted her as he had never wanted another woman in his life. Before their marriage there had been many nights that he had lain awake, his body hard as he had envisioned making love to her, kissing that cherry red mouth; stroking those soft, lush breasts; cupping those firm buttocks and losing himself in her tight warm silkiness. Reality had been beyond even his sweetest imaginings. She had been everything he dreamed of, but something was missing, some vital spark was absent when they came together.

Hugh scowled fiercely. In many respects the marriage he had with Micaela was the marriage he had often envisioned with Alice Summerfield, and he was suddenly startled to discover how very much his marriage resembled the one his stepfather and mother had shared. He should have been happy. Ecstatically so. Aside from gaining an enchanting creature for his bride, he had also strengthened his hold on the company and elevated his position in the city—at least, he thought wryly, amongst the Creoles. His problem was that he was not finding his marriage as pleasurable as he had hoped. It wasn't enough to have a lovely bed mate and a competent, utterly charming housekeeper. He wanted more, much more, from Micaela than mere acceptance. He wanted . . .

As if he had been stung, he jerked upright, appalled at the direction his thoughts were taking. Surely, he did not want her to love him?

He laughed mirthlessly. The jest was certainly on him, and a bitter one it was at that, if wanting Micaela's love was at the bottom of his dissatisfaction with his marriage. He might as well bay at the moon and expect an answer as expect Micaela to love him! Besides, what did it matter? It was not as if he had been fool enough to go and fall in love with his own wife.

The marriage had been hasty. Perhaps, a brief separation, a time for reflection, would not come amiss. He could settle Micaela, along with her mother, if she wished, at the Justine property for the summer, and come the fall, when she returned to the city, they could begin anew. Of course, he would visit her often. A tight smile crossed his face. She might not be as responsive to his lovemaking as he would have wished, but she had him mesmerized, fascinated and the thought of *not* making love to her for several weeks, months . . . well, it just didn't bear considering.

A surprisingly tender smile, one that would have wor-

ried him a great deal if he had been aware of it, curved his
lips. During the summer, he thought slowly, he could
court his wife. Woo her. And by the time the fall
came . . .

Feeling rather cheerful, he glanced at the troubling inventory. In the meantime, he had much to occupy him.
Turning to the problem at hand, he finally decided that he
could do nothing except watch and wait until the next
large shipment arrived. Even getting his hands on a copy
of one of the originals he had requested was not going to
help him a great deal. It would only prove his theory correct. But it would not allow him to trap his thieves, for he
was positive that more than one person was involved. To
spring a trap he needed some bait, bait which *Le Lys Bleu*
would have provided, but was useless to him now.

Hugh stared off into space, considering the situation.
New Orleans, he was aware, was already being deserted
by those who could afford to leave, and by next week
most Creoles and anybody else with any sense would
have left the city and would not be returning until October or November. Which did not mean his culprits would
not strike if a tempting shipment arrived during the next
few months. Which was another reason for him to remain
in the city.

It would be difficult for him to strike swiftly if he were
to remove himself from New Orleans. Of course, it was
also likely that whoever was behind the thefts would not
be in the city either. Someone would have to alert them to
any prospective arrivals. And if Hugh were *already* in the
city, not only would he be able to lay a trap to catch them
in the act, he would also have a very good idea who was
supplying them with information.

Hugh grimaced. He was fairly certain he already knew
who was alerting the thieves—Etienne Gras. He liked the

young man and hated to think of him involved in the situation, but it seemed pretty evident. Etienne's position in the firm made him the most obvious culprit, and, coupled with his gambling habits, the fact that he had been in debt to Alain Husson once made him even more suspect. Nor was Hugh forgetting the young man's obvious nervousness when questioned about any early notice of the arrival of *Le Lys Bleu*.

Etienne could have been merely uneasy at being called before his employer, but Hugh did not think so. He had been a little *too* nervous under the circumstances. A grim smile crossed his face. Perhaps it might be revealing to spend more time in the company of young Gras?

Hugh rose to his feet and, with the inventory of *Le Lys Bleu* in one hand, left his office. He stopped only long enough to request that Etienne accompany him to the firm's warehouses. It was a good walk to the warehouses on Tchoupitoulas Street, but the hour was still early and the humid heat had not yet reached its zenith.

As they walked, Hugh made small talk. While obviously wary to begin with, by the time the company warehouses came into sight, Etienne had relaxed and was animatedly telling Hugh about the latest cockfight he had attended. His face full of pleasure, Etienne exclaimed, "And the black cock, he was most ferocious, *monsieur*! The red fought very hard, but he was no match for the black cock. It was a very very good fight and I am happy that I had put my money on the black. It was a very exciting fight and to win . . . ah, that makes it even more thrilling."

"Indeed," Hugh returned lightly. "Do you win often?"

Etienne's face fell. Somewhat reluctantly, he admitted, "*Non*. Sometimes I-I-I lose more than I should. I have tried to curb my gambling—it worries *Maman*, but it is

something in the blood, *oui*? A man cannot help himself."
Risking a quick look at Hugh's impassive features, he
added hastily, "But I have always paid my debts."

"Excellent!" Hugh answered, wondering cynically if
helping Husson steal from the company was one of the
ways in which Etienne paid his debts. Having concluded
that Etienne was the most likely person to be feeding information about shipments and arrivals to the thief, it was
an easy step to name Husson as the receiver of that information. Hugh had no trouble picturing Husson as the person behind the thefts and probably behind the attack on
him several months ago, too. It seemed the sort of petty
spiteful act that would appeal to Alain.

Etienne immediately took Hugh to the area in the
sprawling building where the shipment from *Le Lys Bleu*
had been placed. Glancing around at the murky interior
of the warehouse, the concealing shadows and rabbitlike
warrens which interspersed the piles and stacks of crates,
barrels, bales and boxes scattered about, Hugh sighed.
Who would notice if anything went missing?

Several brawny, half-naked men labored in the stifling
heat inside the warehouse, laughing and talking, cursing
and shouting, as they carted various bulky objects from
one location to another. There seemed to be a constant
flow of traffic inside the building, crates coming in; barrels and boxes leaving. The air was redolent with odors;
the smell of the Mississippi River itself; the scent of
spices and herbs. Cloves, ginger, cinnamon, and sandal-
wood mingled with the lingering odor of tobacco, indigo,
and cotton, and that faint musty smell endemic to all
buildings near the river. Dust motes floated lazily in the
shafts of hot, yellow sunlight which poured in through
the cavernous doors and from outside came the rattle and
bang of horse-drawn vehicles and the cries of street ven-

dors, hawking their wares—dewberries, strawberries, sweets, fish, and figs.

Determinedly shutting out the sights and sounds and smells which accosted him, Hugh turned his attention to the huge sprawling pile of crates and barrels which Etienne indicated had come from *Le Lys Bleu*. Observing it thoughtfully, Hugh asked, "And you compared what we received with the inventory which accompanied it?"

Etienne swallowed. "*Oui, monsieur.* That is the first thing I do once it has been unloaded."

"I see. And, to your knowledge, has anything been taken from this shipment since you completed the inventory? You mentioned, did you not, that you had just finished tallying it up yesterday?"

Etienne nodded. "*Oui, monsieur*, yesterday."

"And does it look the same? Nothing that at first glance appears missing?"

"*N-n-non*—nothing that I can see without further investigation. There are customers waiting for their orders, but it will be another few days before we start dispersing items."

Hugh's gray eyes suddenly met Etienne's. "Tell me, Etienne, are you happy with your position at Galland, Lancaster and Dupree?"

"H-h-happy, *monsieur*?" he repeated uncertainly and at Hugh's nod, exclaimed, "Oh, *oui*! My *maman* is very proud of me, and many of my friends are envious."

"Then you would not wish to lose your position, would you?"

"*Non*, I would not," Etienne replied, clearly appalled at the idea.

Hugh nodded again, and said casually, "Well, then you are going to have to help me, young man, because if something is not done and done swiftly, there may not be a Galland, Lancaster and Dupree to employ you much longer. We have a thief, a clever one, to be sure, but a thief nonetheless. I need you to help me catch him."

"A-a-a thief, *monsieur*? How can you be certain?"

It was an interesting question, and not the one Hugh would have expected—from an innocent man. Etienne did not seem to be the least surprised by the revelation of thievery. His only interest was in how the thievery had been discovered.

"The inventory," Hugh said gently. "I am convinced that someone has altered it. I need you to tell me if you remember what was on the pages that have been changed."

With all the pleasure of reaching for a deadly viper, Etienne took the inventory Hugh held out to him. Clasping it gingerly, he looked at Hugh. "What do you want me to do, *monsieur*?"

"Go over the inventory again. See if it still agrees with what is stacked here and try to remember if you notice anything missing."

Etienne nodded, his face looking pale in the murky light of the warehouse. "I will do it, *monsieur*."

"I am sure you will," Hugh said quietly. "Just as I am sure there is an easy explanation for what has been going on." Hugh's gaze rested steadily on Etienne's unhappy features. "I am not a vindictive man, you know. If someone who had helped, or who had been forced to help, steal from the company were to come forward and confess, I would treat him generously. And if he were to assist in the capture of the thieves, there is much that I would be willing to overlook. I am a discreet man—no one who came to me with the information I need would ever need to fear reprisals. I would be quite, *quite* grateful to them. However, if no one comes forward . . ."

Hugh's gaze hardened. "Then I am afraid when the thieves are exposed—and they *will* be exposed—he will suffer right along with the others. Do you understand me?"

Etienne swallowed with difficulty. "*Oui, monsieur*—I understand."

Hugh looked at Etienne for a long moment. "Starting tomorrow," he said finally, "and for the next few days, I may be out of the city, but after Thursday I will be home most evenings, should someone care to speak privately with me."

Feeling he had done what he could for the moment, Hugh left Etienne to begin work on the inventory and walked from the warehouse. Revealing to young Gras that he knew of the theft and suspected how it was being done had been a gamble. Would Etienne break and try to save his own neck, or would he run straight to his cohorts and pour out all he had learned? Hugh hoped it was the former.

The day was growing oppressively hot and muggy, and Hugh was glad to reach the cool comfort of his own home. He joined his wife in the courtyard, where she was seated in the shade of an arched trellis covered with scarlet bougainvillea. It was pleasant in the courtyard and Hugh was beginning to understand the Creole love of their secluded courtyards. Palm and banana trees, attractively scattered about, gave the place a tropical air, and the relaxing sound of bubbling water came from a double-tiered fountain positioned in the center of the area. The courtyard was private and intimate, completely shut off from the rest of the world. Covered walkways, with balconies above, adjoined the house and formed two of the enclosing arms of the courtyard, festooned with vines and sweetly scented flowers. The perfume of yellow roses and white jasmine filled the air. Honeysuckle and purple bougainvillea draped the other two walls, softening their stark outlines; flagstones the color of faded charcoal paved the floor.

Micaela greeted him with a smile, her heart leaping as it always did when she first caught sight of his tall form. Dropping her gaze to hide the sheer pleasure she felt in his company, she offered him a tall glass of the ever-present lemonade. Seated across from her with a black wrought-iron table separating them, Hugh took a long swallow of the cool liquid.

Putting the half-empty glass down, he looked across at her and asked abruptly, "Have you thought any more about the Justine place?"

She nodded, and admitted, "I have thought of little else. May I see it before we actually move into the place?"

Hugh grinned at her. "I was planning on taking you there tomorrow if you were agreeable—we could leave early in the morning and probably be back in the city just after nightfall. It would be a swift trip, but it would give you time to make note of any supplies or furnishings you might want to have sent out from the city."

Micaela smiled ruefully. "I will be honest. We have barely settled into this house and now to face another . . . It is somewhat daunting, *hein*?"

"I suppose it is, but again we are very fortunate in the fact that *Madame* Justine was willing to sell the house with many of its furnishings. At least you will not be presented with empty rooms and bare floors."

Despite her initial dismay at the news of the purchase of the Justine plantation, Micaela fell in love with it at first sight. They had left New Orleans just an hour after dawn that morning. Seated beside Hugh in a well-sprung gig pulled by a pair of spanking bays as they traveled along the River Road, Micaela had thoroughly enjoyed the trip. Sunlight sparkled like splashes of pure silver off the waters of the wide Mississippi, and the vivid green of the swamp and forests and fields which meandered along the road provided an ever-changing scenery.

Micaela was almost sorry when, a few hours later, he finally slowed the horses and guided them away from the river, toward an impressive alley lined with magnificent live oaks. Shaded by the huge limbs of the trees which met overhead, Micaela sat up straighter, eager for the first glimpse of her new home. A quarter mile later the road curved and suddenly, there before her, was the Justine house.

It was not more than a decade old, having been built on the site of the original home, which had been destroyed by fire after having stood in this spot for over seventy-five years. The new house was a charming affair, built in the raised-cottage style, with wide covered galleries extending around three sides of the large structure. The turned wooden colonnades of the second story were supported by heavier brick and plaster pillars below, and delicate balustrades lined the upper gallery. In the sunlight the house gleamed whitely, and the narrow shutters which hung at the long windows were painted dark blue. The roof was slightly hipped and dormered, the cypress shingles a pleasing shade of silvery gray. A pair of octagonal *garçonnières* flanked either side of the house, giving it an impressive air.

There was a broad expanse of lawn in front of the house. Live oaks and magnolia trees were scattered around and behind the house. Micaela caught sight of the outbuildings—the slave cabins; the barns and stables;

kitchen and overseer's home. The driveway made a graceful curving swath through the grounds, and Hugh expertly brought his horses to a stop in front of the wide, broad steps at the front of the house.

A pair of young black boys appeared out of nowhere to hold the horses' heads, and, after dismounting, Hugh came around the other side of the gig and lifted Micaela down. Looking toward the boys, Hugh said, "See that they are cooled down before turning them out. We won't need them until five o'clock this evening."

"Did the widow Justine sell you her servants, too?" Micaela asked tartly.

Hugh grinned. "Yes, those that I wanted, and the four thousand acres of land that goes with the house. Less than half is under cultivation—cotton, a little sugar and corn—the majority is swamp and forest."

It was a considerable plantation, even by Louisiana standards, although Micaela knew that there were several larger estates in the Territory, but she was impressed nonetheless. "Do you intend to become a planter, too?"

"My stepfather and I," Hugh said lightly, "have always been planters. We raised cotton in Natchez, but I am considering trying my hand at growing sugar cane here in Louisiana."

A little frown wrinkled Micaela's forehead. "But what about the company? To become a sugar-cane planter will require much of your time. Will you abandon the company?"

"No, I have no intention of turning my back on it. But once I have affairs there under control, it will not be necessary for me to keep such a tight rein on the day-to-day running of the business. I intend eventually to hire a competent manager to handle the company."

Micaela was aghast. Hardly aware of being escorted up

the broad steps and across the wide gallery to the massive twin doors of the house, she exclaimed, "A manager! But that is preposterous! A member of the family has always managed the company."

"Yes, and look where it has gotten us," he replied dryly, as he pushed open the doors and ushered her into the cool interior.

"You, *monsieur*, are insulting my family!"

Micaela might have argued more, but Hugh suddenly pulled her close and pressed a hard kiss on her half-open mouth. Lifting his lips slightly from hers, he said huskily, "I do not want to talk about the blasted business right now. Right now, I want to show my bride her new home. May we, please, for the present forget about Galland, Lancaster and Dupree?"

Micaela's dark eyes met his. Something in the gray depths of his heavy-lidded gaze stirred a powerful response within her, and for a long moment their gazes clung. Hardly aware of what she was doing, too aware of his lean, warm body next to hers, Micaela slowly nodded. "*Oui*," she finally said. "Let us forget the company for the time being."

The following hours were some of the most memorable and enjoyable they had spent in each other's company. Micaela was delighted with the house, and she was undeniably excited at the prospect of buying all the new furnishings that would be needed—rugs, curtains, linens, beds, and tables. A lazily contented smile on his face, Hugh followed her about from room to room, thinking his bride had never looked lovelier—her cheeks were as rosily flushed as her lips, and her magnificent dark eyes were glistening with pleasure.

They enjoyed a light repast in the gazebo overlooking the man-made lake, which had also been constructed

about the same time as the house. It was a charming
place. Cedars, chinaberry trees and magnolias dotted the
area; shrubs and fragrant flowers and vines had been
skillfully planted about the edge of the lake to enhance
the effect of a natural setting.

Pushing aside her half-empty plate, Micaela stared
dreamily out over the placid waters. The scent of magnolias, water lilies and honeysuckle gently perfumed the air.
She was going to enjoy living here with her husband.

She glanced across at him. He was seated comfortably
on the other side of the table, with a lock of thick, dark
hair fallen across his forehead, his gaze on the water.
There was so much about him that she did not understand. And while she wished that their marriage had come
about in a more normal fashion, she discovered that she
did not regret their union. How could she? He had been
everything that was kind and generous and she was a fool
to wish for more. But the knowledge that Hugh had
plainly stated that he'd had *no* intention of marrying her
and that he firmly believed that she had contrived to trap
him into marriage kept her from feeling truly confident in
her marriage. And she could not banish, though she tried,
that unpleasant and painful exchange with Alice Summerfield. Telling herself that the other woman had been
upset and hurt did not lessen the impact of what she had
said. Alice's words still lay like a canker on her heart.

She glanced at her husband, wishing she knew him
better, wishing she had the courage to speak her doubts
aloud. But he was, in so many ways, a stranger to her,
an alien being with ways very different from her own.
They seemed to exist on two different levels—the exciting intimacy of the bedroom and the pleasant, do-
mestic day-to-day living, but they never talked about
the unacknowledged gulf that lay between them. They

never, she realized unhappily, talked about the matters closest to their hearts. She knew she avoided subjects that might cause dissension between them—did he?

And if she found the courage to ask him about Alice, did she really want confirmation? Did she really want to hear that he had been in love with another woman and that he had planned to marry her? Did she really want to risk destroying the fragile facade of tranquillity they had erected? Micaela tried to tell herself that none of it mattered now, but deep down inside she knew that it did matter, it mattered a great deal.

"What are you thinking about?" Hugh asked abruptly, startling her.

She looked across at him and was instantly uneasy to find his eyes fixed on her face. It was apparent that he had been watching her for some time. "Why, nothing," she said quickly, her eyes averted from his searching gaze.

"You looked unhappy. Are you?"

She forced a smile. "Of course not! Why should I be?" With real pleasure in her voice she went on, "This is a wonderful place. We shall like living here very much, I think." A teasing gleam in her eyes, she added, "It is a good thing that you waited to show me the place until after *Madame* Justine had agreed to sell it to you—just as you suspected, I would have been devastated if I had seen it and then she refused to sell after all. You were wise to wait."

"I am glad you like it," he said slowly, aware that she had not told the complete truth. She *had* looked unhappy, and it troubled him. Was being married to him so very awful? And wasn't it what she had schemed for? She had no business, he thought with sudden irascibility, being unhappy. She had gotten what she wanted. What more did she want?

He stood up and, with an edge to his voice, said, "If we want to get back to the city before too late, I suggest we get ready to leave."

Confused by his manner, Micaela nodded, wondering why he was looking so sour. Thinking to ease the sudden tension between them, she asked, "How soon will it be before we remove from New Orleans for the summer?"

Taking her arm and walking beside her as they made their way to the main house, he said, "Next week. Tomorrow you may start ordering the things you need, and I shall see to it that they are delivered directly here." He slanted her a glance. "Are you going to invite your mother to stay with you?"

"Oh, *oui*, if you do not mind. I know *Maman* will enjoy helping me arrange the house."

"I do not mind. In fact, I shall be very glad of it. You will not get too lonely with your mother to keep you company, while I am in the city."

Something in his voice made her look up at him. "Do you intend to be in the city often?" she asked quietly.

Hugh hadn't meant to tell her now, but that unhappy look on her face had been goading him. If she was so damned miserable with him, he thought viciously, he would be doing them both a favor by staying in the city.

"It is not convenient for me to be away from the business for very long right now," he said in a cool voice. "There are things that require my attention, but I will see to it that you and your mother are situated here before I bury myself in work." He sent her a sardonic smile. "You shall not have to endure my company very often during the next months. I shall, of course, come to see you from time to time—as business permits."

Every word was a knife blade in her heart, and any doubts she might have had about his reasons for marrying her were banished. It was clear, having married her and gotten what he wanted, he was now prepared to exile her in the country, while he cavorted and no doubt lived a bachelor's existence in New Orleans. Would there be another woman? Alice Summerfield, perhaps? Was there *already* another woman? Had he and Alice become lovers? The ache in her heart became almost unbearable. How, she wondered sickly, had he come to mean so very much to her, so suddenly?

Her face shuttered and outwardly serene, she said slowly, "I see. Business would, of course, be a priority with you."

"It is why I came to New Orleans in the first place—or have you forgotten?" he said curtly. Her apparent indifference to his decision to remain in the city was a lash on his already uncertain temper, and he was stunned at how angry he was at her reaction. He never got angry! And not over something so silly as a woman's tone of voice. Scowling, he quickened his pace. The separation couldn't come quickly enough for him. He wasn't going to push himself where he wasn't wanted!

It was a fairly silent, almost tense, ride back to New Orleans, and Micaela longed for the easy companionship they had shared during their outward journey. She should not be hurt over his decision, she told herself repeatedly. She knew he had married her for business reasons, and she should be grateful that he had been as kind and considerate to her as he had been. The problem was, she didn't feel very grateful—she felt abandoned. Deserted. And very angry.

Dinner that evening was a stiff, stilted affair. Neither of them could wait for it to be over. It was with obvious relief that they departed the dining room. For the first time since their marriage, Hugh went out, leaving Micaela home alone. More telling, it was also the first night that they slept in separate bedrooms.

Staring dry-eyed at the linen canopy over her bed, Micaela tried to tell herself she was glad that he was finally showing his true colors. Elated that there was no longer any pretense between them. Now she understood precisely where she stood. Their marriage was nothing more than a business arrangement to him. Oh, he was generous and had treated her considerately; he had done his duty by her and now, except for occasional visits to her bedroom when the mood struck him, she would simply be his social hostess. Despair crashed down on her, and her heart felt like ice in her chest. Even worse, she feared that these emotions would visit her often in the coming years, for she realized with a stab of anguish that she had committed the greatest folly of all and had fallen deeply in love with her husband.

Chapter Twelve

*T*he constraint which had risen between them the day they visited the Justine property did not dissipate during the following week. Like an untreated wound, it festered and throbbed, and the distance and chilliness between them grew, until they each stood on opposite sides of an ever-widening, ever-deepening chasm.

Micaela retreated behind an icily polite barrier. So hurt by his defection from her bed, and by the bitter knowledge that he seemed thoroughly content to banish her to the country, she couldn't do anything but act as if it was a matter of supreme indifference to her. Briefly she considered discussing the situation with Lisette, but in the end she decided against it. Micaela had a great deal of pride, and things would have to get much worse before she ran to Lisette like a child with her difficulties. Certainly her mother could not change the fact that she had been fool enough to fall in love with him—which only made her more sensitive and wounded by the situation and unwilling to discuss it with anyone. Determined never to let him know how very much he had come to mean to her, vowing fiercely never to let him know how deeply he had hurt her, she kept a cool smile firmly planted on her lips and treated him with a scrupulously polite manner. Seeing the serene expression on her lovely face, no one would have ever guessed that she felt as if she were dying inside.

For Hugh the situation was not much better. If anything it was worse, because it had been his decision to abandon her bed and his decision not to accompany her to the Justine property, and he was bitterly aware of it. But having carved out a position, he found himself with no way of retreating—not without sinking his pride, and God knew his wife gave him no indication that she would care if he *did* sink his pride and ingratiate himself into her bed. After allowing his anger to dictate he sleep alone that first night, Hugh found himself unable simply to stride into her room the next night and resume his place in her bed, though he wanted to badly. There was too much unsaid between them, and he was damned if he was going to apologize for simply deciding to remain in the city. With righteous indignation, he told himself that he had business to attend to, and Micaela was just going to have to learn to accept it! His decision was a perfectly logical and necessary one, he reminded himself virtuously. And yet he would concede that he would have given much to change the situation. But in the face of her cool indifference, he found the conciliatory words dying on his lips. He cursed himself for a weak-willed creature, but every day it became harder and harder to reestablish the rapport of their first weeks of marriage.

The time had passed swiftly, however, and both had been extremely busy. Frustrated and angry at the increasing distance between them, yet unable to breach it, Hugh had buried himself in work at the firm. It was very late most nights when he returned home. Micaela, skillfully hiding the ache in her heart, had spent several mornings, with Lisette at her side, picking out furnishings and what-nots for the new house. There had also been packing to oversee and the partial closing of the house in the city to manage. Hugh, never realizing that each word was more salt rubbed into Micaela's already wounded sensibilities, had stated that the did not intend to spend a great deal of time at the house, that he would be occupied with busi-ness the majority of the time and that he only needed a few rooms for his own use. The rest of the house could be closed, the rugs rolled up; the furniture stacked and pro-tected by dustcovers until Micaela's return in the fall. Ex-cept for a few servants necessary for Hugh's comfort, the remainder would be put to work on the Justine property.

Since everything needed from the town house had been sent ahead, that last morning in New Orleans, there was nothing to be done except for Hugh to escort his wife and mother-in-law to the plantation. The three of them would not have fit comfortably in Hugh's gig and Lisette had sensibly suggested that they use the Dupree family carriage. Hugh had readily agreed and made a mental note about seeing to the purchase of a carriage for future use, and perhaps a well-sprung cart for his wife's use. A wry grin crossed his face. It was a good thing, the way he had been spending money lately, he admitted to himself, that his purse *was* a rather full one.

The departure from the city went smoothly, Lisette's pleasant chatter covering any uncomfortable silences be-tween the newlyweds. If Lisette had noticed the coolness between Hugh and Micaela, she had wisely not com-mented on it.

Micaela was overwhelmingly grateful for her mother's company. It would have been agony to be alone with Hugh, knowing that these few, precious hours might be the last she would share with him for some time. Without her mother's presence, she might have thrown herself into his arms and begged him not to leave her. She shuddered at the thought. How could she be so weak? And when had she turned into such a mewling, clinging creature?

Giving herself a stern lecture about the importance of maintaining the stiff facade which she had erected this past week, she straightened in the seat, and said gaily, "I am so pleased that you are going to be staying with me, *Maman*. I shall be glad of your advice on some of the furnishings and their placement in the house on the Justine property."

"Are you always going to call your new home the 'Justine property'?" Lisette asked curiously. "I believe when *Madame* Justine's husband built the new house for her, he named the place *Par Amour*. I have always thought it a most romantic name. Will you keep the name, do you think?"

A distinctly sardonic expression crossed Hugh's face. *Par Amour*! For Love! He nearly laughed aloud. Nothing could be farther from the truth! He and his bride were not in a state of armed war, but they were not far from it.

"It has a nice ring to it," he said carelessly. His eyes on Micaela's averted features, he asked politely, "What do you think, my dear?"

For a brief second their eyes met. Then glancing hastily away from the steady gray gaze, Micaela murmured, "It sounds fine. Whatever you think is best."

"Well then," Hugh said with false heartiness, "our new home is no longer the Justine property, but *Par Amour*."

The trip passed swiftly, the day pleasant despite the increasing heat and humidity. Any awkwardness between Hugh and Micaela was covered by Lisette's enthusiasm for the journey and her excitement to see the house. A rapt expression on her face when the main building came into view, she exclaimed, "Ah, *petite*, it is everything I could have wished for you. It is beautiful! And you say that there is a lake, too? We shall have a wonderful summer here, *oui*?"

Micaela forced a gay note into her voice. "Oh, *oui*, *Maman*! There will be much for us to do and explore."

Hugh felt a stab of envy. He would have, he realized uneasily, given much to be the one to discover the delights of the property with his wife. It was obvious, however, that his wife could hardly wait to see the last of him. He scowled.

Having seen Micaela and Lisette settled into the house, and having been treated to more of Micaela's chilly indifference, Hugh decided that there was no reason to continue to inflict his unwanted presence upon her. After a light repast, Hugh rose from the table, which was situated on the charming, flower-ringed terrace at the side of the house. He said abruptly, "I think I should start back to the city now." He sent Micaela a long look. "There is no reason for me to remain any longer."

Micaela's face froze. Concealing the knife blade of agony that had gone through her at his words, she said calmly, "Naturally, you wish to be back in the city." She flashed him a blinding smile, and added, "We shall not keep you." Only she knew how much it cost her to act so careless.

Hugh's jaw tightened. "Will you walk with me to the carriageway?" He glanced at Lisette's serene face. "Do you mind if I take your daughter away for a few minutes, *madame*?"

Lisette smiled at him. "I would have been surprised if

you did not seek a few private moments in which to say good-bye. Go."

Micaela schooled herself to remain outwardly sedate, a polite smile firmly plastered on her lips, but inwardly . . . ah, inwardly, she was fighting the desperate urge to clasp his arm, his hand, and plead abjectly with him that he not leave her like this. That he stay and they attempt to heal this horrible, stupid rift that had grown up so suddenly between them.

When they reached the front of the house where the coach and horses were waiting for him, Hugh stopped and stared down at Micaela, his face unreadable. "If you need anything . . ."

"If I need anything," she said calmly, her heart aching and bleeding inside of her, "I shall write to you and let you know." Her fingernails were biting into the palms of her clasped hands to keep them from touching him, and her throat was tight with unshed tears. Ah, *Dieu*, but this was killing her!

A stiff silence fell between them and Micaela was horrified to hear herself suddenly asking, "When shall we expect your return?"

"Does it matter?" Hugh inquired coolly, smarting from her nonchalant attitude. They would not see each other for several weeks! Couldn't she at least act as if she would miss him a little? Harshly, he said, "I think you and your mother will do just fine without me, and I intend to be very busy."

"Of course, I do not doubt it for a moment," she retorted swiftly, her fingernails almost drawing blood at the effort not to touch him.

"Then I suppose we have nothing else to say, do we?"

"*Non!*"

His mouth grim, Hugh started for the coach, then

abruptly he swung around. "The hell with this!" he snarled, and dragged Micaela into his arms.

He kissed her a long time, his mouth plundering and pleasuring at the same time. Her lips parted easily for him and without volition her arms crept around his neck and her body swayed into his. They remained locked together for endless minutes, then, with a muttered oath, Hugh thrust her from him. His eyes glittering with tightly controlled emotion, he muttered, "Something to remind you of me while I am gone!"

Without another word, he leaped into the coach and barked out the command to leave.

Her mouth swollen from his kiss, Micaela stood there staring until the coach disappeared from sight, unaware of the tears slowly leaking from her eyes. She was so lost in her own misery that she didn't hear Lisette softly call her name or hear her mother's approach. It wasn't until she felt her mother's arms around her shoulders that she became aware of her presence.

"Oh, *Maman!*" she sobbed quietly. "I just want to die! Everything is so awful, and I do not think it can ever be fixed!"

"Shh, *ma mie*. Nothing is ever that bad, I can tell you, though you may not think so at this very moment. In time we will either fix it or you will learn to live, if not contentedly, at least *not* unhappily, with it. Come, let us go inside and you will tell me everything, *oui?*"

Micaela would not have been human if she had not let Lisette comfort her, but by the time they reached the house she had more control over her emotions. Embarrassed that her mother had found her sobbing over an arrogant creature who did not deserve her tears, instinctively Micaela had sought to quickly disabuse Lisette that anything was wrong with her marriage.

They seated themselves at the table on the terrace, and, sipping her lemonade, Micaela said quietly, "You must think me a goose to carry on in such a fashion!" She attempted a misty smile. "I was just being silly—I have grown spoiled at having him around all the time, and I did not know that parting from him would be so painful."

Lisette did not say anything for several moments, her eyes on Micaela's face. "Is that all it is, *petite*? Just sadness at parting?"

"*Mais oui!*" Micaela said airily. "What else could it be?"

Lisette stared at her glass. "I thought that I had noticed a coolness between the pair of you, and I wondered if there had been a misunderstanding."

It was as close to asking for Micaela to confide in her that Lisette could come. She had told herself firmly when Micaela married that she would *not* be a meddling *maman*-in-law. But, *Dieu!* It was impossible not to say *some*thing when one's child was sobbing as if her heart were breaking!

Micaela sighed. "A little one, perhaps," she finally admitted huskily. And having confessed that much, she burst out resentfully, "We have only been married a short time . . . and he is perfectly happy to abandon me here in the country while he remains in New Orleans!" A fiery blush stained her cheeks. "He has left my bed, too. He has made it clear to me that he is already tired of me!" She could not bring herself to mention her fears of another woman.

Lisette laughed. "Ah, *petite*, is that what this is all about? You think Hugh is tired of you?"

Micaela nodded curtly, thinking that there was nothing amusing about the situation.

Lisette smiled at her expression and asked gently,

"And have you done anything to make him realize that being away from him makes you unhappy? Or that his absence from your bed troubles you, hmm? It seems to me that lately you have treated your husband with an aloofness and indifference that I find rather astonishing in view of the way you cried when he left."

"I only acted as a proper Creole wife should," Micaela returned stiffly, remembering uncomfortably the cool, icily polite exterior she had shown Hugh these past days.

Lisette made a face. "And what is a 'proper Creole wife,' pray tell me?"

"Like you. You were always serene and unruffled, even when *Papa* was sometimes difficult. *Papa* never made you cry. He always treated you with kindness and respect and you were always charmingly cordial to him." Her words suddenly sounded silly to her and she ended lamely, "I know that *Papa* was away a lot of the time, but he never abandoned *you* for weeks on end in the country!"

This time it was Lisette who sighed. Her finger running around the rim of her glass, she murmured, "I did not know that I was such a good actress." At Micaela's astonished expression, she added with stunning bluntness, "You are old enough to know the truth—I despised Renault Dupree. And I hated your *grand-père* for forcing me to marry him."

"B-b-but, but you—!"

"Presented the world with a pleasant facade? *Oui*, indeed I did! What else could I do once the marriage was fact? Weep and beat my breast? Shame myself before our friends and neighbors?" Her voice hardened. "*Non*! I did what other women have done before me—I forced myself to be a 'proper Creole wife'! I compelled myself to accept the caresses of a man who made my flesh crawl with revulsion. I made no complaint or mention of the women he kept, nor of the thousand slights I endured while he was alive. To you, the family, the servants, I acted the role that fate had assigned to me. I was a good, understanding, *proper* Creole wife—and I can think of no worse fate than that for you, *ma chérie*." She leaned across the table and took one of Micaela's hands in hers. Staring intently into Micaela's dark eyes, she said earnestly, "You have the chance that I never did—you have married an *honorable*, generous man. It is my dearest wish that you shall have what was denied me—a happy, *loving* marriage. And I think that if you will put your pride and hurt feelings aside and be honest about what you feel for him, you shall have it with Hugh." She smiled gently. "Hugh is a fine young man, *petite*. He has been very thoughtful and kind—the fact that I am staying with you this summer is an indication of his concern for your well-being." Lisette gave Micaela's hand a reassuring squeeze. "I know you were coerced into this marriage, *ma chérie*, but I would never have allowed the wedding if I had not been certain that he would do much to make you happy. I knew that he would make you, not only a good husband—Renault was, in Creole terms, a good husband—but with Hugh you have the chance of having a loyal, honest, loving husband!"

"You did not l-l-like *Papa*?" Micaela asked aghast, as she tried to grapple with what her mother had revealed.

Lisette sat back. "*Non.* I did not like him. It is true that at one time there was talk of a marriage between us and that I was not indifferent to the idea, but that was before . . ." She stopped abruptly, her inward gaze seeing something that Micaela could not. Lisette's face softened and a dreamy expression entered her dark eyes. "But that was before I met someone else. . . ." She looked at Micaela, and her face grew even more tender. "Someone who taught me what love could be like. . . ."

Fascinated and intrigued by this glimpse into her mother's life, Micaela asked breathlessly, "But why did you not marry him? If you loved each other . . . ?"

Lisette seemed to give herself a shake. A bitter note entered her voice. "He loved me, I always believed that even after . . ." She took a steadying breath. "He loved me," she went on briskly, "but not enough to stand up to *Papa. Papa* was completely against a marriage between us. *He* wanted me to marry Renault. It was unthinkable that I marry—!" She hesitated, Micaela's riveted stare and rapt expression reminding her of just what she was revealing. Vexed with herself, Lisette smiled ruefully, and muttered, "It does not matter anymore. It all happened a long time ago. I married Renault, and I cannot complain of the life we led. Renault was not a cruel man, just a selfish one, and, most of the time, he was very good to me."

"But the man you loved? What happened to him?"

A sad smile on her face, Lisette said simply, "Oh, he went away and never came back. . . ."

Micaela gasped, everything her mother had just told her suddenly coming together. The most outrageous thought occurred to her. Her eyes wide and startled, she breathed, "You were in love with Hugh's stepfather, John Lancaster!"

Lisette stared at her for a long time, and then she said simply, "*Oui*. Very much so."

Hugh rode back to New Orleans, staring moodily at the passing countryside. His heart felt like lead in his chest, and he was conscious of a strong inclination to get very drunk and get into a brawl in some rank den of vice. The only ray of light in his black gloom, and it was faint at that, was Micaela's generous response to his frantic embrace. He grimaced. But then what else had he expected? She was a good *Creole* wife, he thought sarcastically.

She could despise him utterly, but her upbringing would not allow her to repulse him or, God forbid, cause a scene. He almost wished she had slapped his face and screamed at him than to have melted against him and made him hungrily aware of all that sweet warmth and silky delight he was denying himself.

Once the coach reached New Orleans and he had been set down in front of his home, he dismissed the driver and vehicle. His temper and strong sense of ill use had not abated, and, cursing Micaela and his own unruly emotions, he reluctantly entered the house. The place felt empty and uninviting as he wandered through the premises, and he cursed himself again for not damning the consequences and remaining at *Par Amour*, and in his wife's bed! It didn't help his temper any to admit that he could have stayed in the country. Staying at *Amour* might have meant frequent trips into the city, but he wouldn't have exiled himself from the very thing that he wanted with an almost painful intensity—his wife, in his arms and in his bed!

He spent a restless night, tossing and wrestling with his bedclothes, the knowledge that he had deliberately sent his wife away eating at him like acid. If he hadn't been so full of stiff-necked pride, he could have been at *Par Amour*, taking his pleasure of his wife, instead of sleeping, alone in his very big, very empty, bed.

His mood was not greatly improved when he finally rose the next morning. But stubbornly telling himself that he really had made the right decision, he dressed. After a lonely breakfast, without much enthusiasm, he walked to his office.

And of course, there was little there to occupy his time or thoughts. He would give Jean credit for having competent men working for them—men who knew their jobs and made, for the most part, the owners' presence superfluous. Besides, he was sick of looking at cargo lists, and he had already discovered what he needed to know. Until something new was added to the current state of affairs, there was nothing for him to do but sit and wait . . . and brood. Not a happy prospect.

Seated at his desk, he stared grimly at the litter of papers which marred its smooth gleaming surface, his thoughts irresistibly straying to his wife. What was she doing now? Had she slept well last night? His lips tightened. No doubt! *He* wasn't around to distress her with his unwanted presence.

Impatiently he rose from his chair. Stepping from his office, he walked over to where Etienne was working. With deceptive idleness, Hugh glanced around. Seeing that no one was nearby or paying any attention to them, he asked softly, "Did you find any discrepancies in the invoice I asked you to go over?"

Etienne started and flushed. "*N-n-non, Monsieur* Lancaster. Everything was in order."

Hugh stared at him thoughtfully. "Do you remember what we talked about at the warehouse?"

Etienne nodded and swallowed. "*Oui, monsieur*, I have not forgotten your words."

"The offer is still open, but I would suggest that for anyone who wishes to take advantage of it, they not delay."

His voice barely above a whisper, Etienne muttered, "I understand."

Having done what he could to move things along, Hugh returned dispiritedly to his office. Seated once more behind his desk, he glared at the papers scattered across the surface. He had remained in town for this? To sit here and stare?

Inevitably his mind wandered to Micaela, and he found himself wondering again what she was doing at this very moment. Enjoying a leisurely breakfast with her mother on the terrace? Strolling near the lake? Sleeping late? A tight ache in the region of his groin at the thought of Micaela lying in bed provoked something very near a growl from him.

Furious at the way she dominated his thoughts and not liking his own company very much, he stood up abruptly. He would go to one of the coffeehouses. Perhaps Jasper had not left the city yet and he could find some congenial company.

He had just started across the room when there was a knock on the door. "Yes? What is it?" he snapped as he flung open the door.

A tall, distinguished gentleman stood there before him, a faint smile on his darkly handsome face, a dimple lurking in his cheek. The gentleman was nearing fifty but wore his age lightly, his shoulders broad, his body still lean and well muscled, and though the majority of his hair was still thick and black, there were striking silver wings at his temples. "Am I interrupting something?" he asked, a twinkle in his dark eyes.

"*Papa*! It is *damned* good to see you, sir!" Hugh exclaimed delightedly, a wide smile crossing his face, his bad mood vanishing as if it had never been. Impulsively locking his stepfather in a powerful hug, he added, "When did you arrive? I have been half-expecting you, but I thought I would have advance word of your arrival."

Putting his elegant curly-brimmed hat on one of the chairs Hugh indicated, John Lancaster seated himself in another, and murmured, "It has been rather lonesome since you left, my boy, and when I received your letter telling me of your sudden marriage, why nothing would do but that I immediately order my bags packed and take the first ship leaving Natchez for New Orleans." The twinkle became more pronounced. "You are not the only one who can make swift, decisive plans, you know."

Hugh laughed. "I never doubted it, sir." Taking another chair near his stepfather's, he leaned forward eagerly. "How long will you stay? I hope for a very long time. Now that you are here, mayhap, I can convince you to move to New Orleans permanently."

"Perhaps," John said. "I have put most of our affairs in the capable hands of Mr. Norton, our esteemed business agent in Natchez, and have told him to expect me when he sees me. I am sure that he will continue to do the same admirable job he has always done for us, so I am here for as long as you wish."

"Excellent!" The gray eyes warm with deep affection, Hugh said huskily, "I have missed you, sir—I did not realize how much until this very moment. It is good to see you."

John nodded. His face reflecting the same affectionate expression on Hugh's, he said quietly, "I missed you, too, my boy—more than I thought possible. I decided that it was foolish to let an old vow keep me from being with the one person who means the most to me in the world." A smile lit his features. "And so here I am, in a place I swore over twenty years ago that I would never set foot in again!"

"Is that why you never came back to New Orleans?

Because you swore not to?" Hugh asked with a faint frown.

"Indeed, yes. I left this place, swearing never to return, with what I thought was a bitter, broken heart and my pride in tatters. But that was in the past and does not matter now. All that matters is that you are here—and married! Now tell me about this bride of yours. All that ridiculously brief note of yours stated was that by the time I read your words you would be a married man! Who is she? The Summerfield chit? You never even mentioned a name." John grinned at him. "You really must improve on your writing skills, my boy. I have been in a fever of impatience to learn more about this paragon who swept you so willy-nilly to the altar. Who is she?"

Hugh made a rueful face. "Not Alice Summerfield. She is a young lady from a prominent Creole family."

John looked astounded. "A Creole? Good God! How did that come about?"

It was on the tip of Hugh's tongue to tell his stepfather the true circumstances surrounding his marriage, but discretion held him back. He did not like lying to John— they had few secrets between them. But there seemed no point in telling him how Micaela had trapped him into marriage. For some reason, and it eluded him, he wanted his stepfather to think well of his bride. He wanted John to like Micaela.

So instead of a bald recital of the unpleasant facts, Hugh smiled and muttered, "She is very beautiful, Papa. I took one look at her and . . ." His voice thickened. "And I fell in love with her." With all the power and speed of a thunderbolt, Hugh realized that it was true. He *did* love Micaela! And she hated him.

He took a deep breath, his thoughts spinning. Forcing himself to act casually, despite the turmoil in his brain, he continued, "There did not seem any reason to wait, although if it could have been arranged, I would have wanted you there beside me the day I married."

"Ah, you young bucks, you are always so impatient," John said with a roguish smile. "And as I was young once and thought myself wildly in love, I understand. I am just surprised that one of those proud-as-sin Creole families was willing to let one of their daughters marry an American!" With a bitter cast to his face, he added, "Believe me, it was not always so!"

Hugh shot him a keen look, his own troubles forgotten for the moment. "Is that why you swore never to set foot in New Orleans again?"

John shrugged. "It may have had something to do with it. But it no longer matters. Let us not talk about me. It is you and your bride who are the more interesting topic."

"There is not much more to tell. I saw her and I had to have her. The family was not averse to the suit, and so you see before you a married man."

"I find it hard to believe that there were no objections to your suit. My memory of the Creoles is that they would sooner have a slave married into the family than an American!"

"There were, uh, good reasons why the family accepted me so readily," Hugh said carefully. "You might say it was as much a merger of interests as a marriage."

John's arrogant black brows met in a frown above his eyes. "A merger of interests? Who *is* this girl?"

"Micaela Dupree. Old Christophe Galland's granddaughter. It consolidated some of the shares in the business. In addition," Hugh added hastily, "to giving me a most charming wife."

John stiffened. "Christophe's granddaughter?" At Hugh's nod, he asked grimly, "And her parents?"

"Lisette and Renault Dupree—although as you know, Renault has been dead for a number of years. His widow, *Madame* Dupree, was Galland's only daughter. I believe you may have met her when you were here setting up the business. She has been extremely welcoming to me. In fact, if it had not been for her warmth and charm, I would have gotten a very cold reception from the remainder of the business partners." Hugh grinned. "With the exception of Jasper, of course. But then you know Jasper."

"Yes, I know Jasper. I seem to remember several harrowing visits from him when the two of you attempted in various hair-raising manners to get yourselves killed," John replied easily, seeming to lose interest in Hugh's bride and her family. "As a matter of fact," he went on, "I had my bags sent to his house, since I did not have your direction."

Hugh stood up again. "I was on the point of leaving when you arrived. Shall we go find your baggage and get you settled in at my house?"

Smiling and nodding, John rose to his feet, and the two men departed a few minutes later, after Hugh had introduced him to several of the employees in the office. It did not take long to get John's baggage sorted out. Luckily Jasper was still in residence, and, finding that he was leaving for his country estate on the morrow and would be out of the city for several weeks, Hugh pressed him to join them for dinner and renew his acquaintance with John. Jasper accepted.

As Hugh and John walked the short distance between Jasper's house and Hugh's, Hugh coolly mentioned that Micaela was not, at the moment, in New Orleans. If John was disappointed or surprised to discover that Hugh's wife of barely six weeks was living in the country apart from her new husband, he kept his reactions to himself.

Instead, he exclaimed with pleasure at the house and stated that he was looking forward to the evening and reacquainting himself with Jasper.

Jasper arrived early, and the three gentlemen enjoyed a long, leisurely meal, reminiscing and discussing the latest events at Galland, Lancaster and Dupree. After dinner, they moved into Hugh's study, enjoying a snifter of brandy as they continued their conversation.

A tap on the door broke the relaxed mood. Sampson, one of Hugh's servants, announced that there were visitors who had come to call on John Lancaster. After he had sent Sampson to bring the guests to the study, Hugh turned to his stepfather and murmured, "One of the Duprees must have gone to the office this afternoon and learned of your arrival. It seems Jean and François have come to call . . . as well as Alain Husson."

John frowned. "Husson? I do not recall that name."

"Like me, he won his shares from Christophe shortly before the old man's death," Jasper said. "The Husson family is well-known and respected in the city, although your stepson and I have had our disagreements with Alain."

"Disagreements?" John asked with a raised brow.

"We do not know if he is behind the troubles at the firm, but we suspect he may have a hand in it," Hugh said casually. "And of course, there is the fact that I fought a duel with him several weeks ago." Hugh grinned at his stepfather. "I won."

There was no time for further conversation. Sampson opened the door, and the three guests entered the room. Everyone was on his most polite behavior, but there was an understandable tenseness about the meeting. Hugh and Alain had not met privately since the duel, and, of course, John had not spoken with Jean Dupree for over twenty years. Everyone was standing as introductions were made and greetings exchanged.

Jasper's presence helped enormously to smooth over any awkward moments and François was clearly impressed by meeting the legendary John Lancaster.

In the French manner, François impulsively kissed John on both cheeks and declared, "*Monsieur* Lancaster! I am most delighted to finally meet you. I have heard of you all my life, and it is a pleasure to see you face-to-face. Welcome to New Orleans!"

John smiled at François's apparent enthusiasm, but his eyes were on Jean's face, as he said dryly, "I wonder if all you have heard of me is good."

Jean grimaced. Coming to stand in front of John, he muttered, "The past is the past, John. Shall we start anew?" And astonishing everyone, he stuck out his hand in the American manner.

John hesitated only a second, then he firmly clasped Jean's outstretched hand, shaking it vigorously. "I will not say that it is good to see you again," John murmured, a faint, sardonic smile curving his long mouth, "but I will say that the years have treated you kindly."

Jean bowed. "And you. You have not changed a great deal, except, perhaps, for the silver at your temples."

Aware of Alain Husson standing quietly in the background, closely observing the situation, John turned to him and gave him an encouraging smile. "I understand that you, like Jasper here, also owe your membership in the family business to Christophe's penchant for deep gambling."

Alain bowed politely. "Indeed that is true, *monsieur*. I trust you do not object?"

John shook his head. "No, of course not."

Hugh indicated several chairs. "Please," he said, "be

seated." Once everyone had been settled comfortably and had been served brandy, Hugh looked across at Jean and asked, "How did you know that my stepfather had arrived in the city?"

"Oh, that was because of me," François said eagerly. "I went by the office this afternoon to see you, and everyone was full of the news of *Monsieur* Lancaster's visit. I told Jean and Alain, and we decided to come to call this evening, since there was every chance that tomorrow you would be taking your step-*papa* to your new home in the country."

"You wanted to see me?" Hugh asked with a frown. "Why?"

François looked embarrassed. "I wanted," he said with a particularly winning smile, "to convince you to let me come and visit with Micaela and *Maman*. They have hardly been gone for forty-eight hours, but I find that I miss them." He grinned at Hugh and admitted with charming candor, "And of course, I am quite curious about your new property. Will you mind if I stay with them for several weeks?"

Hugh shrugged. "Why not? We are, after all," he said dryly, "family." He glanced at Jean. "Of course that extends to you also."

Jean nodded. "Perhaps I will take you up on that," he declared. "It might prove interesting."

The conversation became general, all six gentlemen conversing, as if there were no undercurrents, no hidden rifts to mar the polite discourse among them. Alain was still wearing his sling, but it was obvious his wound was almost completely healed. No reference to the duel was made, nor was any other unpleasant subject introduced. On the surface, everything was most proper and polite. Just six gentlemen sitting around, enjoying a snifter or two of fine brandy with congenial acquaintances.

When Sampson tapped on the door again sometime later and announced that there was another visitor, Hugh looked surprised. The hour was late, after midnight. His stepfather's unexpected arrival today, as well as the visit from the Duprees and Husson, had pushed other thoughts from his mind.

"Who is it?" he asked with a frown.

"The gentleman would not give his name," replied Sampson. "He did say that it was a business matter—one you had discussed with him previously."

"Ah," Hugh murmured, suddenly knowing that it could be only one person—Etienne Gras! "Show him into the front salon and offer him some refreshments, will you? Tell him I shall be with him shortly."

"Business at this hour?" Jean drawled, his eyes full of speculation.

Hugh shrugged. "A minor affair."

"It does not sound so minor to me," Alain murmured, "if it must be conducted at this time of night."

Hugh hesitated. The last thing he wanted was to reveal Etienne's name. Yet if he kept silent, it would only further arouse the suspicions of the others and give his unexplained visitor more importance. Hoping he sounded utterly indifferent, he finally said, "It is no doubt just Etienne Gras—I asked him today to look over some papers and deliver them to me tonight." Hugh smiled. "I think the young man attached more importance to my request than it needed. Tomorrow would have been just fine to give me the information, but, as you probably already know, Etienne is extremely conscientious."

An icy stillness entered the room, but Hugh was unable to place its source amongst the men seated around him.

The unpleasant sensation lasted only a second, before someone laughed and conversation began again, but Hugh had an uneasy premonition that he had just placed Etienne Gras in danger.

Chapter Thirteen

*J*ohn glanced across at Hugh. "Why do you not go ahead and see this young man. No one will mind if you desert us for a few minutes."

Jean stood up. "*Non*. We will leave. We only came to welcome you to the city, and it is time we were on our way." Shaking John's hand once more, Jean said ruefully, "I have enjoyed our talk this evening—and I did not expect to!"

"Surprisingly, so did I," John admitted with a crooked grin. "Perhaps we have both grown mellow with age?"

Smiling and shaking his head at the same time, Jean murmured, "Who can tell? This promises to be a most interesting summer, that I can tell you!"

The two Lancasters politely escorted their departing guests to the front door. Shutting the door behind them, Hugh said, "I shall see Etienne now. I do not know how long I shall be."

John shot him a shrewd glance. "It appears that Mr. Gras's arrival is a bit more than just the innocent business matter you described to the others."

"Yes, it is. I would have preferred that our guests had

not learned his name or of his visit. I am hoping that Mr. Gras will prove to be the weak link in the chain of our thieves."

"You suspect one of them? Certainly not Jasper!"

"No, not Jasper," Hugh said with a laugh. Then he turned somber. "But as for the others . . ."

The two men parted, John deciding to seek out his bed and Hugh to meet with Etienne. After bidding his stepfather good night, Hugh entered the small parlor at the front of the house. Etienne was nervously pacing the floor, his young face white and tense. The mere opening of the door had him starting like a hare flushed by a hound.

His eyes wide and fearful, he stared at Hugh as if he had seen a ghost. "*Monsieur!*" he cried. "You did not tell me that you would have guests. I never would have called tonight if I had known."

There was a slightly accusatory edge to his voice. Hugh indicated that he should be seated and murmured, "I am sorry. I had no idea that I *would* have guests this evening and I did not know that you would choose to call tonight." He glanced unhappily at Etienne as the young man gingerly sat down. "The men who just left are all known to you—Jean Dupree, François Dupree, and Alain Husson. All, one, or none of them *could* be involved in the thefts at the company—until we know differently, you would be wise to be on your guard against all three of them." Hugh grimaced. "It was *most* unfortunate that they were here tonight of all nights."

Etienne swallowed uncomfortably and muttered, "*Sacrebleu!* Unfortunate does not describe it. It could mean my *life* if anyone suspects that I am meeting with you."

Hugh uneasily remembered that odd moment when he had reluctantly mentioned Etienne's name earlier. "Just meeting with me would put you in danger?" he asked slowly, his eyes fixed on Etienne's pale face.

Etienne gave a bitter laugh. "Oh, *oui*! The men who steal from your company are powerful. They will kill me if they even *think* I mean to cooperate with you."

Hugh said nothing for several seconds. The news Etienne imparted was unsettling. He had been so intent upon his own goal that he had not considered he could be putting Etienne's very life in danger by wooing him to his side. Silently Hugh cursed himself for not realizing that he might be dealing with coldly ruthless men—men who would apparently kill without mercy. But would these men really kill, he wondered, or did Etienne merely *believe* that they would?

Hugh sighed. In his innocence he had assumed that the situation facing him was relatively simple; the company profits were falling and he intended to find out why. He had suspected thievery and/or embezzlement all along, but he had not immediately thought that any of the company's partners were involved. That suspicion had come later, although not much later. It was still possible that whoever was behind the losses was someone with no connection to Galland, Lancaster and Dupree. New Orleans was rife with a criminal element, but he strongly doubted that the thief was an outsider. And it was highly unlikely that the problem was confined to mere employees of the firm. No, Hugh was almost certain that the person who pulled all the strings was one of the partners. But which one? A tigerish smile curved his mouth. It would be nice if it turned out to be Alain Husson—he would enjoy destroying that particular arrogant son of a bitch!

"You find my peril amusing?" Etienne asked sharply.

Hugh's smile vanished, and he shook his head. "No. I do not!" He admitted, "But I wonder if you have not overestimated the danger. Thievery is one thing, cold-blooded murder another. Will these men really kill you?"

"They will."

There was such honest conviction in Etienne's voice that Hugh put his own doubts to rest. Not only, it seemed, was he dealing with thieves, but men who practiced murder as well. He grimaced. Not a pleasant situation. Another equally unpleasant thought struck him—if the person who was behind the thefts was actually one of the partners, this evening he might very well have signed Etienne's death warrant by having identified him as his visitor.

Across the brief distance that separated them, Hugh studied the younger man. Etienne's face was pale and haggard, and there was a quiet desperation in his dark eyes. His decision to help had not come lightly, and Hugh admired his courage.

"You are a brave young man," Hugh said softly.

Etienne shook his dark head and said tiredly, "Indeed, I am not, *monsieur*." He rubbed his fingers across his forehead. "I am my mother's only son, you understand? My father died nearly three years ago, and I have five younger sisters who must be provided for." He smiled sadly and met Hugh's eyes. "My *papa* was a good man, but he did not leave *Maman* or any of us a great deal when he died. Oh, we are not destitute, but *Maman* is relying heavily on what I earn to provide respectable dowries for my sisters."

"I understand," Hugh murmured, his gray eyes full of sympathy, but no pity. To pity this young man would be to offend him.

Etienne's gaze dropped from Hugh's. "It was to earn more money that I gambled," he admitted unhappily. "I thought . . ." He gave that bitter laugh again. "Oh, it does not matter what I thought. I became heavily in debt and it was then that . . ." He swallowed and stared at the floor in front of him

"It was then," Hugh said softly, "that someone approached you with a way to pay off your debts as well as earn extra money, yes?"

"Oui."

"Who was it?"

Etienne slumped in his chair. "I do not know," he said almost under his breath.

Hugh frowned. "What do you mean? Surely you know his name?"

"I do not. I swear it, *monsieur*! I received an unsigned note outlining a way in which I could redeem my debts and, as you say, obtain extra money. I threw it away." He glanced at Hugh. "I like to think that I am an honest man, *monsieur*. I did not want to steal. I did not want to become a thief, but *Maman*, my sisters, my debts." He buried his head in his hands. "We would have been ruined! There would have been no husbands for my sisters; *Maman* would have been disgraced. And my debts . . ."

"A difficult situation," Hugh said gently.

"Several weeks went by, and I heard nothing more. I thought that was the end of it, but it was not. Another note was delivered to me, with the same message. I threw that one away, too . . . but not right away." He looked at Hugh. "I was tempted, *monsieur*. Vastly. I had lost more money, and the man who held my notes was pressing me to pay.

"Would that have been Alain Husson?" Hugh asked idly.

"It was. How did you guess?"

Hugh shrugged. "*Monsieur* Husson's penchant for gambling and winning is common knowledge. As is the unfortunate luck that seems to befall people who do not pay their debts to him promptly. But go on with your tale."

"There were two more notes to me, each delivered a few weeks apart and finally . . ." Etienne swallowed painfully, his gaze fixed unhappily on Hugh's face. "And finally, I gave in. I agreed to help. For one shipment only."

"How did you contact the sender of the note? You said you do not know him?"

"I do not. As always, I was given instructions that if I agreed, I was to go to the Silver Cock and leave four silver bits on a specific table. Then I was to leave. I did as I had been instructed."

"The Silver Cock—I do not believe I am familiar with that place."

Etienne gave a mirthless smile. "You would not be. It is a low tavern, a vile den of thieves and vice, located in the Swamp."

Hugh nodded. The Swamp was a notorious area a dozen blocks from the waterfront. Gambling dens, houses of prostitution, and unsavory taverns abounded. The population was composed of ruffians and rogues, whores and pimps, and the unruly riverboat men and others who were not too choosy where they spent their money or laid their heads. Robbery, murder, and rape were common occurrences. It was not an area a respectable man would have normally frequented. The Swamp was a law unto itself.

"I see," Hugh murmured. "And after you followed your instructions?"

Etienne sank back into the chair. "A few days passed, and I heard nothing. I wondered if my message had been received. Then one evening as I was walking home, a hood was dropped over my head, and I was pulled into an alley. I was terrified, *monsieur*! All I could think of was my poor *maman* and my sisters—how alone they would be if I died." He swallowed again. "But I was not to die. A man with a gruff voice told me precisely what I was to do. Where I would find the supplies I would need. It was a perfectly normal printer's shop and a package was waiting for me. It had my name on it. In the middle of the stack of paper was a note. I had been told to look for it. I was to keep the paper safe and I would be contacted and told more when necessary. Again several weeks went by." Etienne sighed heavily. "And then the ship *La Marie-Rose* arrived from France. Almost the entire ship's cargo was for the company—it was a very large shipment. I started work as I usually do on the inventory that afternoon. That very night I was roughly awakened in my room and found to my terror that these men had dared to enter my home—*Maman* and my sisters were asleep just down the hall. Despite the darkness, they hooded me again, a knife was held to my throat and after swearing to do terrible, *terrible* things to my family if I made a sound, they gave me my instructions." A shudder went through Etienne. "They must have eyes everywhere, else they would not have known that I had even started the inventory. I was told precisely what to do. I was to *pretend* to continue the inventory and to make excuses if *Monsieur* Brisson or anyone else who wanted to know why I was not done with it asked. In two days' time, I was to begin anew and to make note of any differences. On the special paper I had already been given I was to make a false copy, making it agree with what actually remained in the warehouse and substitute it where necessary in the original lists. I was to destroy any original pages which would have revealed the actual theft and keep my mouth shut—

they would see to everything else. My money would be paid as soon as the goods were sold."

"And was it?"

"Oh, *oui*," Etienne said wearily. "It was a grand sum. Enough to pay off all my debts. I felt a new man."

"And?"

"And I was a thief, and I did not like myself very much. I thought that that would be the end of it."

"But you gambled again," Hugh said grimly.

"A little," Etienne answered honestly. "But not a great deal. I *had* learned my lesson. It was not the gambling which trapped me—it was agreeing to help them in the first place. I thought that I would only need to do it that one time, but I had not reckoned with the men who used me. They came back, meeting with me the same way, in an alley with a hood over my head. And they wanted me to do it again and again." Etienne fixed a pleading stare on Hugh. "*Monsieur*, you must believe me when I say I resisted. I did. I wanted nothing more to do with them. But it was made clear that having helped once, if I refused to help again, *everything* would be blamed on me! I *had* to help them or face total ruination." His voice thickened. "I did what they wanted."

There was a brief silence. It was obvious that Etienne was exhausted. He was slumped in the chair, his head in his hands.

"You never saw their faces?" Hugh asked with a frown.

"Never." Etienne lifted his head and smiled bleakly at Hugh. "I have nothing to prove my story. Not a scrap of paper. Not an identity. Not a thing."

"Did you talk to anyone at the Silver Cock? Or at the printer's shop? Did you try to find out who picked up the silver or who had ordered the paper for you?"

"The Silver Cock is not a place where one asks questions. As for the print shop, I did go back and ask who had placed the order, but no one seemed to know. They were polite and, I am sure, honest. Whoever is doing the stealing," Etienne said heavily, "is very, *very* clever—and has taken great pains to keep his identity a secret."

It made for an outrageous tale, but Hugh did not doubt a word of it. Careful questioning of Etienne brought little more to light, and by the time Hugh had picked Etienne's brain clean, he knew everything Etienne knew about the thefts. Despite his disappointment with what he had learned, he reassured the young man that his part in the thefts would be kept secret and that he would be rewarded for his help. Showing Etienne to the door, Hugh said quietly, "For the time being you should do your job as you normally would. Until another large shipment arrives they are not likely to contact you." Hugh shot him a piercing look. "The moment you do hear *any*thing, let me know *immediately*! Do not hesitate an instant."

"What will you do?" Etienne asked fearfully.

The young man deserved honesty. Bleakly Hugh admitted, "I do not know yet. But do not be alarmed. I will keep my word and keep you out of it as much as possible."

They said good night and parted. Hugh spent what remained of the night pacing the floor, considering all that he had learned. It wasn't, he thought grimly, a very great deal, and most of what Etienne had told him, he had already suspected. It was comforting to know that he had not been far off in the manner of the thefts, but it galled him that he had not learned more about the men involved. He grimaced. All he had learned tonight simply confirmed his suspicions.

Hugh had guessed that several men were involved—

there had to be to move the goods. Gangs in New Orleans were common, and Hugh did not doubt that he was dealing with a well-organized, ruthless group of criminals. It was also clear from things Etienne had told him that the first thefts had not been as large or as frequent as the ones that had taken place in this past year or so. The thieves had been cautious at first, but as they had met with success after success and no hint of suspicion fell upon them, they had grown greedy. If they had continued to keep their plunder small, who knew when their tactics would have been discovered? Fluctuating profits were to be expected in his kind of business, and Hugh doubted that even he himself would have questioned a slight drop here and there.

But this last year they had grown very greedy indeed. Why? Simple greed? Or need? And what need? During his questioning Etienne had admitted that his payment for each theft had remained the same, no matter the size of the booty. More men to pay? Hugh did not think so. In fact, he did not believe that he was dealing with a large gang of thieves. It probably, excluding Etienne, consisted of no more than half a dozen carefully picked men. Eight maximum. And the leader.

So who was behind it? Hugh liked Alain Husson for the position, and it was not just his own prejudice against the man which led him in that direction. Alain's unsavory connections and his reputation for being ruthless in pursuit of money owed him were already known. A man who, if rumor was to be believed, hired scoundrels to terrorize and brutally attack his debtors would not hesitate to use such tactics in other matters. He obviously was acquainted with the denizens of New Orleans' underbelly. But was it Alain?

And if the mastermind was not Husson, then who?

Jean? François? The notion that it could be one of his wife's relatives had not escaped him. Gloomily Hugh admitted that he had always believed that one of the reasons Micaela had trapped him into marriage was to protect her family.

But if it had been for her family's sake that Micaela had gone to such lengths to marry him, did she know something? Suspect something? Hugh's jaw clenched. The next time he was face-to-face with his charming wife, he was going to have a rather frank conversation with her.

Determined not to think of Micaela or her part in the difficulties at the family company, Hugh shut his mind to the tempting image which erupted in his brain—Micaela standing before him, her dark eyes soft and welcoming, her mouth warmly smiling . . . With a muttered curse, he damned himself for a fool. As for loving her—he did, he would not deny it, but he sure as hell was not happy about it!

Dawn was breaking when he finally decided to seek a few hours of sleep, and it was midmorning when he awoke. After a hasty bath, he dressed and hurried down the stairs. A brief word with Sampson elicited the information that John Lancaster was in the courtyard. Asking Sampson to bring food and coffee out there, Hugh walked out to the courtyard. After greeting his stepfather and apologizing for sleeping late, he took a seat at the iron table where John sat sipping a cup of coffee.

Conversation between the two men was inconsequential until after Sampson had appeared and served Hugh his breakfast: John had eaten earlier. Once Hugh's crawfish omelette, fresh strawberries, and *pain perdu* with cane syrup were served, and a piping-hot pot of coffee placed on the table, Sampson withdrew, and the two men were able to talk seriously.

Between mouthfuls of food, Hugh told John everything that he had learned from Etienne the previous night. It took a long time as he had to backtrack occasionally to explain a particular aspect or point. There was much discussion between the two men about the situation, even more speculation about who the mastermind behind the thefts could be, and several fruitless minutes were spent trying to devise a way to flush their quarry.

The day was growing increasingly humid and warm, the air still and heavy. Around two o'clock in the afternoon, Hugh raised his eyes and scanned the dirty-skirted clouds drifting serenely across the blue sky. "It looks as if we may get a thunderstorm, shortly," he said. "Shall we go inside? It will be cooler in the house anyway."

Settled in Hugh's study, they continued to discuss their problems. John had wanted to know more about Alain Husson, and Hugh complied.

When Hugh was finished speaking, John leaned back in his chair and steepled his fingers in front of him. "I cannot," he began quietly, "believe that both or even one of the Duprees is involved in this. Jean and I have had our disagreements in the past, but he is basically an honorable man." John grinned at Hugh. "Perhaps not as good a businessman as he would like to think, but an honest man. He is loyal to his family, mayhap too much, and I am convinced that he would do nothing to harm the company. As for young François . . ." John's face hardened. "I will tell you the truth—I did not like his father." He sent Hugh a glance from under his elegantly arched brows. "Did you ever meet Renault?"

Hugh nodded. "Once, on my first trip down to New Orleans—Jasper introduced us."

"Like him?"

Hugh smiled. "Not particularly. He was very haughty, very condescending. I thought him a cold, calculating bastard—not someone I would turn my back on for fear of finding a dagger plunged into it."

"That was Renault," John said grimly. "I only met the boy last night, and I see flashes of his father in him, but I also see a great deal of his mother in him. You know him better than I—is it likely that François could be behind our troubles?"

"I doubt it. And yet, I cannot entirely exonerate him. If Husson rubs shoulders with the criminal element in the city, François is the one most likely to be in financial difficulties. In much the same way that Etienne was drawn into their intrigue, I could see François being done the same way. It is common knowledge that he owes Husson a tidy sum of money, just as Etienne did. It is possible that François is an unwilling tool."

"Possible, but likely?"

"I do not know," Hugh said disgustedly. "François was not happy about my arrival or my marriage to his sister. Last night you saw him at his most charming, believe me."

They speculated on the problem for several moments longer, then John said heartily, "Enough of this for now. Tell me more about your bride. When do we go to *Amour*?"

Hugh hesitated. He had known this question was coming and he had not yet decided how he was going to handle it. Walking a narrow path between truth and mendacity, he said slowly, "Etienne admitted to me last night that upon orders, he had destroyed the message which had arrived several weeks ago alerting us to the possible arrival of *Le Lys Bleu* and her cargo. Apparently *Le Lys*

Bleu herself also carried a message for us, which Etienne also destroyed, about another ship which would be sailing approximately six weeks behind her. Assuming she sailed as indicated she should be, barring pirates and storms, arriving around mid-July. Etienne said that *Le Coq* will be carrying another large consignment for us. I want to be here when she arrives."

"I understand, my boy, but there is nothing stopping us from leaving the city for a few days, is there? Perhaps even a week or more? Nothing is likely to happen until *Le Coq* arrives. And it *is* the fever season. Anyone with any sense has already left the city." He smiled. "I did not travel all this distance to die of fever in New Orleans, did I?"

"Of course not," Hugh said easily. "It is too late today to start for *Amour*, and after last night I am longing very much for a good night's sleep. I shall send a servant tomorrow to let Micaela know that we shall be arriving on Thursday. That will give me tomorrow in which to make certain that all is well at the office, and that Etienne is following my orders."

On Wednesday, as he had planned, Hugh went to the office. He finished up a few details and was pleased to see Etienne, looking a little haggard-eyed, busy at work. Except for a sudden paling when Hugh casually asked him to join him in his office, Etienne seemed as always.

Hugh did not keep him long. Only long enough to let him know that he would be leaving the city on Thursday and would not be back for a week, ten days.

"If you need me," Hugh said, "for . . . *any*thing, send someone you can trust with a message. *Amour* is not above a hard three-hour ride from the city. I can be here the same day I receive any message from you."

Etienne nodded. He turned to go, but Hugh called him back.

"You have placed enormous trust in me," Hugh said quietly. "I shall not fail you." He hesitated, then added softly, "I do not believe that any harm should come to you. I would not willingly place you in any danger, nor ask you to risk your life. But if these men are as ruthless as you say, if something were to happen, I promise you that your mother and sisters will not suffer."

Etienne's eyes searched Hugh's. What he saw there must have reassured him, for he said huskily, "Thank you, *monsieur.* I have worried much over my decision to talk to you. You have relieved my mind."

A half hour later, having told *Monsieur* Brisson where to reach him and approximately when he would be returning to the city, Hugh left the office. Upon his return home, he found that a message from Jean Dupree had arrived. Sipping a glass of port in a shady corner of the courtyard, Hugh read the message. He glanced across at his stepfather, who was sitting beside him.

"We shall have company at *Amour,*" Hugh said. "Jean writes that he and François will visit on Monday or Tuesday. They are going to Riverbend for a few days and then will come to *Amour.*" Hugh smiled dryly. "They do not say for how long they intend to stay."

John laughed and shook a teasing finger at him. "Ah, my boy, that is what you get for marrying a Creole girl— have you not heard the saying that when you marry a Creole bride, you marry her *and* her five hundred relatives! Be happy that the Dupree family is exceptionally small."

They spent a pleasant afternoon and evening and around eleven o'clock they had just decided to retire for the night, when Sampson knocked on the study door and entered with a note for Hugh. Puzzled, Hugh slit open the sealed missive and quickly read the contents. His face tightened.

Having dismissed Sampson, he said to John, "It is from Etienne. He writes that he has important news for me, news that will not keep, but that he is afraid to come to the house. I am to meet him at midnight at the company's warehouses."

"It could be a trap," John said slowly, his eyes troubled.

"It no doubt *is* a trap," Hugh replied grimly, "but if this note is not from Etienne, it is the first time that I have had any direct message from the men who are stealing from us. If only Jasper had not left the city today! I will have to go. It may be the only way I can find out more about them."

"More than likely," John snapped, "you will find out how a broken head feels!"

"Perhaps. But I am not going in blind. I will be ready for treachery, and I will be armed."

"I am going with you. I may not be Jasper, and I may not be a young buck anymore," John muttered, "but I can still shoot and I am handy with my fives."

Hugh hesitated, but the stubborn expression on his stepfather's face stilled any remonstrations. "Very well," Hugh said with a grin. "I shall be happy to have your company."

There was no conversation between the two men as they left the house less than an hour later and swiftly made their way to the warehouses. Both were heavily armed, Hugh comforted by the feel of the pair of heavy pistols hidden on his person and the knowledge that John was similarly armed. The knives they both had concealed in their boots added to his sensation of being prepared for whatever might come from this nocturnal visit.

As they drew near their destination, the scent of the river came sharply to their nostrils, and the warehouses loomed up in black bulky shapes against the starlit sky. The flickering glare from the Carondelet lamps which hung from chains on the corner posts at each street intersection lent only fitful light, and Hugh was very aware of how easily an ambush could be launched from any of the dark alleys, as he had once already experienced!

Approaching the warehouse, Hugh was startled to see that one of the large doors was standing wide-open, clear yellow light spilling out into the darkness. He and John exchanged glances.

"It would seem," John whispered, "that whoever sent you the note is already inside."

"And not hiding that fact either," Hugh retorted dryly.

Cautiously the two men entered the cavernous building. The light came from a lantern which had been left sitting on top of a large crate near the entrance of the warehouse. It was still and silent inside, and Hugh took a dozen or more wary strides into the warehouse before he stopped so suddenly that John, following closely behind, nearly barreled into him. Grimly the two men stared at the scene that lay before them.

At the edge of the cheerfully dancing yellow light lay the body of a man, wide scarlet rivulets of what could only be blood radiated outward from the still form. Snatching up the lantern, Hugh brought it closer to the body.

Etienne Gras lay dead on the floor of the warehouse. His throat had been savagely cut, the vicious wound extending nearly from ear to ear. He looked much the same as he had when Hugh had seen him earlier, except now the dark eyes revealed the stark terror of his final moments. . . .

Chapter Fourteen

———⋙•◦•⋘———

*T*he company routinely hired night watchmen to patrol the premises, but it took Hugh and John several minutes to find the pair of them sleeping off a night of hard drinking in a small room at the back of the warehouse. Staring at the bleary-eyed sots who were supposed to be guarding the place, Hugh was not surprised that those behind the thefts and Etienne's death felt they could do as they wished with impunity.

The city guards were sent for, and by the time they had arrived and Hugh and John had explained their finding of the body and had answered the questions of the local authorities, it was nearly three o'clock in the morning. The two Lancasters decided that no good would be served by waking *Madame* Gras at that hour of the morning to tell her that her only son was dead.

An hour after first light, Hugh bathed and changed his clothes and prepared to wake *Madame* Gras with the tragic news of Etienne's death. It was one of the hardest things he had ever done in his life, and it did not help that he was consumed by guilt. He might not have wielded the knife which had killed Etienne, but it certainly had been his actions which had set in motion the events which had led to the murder. A tight ball of fury fought with his guilt, and he swore to himself that Etienne's murder would not go unpunished.

The meeting with *Madame* Gras was every bit as grim as Hugh had thought it would be. The family was shattered, and he spent several hours with Etienne's relatives genuinely commiserating with them for their terrible loss. As the word spread of the horrible tragedy, other relatives arrived, and by the time Hugh departed from the modest Gras home, it was filled to overflowing with grieving family members—grandparents, uncles, aunts, nieces, and nephews. Hugh was able to depart knowing full well that *Madame* Gras and Etienne's sisters were being gently enfolded into the extended Creole family bosom. Before he left Hugh had a private word with *Madame* Gras and her elder brother, Laurent Cloutier, who seemed a sensible man. With delicate tact he explained that Etienne's family would suffer no financial hardship because of his death. The relief in Madame's grief-ravaged face did little to soothe Hugh's sense of guilt. As he walked away, he was conscious that it would be a long time before the image of Etienne's dead body faded from his mind.

The trip to *Amour* had naturally been postponed until after Etienne's funeral, which was held on Friday. Hugh had sent word to Micaela that they would be delayed, but he had not mentioned why. Hugh had also notified the other partners of Etienne's death and had requested their presence at the funeral. It was then that he discovered that none of them, despite having said differently, had actually left the city. Their various reasons for remaining in New Orleans, even Jasper's, seemed specious, although Hugh could find no obvious faults.

But watching the four men as they expressed their sympathy to a heavily veiled *Madame* Gras at the cemetery on Friday, Hugh speculated about them. Which one, he wondered savagely. Which one of those men had either murdered Etienne himself or had ordered it done.

Hugh automatically dismissed Jasper from his list of suspects—might as well suspect his stepfather as Jasper! To his surprise, he found that he did not feel very comfortable putting Jean on his list either. He and Jean had come a long way these past months and whether it was simply that closer association had engendered a mutual respect for each other or whether it was just that they were both older and less inclined to take offense so easily, he did not know. It was probably a bit of both, but Hugh found himself hoping that when the guilty party was unmasked, it would not be Jean Dupree.

He still favored Alain as his villain. For obvious reasons he did *not* want François to be the culprit behind the ugliness. But watching Alain and François walking off with their heads close together as they conversed, Hugh was aware of a sense of unease. He could not ignore the fact that François was very good friends with Alain, and that old adage, "birds of a feather, flock together," ran through his mind.

Hugh had called a meeting at his house immediately following the funeral. Originally he had been determined upon using his personal fortune to pay for the generous sum which would be settled upon Etienne's family, but after a great deal of argument, John had convinced him that the company should pay the money—Etienne had been an employee, and whatever guilt Hugh might feel, what had happened was not his fault. Hugh didn't like it, but he could see the sense of it and he took a certain grim satisfaction in knowing that whoever had killed Etienne was going to be livid that company funds were being expended in such a manner. Picturing the chagrin of the murderer, he smiled without mirth. He was looking forward to watching the expressions on the faces of the others when they heard the news.

Everyone gathered in the main salon of the house. After some brief comments about the tragedy, Hugh immediately explained the purpose of the meeting. There was an astonished silence when he finished speaking and though he was watching closely, no one reacted significantly.

"But why?" exclaimed François in obvious puzzlement. "It is not *our* fault that Etienne died."

"You think not?" Hugh inquired with a lift of his brow. "He worked for us, and he was killed in one of our warehouses. I think we bear some responsibility for the tragedy."

"Then pay him out of your own fortune!" snapped François.

"I find that I agree with my friend," Alain said smoothly. "It is no concern of ours. It is unfortunate, but . . ." He gave a very Gallic shrug.

"Well, I, for one, see nothing wrong with the idea," said Jasper. "The sum will not hurt the company, although our profits may dip a little more for the time being."

François glared at Jasper and slumped back disgustedly in his chair. A muscle jumped in Jasper's jaw, and he sent François a hard look. "I thought Etienne was your friend—will you see his mother and sisters brought to ruin?"

It was Alain who answered. "Friendship has nothing to do with it. It is a matter of business, of money. I would not have accepted Christophe's shares in the company if

I had known," he said in a sneering voice, "that it was going to be turned into a charity."

"If that is the way you feel," Hugh retorted, "I am willing to buy your shares right now."

Alain sent him a hooded glance. "Are you?" he purred. And at Hugh's nod, he named a price nearly five times their value.

His gray eyes hooded, Hugh said, "If you will sign an agreement to that effect this afternoon, I shall have the money transferred to you on Monday morning before I leave for *Amour*."

Rising gracefully to his feet, Alain bowed. "Prepare the agreement."

Alain's offer and Hugh's swift acceptance of it struck the others speechless, and it wasn't until after Alain had signed with contemptuous flourish the hastily drawn document that the silence was broken. Preparing to leave, Alain murmured, "I will not say that it has been a pleasure to do business with you, *Monsieur* Lancaster, but I will say that I am very happy no longer to be one of your partners!"

Hugh smiled like a tiger. "And I, *monsieur*, am overjoyed that Galland, Lancaster and Dupree will no longer have you meddling in its affairs. Good day."

Alain's hand tightened on the stylish malacca cane he was carrying, but he merely tipped his head and glanced at François. "I shall see you before you leave the city?"

François nodded.

When the door shut behind Alain's form, John Lancaster let out his breath in a rush. "Whew! For a few minutes there, I thought you might be fighting another duel with that young man."

Hugh smiled. "So did I." Looking at the others, he

said, "Are there any more objections to settling the money on Etienne's family?"

Jean stroked his chin, looking thoughtful. "We have never done such a thing before, but then we have never had someone who worked for us murdered before either. I regret the necessity for it, but I do not think that I would rest easy knowing that *Madame* Gras and her daughters were destitute. It is only honorable that we do something for his family."

François snorted. Springing to his feet, he muttered, "I do not see why you called us all together—the decision had already been made. You have wasted my time."

The door shut resoundingly behind him. Jean looked embarrassed. "He is young," he said as he rose from his chair, "and much spoiled. I apologize for him." Glancing at Hugh, he asked wryly, "Is the invitation to visit you at *Amour* still open?"

Hugh grinned. "Do you think my wife or mother-in-law would allow me to bar their relatives from their home?"

Jean smiled crookedly. "Very well then. We shall see you on Wednesday or Thursday. Or at least I will. Who knows what that hotheaded young fool François will do!"

Jean started toward the door, but Jasper said, "Wait, *mon ami*, I shall walk with you." He bowed to Hugh and John. "I assume there is no other business you wish to discuss?"

Hugh shook his head, and Jasper said, "Then I shall wish you a pleasant trip to *Amour* on Monday and look forward to seeing you and your charming wife sometime later in the summer."

When Hugh and John were alone, Hugh sat down in a large, overstuffed chair of burgundy and gray cut velvet and murmured, "That went rather well, do you not agree?"

"Better than I expected," John said slowly. He frowned. "I am rather surprised at how easily Husson gave up his shares, even if he did charge you an outrageous sum for them."

Hugh shrugged. "I would have paid double that amount if it got rid of him. And as for the ease with which he sold them to me, if he *is* the one behind our troubles, he has to know that the days in which he could loot the company at will are swiftly coming to an end." Hugh grinned a nasty grin. "Perhaps, like the rat I believe him to be, he has decided to desert the ship while there is still time."

"Perhaps. But I still do not like it. I feel there is something almost *ominous* about his actions."

On Monday morning when Hugh transferred the money to the account which Alain had specified, they were still discussing Alain's motives as well as the tragedy of Etienne's death and the events surrounding it. Feeling as if he had made little progress in the situation at Galland, Lancaster and Dupree, Hugh was reluctant to abandon the city, but John had made him see that he would accomplish little by remaining in New Orleans.

"The fever season, you know," John said gently. "And it is unlikely that anything of note will happen until *Le Coq* arrives, which you yourself have admitted will not be for a few weeks yet. You have hired new guards and tripled their number, and terrified *Monsieur* Brisson within an inch of his life at the fate that will be his if he does not *instantly* notify you of the ship's arrival. There is nothing else you can do. Put it behind you for now."

Hugh had grimaced, but privately agreeing with his stepfather, he had prepared for their journey to *Amour.*

Having decided for the next few weeks to close up the house, all the remaining servants had been sent ahead to *Amour* earlier that morning. Ordinarily John and Hugh would have ridden horseback and made swifter time on their journey, but they would be driving, owing to the fact that Hugh wanted to leave Micaela with the curricle when he did return to New Orleans.

They had left the city immediately after Hugh had taken care of the Husson business. It was midmorning, and the heat had not yet reached its zenith, although it was already extremely warm and muggy. The pair of elegant bays which pulled the curricle moved out smartly, and so the gentlemen were afforded a pleasant, cooling breeze for the start of their journey.

As they swiftly left the environs of New Orleans behind them, they seemed to leave behind their troubles also, and by the time they had been on the road for an hour, both men were thoroughly relaxed as they conversed idly and enjoyed the passing scenery. Hugh was aware of a burgeoning excitement, a growing eagerness to see Micaela, the brief time they had been parted suddenly seeming endless. He wondered just what sort of reception he would receive from his wife. Cool? Wary? Indifferent? Warm?

In the time that had passed since he had realized that he loved his bride, there had been no truly free moment in which to explore his startling discovery of the state of his heart. He had come to accept it as fact that he *did* love her—deeply—and it seemed incredible to him that he could have been so blind to his own emotions. He had known that Micaela had fascinated him, almost from the moment he had met her. He had also known that he lusted mightily after her lush body, but he had not thought that there had been any lasting emotion behind those feelings.

Yet he had taken her as his wife, even knowing that she had connived and tricked him into marriage—even knowing, if Alice was to be believed, Micaela had openly admitted theirs was a business arrangement. His lips quirked into a rueful smile. He had been a thickheaded fool! He had told himself, convinced himself, that marrying Micaela had been simply an expeditious way to gain her bed and also to make certain that her shares in the company had not ended up in the hands of someone like Husson. His reasons, he now admitted with a certain amount of amused chagrin, had been foolish in the extreme and composed of sheer unadulterated nonsense! *He loved Micaela!* And had, he realized with equal parts of despair and satisfaction, for a long time. With a silly smile on his face, he was only partially aware of his stepfather seated beside him and the road ahead of him. Most of his thoughts dwelled dreamily on his future with his dark-eyed, sweet-lipped love at his side.

The dusty, rutted road they were driving upon ambled lazily along the Mississippi River, haphazardly following parallel to the channel of the river. Heavy vegetation obscured the river occasionally, but during other stretches, the edge of the road was not twenty feet from the sluggishly drifting water. There were places where the rampant greenery pressed close to the narrow trail, leaving a scant foot or two between the dust-rimmed leaves of brush and berry vines and the sides of the curricle; other areas were more broad and open, the vegetation growing low and more sparse.

At present, they were driving through an area where the road was fairly wide and straight, the gray-blue river was on one side; on the other lay the tangled brush and swampy undergrowth. The lush, verdant foliage was not as encroaching along this section of the trail, and there was a decent amount of openness, perhaps thirty feet between the edge of the road and the thickly massed green wilderness. It was, Hugh would realize later, a perfect location for an ambush.

Suddenly, several things happened almost simultaneously; a ground-nesting bird at the edge of the road erupted into flight, startling the horses; the curricle swerved wildly as the horses plunged and shied; and the crack of pistol fire rang out. Hugh owed his very life to that nesting bird, the bullet merely grazing his arm instead of finding his heart as it would have if the curricle had not swerved so unexpectedly. He took a deep breath. Though he did not yet realize it, a few inches to the right and he would have been a dead man.

"Get down!" he yelled at John as he slapped the reins on the backs of the horses and brought his whip into play. At the first stinging lash of the whip, the horses leaped forward, even as a second shot buried itself in the cushion of the backrest near Hugh. Too damn near for comfort, Hugh thought grimly, as he exhorted his pair into a dead run. The horses responded like the thoroughbreds they were, their long necks outstretched, their powerful black legs gleaming in the sunlight, the curricle fairly flying down the dusty road.

Ambushes by murderous scoundrels were not uncommon along any road, but instinct told Hugh that this was no simple robbery. Someone, concealed in the undergrowth, had just tried to kill him, and he sincerely doubted that it had been a mere bandit with a penchant for killing his victims.

A third bullet smacked into the rear of the curricle and then the horses, black manes and tails flying, were thundering around a curve in the road, the curricle tipping precariously as they tore around the bend. The curve was sharp and one wheel left the ground, spinning uselessly in the air as the curricle rounded the curve. Hugh and John hastily threw their weight in that direction and the curricle bounced down jarringly as the wheel found earth again. Two miles down the road and no sign of pursuit, Hugh finally slowed his horses to a trot.

His mouth set, he glanced at John. "Are you all right?" John nodded. "You?"

Hugh looked down at his arm, noticing for the first time the tear in his coat and the faint gleam of blood on his sleeve. "I think I have been hit, but it does not feel serious." He grinned at his stepfather's expression. "A mere scratch, sir. I assure you."

A closer examination of the wound proved Hugh's words correct. The bullet had ripped a gash in his upper arm, but beyond a burning sensation, Hugh seemed none the worse for his ordeal. Shrugging quickly back into his coat, Hugh said, "I do not want to linger here any longer than necessary. I don't think our attacker will follow us, but I would just as soon take no chances."

Despite what he had said for John's benefit, Hugh silently considered briefly the possibility of going back and taking a look around. Wisdom dictated otherwise—a lone horseman could easily disappear into the forests, while any attempt to follow in the curricle would prove disastrous. Besides, whoever had shot at them was more than likely gone from the scene by now. And John was with him. The shock of Etienne's death had left Hugh feeling particularly wary about involving others in what was clearly becoming a deadly enterprise. There was no way in hell that he would risk harm coming to his stepfather. The need for direct and decisive retaliation gnawed at him, though, and it was only with great reluctance that he finally snapped the reins and started the horses into motion.

As was their wont when traveling, Hugh and John had brought pistols with them. But there had been no time to bring their own weapons into play, and since their attacker had been well hidden, to have fired upon him would have been a waste of precious seconds and ammunition. But the next time, Hugh thought fiercely, they would be prepared, both pistols now lying handily on the seat between them, ready to be snatched up in a moment. They would not be caught by surprise again.

The remainder of the journey was without incident, but both men were tense and alert, their narrowed-eyed gazes carefully scanning the passing countryside. Hugh kept the horses at a swift pace, slowing only long enough from time to time for the animals to restore their vigor, before pushing quickly onward.

They had driven in silence for several minutes before John said, "A robber with murder in mind, do you think? Or something more sinister?"

"More sinister," Hugh replied bluntly. "It *could* have been an attempted robbery, I will not deny it, but you will have a hard time convincing me that someone did not just try to kill me."

John agreed. "My opinion also. Etienne's killer?"

"I do not know. Probably. There are lawless, murderous men aplenty in this area, but it would seem too much of a coincidence that Etienne and I would cross paths with two different such men."

"But who?" John demanded with thwarted fury. "If it is the same man who killed Etienne . . . One of our erstwhile partners, do you think?"

That dangerous tiger's smile crossed Hugh's face. "I do not know, sir, but I certainly intend to find out—

soon!" His expression grew hard. "Everyone knew that we were leaving for *Amour* this morning. And knowing that, it would have been a simple task for anyone to set up the ambush."

"I do not like this at all," John admitted uneasily. "This person is becoming more vicious by the hour. Etienne is dead, and you were just shot at." He looked worriedly at Hugh. "If they tried once, what is to stop them from trying again?"

"Nothing, except that now they have lost the element of surprise and believe me, Papa, I do not intend to make myself an easy target for them again."

"Who do you think it was?"

Hugh slanted his stepfather a mocking look. "Well, and I could be wrong, but I suspect that we have discovered why Husson was so easily convinced to sell me his shares—even at an inflated price."

John frowned. "What do you mean?"

"I think," Hugh began slowly, "that it was Husson back there who tried to kill me. He is no friend to me, and he had nothing to lose by my death and everything to gain— I had already bought his shares and paid him for them. More importantly, before I came to New Orleans he was a suitor for Micaela's hand. . . . I think *Monsieur* Husson saw a way to dupe me twice. The first by making me pay an exorbitant price for his shares while I was alive and the second, in due time, after he had murdered me, by marrying my widow and gaining control of a majority interest in the firm, including the shares he had made me buy from him."

"How very *diabolical!*" exclaimed John, horrified.

Chapter Fifteen

*W*hen Hugh's first note had arrived, Micaela had been overjoyed, *thrilled* that their separation would be so brief. She was miserably aware of the constraint that still lay unresolved between them. But the conversation with her mother had given her much to think over and she had concluded that she was a silly goose for letting the situation happen in the first place. And she would be a fool ten times over, she told herself sternly, if she did not attempt to breach the gulf between them before it became any wider. Hugh's unexpected return would give her a chance to make amends.

Micaela and Lisette had been sitting in the shade of a sprawling magnolia tree near the house, enjoying the faint breeze from the river, when the servant from New Orleans had arrived with Hugh's note. Since Hugh left the ladies had been busy exploring the house, outbuildings, and gardens. They had met with the various new servants and organized a thorough cleaning and inventory of the place. The house had fairly vibrated with all the activity and only today had the two women begun to plan the furnishings that would be needed. It was highly pleasant to spend money, especially when one had a generous husband!

Seeing the color blooming in Micaela's face and the glow in her eyes as she read the note, Lisette laughed. "Now let me see," she began teasingly, "what can that little piece of paper contain that makes you look so? Could it be? Is it that your so virile and handsome husband is returning?"

At Micaela's smile and nod, Lisette murmured, "And you thought he was tired of you! For shame, *petite*, it is obvious that the man cannot stay away from you."

Thinking of what else Hugh had written, Micaela laid aside the missive and, a mischievous gleam in her eyes, murmured, "He writes that he will be returning to *Amour* tomorrow and bringing a guest . . . John Lancaster."

Her words had all the impact she could have wished. Lisette's beautiful eyes widened. She paled, and her breath caught audibly in her throat. "*Here*? He is coming here?"

"Of course," Micaela replied demurely, her eyes dancing. "Where else would my husband bring his stepfather? I suspect that *Monsieur* John Lancaster will stay here for several weeks."

Lisette surged to her feet. "Oh! *Merci*! I did not think to meet him again so soon! I knew he was coming, but I did not—And to be living in the same house! *Dieu*! I must leave! Oh, what will he think to find me here?"

Fondly Micaela watched as Lisette took several agitated steps around the area, and she decided that her flustered and very pretty *maman* did not look as if she were old enough to have two children who were now adults. She looked like a woman half her age, her creamy skin firm and glowing, her black hair without one strand of silver in it and her form as generously rounded as a young girl's. With midnight black eyes full of uncertainty, Lisette swung around to stare at Micaela.

"I cannot stay here!" Lisette said almost desperately.

"Why can you not?" Micaela asked interestedly, feeling very wise and mature in the face of her mother's obvious agitation. "The man is only my *papa*-in-law. He will not eat you, *Maman*, no matter what happened between you in the past."

"But you do not understand! We were to run away together, it was all planned." Lisette's voice thickened. "We were to meet at the gazebo near the river, and he was going to take me away with him to Natchez, only *Papa* and Renault were there instead." Lisette looked away, her eyes filling with tears, even after all these years, as she remembered her shock and anguish at John's bitter betrayal. She took a deep breath. "They told me that John had confessed our plans to them that afternoon—and that he had admitted that he did not want to marry me—that he had only been amusing himself with me. He abandoned me. Deserted me, even knowing that I—"

"But, *Maman*, that is awful!" Micaela cried out, furious at Lisette's callous treatment at the hands of John Lancaster. But she was puzzled, too, and she said slowly, "And yet you spoke so fondly of him, almost as if you still cared for him."

Lisette gave a twisted smile. "I loved the man I thought him to be. And I can never forget that the time we had together was the most precious in my life. Sometimes I hate him very much, but then I remember—" She smiled sadly. "We French have an old saying. 'The heart has its reasons that reason knows nothing of.' I can know with my mind that I was betrayed and abandoned by him, but my heart only remembers the love I had for him."

"But if he abandoned you, if you misjudged him so

badly, how can you believe that his stepson will make me such a wonderful husband?" At her mother's stunned look, Micaela asked gently, "Were you hoping that we would have the happy ending you did not?"

A stricken expression on her face, Lisette's gaze met Micaela's. "I do not know," she said in a low voice. "I do not know."

Some of the confidence that had been hers faded for Micaela. If her mother had been so very wrong about John Lancaster, what was not to say that she had also badly misjudged Hugh? Except, in the deepest recesses of her heart, Micaela simply did not believe it. She knew that her husband did not love her, but at least he had spared her the pain of seeing him pretend that he did. And yet, he had been so very kind, extremely generous, and considerate toward her. Her throat grew tight as she remembered the nights they had lain together as man and wife. He had also been so *very* tender with her.

Giving herself a decided shake, she asked curiously, "Are you not curious about Hugh's step-*papa, Maman*?" Her eyes suddenly twinkled. "Have you thought that he may be bald and fat? Or so dissipated with drink and wild living that you find him repulsive? Are you not the least curious about what the years have done to him?"

"Perhaps a little, but it will be very hard to see him again, knowing that in the end he did not want me."

"Bah! He was a fool then!"

Lisette stared at Micaela, uncertainty in her eyes. "There is much that you do not know, *petite*, but I think you may be right. He *was* a fool!"

"*Bon!* And now we will talk of something far more pleasant," Micaela said. Her voice taking on a teasing tone, she murmured, "Just what do you think we should wear to greet the gentlemen when they arrive? Something, perhaps, to make old *Monsieur* Lancaster's eyes pop out of his head, *oui?*"

Lisette laughed. "You are an extremely wicked child! I must have raised you badly."

The two women smiled at each other and then went on to other topics. On Thursday morning, they arose early and spent a frantic morning, instructing Cook on the lavish and mouthwatering meal they wanted for the gentlemen and then retiring to their rooms, respectively to tear their wardrobes apart searching for the perfect gown in which to stun the gentlemen.

Both women were looking fetching in the extreme by midmorning, Lisette in a gown of pale plum muslin and Micaela dressed in a frock of butter yellow jaconet. Lisette's hair was confined in a sophisticated chignon, while Micaela had chosen to wear her hair in a pretty coronet of thick black braids wrapped intricately around her head. They were ready hours ahead of time and were seated under the shade of one of the many trees near the house, when the message that his trip would be delayed arrived from Hugh.

Micaela's face fell, and her pleasurable excitement faded as she read Hugh's brief note. Disappointment evident, she said, "They are not coming. My husband writes that they are 'delayed.' He is not certain when they will come—he thinks on Monday."

Some of the glow went out of Lisette's face. "Ah, I see," she said smoothly. "Does Hugh say why they are delayed?"

Micaela shook her head. "*Non.* Here, you may read it yourself."

Lisette read the note. Pasting a smile on her face, she rose determinedly to her feet. "I think we had better tell Cook that we are not having company today, after all," she said firmly. "And then we shall change our clothing and finish our list of items that we need for the house from New Orleans. We can send it off today with Hugh's servant when he leaves to return to the city, *oui*?"

They did exactly that, and if the day had not turned out as they expected, both felt pleased with their endeavors. The list, and it was a very long list, had been sent off as planned and they now had the happy prospect of the eventual arrival of wagonloads of new furnishings to contemplate. It was only that night as she lay alone in one of the big beds which had come with the house, that Micaela admitted how very disappointed she had been by Hugh's unexpected postponement of his trip. She was mortified that she had been so excited by the simple prospect of seeing her husband again. She was also grimly determined not to let him raise her hopes again. Completely forgetting the icy cordiality that had existed between them prior to the move to *Amour*, or the fact that Hugh had had no way of knowing that she would be crushed by his delay, she honestly believed that his delay had been deliberate. He was clearly and cruelly showing her just how very little she meant to him. *Zut!* She would not allow him to hurt her this way. What did she care whether or not he came? When he did finally put in an appearance, she would meet him with a charmingly indifferent smile. He would, she vowed fiercely that night, never, *ever* suspect how hurt and wounded she had been by his delay.

Over the next few days mother and daughter had time to repair their damaged feelings, and when Hugh and John finally did arrive at *Amour* on Monday afternoon, they were eventually greeted by two obviously busy women wearing their oldest gowns, who had been industriously overseeing the cleaning of the enormous attics.

Both had studiously polite smiles on their faces and a cobweb or two clinging to the gaily colored tignons they had worn on their heads to protect their hair from the worst of the dust and debris.

"Oh! You are here," Micaela said with artless surprise as she walked into the second salon, the only one with any decent furnishings at the moment. "Did you have a pleasant journey?"

Her gaze barely touched her husband before she glanced shyly at the tall, older man standing beside Hugh. He was very handsome, this John Lancaster who had claimed her mother's heart and then abandoned her so long ago, she thought. Not at all bald and fat! To her surprise, she found the friendly glimmer in his dark eyes and the winsome smile on his dark, lean face vastly appealing. His features were full of character, and Micaela sensed an innate honesty about him—he certainly did not look like a man who would have deserted a woman he had claimed to love, and she wondered briefly if events had happened precisely as Lisette remembered them.

With a much friendlier smile than she had given her husband curving her mouth, she said, "And you must be my new *papa*-in-law! I am Hugh's wife, Micaela. Welcome to *Amour, monsieur*." And astonishing herself as much as it did everyone else, she crossed the room on light feet and warmly kissed John on both cheeks in the French manner of greeting. Her dark eyes shining, she murmured, "We hope that you will enjoy your stay with us."

"After a greeting like that, I can assure you that I certainly will!" John exclaimed, plainly enchanted by Hugh's bride. She looked, he thought with a sharp pang, very like her mother. And yet, as he gazed down into her lively features, he was aware that there was something disturbingly familiar about her that owed nothing to

Lisette, something about the shape of that sturdy little chin and that finely molded nose. Renault? he speculated to himself, ignoring the tight ball of rage that suddenly bloomed in his stomach.

"And this," Hugh said dryly, breaking into the little silence that had fallen as John and Micaela studied each other, "is my *maman*-in-law, Lisette Dupree. I believe that you may have met her when the company was first founded."

With a jerk, John tore his gaze away from Micaela and his breath caught painfully as his eyes met Lisette's across the room. My God! he thought stunned. She has not changed a bit. She looks just as lovely as she did over twenty years ago.

Mindful of the estrangement and the gulf of the years between them, as well as the presence of the others, John bowed stiffly. "*Madame*. The years have been exceptionally kind to you."

"And you, *monsieur*," Lisette said with equal restraint despite the painful thudding of her heart. *Dieu!* But he was still a handsome devil! With his dark, almost swarthy skin, the silver wings at his temples only increased his attractiveness. Lisette was terribly conscious of the leap in her pulse when he reached out and kissed her hand with cool politeness.

Their eyes met and for a long moment, the world fell away, and there was just the two of them. Then Hugh coughed politely and Lisette started violently; John dropped her hand as if stung. Almost as one they sprang apart, putting the width of half a room between them.

Lisette gave a strained little laugh and babbled, "If you will excuse me, I must go and see that Cook is—um—following instructions for our evening meal."

Under Micaela's bemused stare, Lisette bolted from

the room. *Monsieur* Lancaster obviously still had the power to overset her usually so calm and collected *maman*. Consideringly she eyed him, noticing that he seemed almost as affected by the meeting with the woman he had apparently deserted over twenty years ago as her mother. His color was high, and he appeared greatly disturbed. This was most interesting!

Micaela glanced at Hugh to see what he had made of the situation and it was then that she noticed for the first time the torn sleeve of his jacket and the dried blood-stains. Her face paled. "*Merci! Merci!* What has happened to you?" she cried. "Are you hurt?"

Amusement glittering in his gray eyes, Hugh looked down at his wounded arm. "Oh, that. It is just a little wound. Nothing to worry about."

"Nothing to worry about!" Micaela exclaimed as she skimmed across the room to see for herself the extent of the damage. Any notion of treating him with cool polite-ness vanished the instant she spied the bloodstained sleeve. "Please you must sit and let me see for myself. But first let me ring for a servant to bring us something to clean it with and some cloth for bandages."

As Hugh obediently sat, Micaela rang for a servant. Turning back to her husband, she fussed over him, help-ing him so gently out of his jacket that one would have thought he was near unto death. Once the jacket had been removed and his shirt partially undone, Micaela sank to her knees beside his chair, scrupulously ignoring the tan-talizing expanse of his broad chest. The sight of the deep angry red furrow along his muscular upper arm brought a dismayed gasp from her. "How did this happen?" Her voice dropped. "Not another duel?"

Rather enjoying having his wife minister to him, Hugh shook his head and murmured, "No duel, sweetheart.

Someone shot at me on the road this morning." His eyes met John's. "We think it might have been a bandit."

"A bandit. *Dieu*! But this is terrible." She swallowed and looking at the wound once more, said softly, "You might have been killed."

Hugh lifted her chin. Unable to help himself, he dropped a kiss on her tempting, trembling mouth. "And would that have bothered you, hmm? You would be a very rich widow."

Micaela scowled at him. Impatiently slapping his hand away, she replied crossly, "I do not want to be a widow! I have barely begun to be a wife."

Hugh grinned and settled back more comfortably in the chair. Not for the world would he admit that he would suffer a hundred wounds, ten times worse than this, just to have her looking at him as she was right now. Perhaps she had begun to care, just a little, for him?

The servant, a slim, black man named Michel, entered the room and, after hearing Micaela's instructions, returned presently with the items she had requested. With John watching, she efficiently cleaned the wound, slathered on a cooling salve of herbs, then tenderly wrapped the area. Despite Hugh's protests, she convinced him that for a day or two at least, he should keep the arm in a sling.

"It will heal so much faster, you understand," she said earnestly.

"If it pleases you, sweetheart," Hugh replied meekly, beginning to think rather fondly of the gentleman who had shot him.

"Do you wish to lie down and rest? Shall I help you to your room? Or should I ring for Michel?" Micaela asked anxiously, when a square of black silk had been procured and fashioned into a sling for his arm.

Feeling as if spring had finally arrived after a long, cold winter, Hugh was not about to allow Micaela to revert to her previous manner. Taking full advantage of her tender concern, he sighed and murmured in a suitably weary tone of voice, "I *am* somewhat exhausted. If you will just let me lean on you a trifle, I should be able to make it to our rooms."

Ignoring the dancing amusement in his stepfather's eyes, Hugh draped himself comfortably around Micaela and managed, with her help, to totter toward the door. The sensation of feeling her arms around him again, even if he'd had to practice guile and craft to accomplish it, was sheer delight. It was worth getting shot, he thought cheerfully, to have Micaela's slender shoulders tenderly supporting his drooping body and her arms locked securely around his waist.

Reveling in the sound of Micaela's soft, concerned voice washing sweetly over him, he had entirely forgotten about John. It was only when they reached the door and John rather loudly cleared his throat that Hugh and Micaela were recalled to his presence.

"Oh, *monsieur*! Forgive me!" she cried in deeply mortified accents as she glanced back at him. "Would you like for me to ring for a servant to bring you some refreshment or to show you to your rooms? If you like, you may rest and refresh yourself before we dine at seven o'clock."

"Oh, that will not be necessary," John said smoothly. "You run along with Hugh." He sent Hugh a mocking look. "I completely understand that your husband's health is of the utmost importance to you at this moment. I think, however, if you have no objections, that I shall wait here for the return of *Madame* Dupree. Perhaps you could arrange it so that she could give me a brief tour of the place before I see my rooms and change for dinner?"

Micaela studied him for a moment, beguiled by his smile and the tiny twinkle in the depths of his handsome eyes. *Dieu! Maman* was going to kill her! She dimpled at him and said, "Of course, *monsieur*! I shall send a servant to find her immediately."

"Thank you. Thank you very much," John replied gravely.

Hugh managed to maintain his air of suffering all the way up the stairs and into their rooms. He had left the choice of their bedchambers to Micaela, and he was pleased with the suite she had selected. It consisted of two large rooms, each with its own separate entrance from the main, broad hallway and each with its own private sitting area. A pair of spacious dressing rooms separated the two bedrooms, and there was a wide interior hallway which gave private access to the sleeping chambers.

Beyond an enormous high-poster bed with a faded canopy of blue-and-white printed linen there was only one other piece of furniture in his bedroom—a huge rosewood armoire which sat against one wall. Curtains in the same faded blue-and-white linen draped the many windows, blocking out the hot sunlight, and the room was dim and cool. There was a pair of wide French doors which opened onto the upper gallery, and a faded painted canvas rug of various shades of blue lay upon the yellow-pine floor.

In anticipation of his arrival, Micaela had had the bed freshly made up that very morning, and, closing his eyes as he sank down onto the sunshine-scented sheets, Hugh sighed with bliss. He was, he realized with amusement and despair, precisely where he most wanted to be—in his own bed, in his home, and with his lovely wife hovering attentively nearby. What more could a man ask for? He carefully opened one eye a crack. Micaela's sweet face filled his gaze as she stood uncertainly by the door to the main hallway. His wife. That was what he wanted. His wife, in his bed, lying right by his side.

"Will you be all right if I leave for a little while?" Micaela asked softly. "I really should go and see that all is well in the kitchen and that *Maman* is entertaining your step-*papa* properly."

Hugh groaned with heartrending realism. "Must you?" he asked weakly.

Micaela sped to his side. "*Merci*! Are you all right? Where does it hurt? What can I do to make you more comfortable?"

A particularly vivid and explicitly erotic image floated across his mind. A rush of heat charged through his body, and he was conscious of the sweet biting ache of desire churning low in his belly. If Micaela's eyes happened to fall on a certain part of his suddenly rigid anatomy, she would have no trouble, he thought ruefully, guessing what would make him comfortable.

Half propping himself up with his good arm, he murmured pathetically, "Perhaps you could help me out of my shirt and pull off my boots for me?"

It never occurred to her that a servant could do all that as well. "Oh, *oui*, of course!" Micaela replied as she set to work to accomplish his request.

His boots were easily discarded, but she seemed to have an inordinate amount of trouble getting his shirt off of him; his arms kept sliding around her, his hands, accidentally she was sure, kept brushing against her hips, the back of her neck, and the sides of her breasts. He seemed to have trouble controlling his head, too, his lips nuzzling her temples and hair. By the time his shirt was finally laid on the end of the bed, Micaela was flushed and thoroughly flustered.

The occasional scrape of his warm face against her cheek as they struggled to remove the offending garment, the musky intoxicating scent of his body, and the accidental brush of his lips on her skin were stunningly arousing, and she was mortified by her response to his nearness. He was wounded! He had been shot! she reminded herself fiercely. And she was determined to hold herself politely aloof from him, wasn't she? It was all well and good to remind herself of those things, but she was very conscious of the half-naked man on the bed, tinglingly aware of every muscle, every sinew that lay bare to her gaze. It seemed like an eternity since she had lain in his arms. She was embarrassingly conscious of the slow, sweet ache that was building between her thighs and the throbbing swell of her nipples.

Averting her gaze from his all-too-appealing charms, she said breathlessly, "I must go. I shall send a servant with some broth and some wine and bread for you."

His voice warm and husky, Hugh reached out a hand and caught one of hers. "Do not," he murmured. He pressed a gentle kiss to the back of her hand. "Stay with me . . . please?"

Their eyes met, and what she saw in the depths of those intent gray eyes made her knees go weak. He did not love her, she reminded herself sternly. He had married her simply because of the business. And had abandoned her in the country, while he, no doubt, caroused and womanized in New Orleans. She was angry with him, hurt by him. It did no good. Her heart was not listening to her brain. Her body did not wish to listen to cold, hard reasoning either.

As she stood there hesitating, heart and body locked in a powerful struggle with what she was certain was clear-thinking logic, Hugh gave a tug to her hand. "Please?" he said again, so softly she almost did not hear him. But her heart did. Her body did.

She did not pretend to misunderstand him. Heart thudding, excitement welling deep inside of her, she managed to ask, "Your wound?"

Hugh smiled, such a tender, knowing smile that every nerve in Micaela's body rejoiced. "My wound," he said thickly, as he effortlessly pulled her onto the bed and into his embrace, "will do just fine."

Their lips met, and the kiss was everything each had dreamed it would be. Each was vaguely conscious that there was a new element between them, but the warmth and utter sweetness of that kiss drove coherent thought from their minds.

With astonishing speed, Micaela's garments as well as Hugh's disappeared, and the next instant they were lying side by side, Micaela's breasts crushed against his chest, her fingers buried in his hair, and their legs locked in an erotic tangle. His kiss deepened, became hungry and ravening, his lips hard and greedy against hers, his tongue eagerly claiming the moist depths of her mouth. Joyously, she gave herself up to the demanding desire that flooded through her. He was her husband. *She loved him!* And, oh, *Dieu!* She wanted him.

Helplessly she pressed closer, and Hugh groaned with delight. Her nipples burned into his chest, her roving hands caressed his shoulders and his back, and her thighs rubbed erotically against his, making his entire body clench with need.

He shifted slightly, mindful of his wound, and dropped his head to her breast, his mouth closing hotly around her nipple. Ah, dear heaven! Nothing had ever tasted so sweet, so intoxicating.

Despite the urge to take her swiftly, Hugh tried to slow down, tried to tamp down his desperate need to join them, to sink his heavy, swollen manhood deep inside of her. But recklessly driven by the urge to mate, the incessant urge to reclaim her, he could not slow the demands of his body. He sought the thick thatch of curls between her legs, excited and unbearably aroused to find that she was already wet and slick and ready for him. Holding his own devils at bay, he toyed with her there, exploring and teasing her, tearing a soft, shaken sigh from her.

Frantically trying to remember why she was to be docile in his arms, trying to remember why she was not to respond too wildly to his touch, Micaela trembled under the onslaught of his mouth and hand. The taste of Hugh on her lips, the frankly carnal movements of his hand between her thighs burned away any thought of lying passive beneath him. She could not.

Uncontrollably she arched up, her legs half–splayed open for him, for the first time ever, actively seeking his possession, and Hugh's frail leash on his own hungers snapped. He reared up, intending to mount her, but his wounded arm failed him, crumpling painfully under him. With something between a curse and a heartfelt groan, he fell back to the bed.

Micaela jerked upright. "Your wound! I forgot. Oh, what have I done? Did I hurt you? This is madness, we must stop!"

With his good arm, Hugh pulled her across his chest. Kissing her urgently, he muttered, "It will hurt me far more if we do not finish what we have started—and I assure you that I shall go quite, quite mad if I do not have you—now!"

"But, but your arm— You cannot—"

A distinctly sensual smile crossed his face. "There are ways, sweetheart. There are ways. . . ."

She gasped in surprise as Hugh gently positioned her over the top of him, her thighs on either side of his lean hips. Her eyes widened in astonished pleasure when a second later he shifted slightly and fully impaled her on his broad shaft. She marveled at the wonderful sensation, fascinated by this new dimension to their lovemaking. She wiggled experimentally, the jolt of pleasure that shot up through her making her moan helplessly.

Her face flushed with passion, she asked breathlessly, "Your wound? This will not hurt you?"

His breathing uneven, those temptingly generous breasts inches from his hungry mouth and the feel of her hot, silken flesh clinging tightly to his aching shaft, made it woefully difficult for Hugh to concentrate on anything but the sheer pleasure coursing through him. "Wound?" he asked fuzzily. "What wound?"

Micaela giggled and wiggled again. Hugh's eyes darkened and then he touched her between her legs, stroking her, and her amusement fled. Despite the pain in his arm, he managed to grip her hips with both hands and began to guide her, teaching her the rhythm. She was a joyous and willing pupil.

Taking as much pleasure from the dazed expression on her face as the sweetly punishing movement of her body sliding up and down on his near-to-bursting member, Hugh was certain he had never experienced anything quite so exquisitely divine.

During the time since their wedding night, Micaela had thought that she had learned all there was to know about lovemaking, but she was discovering that she had been wrong. Oh, so very wrong. It was exciting, so very erotic to feel him beneath her, to feel his solid shaft fitted snugly inside of her and to feel his lean hips between her thighs. When Hugh pulled her head toward him and kissed her hungrily, the burning coil in her belly tightened almost unbearably. When he touched her, when his hand left her head and slid down past her breasts, skimming her flat stomach, traveling ever lower and he finally stroked and fondled her there where they were joined together, she almost screamed with pleasure. Panting, moaning aloud, she rode him harder, increasingly frantic to assuage the demands of her body. He touched her again and she seemed to explode inside, quaking and crying softly as ecstacy, intense and emphatic, swept over her. Limply she sank down on his chest, her body quivering, spent.

The muted sounds of her pleasure were music to Hugh's ears, the convulsive clasp of her flesh around him sending a sharp spiraling delight through him and pushing him over the edge. He gave one powerful lunge upward, driving himself deeply into her, then shuddered and groaned as he, too, found that same elemental ecstacy.

They lay locked together for several moments, each too sated to move. Eventually Micaela slid reluctantly from him. With his good arm, Hugh instantly pulled her next him, brushing a warm kiss against her cheek. Snuggled by his side, Micaela thought giddily, Hugh had been right—there were ways . . . and then there were ways. . . .

Chapter Sixteen

*L*isette almost ignored Micaela's plea to entertain John Lancaster while she tended her husband. She had been shocked to learn of Hugh's wounding, but she was even more dismayed to learn that it would be up to her to act as hostess for a few hours. She seriously considered ignoring the message, but then she put on her most polite expression and strode determinedly from the kitchen where Michel, with Micaela's request, had found her.

John Lancaster meant nothing to her, she told herself firmly. She was *not* a young girl, easily enthralled by a dark, exciting stranger. She was a grown woman. A widow. She had borne two children. John Lancaster did not intimidate her!

Which was all very well and good as far as it went, she thought uneasily, as she walked the short distance between the house and the kitchen. But considering the way her heart had pounded when she had seen him! *Dieu!* It did not bear thinking about! And when they had gazed into each other's eyes . . .

She snorted. This was ridiculous. After the way he had abandoned her, she should feel nothing but scorn and contempt for him. And she did, she reminded herself fiercely. She really did, except . . . except that it was very hard to remember what she *should* feel when she was only aware of what she *did* feel, especially when her wayward heart was telling her something far different than her brain.

There was no sign of her inner turmoil when she reentered the small salon. Briskly she said, "Ah, here you are *Monsieur* Lancaster. Since my daughter will be busy for a while with her husband, it will be my . . . pleasure to show you about their new home. Would you care for some refreshments first?"

John shook his head. A winsome smile curving his chiseled mouth, he asked, "Could you not call me 'John'? I remember a time when my name came easily to your lips."

Lisette stiffened. "That," she said coolly, "was many years ago. I was a foolish young girl in those days." She met his eyes steadily. "You can be sure, *Monsieur* Lancaster, that I shall not make the same mistakes I made then."

John's face tightened and a muscle bunched in his jaw. "You were not the only one who was foolish. I was foolish enough to believe you when you said you loved me— foolish enough to believe that you would marry me."

Her eyes flashed. "You dare to say such things to me?" Lisette demanded furiously. She was so outraged that she had to fight the impulse to cross the room and strike his dark face. This was her daughter's father-in-law, she reminded herself. Micaela was married to his stepson. For the sake of the younger ones, they would have to learn to rub shoulders together. She took in a deep, calming breath, forcing the knot of rage in her chest to slowly dissipate.

Her head held proudly, she said, "There is no use for us to discuss what happened a long time ago—it is over and done with. And I suggest that we would both be wise if we simply agreed that we were both fools and let it go at that."

John nodded curtly, an acid taste in his mouth. How many nights had he lain awake savoring the angry accusations he would hurl at her if he ever saw her again? How many times had he alternately cursed her and yearned to hold her again? He sighed. What good had all his private suffering and rage ever done him? Perhaps she was right. Perhaps, they should just let the past go.

"Very well, since we are not to discuss what happened between us, what do you suggest we do?" He smiled sardonically. "Pretend we are strangers? Pretend we have just met?"

"We *have* just met! I am not the young girl that you knew—I have been married, and I have borne and raised two children. You are no longer the man I thought I had fallen in love with—you also married—Hugh is your stepson. We are not the same people we were."

John moved restlessly around the room. He finally stopped a few feet from her. "It will not be easy. Memory has a way of tripping one up when least expected."

"I know," Lisette said softly, wishing he was not standing quite so close to her, wishing that his dearly remembered scent was not in her nostrils, wishing painfully that she did not feel the powerful tug of attraction between them. So it had been, she thought sadly, the first moment they had laid eyes on each other.

Determined to follow her own advice, she picked up her skirts and said briskly, "If you will follow me, I shall show you the main rooms on this floor. They are, as you may have noticed, scantily furnished, and many of the things are somewhat shabby, but it will not be so for long." An impish smile curved her mouth. "Micaela and I composed a very long and *very* expensive list of items we needed and sent it off to New Orleans. It is good that your stepson has a deep purse."

To their astonishment, the time they spent together wandering through the various rooms of the house passed pleasurably. John was very interested in the house, and Lisette happily explained its history and the various changes Micaela intended to make.

"Are you going to be living with them?" John asked at one point.

Lisette smiled and shook her head. "*Non!* At the moment they seem to be very happy to have me around. I intend for them to continue to do so. Not having me underfoot all the time will make us all enjoy the time we do spend together so much more, *oui?*"

"Very astute of you," John replied, nodding his head. "Hugh would like me to leave Natchez and join him down here, but I have not yet made up my mind."

She regarded him thoughtfully for a long moment. "Living near them, as I do," she said quietly, "is not quite the same thing as one living in Natchez. I am only hours away from Micaela, but for you it is a long, arduous journey between New Orleans and Natchez."

His gaze fixed intently on her face, he asked slowly, "And how would you feel if I were to move down here, if I were to buy myself a home that was only 'hours' away from them? Our paths would be bound to cross frequently."

Lisette gave an airy shrug. "For my child," she said tartly, "I would endure even *your* presence!"

A spark lit John's eyes, and he threw back his head and

laughed. "You still," he murmured a moment later, "have a damnably sharp tongue."

Lisette gave a saucy toss of her head. "And now, *monsieur*," she said determinedly, "if you please, I should like to show you the terrace at the side of the house."

Meekly John followed her, realizing somewhat regretfully, that for the moment at least, Lisette was once again firmly committed to her role of polite hostess.

There was no polite hostess, however, to greet François when he called that same afternoon at Alain Husson's town house in New Orleans. He was expected, and the Husson butler immediately showed him to the small salon and indicated that Master Husson would join him shortly.

His attractive features strained, François wandered around the elegant room, wondering uneasily why Alain had wanted to see him. He hoped it wasn't about his debts.

Alain entered the room a moment later, an affable smile on his face. Straightening the cuff of his shirt where it showed beneath the sleeve of his well-fitting plum-colored jacket, Alain asked, "Have you been waiting long? I had an errand to take care of, and have just returned to the city."

François shrugged. "*Non.* I only arrived a few minutes ago."

"*Bon*! Would you care for some refreshments? Some café au lait? With some pastries, perhaps?"

"Just coffee will be fine," François said, seating himself in a chair covered in oxblood-colored leather.

After ringing for a servant, Alain chose an identical chair across from François and settled into it. He cocked a brow and said, "I suppose you want to know why I wanted to see you today?"

François nodded, instinctively bracing himself for Alain's demand for payment of the monies owed him. Monies he had no way of paying.

Almost as if Alain had read François's thoughts, he murmured, "Do not be so tense, *mon ami*. I have no intention of asking for payment. I am very well aware of your means, and I know that raising the amount you owe me is beyond your power at this time."

"I *will* pay you, I assure you," François said stiffly.

Alain smiled. "Oh, of that I have little doubt, *mon ami*."

The butler arrived just then with their coffee, and for several minutes there was no further conversation. It was only when the butler had left that Alain sank back into his chair and, lazily stirring his coffee, said, "I had intended this meeting to be a bit of a private celebration between the two of us, but I am afraid that I—er—*mis*calculated."

"A celebration?" François repeated bleakly. "What would we have to celebrate? I *still* owe you a great deal of money. If things had gone as we had planned, you would now be my brother-in-law and my debt to you would have been paid. As it is, I have no idea how I am to pay you—but I shall—honor demands it." François sighed. "And then there is Etienne's murder."

Alain took a sip of his coffee. "Does that bother you? Etienne's death?"

"*Mon Dieu*! Of course, it does!" François burst out explosively, rising from his chair in his agitation. He glanced back at Alain. "We were friends! I have known him and his family since I was a child—all my life."

Alain looked amused. "I had not realized that you were so close to him."

"Damn you! We were not close, and you know it! But we *were* friends and to have—! François stopped, his fists opening and closing impotently at his sides.

"Sit down," Alain said sharply, "and listen to me. Etienne is dead, and there is nothing you can do about it now. He had to die. Once it was known he was in Hugh's hands, there was no choice. It was necessary. Just as the *Américain's* death is necessary."

François blanched. "*Nom de Dieu*, you *are* serious—you mean to kill him."

Alain nodded. "Of course. And if luck had been with me a few hours earlier, he would be dead already. The, er, unhappy victim of a murderous bandit."

"You tried to kill him? Today?" François demanded, aghast.

"Naturally." His eyes hard, Alain added, "I have every intention of marrying your sister. And I cannot do that if Hugh Lancaster remains alive. You agreed with me. And do not forget, *mon ami*, you are in this as deeply as I am."

"B-b-but murder! I never agreed to *murder*! It is horrible enough that Etienne is dead, but now you tell me you plan the murder of my own brother-in-law—it is despicable."

"Such a tender conscience you have developed, *mon ami*. You were not so high-principled when we first began our profitable enterprise." Malice evident, Alain added, "If memory serves me, it was *your* idea."

François swallowed with difficulty. "I cannot deny it, but I never expected . . . it was only to have been . . ." He stopped, clearly distressed. Then, taking a deep breath, he went on bitterly, "Once you learned how I meant to pay you, you were the one who expanded upon my idea, the one who volunteered to help me and the one who wanted us to steal more and more. I had meant only to pay my debts to you and then cease the pilfering." François looked thoroughly miserable. "In the beginning with you demanding immediate payment and me with no way to pay you, it did not seem so very bad. I was only taking a little extra from my own company." He flashed Alain a glance of dislike. "When you offered to help me steal, you said that after a shipment or two, I would have completely paid my debt to you." François's jaw clenched. "But then when you saw how easy it was, you grew greedy."

"And you," Alain said softly, his eyes cold and unblinking, "could not stay away from the gaming tables. I was not the one who continued to lose money I did not have."

François looked away. "You are right," he said unhappily. "I was a fool! I kept thinking . . ."

"You wanted," Alain drawled unkindly, "to show everyone how very adult and sophisticated and clever you were. Worse, you kept thinking you could best me and impress everyone. You were indeed a fool if you thought that I would allow that to happen. I do not lose. And I do not intend to lose now." Almost pityingly, Alain continued, "You are in far too deep to escape, *mon ami*."

"Do not call me that! I am not your friend! You have used me and maneuvered me and forced me upon a path I never intended, just as I suspect you did to Etienne!"

"Ah, I see that perhaps I was mistaken in you. I thought you were your own man, answerable to no one." His voice cruel, Alain continued, "You boasted of it often, if I recall correctly. All that righteous anger you so frequently and vocally expressed against the *Américains* was just for show, *oui*? You like the *Américain* lording it over you? You are pleased that your sister is married to that mongrel? An *Américain*, who has practically thrown you out of your own company?"

"I did not like the *Américains* it is true—"

"*Did* not like? Do my ears deceive me? Has the so staid and stolid *Monsieur* Hugh Lancaster won you over to his side? Was it not just a few days ago that you were outraged at his decision to pay Etienne's family a generous settlement from company funds? I do not remember you thinking so kindly of him then—or of your feeling such remorse over Etienne's death."

"Damn your eyes! Can a man not have second thoughts? I had not had time to think about it when Hugh sprang it on us! And to my shame I must admit that I was simply angry at his actions—I viewed it as another example of his high-handedness—but after I thought about it for a while, I realized that he was right and I was wrong. We should have done something for Etienne's family—it was our *responsibility*. Even more so," he ended bitterly, "since I contributed to his death. . . ."

Alain set down his cup and saucer with a clatter. "Do you know that you are growing infinitely boring, *mon am*—. Ah, forgive me, I am not to call you that anymore, am I?"

François drew himself up stiffly. "*Non*," he admitted grimly, "you are *not* to call me 'friend' anymore. I am not your friend. But I *am* a fool. I have acted unwisely, and I have let my temper, my pride and, yes, my prejudices blind me to reality. It is *you* I should have vented my rage against, not the *Américains*. Because of you and my own reckless foolishness, I allowed myself to become involved in something that is totally dishonest and dishonorable. I have ruined myself. And all because I wanted to show everyone—*Maman, mon oncle*, Micaela, you and all my friends that I was a grown man, capable of running my own affairs. All I have done," he said heavily, "is show the world, what a spoiled, immature, and arrogant fool I am."

"Oh my," drawled Alain, spite gleaming in his black eyes, "do I see before me a reformed sinner? A penitent ready to flay himself raw in the name of redemption? Are you wearing a hair shirt beneath your fine clothes today? Do you intend to devote yourself to good works now? Embrace the *Américains*? Work diligently in the family firm? Perhaps you will even lick your brother-in-law's boots, too?"

"*Non*." François answered tiredly, sinking down into his chair once more, ignoring Alain's insults. "I regret, bitterly and deeply, what has transpired, and I hope most fervently that I *can* find a way to redeem myself, if only in my own eyes. I have been a fool, but I do not have to continue to be a fool."

Alain yawned delicately. "As I said, you have become an awful bore. I liked you much better when you were spitting fury and venom at the *Américains* and railing at the unfairness of fate."

"I blamed everyone, but myself," François said slowly, with a note of astonishment, "when no one was at fault *but* myself—"

"Oh, *please*! Do spare me this drivel! Once Hugh is dead and I am married to your sister, you can join a monastery if you like and spend the rest of your life making amends for your sins, but for now . . ." Alain's eyes narrowed and grew hard. "For now you are going to do exactly what I tell you to do."

"And if I do not?"

"If you do not, you will regret it for the rest of your life," Alain threatened softly. "Remember, I can arrange it so that your part in the systematic robbing of your own family's company is made public. I think," Alain went on thoughtfully, "that I can even arrange it so that you are implicated in Etienne's murder."

"And what about your part in all of this?" François asked grimly. "If you expose me, you expose yourself."

"I think not. If you will remember, I have been careful to remain in the background." He smiled benignly at François. "Granted it was my fine hand behind much of what was done, but it was you who first came to me with the idea. Few people, and none that count, I might add, know that I was involved. Certainly the people who work for me will not speak in your defense." His smile broadened at François's expression of dismayed, dawning comprehension. "And if you are foolish enough to attempt to lay the blame at my feet, why, I think most people would see it for what it was—an unscrupulous, spoiled boy's attempt to escape punishment. The fact that you owe me a large sum of money could even be viewed as the reason you were trying to involve me in your schemes. Yes, I think it can be arranged so that *I* appear an innocent victim of your shocking manipulations—you do not want to pay me what is rightfully mine, so you try to lay the blame for your own misdeeds at my door. I do believe that it can be done." He smiled at François. "Would you like to make a wager on it?"

Dispiritedly, François shook his head. What Alain said was all too true. Worse, the thought of his mother, of his family having to bear the shame of his disgrace—even if he could expose Alain as the devious devil that he was and bring him to justice—was too utterly painful to contemplate. His mother would be devastated and blame herself for his misdeeds. His uncle would despise him. His sister would scorn him, and as for Hugh . . . He shuddered, imagining the contempt he would find in his brother-in-law's face. He *had* been a fool. A stubborn, proud, arrogant young *fool*! With unexpected dignity, he said, "*Non*, I will not make a wager with you. I have learned that a wise man does not gamble with you."

"It is too bad that you did not learn it earlier!" Alain retorted viciously, suddenly enraged by François's remorse. "You were such an easy pigeon to pluck that I almost enjoyed watching you fall deeper into debt to me."

"What do you want me to do?" François asked wearily, ignoring the jibe.

More furious than he had thought possible by François's defection, Alain regarded him silently for a moment, fighting to bring his temper under control. The *fool*! How had he thought this would end? And how dare he discover his conscience at this late date! Alain smiled in sudden grim amusement. His own conscience allowed *nothing* to stand in the way of what he wanted. He had thought that François was of the same mold and he felt deeply betrayed by François's unexpected attack of conscience. Once Hugh was dead and Micaela was his, he might just have to do something about François.

François shifted in his seat. "You have not answered me, Alain. What is it you want me to do?"

Cheered by thoughts of the future, Alain laughed. "Oh, come now, *mon ami*—and I am your friend, even if you do not believe it—things are not so bad. And what I want you to do for me is very simple. I want you to invite me to come with you when you go to visit *Par Amour*."

"Why?"

Alain's jaw clenched. "Because I asked you to!"

François regarded him steadily for a long time. "And if I do not?"

"If you do not," Alain said with cold menace, "I shall see to it that your schemes to rob your own company, your blatant stealing from your own family are common knowledge." He smiled nastily. "By the time I am finished with you, just the mention of the name 'François Dupree' will bring a scandalous gasp to the lips of any respectable person who hears it."

François did not doubt him. For weeks now, he had been becoming more and more aware that Alain was not what he appeared to be, that behind his smile and polite manners lay something vicious and unprincipled. Alain knew people: not people François would ever introduce to his family: people who made François distinctly nervous. Alain seemed to have tentacles everywhere in the city, from the homes of the most rigid society matrons to the proprietors of the most despicable dens of sin, and François knew from things that he had learned in the heady days when he had been flattered by Alain's friendship that Alain arranged for unpleasant and shocking things to happen to anyone who displeased him.

Wearily François rested his dark head on the high back of the chair, his eyes closed. There seemed to be no way out. "I go to *Amour* on Thursday. Jean and I are traveling down together in the morning," he said expressionlessly. He opened his eyes and glanced at Alain. "I cannot simply bring you with me, I would have to ask Micaela if she minded if I invited you to visit with me a few days while I am there. She might not comply with my request, you know, and I can hardly insist that you be allowed to come."

"Then it will be up to you," Alain said sweetly, "to ensure that your sister *does* agree to my presence, will it not?"

François nodded slowly. "*Oui*. And not only Micaela—Hugh also must be convinced to allow you to stay. He is not going to be very happy about your inclusion."

At that very moment, Hugh was very happy. Micaela had given herself to him with a delightful abandon that had not been present in their previous lovemaking, and for the first time in their marriage he had the sweet and complete satisfaction of *knowing* that their lovemaking had given her pleasure. The signs and sounds of her enjoyment had been unmistakable, and he felt inordinately pleased with himself. Any doubts he had harbored about his skills in bed or his ability to bring his wife physical satisfaction had fled. And if he'd had to be shot and wounded to accomplish this, it seemed like a more than fair trade to him.

With Micaela's soft form lying next to his, her head nestled on his shoulder, his own body feeling as sated and replete as it had ever felt, Hugh did not want to think about the problems that still lay between them, but he was uneasily aware that he still had much to accomplish—such as making his wife fall in love with him. He also, despite the fact that he would freely admit that he was deeply and irrevocably in love with her, had not forgotten the events surrounding their marriage, nor that it was his fortune which held the greatest allure for her. That damning conversation he had overheard between her and François was still a corrosive, acidic trickle running through his happiness and Alice's words were additional drops of poison.

A tiny frown creased his forehead. He didn't want to think about the reasons for their marriage, especially not right now, but like persistent, irritating mosquitoes, they kept buzzing around in his head.

Micaela's thoughts were equally unpleasant. She was

deeply ashamed of her lascivious behavior in her husband's arms, and she was halfway braced for him to express his disapproval of her wanton ways. That he did not
worried her. Was he too disgusted to speak of it? Had she
repelled him? Was Hugh going to, as that long-ago Creole gentleman had, request a divorce because his wife
had so boldly responded to him?

And then there was the unresolved situation between
them. Nothing had actually been settled. The same problems that had confronted them before they had made love
still confronted them. Micaela would have been a fool,
however, if she had thought after the afternoon they had
just spent in each other's arms that she could retreat behind the coolly polite facade she had shown him these
past weeks. Only a fool would try to pretend this afternoon had never happened. And she did not think she was
a fool.

Lying beside him on the bed, listening to the even beating of his heart beneath her ear, she realized also that this
was precisely where she wanted to be. She did not want
the coolness between them to continue. But neither did
she want to go back to the admittedly pleasant weeks they
had enjoyed in the early days of their marriage. She and
perhaps, Hugh, too, had been pretending that all was well
in their marriage and ignoring reality. They had, she realized with embarrassment, been too busy enjoying each
other's bodies and the novelty of being married and setting up their own household to think very deeply about
the true state of their marriage.

But what *was* the true state of their marriage? Was their
situation so very different from the majority of Creole
unions? Many were almost straight business arrangements; the bride acquired a husband who took care of
providing her basic needs—shelter, food, status and re-

spectability—and the husband acquired a charming hostess who ran his household efficiently and with astonishing regularity presented him with handsome sons and lovely daughters. She knew of several marriages that had been arranged simply because it was prudent for the families to join forces, whether to consolidate fortunes, save plantations, or expand others. Or businesses, she thought with a grimace.

Unable to sleep, Micaela sat up cautiously. When Hugh gave no sign of being disturbed, she slid from the bed and quietly began to search for her clothing. With a wary eye on her napping husband, she dressed hastily.

Staring at him as he lay there on the bed, a lock of dark hair falling across his forehead, his ridiculously long lashes shadowing the cheekbones of his face, her heart clutched painfully in her breast. He was so dear. She loved him so much. She could not imagine life without him. Her gaze fell on his wound. And someone, she thought sickly, had tried to murder him. The terrifying knowledge of how easily, how swiftly he could have been taken from her, made her realize that it was petty to hold against him the manner in which he had brought about their marriage. Her gaze softened. No matter why he had married her, he had proven himself to be a kind and generous husband, and for *that* she would give him the respect and esteem he deserved. She would learn, she told herself sternly, not to harbor doubts. He was much too precious to her to waste time wondering about his motives. She loved him, and that was all there was to it. *She loved him.*

Hugh's eyes suddenly opened, meeting hers. He quirked a brow at the unmistakably tender expression on her face. "What?" he asked. "Why are you looking at me that way?"

She smiled slowly, an achingly lovely smile. "I was just thinking that I am very fortunate to have you as my husband."

Hugh's breath stopped at the sight of that dazzling smile, pleasure at her words spreading warmly through him. Then he scowled, suspicion sliding like a serpent through his mind. What was she up to? What did she want? She'd been treating him like a pariah up until a few hours ago, and while he had not expected her to retreat immediately behind the polite indifference she had shown him lately, he was not prepared simply to accept either her words or her damnably enchanting smile. There had to be a reason, other than the gloriously satisfying time they had just spent in each other's arms, to bring about such a drastic change in her manner toward him.

He was immediately appalled at his suspicions. Utterly aghast at how swiftly he had gone from contentment to being full of doubts and mistrust. In that split second, it became blindingly clear to him that until there was some plain speaking between them, until they were both honest with each other, that there would be no lasting happiness for them. Ugly suspicion and mistrust would be their constant companions, and he was grimly determined that such was not going to be the case.

He started to rise up, but his wounded arm reminded him forcibly, *painfully*, of the reason he was in bed in the first place. With a smothered curse, he fell back against the pillows.

When Micaela rushed forward and would have helped him, he held up a restraining hand. "No. We need to talk, and I will be the first to admit that when you are near me, *talking* is the last thing on my mind!"

Micaela blushed at the implication, her heart melting

with love for him. "What did you want to talk about?" she asked shyly.

Hugh shot her an irritated glance, fighting against the powerful urge to forget the whole thing. Did she have to look so appealing, just when he was ready to have a *very* uncomfortable conversation with her? Did she have to speak to him in that beguiling tone, making his sudden determination waver?

Having struggled up into a sitting position, he eyed her grimly. "You may drop the facade, my dear," he said bluntly, before he could change his mind about the wisdom of what he was doing. "I overheard your extremely revealing conversation that day at the gazebo. And I know precisely *why* you went to such lengths to marry me."

Chapter Seventeen

"*What?*" Micaela asked in obvious astonishment, her lovely smile fading as she stared at Hugh.

Hugh grimaced. She was going to pretend she didn't know what he was talking about, was she? For some reason, he found that deeply disappointing. From what he had overheard of their conversation, he knew that François and perhaps even Jean had put enormous pressure on her to marry him. When she had given into their pleas, she had done so more for their sakes than her own. It still stung him to remember that she had admitted to François that she did not like him very much and that not even his fortune had tempted her. Obviously, she had changed her mind, but he wished she would be honest with him. Marrying a man one did not love in order to save one's family was not such an ignoble act. Which did not mean he was happy about being married because of what he could do for her family. He was not. And the idea that Micaela considered marriage to him a sacrifice for the Dupree family's continued well-being left a distinctly nasty taste in his mouth.

"I said," he repeated coolly, "that I know why you married me. I did not mean to eavesdrop, but I overheard that rather revealing conversation you had with François at the gazebo at Riverbend."

When Micaela still looked puzzled, he went on harshly, "The one where your brother pleaded with you to marry me—I believe he referred to me as 'young and handsome and a man who would someday be one of the wealthiest, most influential citizens in New Orleans'—or something of that nature." He smiled grimly. "And then there is the matter of that sharp tongue of yours. Who else felt its lash as I did?"

Micaela's eyes widened in dawning comprehension. A bitter laugh was startled from her. "You thought that François was referring to *you?*"

Hugh winced at the scorn in her voice. "Considering what happened, I think it was an honest assumption," he replied levelly.

Her eyes flashed, and she was suddenly, blazingly furious at him. To think such a thing of her! "You think that I married you for my family? That I connived and trapped you into marriage so I could get my hands on your money?"

She looked like an angry young tigress as she stood there before him, her hair in wild disarray around her shoulders, her cheeks blooming with angry roses and those dark eyes full of fire. Her hands were on her hips and her temptingly shaped mouth was tight with fury.

Her obvious wrath gave him pause, and somewhat warily, he answered, "It seemed likely, after overhearing that conversation and your subsequent actions. You *did* put us in a compromising situation. A situation which forced our marriage—and gave you access to my fortune."

Micaela's dainty nostrils flared with suppressed fury.

"You arrogant, conceited, snooping *snake*! Do you really think that François wanted me to marry *you*!" She laughed angrily. "Your belief, *monsieur*, in your own charms and wealth is far superior to reality. *It was Alain Husson whom François wanted me to marry.* François is deeply in debt to him, and if I had married Alain, the debt would have been paid. You, I am sorry to say, would have been the *last* person François would have wanted me to marry!"

Hugh's brow snapped together in a ferocious frown. Her anger was very real, and he suddenly realized with a sickening lurch in the region of his belly that what she said made sense. Perfect sense. Of course, François would not have wanted her to marry him. Of course, Alain Husson would have been the logical choice. With growing chagrin, Hugh recalled again that he had even heard gossip that Alain was courting her. And he had known about François's debt to Alain. What a block-headed buffoon he had been to leap to the, no use pretending otherwise, *conceited* conclusion that it was himself François had been urging her to marry. There were, he admitted wryly, other young men who also fit François's description—only he had been too arrogant to realize it. Or perhaps, he simply had not wanted to realize it. He had, it seemed, completely misunderstood the situation.

Like a man grasping at straws, he said desperately, "But you arranged for us to be found in that old hunting shack. You deliberately stayed behind with me. Tell me that was an accident!"

Her lip curled. "*Non, monsieur*," she said sweetly. "That was no accident. It was a simple act of human kindness. I thought that you were hurt. I thought that I was *helping* you."

Appalled, Hugh stared at her, every word she said shattering his conception of the reasons behind their marriage. She had claimed to be innocent before, but he had not believed her. He had thought she was lying, but only because of what he had overheard. If *Alain* had been the man her brother had urged her to marry . . . then their being found alone had just been . . . unfortunate. Her stopping to help him had been entirely innocent and *not* part of a clever scheme to trap him into marriage. He swallowed painfully.

Of course, he reminded himself weakly, she could be lying now. Alain might not have been the subject of that overheard conversation, no name had ever been mentioned, but Hugh knew that he was only chasing will-o'-the-wisps. The conversation made entirely too much sense if he substituted Alain for himself. He had, he realized uneasily, blundered badly—at least in one respect. But remembering Alice's words that Micaela had admitted to her that their marriage was purely business, he said, "On our wedding day you told Alice Summerfield you had only married me because—"

Micaela did not allow him to finish. "*Alice Summerfield!* How dare you say her name to me! I told her nothing! Why should I? She was a stranger to me. But you!" Her lip curled contemptuously. "She told me a great deal about you! You married me, loving her—you deserted her, broke your promises of marriage to her to marry me. What does that make you?"

Hugh's brows snapped together. "What the devil are you talking about? There was never anything between Alice and me except friendship." Suddenly he looked a little guilty. "There was a time that I . . . did consider marriage with her, but nothing came of it—I never loved her, nor did I ever say such a thing to her—or offer marriage to her. And if she said any differently, she was lying."

Even as he defended himself, Hugh realized precisely how Alice had played them one against the other. He and Micaela had been strangers forced into marriage—they had known little about each other, and there certainly had been no trust between them. How easy it had been for Alice to meld fact and fiction, to plant seeds of doubt in Micaela's head, as well as his own. He could not excuse himself for misunderstanding the conversation he'd overheard between Micaela and François, but he should have recognized Alice's words for what they were—the mendacious jabs of a jealous woman. Alice had confirmed his own worst fears, and she had obviously given Micaela an entirely erroneous impression of their relationship.

Across the short space that divided them, he eyed his wife. His very beautiful, very *angry* wife. She did not look, he decided ruefully, to be in the mood to listen to any apologies or explanations he might offer. And he was very aware that there was little he could say to excuse his arrogant assumptions. But he had to try.

Attempting a smile, he said helplessly, "Micaela, I owe you—"

"Ah, bah!" she snapped. "I do not want to hear any more silliness from you. You have blamed me from the beginning for our marriage when it is *you* who connived and schemed."

"I most certainly did not!" Hugh said indignantly, outraged that she thought such a thing of him.

"*Non?* Forgive me if I doubt your word. Is it not true that when we married, Jean turned over control of my shares to you?"

"Well, yes, but that was only because I am your husband, dammit. They are not my shares, however, they are yours. I am only holding them for you much in the same way your uncle did."

"Ah, so then, my shares in the company mean nothing to you? I could demand that you give them to me and you would? I could say, give them away to . . . Alain, and it would not bother you?"

Hugh hesitated, fatally. Micaela smiled grimly. "Never mind," she said coolly. "I do not want to hear your lying answers." She pointed a slim, accusing finger at him. "It is you, *monsieur*, who trapped me—you who pretended to be hurt and who pretended to fall asleep so that we would be found in such a compromising situation. That is what François believes. He believes you did it deliberately in order to force me to marry you and gain control of my shares, thereby increasing your control of the company."

"*Blast* the damned company!" Hugh burst out angrily, just as furious as she. His gray eyes glittering dangerously, he demanded, "And what do you think? Do you really think that I would stoop to such dishonorable tactics?"

She regarded him for a long moment. "Why should I not?" she finally asked. "You believed it of me." And she spun on her heel and stalked from the room.

"*Micaela!* Dammit, do not walk away from me!" Hugh shouted after her departing form, but she ignored him, and, a moment later, he was alone. Alone to contemplate the quagmire into which he had blindly stumbled. Or perhaps, not so blindly, he thought furiously. Pigheadedly was more like it.

Hugh spent the remainder of the afternoon alone in his bedroom brooding over his mistakes, planning and discarding a dozen schemes to redeem himself with his angry wife. Nothing terribly useful came to mind. He had erred, badly, and it appeared that he was going to have to suffer for it.

Dinner that evening was a peculiar affair. On the surface, everything was as it should be; Micaela was lively and full of smiles, Lisette continued her role of polite in-law toward John Lancaster, and the two men both acted as if they had not a care in the world.

Still smarting from the argument with Micaela, Hugh was on his best behavior. He warmly complimented his wife on the meal, wild duck stewed with young turnips; commented approvingly on the changes she had wrought in the house and mentioned how charming she looked in her gown of jonquil silk and lace, but all his efforts gained him was a cool stare. John did not fare much better. The conversation during dinner was naturally of a general nature, but after dinner, it was decided that the four of them would brave the mosquitoes for a few minutes and take a short walk in the warm, moonlit evening. When the younger couple strolled ahead of them, John hoped for a private word or two with Lisette, who was walking sedately beside him, her hand resting lightly on his arm.

He thought she had never looked lovelier. Her dark eyes here bright and glowing, her black hair was worn swept up on top of her head, affixed with a gleaming jeweled comb that winked in the moonlight, and the ruby-colored gown she was wearing intensified the ivory hue of her shoulders and arms. Aware of the powerful attraction she still exerted over him, John said softly, "You look very beautiful tonight, more beautiful than I ever remember seeing you."

Lisette glanced at him, one slim brow arched. "Indeed,

monsieur. Does that mean I looked like a hag previously?"

John scowled. "That was not what I meant, and you know it."

Lisette shrugged. "It is not necessary for you to pay me compliments. I am long past the days when pretty words turned my head."

John bit back a curse. Controlling himself with an effort, he muttered, "I was not trying to turn your head—I was merely commenting on how nice you look this evening."

"*Merci,*" she said coolly, "but I would prefer if you did not make personal comments. We are nearly strangers to each other and only the marriage of my daughter and your stepson forms any sort of bond between us. Please remember that in the future."

Gritting his teeth and stifling a strong urge to shake her . . . and then take her into his arms and kiss her senseless, John wisely made no further attempts to breach the wall she had placed between them.

The arrival of Jean and François two days later, on Thursday, was greeted with great relief by everyone. The intervening time had not been *un*pleasant, but Hugh and John were very conscious of treading on thin ice around a pair of unfailingly polite, but frustratingly elusive ladies. The two men viewed the arrival of another pair of males almost as much-needed reinforcements in a war they seemed to have no hope of winning. As for the ladies, they, too, were delighted at the influx of company, the strain of trying to keep two determined men firmly in place and at arm's length beginning to fray their nerves.

Hugh was still wearing his arm in a sling, but the wound was healing nicely, and in a week or two he would

be completely recovered. Naturally, the attack on him
was of great concern to Jean and François. After the first
flurry of greetings had been exchanged, the attack became the topic of conversation when the group retreated
inside to the relative coolness of the house.

Once refreshments were served and consumed, and all
aspects of the attack on Hugh and the condition of his
wound had been thoroughly explored, the two guests
were shown to their rooms. It was midafternoon, the air
still and muggy, the sun a great blazing orange globe in
the cloudless blue sky. Everyone wisely chose to remain
inside relaxing, until the worst of the humid heat had dissipated.

Since Micaela was not sharing his bed again, and had
not since their disastrous argument, Hugh found time
heavy on his hands. He was not used to indolence and his
wound, while not really incapacitating, did hamper his
activities. It would have helped if he could have en-
meshed himself in the affairs of the business, but here in
the country even that escape was denied him. Restless
and bored, he had already gone over the account books of
the plantation and yesterday had conferred a long while
with the new overseer about plans for the future of
Amour.

Ordinarily, Hugh enjoyed living in the country, partaking eagerly of those activities which were common occurrences, but there would be no hunting, fishing, or
riding for him for a few days yet. Nor, in the face of the
oppressive heat and humidity, which caused even the
lightest clothing to cling damply to one's skin, did Hugh
view a drive with any great enthusiasm.

Neither did his rather lonely bedroom hold much allure. Wistfully, he looked at the big inviting bed, remembering the joy he had shared with Micaela there just a few

days ago, and he wondered if those moments would ever come again. Realistically, he knew that they would—he certainly did not envision spending the rest of his life barred completely from his wife's dazzling smiles and warm laughter, or her distractingly enchanting body—but he knew that her anger at him was not going to abate anytime soon. He did not blame her for feeling as she did.

Deciding that he had nothing to gain by brooding in his bedroom, he sought out more congenial surroundings. It was quiet in the big house this time of day. Seeking out the cheerful, airy room on the east side of the house that Micaela had chosen for his study, he was pleased to find John sitting there browsing through a copy of *Le Moniteur de la Louisiane*, the New Orleans French newspaper, which Jean had brought with him.

Seeing his stepson in the doorway, John happily tossed aside the newspaper. Smiling he said, "I will be glad when John Mowry's *Louisiana Gazette* is published next month. *Le Moniteur* seems to be full of nothing but business advertisements and bills of lading—only occasionally is there any mention of anything of interest happening. I hope Mowry's paper, when he finally begins publishing, will prove to be more informative."

Hugh shrugged. "Who can tell, but I am certain that the Americans who do not read French will welcome it."

Like most of the house at present, the study was sparsely furnished. A fanciful carved mahogany framed mirror hung over the black marble mantel of the fireplace; a brass and crystal candelabra sat at either end of the mantel. Fresh, sweet-smelling straw matting covered a portion of the gleaming cypress floor, and from the furnishings that went with the house, Micaela had selected for use in the study a pair of large comfortable chairs covered in russet leather; a long, narrow walnut table, and four cane-bottomed chairs which she had scattered about the large room for the time being.

Choosing the leather chair opposite John, Hugh sat down, stretched his long legs out in front of him and gave a contented sigh. "I think that I am very pleased with my new house. What is your opinion?"

John smiled. "It is a fine house, Hugh. And I dare say that once Micaela and her mother finish furnishing it, it will no doubt be an exceedingly grand home."

"And I shall more than likely be destitute," Hugh returned grinning.

The two men talked desultorily for several moments, then Hugh asked abruptly, "Have you thought any more about selling out in Natchez and joining me here in Louisiana?"

"I have thought of little else these past few days," John replied with unaccustomed moodiness.

One of Hugh's brows rose. "And?"

John shot him a dark look. "Did you know," he suddenly asked, "that I once thought to marry your very beautiful mother-in-law?"

Hugh jerked upright. Astonishment evident on his face, he exclaimed, "Sweet Jesu, no! I knew that there had been another woman in your life before you and Mother decided to marry, and that she was the reason you were willing to settle for a marriage of convenience, but I never guessed—"

"My marriage to your mother was one of the best things that ever happened to me. I knew how she felt about your father, and she knew how I felt about Lisette, although she did not know her name. She only knew that there had been someone, someone else who still held my heart." John sighed and stared out the bank of tall windows which flanked a pair of French doors and overlooked an oak-and-magnolia-shaded expanse of lawn. "Despite both of us knowing our hearts were given elsewhere, jealousy," John said slowly, "was never an emotion between us. We respected how the other one felt and we were grateful for the companionship and affection that we were able to share." He flashed Hugh a fond look. "I was especially happy to be your stepfather. You are a fine man, and I hope you will allow me to take a little of the credit for that fact."

"Gladly, sir, you know that. After Mother died, I do not know what I would have done without you. I barely remember my own father, and I do not think it cruel of me to say that you are the only father I have ever known. I am proud to be your son."

"Perhaps," John said slowly, "fate really does arrange events to work out for the best. If I had married Lisette, you would not be my stepson, and your very lovely bride would never have been born."

"May I say, though you suffered for it and I am sorry for that, I am very, *very* grateful you did not marry Lisette. I could bear much, but not a world in which there was no Micaela."

"A very handsome sentiment, my boy, one I am sure would please your wife."

Hugh snorted. "The way she is feeling about me right now, I doubt it."

"Trouble?"

"Nothing that will not pass. The silly little fool believes I married her to gain control of the company! Anyone with a pair of eyes can see that I am thoroughly besotted by her." He grimaced. "Everyone but the lady in question."

John grinned. "And have you told the lady in question how you feel?"

"I have tried, dammit, but it is deucedly hard to lay one's heart bare when the object of one's devotion is determined to meet any attempt at reconciliation with an icy stare and a haughty toss of her head."

"I know precisely what you are going through," John replied with feeling.

"My esteemed and utterly charming *maman*-in-law?"

John nodded, his expression grim. "Noticed that, have you? I do not know how she has done it, but she has managed to make me the guilty party in what happened between us years ago—when she was the one who jilted me! And worse, dismissed me with a mere note and sent her father and that bastard Renault to confirm the shattering news that she did not want to marry me after all. They took great pleasure in telling me that she was going to marry Renault before the month ended." John took in a deep breath. "I did not believe them at first when they confronted me and told me, but her note and the fact that they seemed to know all about our plans finally convinced me. I knew she was devoted to her father—I will agree that the note was probably coerced out of her—but in the end she did write it." He sighed. "I knew that Christophe had been eagerly pushing a match between Lisette and Renault, but I was certain our love was stronger, that she could hold out against their pressure. I was obviously wrong." A faraway look entered his eyes. "And yet, and yet she had given me the most incontrovertible proof of love a woman can give a man. I would have sworn on my life that she loved me! What folly! I should have been prepared for what happened, and I would have been, if I had not taken one look at her and fallen deeply in love." He shook his head. "I was a fool! I knew right from the beginning that one of the reasons the Duprees were brought into the business in the first place was because of the hoped-for marriage between Lisette and Renault. Christophe's reasons were strictly practical, aside from the fact that Renault was considered quite a catch. By marrying Lisette to one of the other partners, he would not have to take as much money out of his own pockets to put into the partnership. To his way of thinking, it kept the business in the family. Of course," John said bitterly, "marriage to me, the largest share-holder, was out of the question. I was an *Américain!*"

Thanks to Jasper's determined partisan sponsorship of him, he had not been the victim of that sort of open prejudice himself, but Hugh understood exactly how John felt. And, he reminded himself with a funny little leap in his pulse, I am far luckier than my stepfather. I was able to marry my own little Creole enchantress.

"How do you feel about Lisette now?" Hugh asked quietly. "Is it uncomfortable for you to be around her?"

"Hell, yes! It is uncomfortable, damned uncomfort-able, I can tell you, but having seen her again, it would be a thousand times worse *not* to be around her!"

"Ah," Hugh murmured, a knowing grin curving his mouth, "so that is the way the wind is blowing. I had wondered. One could not help noticing the impact the pair of you have on each other."

John flashed him a dark look. "Get that smug expres-sion off your face, young man! And stop grinning. There is nothing amusing about my situation."

"Of course not," Hugh replied meekly, but his grin did not abate. "What are you going to do about it?"

"If I can ever get a moment alone with the tart-tongued little witch, I intend to make her listen to me and make it clear to her that I did *not* desert her—she deserted me! After that I will make *her* explain precisely where she got such a foolish notion and why she sent her father and the

Duprees to send me away in such a cruel manner. And then, as insane as it may sound, I intend to propose to her again and again, until she finally comes to her senses and realizes that I am the only man for her." His jaw hardened. "That I was *always* the only man for her."

Hugh did not envy his stepfather his task. Micaela was very like her mother, and, with a distinct feeling of unease, he realized that his situation was not so very different than John's predicament. Micaela blamed him for their marriage and believed that he had married her only for the business. Since Lisette blamed John for what happened years ago, it appeared that Lisette, in spite of her own note to him, believed that John had simply deserted her. But notes, he thought suddenly, could be forged.

Hugh stiffened. His gaze intent, he leaned forward. "You recognized her handwriting? And you never spoke to Lisette again until you met her here on Monday?"

John nodded.

"You said she loved you and had agreed to run away with you. Did you believe her, or did you think she was lying when she said those words?"

John's face softened. "I believed her. It took me a long time before I realized that Christophe must have played upon her affection and family loyalty in order to convince her that it was best that she not marry me."

"But at the time you never talked about it with her? You simply took your wounded heart back to Natchez and put it from you?"

"Well, yes," John said, puzzled. "I did not have much choice."

Hugh smiled grimly. "If you did not talk to the lady yourself, then how do you know that *she* sent Galland and the Duprees to meet with you? How do you know *she* wrote the note? I have heard often enough what an underhanded schemer Renault Dupree was and what a crafty devil old Christophe was. Is it not possible that somehow they got wind of what was planned and confronted you each separately, telling each of you that the other had changed their mind?"

John looked thunderstruck. He paled, then flushed. His eyes widened. He opened his mouth to speak, then shut it with a snap.

Hugh leaned back in his chair. Amusement in his eyes, he murmured, "I see that such a thought never occurred to you. But it is possible?"

John nodded slowly. Recovering himself somewhat, he muttered, "Those *bastards*! The events you put forth sound exactly like something that Christophe and Renault would have done—and I can easily surmise the identity of the person who exposed our plans—that blasted French maid of Lisette's! She was always spying on her, snooping through Lisette's things. Lisette was fond of her, could never believe that Musetta, or whatever her name was, would ever do any harm. Ha! I cannot prove it, but I'd wager half my fortune that she was the one who ran to Christophe with the information that Lisette and I were planning to run away together."

"So what are you going to do about it?"

"There is precious little I can do about it now—both the men are dead—but I can confront Lisette with what we suspect and find out if she did write the note. If the note *was* forged, I intend to make her see that I never deserted her." A glow entered John's dark eyes. "And that I never stopped loving her. . . ."

"What about Jean? How much do you think he knew?"

John hesitated. "In those days, he was just a boy, and he was fervently attached to Renault. It is possible that he did not know the whole truth. He may have believed implicitly the tale concocted by Renault and Christophe."

"Since it is mere conjecture that brought us to these conclusions, before we proceed further, I have to ask you: are you absolutely convinced that Lisette is innocent? That she did not do precisely as you were told?"

A grim smile played at the corners of John's mouth. "There is only way to find out, is there not?"

With the influx of company, dinner that evening was an enjoyable affair. Though Hugh's thoughts were on the thorny problems that existed between him and Micaela, he was reasonably confident enough of the outcome that he could relax and find, much to his surprise, that Jean and François could be very entertaining guests when they put their minds to it.

Jean seemed finally to have accepted the unpalatable fact that a despised *Américain* was now part of his family and that the very same *Américain* was going to continue to play an active role in the affairs of Galland, Lancaster and Dupree. The unexpected rapport that had sprung up between Jean and John did not appear to be abating, and Hugh wondered how much of Jean's dislike of things and people American had had to do with Renault's attitude toward them. Perhaps, he was discovering that Americans were not the grasping, greedy, barbaric monsters he had first thought?

As for François, there was something different about him this evening that Hugh could not quite put his finger on. The young man was polite and charming enough, but he seemed preoccupied, and from the surreptitious glances sent his way, Hugh suspected that it had something to do with him. But what? More displeasure about the running of the company? Hugh did not think so.

François was being too friendly and undeniably pleasant for it to be something disagreeable. Mayhap, like Jean, François had finally come to accept the situation gracefully? Hugh hoped so, but he had the uneasy feeling that trouble with François was not yet a thing of the past. The young man was too hot-tempered, too volatile for his own good. But it was most enjoyable, for the moment, to have the two Creole men in his house and at his table and displaying all the good manners and vaulted charm of their culture.

As for John and Lisette, it was apparent from Lisette's chilly, polite expression whenever she replied to his stepfather that John had not yet had a chance to speak to her alone. Hugh smiled. It was going to be interesting having Lisette as not only a mother-in-law, but a stepmother, too. And he had no doubts about *that* outcome.

Hugh shot a considering glance down the long length of the linen-covered table to where his wife sat at the other end. Was he being overly confident, feeling that he could gain her good graces once more?

A warm light in the depths of his gray eyes, his gaze ran over her. She was, in his opinion, the dearest thing in the world. Watching her laugh at some sally of François's, his heart clenched. He wanted that laughter for himself. And she was a damned silly goose if she believed for one moment that he had married her for the blasted company! He had been in love with her for a long time—a long time before he had realized it himself. Now, he thought wryly, all he had to do was convince her of it. His mind momentarily taken up with considering the best method to change her stubborn mind, and the marriage-bed delights that would be his, Hugh was not paying close attention to the conversation. It wasn't until he realized that everyone was staring at him that he became aware that his wife had posed a question for him.

A set smile on her lovely face, her dark eyes glittering with a challenging light, Micaela said for obviously the second time, "François has just asked if he might invite Alain to stay here at *Amour* for a few days." Fairly daring him to contradict her, she added demurely, "I told him that I would be delighted to open my home to such a dear, *dear* old family friend and that, naturally, you would have no objections."

Chapter Eighteen

*T*orn between laughter and a strong desire to swear, Hugh stared back at her. Lifting his wineglass in a private toast to her audacity, he murmured, "Of course I have no objections to Alain's presence in my home, if that is your wish, my love." He smiled like a tiger. "Any friend of yours, my dear, is naturally a friend of mine. I shall look forward to his visit." He glanced at François. "And when," he asked with nothing more apparent than courteous interest, "would *Monsieur* Husson be arriving?"

Uneasily, François looked from Micaela to Hugh. "I—uh—thought that if it was agreeable I would write him a note tomorrow and have a servant deliver it to his home in the afternoon. It would probably be at least Saturday or Sunday before he arrived."

"Good!" Hugh said heartily. "We shall look forward to his visit." He sent his wife a bland look. "Will we not, my dear?"

Nonplussed, Micaela stared back at him. She had not expected him to create a scene, but she certainly had not been prepared for him just calmly to accept Alain's intrusion into what was essentially a family gathering. She had been positive that he would attempt, even if only briefly, to wiggle politely out of inviting Alain to stay with them, and she had been looking forward with relish to watching him squirm. Instead he had turned the tables on her and had graciously acceded to François's request. Feeling slightly deflated and losing all interest in Alain Husson's proposed visit, she shrugged and muttered, "*Oui*. It will be most pleasant."

The conversation passed on to other topics, but Micaela only paid half a mind to what was being said. Watching her husband's dark face as he laughed at some comment made by Jean, she was aware of a sensation of despair. She loved him—the handsome, unfeeling wretch! And he obviously did not love her—during the past two days he had made no *real* attempt to heal the breach between them and had apparently calmly accepted her cool rebuffs to the few overtures he had made. If he cared anything at all for her, he would not have let the strained situation between them continue. Nor, she admitted miserably, would he have allowed them to sleep apart. It was insultingly clear to her from the way he was acting that he felt only the most tepid of emotions where she was concerned. Why else would he have agreed so easily to have as a guest in their home a man he knew had been a rival for her hand? Bah! She did not understand him at all!

There was one tiny glimpse of light on her dark horizon—Hugh's denial of Alice Summerfield's assertions. The American woman's words had long haunted Micaela, and his statement that there had only been friendship between them rang true. Besides, Micaela desperately wanted to believe him. If she took his words as fact, at least she would be able to banish the specter of being married to a man who loved another. Of course, she admitted gloomily, he could be lying, but in this instance, she did not think that he was. She was wise enough to realize now, with the aid of hindsight, that Alice might just have been spewing venom hoping to cause problems between them—which was precisely what had happened. Alice's words alone would not have been enough, but, coupled with the circumstances, they had certainly added their own share of misery.

But why, she wondered unhappily, had he agreed so amiably to Alain's inclusion in what was primarily a family gathering? Perhaps, she mused with an ache in her heart, she meant so little to him that Alain's presence meant nothing to him?

With her vivid imagination easily conjuring up a bleak future, she felt a profound sense of relief when she finally rose from the table at the end of the meal. Leaving the gentlemen to their Madeira and sherry, she escaped into the sitting room with her mother. While Lisette sank gracefully into a delicate rosewood chair covered in pale green damask, Micaela moved restlessly about the room.

After watching her pacings for several moments, Lisette asked quietly, "What did you hope to accomplish by staging that scene tonight, *petite*? Inviting Alain Husson to come and stay here was not a very wise thing to do. It was foolish of François to make such a request of you in the first place, but you were twice as foolish to challenge your husband in that manner." She hesitated, then went on slowly, "I trust that you have not come to regret that you did not accept Alain's offer when you had the chance?"

Micaela made a face. "*Non.* I do not care a fig for Alain Husson. I love my husband—but he is *such* a dolt!"

Lisette smiled, the faint frown of worry which had creased her forehead vanishing. "Ah. I understand completely. Men can be so, so, stupid sometimes, can they not?"

Micaela eyed her mother speculatively, her own troubles suddenly forgotten. "Oh? Is any particular male proving to be annoyingly stupid these days, besides my husband, of course?"

It was Lisette's turn to make a face. "It shames me to admit it, but even knowing that he abandoned me all those years before, I still find John Lancaster far too attractive for my own good. For my peace of mind I wish he *had* been bald and fat!" She sighed. "When he smiles at me, when he looks at me, I forget everything and remember only that I loved him passionately once. I have tried keeping him at arm's length, but he is doggedly persistent." An angry sparkle lit her fine eyes. "Perhaps," she muttered, "if he had been as persistent years ago as he is now, things might have been different. But too much has happened. He betrayed me and hurt me immeasurably. I cannot forgive him, nor could I ever trust him again. But he still has the power to charm me, and it frightens me. I am afraid that if he decides to make a long visit with you, I may go home early." She glanced uncertainly at Micaela. "Will you mind?"

Considering her own troubles, Micaela understood perfectly how her mother felt. She shook her head, and said gently, "I will miss you, but we shall have other visits when there are no annoyingly stupid males around, *oui*?"

"Or at least," Lisette replied with a twinkle, "you shall have ceased feuding with your husband and decided that he is not quite so annoyingly stupid?"

Micaela looked wretched. "I do not think that he cares anything for me, *Maman*." Too ashamed to admit that Hugh had thought her the greatest conniver alive, she stared blankly out the windows, furiously blinking back an embarrassing rush of tears.

Lisette smiled. "*Petite*, you do not see the way he looks at you. I cannot say whether he loves you or not, but he cares a very great deal for you. As I mentioned previously, it is obvious to anyone who is in the same room with you both."

"Oh, *Maman*, are you *sure*?"

Lisette's smile became incredibly tender as Micaela swung around to face her. "As sure as I can be of anything, *ma chérie*." She looked down at her hands folded in her lap and said slowly, "Micaela, I have warned myself against being a meddling *maman*, but I would give you some words of advice. Do not let pride and little misunderstandings destroy what you and Hugh already have. Talk honestly to your husband, let him know how you feel about him, tell him that he has made you unhappy and why. If after that, he still continues in the same manner, then you will know that his actions are deliberate and not just unthinking or unknowing."

Micaela bit her lip. "But suppose you are wrong? Suppose he does not care as deeply for me as you seem to think? I will have humiliated myself—and for nothing!"

Lisette sent her a long look. "Pride is a cold companion. Do you wish to share your bed for the rest of your life with only your pride to keep away the night's chill? Or do you want a warm and loving husband by your side? It is true that I might be wrong. Hugh might not love you; he might have simply married you because of the business. Do you not want to find out the truth?"

Her eyes huge in her face, Micaela stared at her mother. "I am frightened, *Maman*," she admitted reluctantly. "I think I almost prefer not knowing how he feels, if it means learning that he really *did* marry me just for business reasons."

"Listen to me, *petite!*" Lisette said urgently. "Your marriage came about as it did because of an unfortunate set of circumstances. Hugh was as trapped as you were. But that does not mean that if you had been given time, he would not have courted you and married you in a more traditional fashion. It is only because you feel you were forced to marry him that you are so uncertain about him. And as for François's opinion that Hugh deliberately arranged events to his own advantage—it is all nonsense! Only the wild conjectures of a hotheaded, foolish, and impetuous boy. François does not really believe it himself, though he would rather choke than admit it to anyone. You know your brother, he is always full of fits and starts." The twinkle suddenly returned to Lisette's eyes. "And since when has your brother's opinion mattered so much to you anyway? Are you not clinging to François's silly idea as a way to protect yourself from possible hurt?" When Micaela remained silent, she asked softly, "Do you really enjoy living in this netherworld you seem to have created? Neither lover, nor enemy?"

Micaela took a deep breath. "*Non!* But I do not feel very brave at the moment. I am angry and confused. And I would not be very sensible if I were to confront him right now."

"You do not have to face him right away, *ma chérie.* Think about it, if you wish. But Micaela," Lisette said warningly, "do not wait too long. You may miss a chance for real happiness and have only yourself to blame. The situation which currently exists could become a habit."

Micaela managed to get through the remainder of the evening, and she even found herself smiling at some of the quips thrown out by the gentlemen when they joined the ladies a short while later. She could not deny, however, that she was grateful when the evening ended and she was able to retreat to her own suite of rooms.

Lying alone in her big gauze-swathed bed, she played over and over again in her mind the evening's events, her mother's words echoing in her head. Her mother was right. Micaela knew that. And she had never considered herself a coward, but when she envisioned seeking out her husband and boldly revealing that she was in love with him and that she wanted his love in return, her courage failed. Even Lisette's reassurances that Hugh *did* care deeply for her did not revive her quailing spirits. Perhaps if they had not had that terrible argument on Monday afternoon. . . .

She spent a restless night and the soft lemony rose glow of daylight found her still with no definite plan. But the situation could not go on, she decided wearily, as she lay there staring at the spreading golden light. *Maman* was right—it could become a habit—a terrible one.

Micaela was not the only one to wake at dawn from a night of less than restful repose. John Lancaster had spent much of the night wrestling with his bedclothes and getting little sleep, the knowledge that he and Lisette might both have been duped revolving like a glowing beacon in his brain. By dawn, he was determined to have a private word with her, even if he had to abduct her to do it.

Springing from his bed, he dressed hastily, his brain formulating several different methods of accomplishing his goal. Having decided upon the most immediate needs for his scheme to work, he raced from his room and though daylight had just broken, instantly set his scheme in motion.

After having taken care of the practical matters, John

went in search of Hugh. Fortunately Hugh was an early riser, and, finding his stepson sipping his first cup of coffee of the day, John asked for a private word with him. Hugh studied his stepfather's face for a second and, rising to his feet, suggested they retire to the study, where they were not likely to be interrupted.

Hardly waiting until Hugh had shut the door behind him, John said bluntly, "If the truth is to be discovered, I must speak privately with Lisette. Since she has thwarted my every attempt to do so, I have decided upon desperate measures." He took a deep breath and blurted out, "I intend to abduct her, and I need your help."

Hugh's brow rose. "Indeed. And how may I help you in this exceedingly—er—desperate endeavor."

John grinned at him, suddenly looking boyish. "You can make excuses for our absence, no matter how long it may be."

A glimmer of amusement lurking in the depths of his gray eyes, Hugh nodded. "Of course. You know that you may depend upon me. Do I dare ask how you hope to accomplish your task?"

The boyish looked increased. "I have already ordered two horses saddled and asked Cook to see to it that suitable food and drink is packed in the saddlebags. It is unlikely that anyone except ourselves and a few servants is awake at this hour. Since there is practically no one to see me, or to give her aid, should I be so foolish as to allow her to seek it, I intend to march up to Lisette's rooms and compel her to come with me."

"And how do you plan to compel her to come with you?" Hugh asked, trying not to laugh.

"By carefully explaining what would happen should I be found in her bedroom at this hour of the morning—or any other morning, for that matter," John replied with a resolute gleam in his eyes. "Though she is a widow and allowed much license, the thought of a man, especially if I am the man, being discovered in her bedroom by a member of her family will, I am certain, make her very agreeable to following my orders. And since I intend to make my threat to create a scandal, either this morning, or another of my choosing, very real, I do not believe I will get much of an argument out of her." John suddenly sighed, looking not quite so cheerful. "I wish there was some other method to obtain a private conversation with her, but she has forced this situation upon me." He glanced almost pleadingly at Hugh. "All I am really asking of her is that she accompany me to someplace private, where we can discuss without interruption what happened to destroy our plans to marry over twenty years ago. It is not too much to ask, is it?"

Hugh shook his dark head. "No," he said quietly. "Not too much at all."

Except for a dicey moment in Lisette's room, when to his dismay, he found that Lisette had already arisen and was seated at her dressing table arranging her hair, John's plan proceeded smoothly. It had been an unpleasant shock even to find her awake, and, spying a cup of coffee and a half-eaten beignet sitting near the edge of the dressing table, he stifled a curse. He had counted on finding her half-drowsy and still abed, *not* fully awake and able to think quickly and clearly. He planned to get her well away from the house before she realized what was really happening, but listening to her humming softly to herself as she finished braiding her lustrous hair and fashioning the two thick braids into a tidy coronet around the top of her head, he knew he would not be able to rely on her befuddled state to aid him.

He hesitated just inside the French doors in her room, which opened onto the upper gallery. Half-hidden by the printed green-and-white cotton draperies, which had been pulled back on either side of the doors, John considered his position. He decided grimly that boldness would just have to carry him through. So when Lisette rose from her dressing table and approached the heavily carved armoire which was positioned against the far wall, he stepped brazenly out from his place of concealment.

Lisette caught a glimpse of him out of the corner of her eye and uttered a startled gasp, whirling to face in his direction. In a flash he was across the room, his hand going to her mouth, his other arm wrapping around her and pulling her next to him.

"Hush!" he whispered quickly. "I mean you no harm, but I must speak with you."

She made a notable attempt to escape him, but finding that she could not, she finally ceased her struggles and contented herself with glaring up at him, her dark eyes spitting fury. She looked, John thought idiotically, utterly enchanting.

"If I remove my hand from your mouth, have I your promise that you will not scream?" he asked softly.

Lisette nodded curtly. The moment his hand was removed, she demanded furiously, "Have you gone mad? What are you doing here? *Dieu!* If you were to be found here, there would be a terrible scandal. What were you thinking? What is so important that you could not wait to talk to me in more appropriate surroundings?" Determinedly she began to propel him toward the French doors. "You must leave immediately! No one must find you here."

John dug in his heels, refusing to budge, and when her efforts to remove him from her rooms proved futile, she stopped and hissed, "Did you not hear me? You cannot be found here. My children would be scandalized. And as for Jean! *Dieu!* I cannot even think of *his* reaction. You *must* leave this instant!"

John smiled down at her flushed, angry features. "Oh, I intend on leaving," he said slowly, "but not without you."

"*What*? Are you mad? *Zut!* I will go nowhere with you."

"Very well," John replied equitably and, selecting a small cypress chair near the French doors, sat down. Still smiling, he crossed his arms comfortably over his chest and said amiably, "Since you feel unable to accompany me at this moment, I shall sit here and wait until you are ready."

Lisette's eyes narrowed. "Have you been drinking? Is that why you are acting like a fool?"

"No, I have not been drinking, and I am not acting like a fool." His voice hardened. "I am, however, acting like a man whose patience has run out. I want to talk to you— privately, and I am not leaving this room until you agree to give me what I want."

Lisette threw a harassed glance around. If anyone, even a servant, were to find him here! She looked down at her simple dimity wrapper, suddenly aware of her nakedness underneath it. *Dieu!* She had to think quickly.

Resentfully she eyed him, deciding waspishly that he looked indecently attractive for this time of the morning, his brown eyes alert and lively, his cheeks freshly shaved, and the silver wings at his temples striking against the inky blackness of his hair. He was wearing a form-fitting russet jacket and buff breeches which carelessly emphasized his broad shoulders and lean legs. For a man of his age, she thought bitterly, he was far, far too handsome. And he was in her bedroom!

Recalled to her senses, she stifled the urge to throw something large and heavy at his head and instead stamped her foot in frustration. Taking a deep, steadying breath, she finally asked, "If I go with you—you swear that you will not bother me again?"

"If you go with me and agree to discuss what happened over twenty years ago."

"*Zut!* What happened was that you abandoned me!"

"Odd, that is exactly what I thought—only *I* was the one abandoned. You deserted *me!*"

Lisette looked taken aback. "I never deserted you," she said with a trifle less heat. She started to say more when the rattle of crockery on a tray in the hallway stopped her. "We cannot talk here—someone is going to interrupt us," she said distractedly.

"My point exactly—which is why you are going to put on your riding clothes and come with me."

She flashed him a furious glance, but from the stubborn jut of his chin, it was obvious that he was going nowhere unless she went with him. Muttering under her breath, she flew across the room to the armoire and hastily extracted a riding costume. Mouth set, she disappeared behind a screen in one corner of the room.

Scrambling into her clothes, she reappeared only seconds later and, sitting down on the bed, yanked on her boots. Fairly quivering with outrage and indignation, she said less than five minutes later, "I am ready. Shall we leave?"

John rose to his feet and smiled. Lisette's palm itched to slap his handsome face. Gallantly offering his arm, he said, "If *Madame* will allow me?"

Lisette snorted and hurried out the doors, her relief

only marginal that they were now on the gallery and not in her bedroom. She still had to go with him, and she was not looking forward to the prospect.

They were silent as they hastily left the upper gallery via the wide staircase at the rear of the house. The horses were tethered at the base of the stairs, and a moment later John had tossed Lisette into the saddle of a smallish bay mare and mounted his own horse.

It wasn't until several minutes later, when they had left behind the immediate grounds of the house, that John let himself believe that his plan had actually worked. He slanted a glance at Lisette's stony features. Getting her away from the house had been the easy part, he realized uneasily. The hard part was yet to come.

They rode for some time through the sun-dappled countryside—oaks, locust, hackberry, magnolias, and cottonwoods growing in wild profusion. Coral honeysuckle and Virginia creeper and other vines ran rampant through the verdant undergrowth, and the vivid pink and purple splashes of the wild azaleas could be seen here and there. They crossed the occasional sluggishly moving bayou lined with spiky-fanned palmettos and once surprised a sleeping alligator on a muddy bank.

As time passed and they plunged deeper and deeper into the wilderness, the silence between them changed. The air was no longer charged with anger. The tenseness which had vibrated between them lessened, and they both gradually began to relax. To her astonishment, Lisette discovered she was actually enjoying the ride. With a steady horse under her, the early-morning air soft and caressing, the myriad, mysterious scents of the bottomland forests wafting in her nostrils, and the sheer variety and number of plants, trees, and animals to catch her gaze, it was no wonder that she found it difficult to focus on her previous resentment and fury.

Yet she did not totally forget why she was here or the underhanded method John Lancaster had used to obtain her presence. But she was very confused about his reasons for going to such great lengths simply to discuss the unfortunate demise of their plans all those years before. Surely, it could not matter to him now? A little frown marred her forehead. What had he meant by declaring that she abandoned him? She never would have done such a thing, she thought passionately. She had loved him! She had longed with the very fiber of her soul to be his wife. If *Papa* had not come to her with the news that John had . . . She stiffened, her fingers involuntarily clenching around the reins. If *Papa* had not come to her . . .

For the first time since that awful day her father and Renault had confronted her about the plan to run away with John Lancaster, she wondered about the sincerity and honesty of the men who had destroyed her dreams. Her mouth twisted. After she had married him, she had learned firsthand that Renault had not always told the truth—only when it suited him, and then only what he wanted anyone to know. There had been countless times during their marriage that she had caught him in lie after lie. And *Papa*. When it came to getting his own way, she admitted reluctantly, *Papa* would have lied to the Archangel Gabriel if he had thought it would gain him anything. John had claimed that she had abandoned him—had she? Unknowingly. Had her father and Renault confronted each of them with a pack of lies? And they, like fools, had believed them?

Ruthlessly tamping down the silly surge of hope which ran through her, she eyed John's broad back as he rode in front of her. She had loved him once. Passionately. Adoringly. He had been everything she had ever wanted in a man, a husband. For years he had haunted her dreams, and she would awaken with her arms aching to hold him just one more time and tears on her cheeks. Even now she had trouble believing fully that he had brutally left her to face her family, alone and disgraced. But had he? she wondered. Had he been told that she did not want to marry him? And had he left New Orleans believing that she had deserted him?

It was a tantalizing thought. She told herself she was being ridiculous to think him innocent, to make excuses for his behavior. He had made no attempt to see her again. In fact, he had never, to her knowledge, set foot in New Orleans again.

Suddenly that fact began to take on enormous importance. Why had he not come back again? Too ashamed to face her? Or had there been another reason? Such as being so shattered by her betrayal that he could never return to New Orleans? Her heart began to beat swiftly, and she was annoyed at her reaction to the possibility that there was more to the sudden ending of their love affair than she had been led to believe. *Ma foi!* she told herself sternly, I am just being a silly old woman. Of course, he had not been shattered by her supposed defection. But the idea would not go away—suppose that he *had* been so hurt to think she would carelessly toss away their love that he could not . . .

Finding a small shady glade, John halted their horses, and, first politely lifting Lisette down, he tied the horses at the edge of the clearing. A huge fallen log lay at the side of the glade, and, after checking around it for any unwelcome wildlife, John spread a blanket on the forest floor, using the log as a backrest. To Lisette's further bemusement, he immediately unpacked a tasty picnic and proceeded to arrange the various packets of food and drink on the blanket to his satisfaction. Only after he had finished setting things to his liking did he turn and look at her.

An unreadable expression in his dark eyes, he held out a hand and said softly, "*Madame*, will you join me for some refreshments?"

Warily, Lisette put her hand in his and allowed him to help her to the ground near the log. The skirts of her riding habit tucked demurely under her legs, she settled comfortably against the blanket-draped log, her eyes never leaving his dark, intent face.

John smiled down at her. "Would you like something to drink? Cook sent along a jug of lemonade, and there is also some orange juice."

Lisette shook her head, her lovely features mirroring all the uncertainties, mistrustfulness, and half-acknowledged yearnings that were within her. "You said," she began quietly, "that you wanted to talk to me where we would be uninterrupted." She glanced around, a wry expression crossing her face. "I doubt that we shall be bothered here."

John nodded soberly. Seating himself across from her, he nervously plucked at a tuft of grass that grew near the blanket. "It seemed so simple," he explained, his eyes fixed on hers, "when I planned this little outing. But now that the moment is upon me, I suddenly find myself at a loss for words."

"I do not remember that you were ever so in the past," Lisette murmured, wishing that her pulse was not acting erratically and that her heart was not behaving in the most peculiar fashion. But so many taunting and tempting thoughts were running through her brain that she could not control either them or her reaction to them. *Had* they been lied to? Had John loved her after all? She had certainly believed so. More importantly, if she had not believed him implicitly, she would never have given herself to him. Confused and yet hopeful, she did not know if she really wanted to find out the truth. Life had been so much simpler thinking him a cad and a liar all these years. Painful and lonely, but simpler. She did not know if she wanted to learn that her father and her husband had blatantly and coldly rearranged her life to suit themselves.

John smiled crookedly at her. "Then I put on a very good act. Whenever I was with you, I felt as tongue-tied as a country bumpkin in the presence of a goddess."

Stoutly ignoring the almost painful thump in her chest, Lisette tossed her head slightly. "You see, you claim not to have a facile tongue, and yet you easily spout charming nonsense."

John shook his head. "It is not nonsense—it is true." He suddenly reached for her hand and pressed an ardent kiss to her warm palm. Then he said, "Lisette, do you not know that I always thought of you as a goddess—that I wondered how I could have been so lucky, so damned fortunate to have gained your love?"

"Then why did you leave me?" she cried, her hand trembling violently in his grasp.

"I did not leave you." His mouth twisted. "At least not until your father and Renault had made it painfully obvious that you were not going to run away with me, that you were marrying Renault before the month was out and that I was just an embarrassment to you."

Her fingers tightened around his. "And you believed them?" she asked in a low shaken voice. "You believed them?"

"Their words alone, no, but, you see, they gave me a note you had written to me."

"What note?" Lisette demanded with a frown.

John released her hand and, from the inside of his jacket, withdrew a much-folded piece of paper. It was obviously many years old and had obviously been much handled. Wordlessly, he handed it to her.

For several long moments Lisette stared at the small, torn scrap of paper in her hands as she might a poisonous snake. Just when John thought he could stand the suspense no longer, she gingerly unfolded the note and read the contents. There was not a great deal written, just a few lines, but those few lines, John reflected bitterly, had utterly destroyed him. Over the years since that terrible day, he had read and reread them, and each time he had read them he had felt as if each word had been etched in acid on his heart.

Please, I beg you, if you care for me at all, do not continue to importune me. I will not marry you. I love another.
Lisette

Chapter Nineteen

"*T*hey tricked us! Oh, you dear, *dear* imbecile—I never wrote this to *you*!" Lisette exclaimed. "It is part of a note that I wrote to *Renault* when I knew that I loved you." Her eyes huge, dark pools in her white face, she said carefully, "Renault wanted to marry me; *Papa* approved, and, before you appeared in New Orleans, I had been drifting into a betrothal with him." She hesitated and, even after all these years, a charming blush stained her cheeks. "But once I had met you . . ." Her eyes seemed to grow even more luminous, more mysterious, her expression indescribably tender. "Once I had met you, I knew that I could not marry him. I loved you. And only you."

John made an inarticulate sound and dragged her into his arms. "I have always loved you," he swore huskily against her lips. "*Always!* Even when I believed that you had lied to me, deserted me, and loved another."

"Oh, *John!*"

There were still many explanations to be aired, but for the moment, John and Lisette cared for nothing but the fact that they were in each other's arms once again. They kissed many times, kisses as passionate and loving as they had shared in their youth, but there were now two new elements in their embrace—an aching sadness for what they had lost and a sweet ecstasy that came from knowing that in spite of deceit and trickery and even marriage to other people, their love had never lessened, never faltered.

It was very quiet in the glade, the only sounds the soft, tender murmurings of two lovers, cruelly, deceitfully parted for decades. Their arms entwined around each other, hands caressing, lips almost touching, they spoke for a long time of things shared only by lovers.

It was the startled snort of a buck which brought them back to the present. Together they stared as the sleek brown form disappeared into the forest once more, then they looked at each other and smiled.

John was leaning back against the log, Lisette's head resting in the crook of his arm. Toying with the button of his jacket, she muttered, "They deceived both of us! Lied to both of us. *Dieu!* It does not seem possible now that they managed to make us believe their lies."

"Your note was pretty convincing," John said dryly. "I was certain they were lying until your father handed it to me. Once I had read it, I was so hurt and stunned that it was fairly easy for Renault to hustle me out of town, while your father no doubt hurried back to you with the news that I was nothing more than a black-hearted scoundrel who had taken base advantage of you."

Lisette squirmed around and sent him a severe look. "You should have tried to see me yourself."

John sent her a look. "I suggested that, my love, but your father informed me most sincerely that I would only embarrass and upset you. He said"—John's voice hardened—"that if I really loved you, I would not cause you any more pain. I followed his advice." He cocked a brow at her. "What exactly did they tell you?"

Lisette sighed and snuggled closer to him. "You put it rather succinctly a moment ago. *Papa* was very kind, but he made it very clear that you did not love me and that you did not want to marry me, that I had thoroughly mistaken your intentions. *Papa* said that you had only been toying with me, amusing yourself, and that I was a silly little goose if I really believed your declarations of undying love. I did not believe him at first." Her lips twisted. "I was very angry with him, and I accused him of lying. He said that if I did not believe him, he would take me to town himself and prove to me that you had no intention of meeting me as we had planned and that you had already left New Orleans for Natchez."

"Which, of course, I had, thanks to him!" John said bitterly.

Lisette nodded. "I did not really begin to believe *Papa* until we had gone to the hotel where you had been staying and the concierge informed us that *Monsieur* Lancaster had paid his bill and had left the hotel that morning for Natchez." Her voice grew very small. "*Papa* even took me to the docks and let me talk to a pair of dockworkers, who described you and swore that you had gotten on a keelboat heading for Natchez not two hours previously." Tears sparkling on her lashes, she confessed, "It was then that I truly believed that you had left me."

John took her into his arms. "In my heart, I never left you, Lisette. Never," he murmured as his mouth found hers. His lips were warm against hers as he kissed her with infinite tenderness, and Lisette trembled from the very sweetness of it. When he finally lifted his head, her eyes were full of stars, and a dreamy smile curved her mouth.

"I love you," he said simply. "I always have. Will you marry me? As soon as it can be arranged?"

Lisette's hand gently caressed his lean, sun-lined cheek. "*Oui, monsieur*. I shall be honored to be your wife."

After that there were no words between them for a very, very long time. . . .

The news that John and Lisette were to be married came as no surprise to Hugh. Watching as John gently lifted Lisette down from her horse and seeing the soft glow on Lisette's face and the tender expression in John's eyes several hours later when they returned to *Amour*, one would have had to have been blind not to understand the situation between them, and Hugh was not blind—at least not where other people's emotions were concerned.

Smiling, he met them at the top of the broad steps, and, after glancing again from one face to the other, he murmured, "I take it that congratulations are in order?"

Two heads nodded simultaneously, bemused smiles meeting his words.

"We are to be married as soon it can be arranged," John said, his hand tightening on Lisette's.

Having heard the horses approach, Micaela came out onto the front gallery, and, like Hugh, she took one look at the other couple's faces and knew immediately what had occurred. An enchanting smile curving her mouth, she flew across the wide gallery and threw her arms around her mother.

"Oh, *là*!" she exclaimed gaily. "Things have been explained? He is not the villain you thought? And I am to have a step-*papa*?"

Lisette chuckled. "Indeed, you are—in a remarkably short time, too!"

The happiness of the older couple was infectious, and, for a little while, the constraint between Hugh and Micaela disappeared. They exchanged looks of amused satisfaction just as if they had planned the entire outcome. Hugh suggested that a toast was in order, and so, laughing and talking at the same time, the four of them went inside.

They had just entered the spacious hallway when they met Jean descending the main staircase. Like Hugh and Micaela, well aware of the past and what had occurred, he took one look at Lisette's and John's faces and realized what must have happened. A silence fell as the four in the hall stared up at Jean's unrevealing features.

"So," he said slowly, "you have discovered the truth."

John nodded curtly, his arm closing possessively around Lisette's slim shoulders. "Yes, we have. How much did you know?"

Continuing on down the staircase, Jean admitted, "Most of it. I knew that they used part of her letter to Renault to drive the final spike in your heart and the fact that you had left town to convince her that you had never meant to marry her."

John's jaw hardened. "It did not disturb you?"

Jean shrugged. "You forget that I was a mere youth, younger even than Lisette. In the beginning, I believed them when they said they were doing what was best for Lisette, our two families and the company. Besides, Renault was my brother, and he wanted to marry her—who was I to question his actions? It was my duty to support his endeavors."

His eyes slid to Lisette's face. Almost apologetically he said, "I know that I was not always fair to you—I blamed you for what happened. I felt for many years that you had betrayed my brother, and I resented you and what you had done. It did not sit well with me to know that Renault had married another man's leavings."

There was a gasp from the two women, color coming and going in Lisette's face and John surged forward, his features dark and dangerous, his intention plain. Hugh intervened swiftly, stepping quickly between the two older men. "It all happened a long time ago," he said quietly, urgently, looking from one tense face to the other. "The two culprits who created the situation are dead. They are the ones to blame—not each other. There is no need to make a tragic ending now."

Jean took a deep breath. "I did not mean to be insulting," he said stiffly. "I was merely, in my clumsy fashion, attempting to explain to Lisette why I have acted as I have toward her." He stepped away from Hugh and bowed deeply in Lisette's direction. "I beg your pardon. I realize now, and have for some time, that what happened was not your fault." He gave a twisted smile. "Unfortunately, my resentment was even a longer time dying, and treating you as I have had become a habit."

His words smote Micaela like a blow between the eyes. She understood now the simmering tenseness she had always sensed between Jean and Lisette, but Jean's mention of his behavior becoming a habit struck her hardest. She flashed a glance at her husband, her heart melting as she stared at his beloved features. *Maman* was right—pride was a cold bedmate. *She must talk to him!*

Jean crossed to stand directly in front of Lisette. Lifting her hand, he pressed a kiss on the back of it. "Will you allow me to make amends? And allow me to offer you my most sincere congratulations?"

Lisette hesitated, then her gentle smile appeared. "*Oui!* Thank you. And perhaps, now with no secrets between

us, we can become the friends we should have been all
the time."

Jean cocked a brow. "If there *are* no more secrets," he
said softly and for her ears alone.

Lisette suddenly became flustered and said hastily,
"*Dieu!* But we have all become very serious, have we
not? Come let us partake of that toast my handsome son-
in-law mentioned."

Hugh laughed, pleased that the sticky moment was apparently behind them, and ushered the two ladies toward
the sitting room. For a moment, Jean and John were left
to face each other alone in the hall. Silently they regarded
one another, then John slowly extended his hand. "My
stepson is right. The past is the past. There is no reason
for *us* to continue to be at odds. Our families seemed determined to commingle. It will be difficult if you and I
continue to hold grudges that were not of our own making."

Jean smiled, albeit ruefully. "I admit that I am torn—
one's loyalty to one's family is very strong, but as you
said, our families *have* become one. You and I are older
now and, I hope, wiser. I find that at my age I prefer
friends to enemies."

They shook hands firmly, and John clapped Jean on the
back. "Come along, my friend," he said heartily. "We
shall drink several toasts this afternoon, not the least to
the demise of an old deceit and a new and lasting friendship."

It wasn't to be expected that François would take the
news of the coming nuptials between Lisette and John
Lancaster as calmly as the others—his mother's and
John's shared history was totally unknown to him, although he was aware that they had met years ago, when

the company had first been formed. He had troubles of his own to occupy his unpleasant thoughts. The terrifying knowledge that Alain would be arriving at *Amour* sometime within the next forty-eight hours with the stated intention of killing Hugh was not exactly conducive to an easy conscience.

He had, with a fervor which surprised him, prayed that the invitation for Alain to join them would be denied. And he had been sunk in black despair when the very thing he had asked for had been granted so easily. It was with very little enthusiasm that he had penned the note inviting Alain to come to *Amour* and seen it sent off to New Orleans.

No one seemed to have noticed that François was unusually withdrawn since arriving at *Amour*, that his merry smile was not much in evidence. If anyone had noticed something amiss, it had no doubt been put down to his being bored in the country. François was not bored. In fact, now that his world was coming down around his ears, he was realizing just how very fortunate he had been before he had allowed himself to be sucked into Alain's iron grasp.

With his newfound sense of responsibility and sudden maturity, François no longer blamed everything and everyone else for his trouble. He did not even blame Alain completely for his present predicament. He knew that he had no one to blame really except himself. Nor could he escape the ugly fact that the idea to pilfer small amounts from the company had originated with him. If only, he thought despairingly, he had not wanted to act the part of a sophisticated, wealthy man-about-town, friend and confidant of the dashing Alain Husson, eager and ready to show his nerve and verve by gambling on everything and anything. If only he had not wanted to prove to everyone just how adult he was, how very "knowing" he was, he would not have acted as he had. He squirmed with embarrassment and shame when he considered his actions. There was also the bitter awareness that he had simply parroted Alain's inflaming statements about the *Américains* and that he had blindly taken Alain's attitude toward Hugh as his own. With a sinking feeling he admitted that he had grown to like Hugh—or at least, he did not *dis*like him.

Alone in his suite of rooms upstairs at *Amour*, François had spent hours pacing and staring sightlessly out the tall windows, desperately seeking a way out of the trap he had dug for himself. Confessing all to Jean was one way out. But while knowing it was what he should do, François could not quite bring himself to expose his own duplicity, his own blatant foolishness and arrogance to his uncle. Telling his mother or sister was not to be considered. And then there was Hugh. . . . His young face bleak, he sighed heavily and turned away from the windows.

How could he quietly stand by and let Alain murder his brother-in-law? Etienne's death, though he had had nothing to do with it, stabbed at him every time he thought of it—which was almost constantly. He could not say that he was deeply fond of Hugh, but he was discovering that he would be pleased to have the opportunity to know him better and to strengthen the tenuous bonds between them. To have Hugh's death on his conscience, knowing he could have prevented it, was unbearable.

He wouldn't have been François if he had not been just a little bit sorry for himself, but he had come a long way since that last shattering interview with Alain, and, as he looked back at what he had done, he was appalled. How could he have been so blindly arrogant? How could he have so carelessly justified stealing from his own company, no matter what the reason? How could he have stolen from his own family that way?

His face twisted. He had been a weak fool! He could not undo what he had done, but he was dimly aware that eventually the truth was going to have to come out—all of it. He would be, he knew, deservedly punished for his part in what had happened, and he almost looked forward to the day his sins were revealed. But he was not yet ready to face that particular debacle, and at the moment his greatest concern was trying to come up with a plan to stop Hugh's murder. Something that at the moment seemed impossible. He sighed again. Deeply and heavily.

The tap on his door broke into his unhappy thoughts, and when his mother entered the room, he was surprised. Forcing a smile onto his lips, he said, "*Maman!* What is it? What brings you looking for me?"

Even as distracted as he was by his own troubles, François could not help but notice the glow of happiness which seemed to surround her. His smile becoming more natural, he approached her and asked, "What is it? Has Micaela told you that you are to be a *grand-mère*? Am I to be an *oncle*?"

Lisette shook her head, suddenly uncertain how to start. She had left the others downstairs, still laughing and discussing wedding plans, and had come in search of her son. Everyone knew where she was and what she was doing. François's probable reaction had already been discussed, and it had been decided that he would take the news of the coming marriage better from his mother, privately. They had all agreed that it would not be wise to spring it on him without warning at dinner tonight.

It was considered an advantage that François appeared to like John Lancaster, and there was the hope that since he had already seemed to have gotten over his resentment of Micaela's marriage to Hugh, the news that his mother was going to marry Hugh's stepfather might not set off the furious explosion they all feared would mar the happy event. But looking at him, seeing the shadows lurking in his dark eyes and the signs of strain on his young face, Lisette was suddenly not so sure of her ability to explain things to him as she had been a few minutes ago when she had slipped out of the sitting room and come in search of him. He looked, to her mother's eye, deeply troubled.

A little frown crinkled her forehead and touching him fondly on the arm, she asked, "What is it, *mon amour*? You look very unhappy."

François shrugged and said, "Oh, it is nothing. I have had the headache today and have not felt like being very gay."

Her eyes searched his, and, seeing that he was not going to say more—if there was anything more to say— she gave his arm an encouraging squeeze and turned away. Wandering over to the windows, she said softly, "I do have some important news to tell you—I hope that you will be happy for me."

When she told him, at first he did not seem to understand what she was saying. His face the picture of confusion and incredulity, he stared at her. "M-m-married?" He finally got out. "You and John Lancaster?"

Lisette nodded, her hands clasped nervously together. "We were always attracted to each other," she began carefully, slowly laying out the story that had been agreed upon. "But I was in love with your father and nothing came of it."

It had been Jean who suggested that there was no reason for François to know of the cruel deceit practiced by his father and grandfather. Let him believe that a fleeting attraction years ago between John and Lisette had recently blossomed into full bloom.

    If François's thoughts had not been taken up with his own worries, it is possible he would not as easily have swallowed Lisette's story. But after his first disbelief and shock, he seemed genuinely pleased by the news.

"I am to have a step-*papa*? John Lancaster will now have two stepsons, *oui*?" he asked eagerly, his dark eyes suddenly alight with pleasure.

Lisette nodded. "You do not mind, *mon cher*?" she inquired anxiously. Nothing would stop her from marrying John, but she had feared that François would not be as thrilled and excited for her as Micaela had been.

François smiled and kissed her affectionately on the cheek. "*Non!* I have always thought that my sweet *maman* was too young and pretty to stay a widow for the rest of her life. He seems a fine man. And since," he said teasingly, "we already have one *Américain* in the family, what is one more?" Laughing he added, "Perhaps I, too, shall marry an *Américaine* some day!"

With François's approval, Lisette's last bar to complete happiness had been lifted and dinner that evening was merry and lighthearted, with toast after toast being offered to the happy couple. The wedding was set for two weeks hence, and it had been decided that it would be a quiet and private affair. Just the immediate family would be in attendance, and it would take place at *Amour.* Jean, in the spirit of firmly putting the past behind them, even offered to make the arrangements with the parish priest to perform the ceremony at the house and François, with a charming deference foreign to him, added quietly that he would be pleased and honored to give his very lovely *maman* away.

It was a very pleasant evening, and, taking advantage of the goodwill which seemed to be flowing so freely, Hugh decided it was as propitious a time as any to attempt to heal the breach with his wife. He had surreptitiously watched as she wandered over to help herself to another glass of the champagne punch which had been brought into the sitting room after dinner. Everyone else was gathered together on the far side of the room, and, under the guise of needing to refill his own glass, he walked up to her.

Smiling, he asked, "Allow me?" And at her nod he proceeded to ladle them both another glass, leaving his own sitting on the table as he handed her glass back to her.

Micaela did not immediately drift away as had been her wont lately, and, taking heart, Hugh inquired lightly, "Are you happy about this?"

She glanced at him over the rim of her glass, her dark eyes unfathomable. A smile that made his heart catch in his chest curved her mouth. "Oh, *oui*! It is most romantic, *non*? To think that they have always loved each other and that now after all these years the way is clear for them finally to wed."

Hugh looked across the room, where John sat casually on the arm of Lisette's chair, their hands lightly clasped. His stepfather appeared dazzled and delighted by what had happened, and the expression on Lisette's face was not much different. Slowly Hugh nodded. "It is too bad that they had to wait over twenty years though," he said carefully. His eyes flicked to hers, and deliberately holding her gaze, he asked huskily, "And what about us? Am I going to have to wait twenty years for you to forgive me for being so stupidly arrogant and conceited?"

Micaela swallowed, her pulse galloping in her veins, her eyes clinging to his, unable to break away from that steady gray look. They were almost touching, and, this close, she could smell that excitingly masculine scent that was uniquely his and feel the enveloping warmth of his tall, solid body. Her mother's words rang in her ears again and, realizing that there was only one place in the world that she wanted to be—in his arms—she said softly, "There is nothing *to* forgive. We were both wrong."

The gray eyes darkened. "Does that mean what I think it does, sweetheart?"

A bubble of joy surged up through her at the hungry note in his voice, and, smiling demurely, her lids half-lowered, she murmured, "And what do you want it to mean, *monsieur*?"

Hugh took an impetuous step toward her. As his arms came swiftly around her, a blush stained her cheeks. Aware of the others in the room, she said hastily, "Hugh! Not right here, not *now*!"

Recalled to his senses, Hugh's arms lessened only fractionally. Grinning down into her face, a glitter in the gray eyes that made her feel weak in the knees, he demanded, "Tell me when and where, sweetheart, and then and only then, will I let you go."

Burningly aware of his arms around her, aware, too, of the sudden sweet ache of anticipation in her own body, she muttered, "My rooms—after we have all retired for the night."

He brushed a swift kiss across her mouth. "Do not," he warned, "even think of changing your mind."

"Perhaps it is you who will change his mind," she said saucily as she slipped from his embrace.

He caught her hand and pressed a warm, ardent kiss on it. "Never!" he swore softly, his eyes full of promises she dared not think about right now.

Her entire body tingling, a decidedly dreamy smile on her lips, Micaela rejoined the group at the other end of the room. Her thoughts were on the private moments she would soon spend with her husband. Perhaps that was why when they all parted to seek out their own beds she did not notice the quiet exchange between Jean and Lisette.

All evening, the conversation had been on the future, but for one person, at least, the past had not been entirely forgotten and as they all bid each other good night and parted, Jean quietly asked for a private word with Lisette. Lisette hesitated, her expression uneasy. It was on the tip of her tongue to deny his request, but there was something in his eyes that made her decide to meet him. What could it hurt? Seeing that John had not noticed them, she murmured, "Meet me on the gallery downstairs in half an hour." Jean nodded and left her.

Having shared a tender goodnight with John, Lisette waited several minutes before slipping out of her door and hurrying silently down the stairs. She breathed more easily once she had stepped outside onto the downstairs gallery. Jean was waiting for her. Politely placing her hand on his arm, they began to walk side by side in the magnolia-scented darkness.

They had barely taken a half a dozen steps before Jean said in a low tone, "He will have to be told, you know. You cannot let this secret lie between you."

Lisette looked at him, her face bleak. Stonily she said, "I do not know what you are talking about. And I must say I am rather annoyed at you for getting me down here where you waste my time by speaking in riddles. It is very late, and I would like to go to bed."

When she started to turn away, he gently held her captive.

"Lisette, we have to talk about this. You cannot pretend that it never happened."

Her eyes searched his desperately. "What do you know?" she demanded. "What is it you *think* you know?"

Jean smiled, more a grimace than a smile. "Very well, we shall do it your way," he said tiredly. He hesitated, and gazing out into the black night, said carefully, "I *think* that I can count on my fingers as well as the next man, *ma chérie*, and according to my calculations, Micaela was born almost seven months to the day after your marriage." He slanted Lisette an old-fashioned look. "Everyone else may have believed that she had been born early, but you forget I was there." He looked away from Lisette's stricken features. "I did not know all the details of your affair with John Lancaster, but I knew enough to figure things out for myself and there was one thing that I was very positive of—even at seventeen . . . my newborn niece was far too fat and lively an infant to have been born two months early. And then there was my brother's reaction to her—he did not exactly ignore her, but I know there was more to it than simply the fact that he doted on his son and was almost indifferent to his daughter. There were times when he looked at Micaela, when he thought himself unobserved, that his face wore a most unpleasant expression."

"Which does not mean a thing!" Lisette said sharply.

His eyes full of pity, Jean said heavily, "On the face of it, no, it does not mean anything. Many Creole fathers prefer their sons to their daughters. But knowing as I did that you had refused Renault several weeks before you ended up marrying him—rather hastily, I might add—and knowing, as everyone else did not, that you were in love with John Lancaster . . ."

Lisette opened her mouth, but Jean shook his head.

"*Non.* Do not try to tell me differently. Let there be no more lies between us." When Lisette would not meet his gaze, he added mildly, "There is one more thing, perhaps the most telling of all: your father's gift of nearly half his stock in the company to Renault on the day you married. Stock that was to be Renault's for his lifetime only and that upon his death was to go to your firstborn child and *only* your firstborn—no matter how many other children were born to the marriage. Rather curious do you not think? It always struck me, very much like a bribe . . ."

Lisette, her jaw set, tears glittering on her lashes, remained silent.

Jean sighed and asked gently, "So, when are you going to tell him that Micaela is his daughter? And how do you intend to explain to Micaela that her father is not Renault Dupree, as she has been led to believe all her life, but John Lancaster?"

Chapter Twenty

*M*icaela paced the gleaming yellow-pine floor of her room, eager for Hugh's arrival, yet just a little anxious, hardly daring to believe that the problems which existed between them could be resolved so easily. Again and again, she reminded herself of her mother's advice. She must not let hasty, hot-tempered words ruin what could be a new beginning between them. A beginning based on truth and not mere speculation and other people's opinions. She and Hugh had both made mistakes, made assumptions about each other that were incorrect. Bleakly she realized that if she was to save her marriage, she had to put away her hurt, her anger, and, yes, her pride. She had to listen to her heart, and she had to stop being a coward! She must speak of her deepest feelings to him, no matter what the cost.

She was wearing a modest, pale yellow nightgown of finest cambric trimmed with lavender ribbons and a filmy, flounce-hemmed wrapper in a pleasing shade of soft spring green. With her hair falling in black, lustrous waves around her shoulders, she looked very young and vulnerable as she paced her room. Tonight would be between just the two of them, and if she were brave enough to bare her heart, to speak honestly of their differences, by the morning, she was either going to be the happiest woman alive or the most miserable. Nervously she clasped her hands together, wishing that it was already morning. This would, she admitted wryly, be all behind her. She would know the truth of his feelings for her.

At the sound of a door opening behind her, Micaela stiffened. Her eyes wide, she swung in that direction. Hugh leaned negligently in the doorway between their two rooms, his broad shoulders propped against the door-jamb. He was wearing a robe of richly embroidered silk; jewel-toned dragons and other mythical beasts rioted across the black background. To Micaela's fascinated gaze, the flickering candlelight gave life to the creatures on his robe, a golden eye here, an emerald tail there.

He appeared tall and rather forbidding as he lounged there, his face in shadows, the thick black hair falling carelessly across his brow. His arms were folded casually on his chest, and, as he continued to silently stare at her, Micaela was aware of a sudden trepidation. Reminding herself that this was her husband, that she had nothing to fear from him, she gave herself a shake.

Forcing a welcoming smile, she murmured, "Good evening."

Hugh grinned, his forbidding air falling away like magic. Approaching her, he lifted her chin with one finger. "Being formal tonight, are we, my love?"

Micaela swallowed, her eyes locked on his. Was she his love? she wondered unhappily. Or was he merely teasing her? Aware that she had been staring at him for several seconds, she found her tongue and stammered, "*N-n-non*." And taking refuge in blunt honesty, she muttered, "I could think of nothing else to say to you."

"Now I find that hard to believe," Hugh said mockingly, his gray eyes glinting in the candlelight. "Considering the number of times I have been on the receiving end of that tart little tongue of yours."

Micaela jerked her chin away. Not looking at him, she said miserably, "Do not tease! I do not want to fight with you."

"And the last thing I want to do, sweetheart, is fight with you," Hugh admitted huskily as he pulled her unresisting body close to his. Resting his chin on her dark hair, her cheek pressed to his chest, he murmured, "I do not know how we got in the tangle we are in, but I do know that I want it to end. We cannot, if we are to have any sort of happiness, continue as we are. You are my wife. I am your husband. Surely, sweetheart, we can do better than we have done so far?"

Micaela nodded, rubbing her cheek against his warm, hard chest. "It is mostly my fault—I am too quick to take offense," she said earnestly. "And I believed François when he said that you only married me because of the company." She felt Hugh stiffen slightly, and she added hastily, "François is very young and silly—I should not have listened to him."

Hugh sighed and dropped a kiss on the top of her head. "I would not be so eager to take all the blame for our situation—I have done my part also to bring us to this point." He gave her shoulder a gentle squeeze and added, "I think it is time that we had a long talk, and if we are going to be confessing our sins, I suggest that we get comfortable." He swung Micaela up in his arms and started toward the bed, but realizing how little talking would get done the moment he laid her on the mattress, he grimaced regretfully and swerved in the direction of a big, overstuffed chair covered in faded ruby damask. The chair had been pressed into service until the new furniture arrived, but settling into its worn comfort, Micaela resting on his lap, Hugh suddenly discovered a surprising fondness for the object.

Neither one of them quite knew how to start, but both were painfully aware of the importance of tonight. Nervously Micaela's fingers crumpled the heavy silk lapel of Hugh's robe, her thoughts darting like fireflies through her mind. The warmth and feel of Hugh's hard body beneath her legs was very distracting, the knowledge that he was probably naked underneath the robe making an aching pulse spring to life between her thighs. Wrenching her thoughts away from his physical attributes was difficult, but she was determined to have her say before her courage failed her.

Hugh was just as aware of Micaela as she was of him, and just as determined that they thrash things out between them before he allowed himself the delight of making love to his wife again. It was not easy. He was already hard and eager, the heavy weight of his manhood making its presence felt against his leg. The fact that her tempting little bottom was pressing against his thighs, her breasts were nestled snugly against his chest, and her mouth was mere inches below his did not help matters. She glanced up at him just then and his eyes locked compulsively on her lips, his hunger to kiss her almost overwhelming him.

Suppressing a groan and his baser instincts, he pressed her head against his neck and muttered, "We must talk! And if you look at me like that, I am afraid that I will forget everything but how very much I want to make love to you."

Micaela smiled tenderly against his warm neck, suddenly feeling more confident. Softly she asked, "Did you really think that I had trapped you into marriage—that you were the person François was badgering me to marry? You truly believed that François wanted me to marry *you*?"

The incredulity in her voice made Hugh wince and realize just how badly he had misunderstood the conversation he had overheard. Above her head, he made a wry face. "Indeed, I am sorry to say that I did, sweetheart. I was positive. And you have to admit, that while it was rather conceited of me, my assumption was not entirely without basis. What François said of Alain could, I think you will agree, have also applied to me—and then when we were found alone in such a compromising situation such a short time later, I was thoroughly convinced that you had planned it all." He tipped her head back so that he could look into her face. "I was even half-convinced that François found us so easily because you had told him where we would be."

Micaela's eyes widened indignantly. "*Dieu!* And I suppose I caused the storm and made your horse act up, too?" Stiffly she added, "You do not hold a very high opinion of me, do you?"

Hugh shook his head. "I did not," he admitted honestly. "But even believing you had deliberately trapped me, you may have noticed that I married you anyway— and in my own clumsy way have tried to make you a good husband."

"Why?" she demanded bluntly, ignoring the rush of tenderness his words engendered.

He brushed a kiss across her mouth that made her lips tingle. "Because," he said huskily, "I discovered, much to my astonishment, that I wanted you—at any cost. And because I found you utterly enchanting and that having you in my arms and as my wife seemed like the most important thing in the world to me."

Her expression rapt, Micaela stared up at his dark face. Gently she caressed one lean cheek. "Truly?" she breathed. "It was not because of the business?"

Hugh smothered a curse. "That blasted company has caused me no end of trouble. There are times that I have seriously considered selling out, just to be rid of that particular entanglement." He glared down at her. "You adorable little fool! Of course, the company had nothing to do with our marriage. It was a side issue." His face softened. "The company brought us together, I cannot deny that or that it gave me an excuse to be around you." Hugh hesitated, then said huskily, "Micaela, you have to know that I love you. A man does not act as I have, with-*out* being driven by some very strong emotions. I do not know when I fell in love with you—it is a feeling that has been with me for so long now that I do not know when it began. I love you! And I want to keep you happy and safe, and in my arms, always!"

Micaela flung her arms around him and pressed urgent, joyous kisses over his face. "Oh, Hugh—I have been so afraid! So afraid that you married me only because of the business and that you left me here while you stayed in New Orleans because you had grown tired of me. I was even afraid you had gone to Alice." A blush stained her cheek. "You did not even seek out my bed anymore," she said in a low, embarrassed tone. "I was miserable when you left. *Maman* will tell you how unhappy I was. I wanted only to be with you and I feared"—she gave a shaken little laugh—"I feared that you had left my bed because I bored you."

Hugh strangled back something between a groan and a laugh. "Bored? My sweet, if you only knew how much I have missed having you in my bed, how much it pained me to leave you here while I went back to New Orleans.

And as for Alice—forget her! She lied about everything. Besides, I was too busy missing you to think of any other woman. The house in town was an empty cavern without your sweet presence in it. Even if we were sleeping apart, I had at least been able to see you and talk to you." He gave her a lopsided grin. "Even if it was only the sharp side of your tongue that I received." His voice deepened. "The last thing I wanted was to be parted from you, but I could see no other solution. Together we were certainly not solving our differences, and I thought that perhaps a little time apart would—"

"And then I *would* act the part of a silly goose!" Micaela interrupted disgustedly. "I should have trusted you. I should have told you, or shown you, what was in my heart."

His face tender, he stared down at her as she lay cradled in his arms. His lips tantalizingly near hers, he asked softly, "And what, my dearest little love, is in your heart?"

Her eyes glowed. "Why, only love for you, *monsieur*." Hugh's eyes darkened, and she said dreamily, caressing his face with her fingers, "My heart is full of love for one man and one man only—my stubborn, arrogant, infuriating and oh so wonderful husband, Hugh Lancaster."

He kissed her then, fully, his mouth hard and tender, passionate and worshiping. Micaela's arms clung to his neck, and she returned his embrace ardently, her lush body straining against his as if she could not get close enough, as if she wanted to crawl right inside of him and become melded forever to him. It was a glorious moment, a moment to be cherished and remembered always. He loved her! She loved him! Nothing else mattered.

Soft, incoherent murmurs came from each of them, and, amazingly, the other seemed to know exactly what was being said. Sitting in that old, shabby chair, flickering candlelight bathing them in a golden glow, their arms around each other, their lips nearly touching, they exchanged the sweet vows and promises that all true lovers have since the beginning of time.

There was a new and different tingling awareness of each other, the knowledge that love brought them together, that it was love which made their bodies yearn and ache for each other, making the moment even sweeter, the anticipation of their joining so much more intense. When Hugh finally lifted Micaela in his arms and walked toward the bed, it was an unhurried and sensuous journey they took together, with many long, decidedly erotic stops along the way, as they tasted and explored and shared the wonder of their love. By the time he lowered her to the waiting bed, their clothes were gone, left scattered haphazardly in a telling trail on the floor behind them. Their hunger for each other was an incandescent demand that pleaded for succor. And as their bodies slowly, sweetly merged, it was like the first time and every time they had ever made love; and it was love that they made all through the night on that large, welcoming bed.

Alain Husson wasted little time in responding to François's invitation. It was not yet eleven o'clock on Saturday morning when he drove up to the main doors of *Amour* in a stylish phaeton pulled by a pair of high-strung grays. His trunks rode in the small baggage rack at the rear of the vehicle.

Watching as Alain descended from his vehicle and was greeted by a surprisingly less-than-jolly François, Hugh smiled to himself. To think that such a short while ago he had been dreading this man's arrival! Knowing that Micaela loved *him* made all the difference in the world, Hugh thought with excusable smugness. Confident of his wife's love, he strolled down the steps and greeted Husson with something almost approaching genuine welcome.

If Alain seemed a bit taken aback by Hugh's warm greeting and François's noticeably cool one, he kept that emotion to himself. Putting on his most attractive smile and displaying the charm for which he was noted, he allowed himself to be escorted to the gazebo near the lake, where everyone else was enjoying the tranquil morning.

When Alain approached the group in the gazebo, there were more greetings, and the conversation did not become general until after he had been served a cup of coffee and had settled comfortably in a sturdy cypress chair like the rest of them. The two women looked cool and charming in their simple garb, Micaela fairly glowing in a pale pink muslin gown; Lisette, in a soft shade of green, had an unmistakable radiance surrounding her. The gentlemen, also casually dressed, were all wearing breeches and boots, Hugh and François even having foregone their jackets, their crisp white linen shirts not yet showing the effects of the debilitating humidity. There was a very relaxed, carefree air about them all—except, though he did his best to hide it, for the faint moodiness of François.

Sipping his coffee, Alain carefully studied the group before him. He could not fail to notice the air of intimacy between John and Lisette. They were discreet but they made no attempt to conceal their affection. Sitting side by side on a wooden settee, their glances meeting often as they exchanged small, private little smiles, their closeness was obvious. Alain's eyes narrowed. He shot a furtive glance around the group. The fact that no one else seemed surprised by their behavior gave him pause.

From where he stood, behind Micaela's chair, one hand lying gently on her shoulder, Hugh watched Alain's reaction with amusement. "You have arrived at a very happy time for all of us, Alain." Hugh said casually. "My very lovely *maman*-in-law agreed only yesterday to become my stepmother." He grinned at the older couple. "Lisette is to marry my stepfather in a matter of weeks. We are all extremely pleased by the news."

Alain was shocked, anger instantly coiling in his belly, and he shot a swift glance at François to gauge his reaction to this astonishing news. François seemed not the least perturbed by the knowledge that his mother was about to marry one of those despised *Américains*—and a damned Lancaster at that! Were none of their women safe from these encroaching vandals? Alain thought furiously. And François! *Mon Dieu!* What was he thinking of, to condone such a thing?

Recovering himself almost instantly, Alain smiled politely, giving no hint of just how infuriating he had found the news of the coming nuptials. "Congratulations to both of you," he said, his voice as smooth and melodious as ever, not even the faintest sign of his anger in his tone. He was even able to bring a warm gleam to his dark eyes as he murmured, "I am honored to be one of the first to hear of your good news."

There was talk of the wedding and of John's plans to settle in the Louisiana Territory. Looking tenderly over at Lisette, John declared, "While I know that my bride would gladly follow me to Natchez, I think that she, and consequently I, will be far happier living near our children. I intend on Monday to write my business agent in Natchez to sell all my holdings, and I shall immediately begin looking for a suitable property for us." He picked up Lisette's hand and pressed a kiss to the back of it. "If we cannot find something with a house already on it that pleases my bride then we shall build ourselves a new home which *will* please her."

"Ah—how very nice," Alain said mendaciously. "I shall look forward to visiting you in your new home."

"It is very exciting, *oui*?" Micaela asked happily. "To think that my *maman* and Hugh's step-*papa* are getting married! We have all been a little giddy this morning." Her gaze slid to her husband, and she smiled lovingly into Hugh's eyes. "We have," she added softly, "much to celebrate today."

The warmly intimate look that passed between Hugh and Micaela, as well as the caressing note in her voice, enraged Alain anew and for the first time he became aware of the changes in the younger couple. Watching narrow-eyed as Hugh ran a carelessly caressing finger down the side of Micaela's cheek and she turned her lips to kiss it, Alain's own fingers clenched painfully around his fragile china cup. A second later it shattered in his hand.

Exclaiming and apologizing profusely, Alain sprang to his feet. Fortunately he had drunk all his coffee, and nothing had been spilt on his clothes. But he used the disruption as an excuse to leave the happy group. A stiff smile on his lips, he murmured, "I find that my early start from the city has tired me. Do you mind if I rest in my rooms for a short while?"

A chorus of assent met his request, and escorted by François—who had only accompanied him after Alain had sent him a speaking look—the two men departed for the house. It was Jean who stated the general impression of everyone else. "Is it my imagination," he asked, after the two young men had strolled away, "or does François seem less than pleased at the arrival of his friend?"

"I was wondering the same thing," John replied. "He did not seem particularly happy at Alain's presence."

"Well, I for one will be glad if my son has finally come to his senses and realizes that Alain Husson is *not* a young man after whom to model himself!" Lisette said tartly. "I have always been of the opinion that young Husson thinks far too highly of himself and has been outrageously indulged by his *maman* and sisters."

"And François has not?" Micaela inquired lightly, a twinkle very like her mother's in her dark eyes.

Lisette flushed faintly, but she said gamely, "It is true that I have—er—"

"Spoiled him?" Jean inquired with a teasing note.

Lisette laughed. "Oh, very well, I have spoiled him, but he is basically a good boy."

"He is not a boy," Hugh said gently, the smile on his face taking any sting from the words. "He is a man. And perhaps, he is discovering that one's first friends are not always one's best friends."

François would have agreed most emphatically with Hugh's assessment of the situation. For as long as he could remember he had admired and aspired to be like the dashing heir to the Husson fortune, but he had discovered during the course of the last several days that he no longer viewed Alain as the epitome of Creole verve and manliness. More and more, he found himself drawn to Hugh, and more and more he had become ashamed of his own actions—not only his part in the blatant robbing of the company, but also his surliness and rudeness toward the *Américains*, Hugh in particular. Thinking of some of the things he had said, he cringed.

François knew himself to be at fault, and he would not pretend otherwise, but he also knew that his youthful admiration of Husson and his willingness to follow blindly where the older man led were at least partly to blame for his present predicament. As he walked with Husson up the staircase and showed him the suite of rooms which had been assigned for his use during his visit, François suddenly realized that he did not like Husson very much. In fact, it was suddenly clear to him that there was little to admire in the other man. What was he after all, François wondered, but a wellborn, wealthy thug? A man who needed to dominate and wield power over others in order to feed his overweening pride; a man who habitually hid behind others and hired brutal underlings to carry out his commands. He was also, François admitted with a guilty pang, a man who could order the murder of a longtime acquaintance and have no qualms about it. And *I wanted to be like him?* François thought incredulously. *How could I have been so mad?*

It didn't help François's frame of mind that Alain took one scornful look at the sparse furnishings and faded window and bed hangings in his rooms, and said sarcastically, "If this is a sample of the *Américain*'s wealth, I am afraid that your sister has made a very bad bargain."

Instead of firing up as he would have not a week ago, or eagerly agreeing with him, François said mildly, "Hugh and Micaela were not yet expecting company. The house is being entirely redone, but it will be some time before all the new furnishings arrive and all the changes are made." Coolly he added, "The only reason you are here now is because you forced yourself upon us. If the surroundings displease you, you may leave."

Alain whirled around, his black eyes narrowed and dangerous. "Feeling brave, are we?" he asked silkily. "Have you forgotten that we are in this together?"

"No, I have not forgotten, but *you* have forgotten a

great deal if you think that I ever agreed to murder," François stated grimly.

"Do not tell me that you have developed a conscience?" Alain sneered. "Do you think to throw yourself on your brother-in-law's mercy? Do you think he will overlook what you have done because he is married to your sister?"

"No, I do not," François replied quietly, his face suddenly looking older, almost haggard. "But I have sworn to myself that no matter what happens to me, I will not stand by and let you kill him."

"You think to stop me?" Alain hissed, his hands clenching into fists. "You would dare?"

François nodded slowly.

Alain's ugly expression suddenly cleared, and, smiling, an open, sunny smile that had always charmed François previously, he threw an arm around François's stiff shoulders and murmured, "Come now, *mon ami*, what are we fighting about? You know that the *Américain* has to die. It is necessary if I am to marry your sister— have you forgotten that I have always wanted her for my wife?"

François deftly stepped away from Alain's clasp. "Have *you* forgotten that she did not want to marry you?" An ashamed expression flitted across his features. "And I was wrong to attempt to force her into a situation where she would have had no choice in the matter but to marry you. It is almost fitting that our plans to compromise her turned out as they did. Some might say that it was poetic justice for her to end up forced to marry Hugh Lancaster." His eyes bored steadily into Alain's. "And perhaps," he said quietly, "I no longer want you to marry Micaela."

"Then perhaps," Alain snapped, "you had better make

plans to see that the rather large sum you owe me is deposited in my bank on Monday morning."

François bowed with exaggerated politeness. "Of course. I intend to discuss the matter with my uncle within the next day or two." Proudly, he added, "You do not have to worry about your money. A Dupree always pays his debts, but not in the blood of other men. You will have your money—leave Hugh alone."

"And if I do not?" Alain asked tightly, his handsome features mottled with fury. "Do you really think that you can stop my plans for him?"

Short of confessing all to Hugh, François saw no way out of his dilemma. Realizing that falling out with Alain was going to gain him nothing, and might actually pose more of a danger to Hugh, he dropped his antagonistic stance and asked reasonably, "Why is it so important that you kill Hugh? I have promised to pay you what I owe you; our plans for your marriage to Micaela did not come to pass, and it is too dangerous to continue embezzling from the company. You already have a large fortune so you do not need the money. Why persist in this unlawful endeavor? Could you not simply stop what you are doing before anyone else gets hurt?"

Alain studied François's face for several minutes, his mouth tight and grim. Then he relaxed slightly and, throwing himself down in a worn black leather chair, said easily, "Perhaps you are right. Perhaps I have thought so long about killing Lancaster that it has become fixed in my mind."

"You will reconsider?" François asked eagerly, hardly daring to believe that he had stood up to Alain and had convinced the other man to change his mind.

Alain's eyes dropped, hiding the fury in their depths. "I will certainly think about it." He glanced up and smiled with apparent ruefulness at François's anxious features, the expression in his gaze hidden. "I would dislike losing your friendship over this matter—after all, I had hoped to be your brother-in-law, and now that I consider it, much of what you have said has merit," he drawled. "You are my dearest friend. I would not want to offend you." Alain stood up, clapped François on the back, and said merrily, "Take that worried look off your face, *mon ami*; you have won. To please you, I shall rethink my plans—Hugh Lancaster will not die by my hand—I swear it to you."

François wanted desperately to believe that he had really changed Alain's mind, and though he nodded and exclaimed his relief at having the matter settled, he did not quite trust Alain. Husson was capable of great villainy and deceit as Etienne's death had shown. Still, when François left Alain's room a few minutes later, he felt that he *had* given Alain food for thought and that Alain might have spoken honestly—and, more important to François, Alain had given his word that he would not kill Hugh. Now, he thought glumly, if I can only bring myself to face up to what I have done, and tell Hugh and Jean.

François was not the only one with a secret weighing heavily on his mind. The previous night's conversation between Lisette and Jean was never very far from Lisette's thoughts, and, a dozen times during the day, she had almost brought herself to the point of speaking privately with John. Every time she thought she had fired up her courage enough, she would look at him and imagine the anger and hurt she would see in his eyes, and her heart would sink. Had they been kept apart all these years by other people's lies, only to stumble on the biggest lie of all? One that was entirely of her own making?

A bleak expression on her face, Lisette wandered through the flower-lined walkways of the grounds at *Amour* late that afternoon, her thoughts heavy and unhappy. John deserved to know, she told herself repeatedly. She could not begin their life together with the knowledge that Micaela was his daughter kept secret. But what if he turns from me? she wondered, anguished. What if he despises me for not having told him before now?

Common sense told her that he could not blame her for not having spoken earlier—until just a day ago they had both believed they had each been cruelly deserted by the other. But I should have told him yesterday, she admitted painfully. And every hour, every minute I delay makes it more difficult.

She was standing in the shade of a towering magnolia tree, the huge creamy blossoms perfuming the cooling air as she stared blankly at the small man-made lake near the gazebo. Intent upon her own thoughts, she had not heard John's approach and she started dramatically when he touched her lightly on the arm.

"I am sorry, my dear," he said apologetically. "I did not mean to frighten you." He grinned at her. "If I did not know better, I would think that you were either planning some dark, dastardly crime, or that you had a terrible secret to hide."

Lisette stared up at his beloved features. How could she bear to lose him again? And yet, his very words had given her the opening she needed.

A quick glance around confirmed that they were all alone, and, taking a deep breath, not allowing herself time to consider what she was saying or to change her mind, she said starkly, "I do have a secret. I did not know it at the time, but I was pregnant when we were parted. That was mainly the reason I agreed to marry Renault so soon after you left." Her eyes met his unflinchingly. "Micaela is not Renault's child. She is yours—ours."

Chapter Twenty-one

John stared at her, his expression a mixture of astonishment and awe. "Micaela is *my* daughter?" he finally managed after several long, agonizing moments.

Lisette nodded, too moved by the dawning delight on his face to speak. What could she have said anyway? Her future, happy or brutally shattered, lay in John's hands. Her body braced as if for a blow, she regarded him, loving him even more at this moment when she might very well lose him again, this time forever. His initial reaction was promising, but when he had recovered from his shock, when he'd had time to think about it, would he hate her? Angrily condemn her and believe that she had practiced the cruelest chicanery of all on him?

"My child," John said dazedly. "I have a daughter." The words were spoken in a manner which strongly suggested that he had to actually say them aloud to understand them. "*Our* daughter, Micaela."

Just when Lisette thought she could bear the suspense no longer, the most tender smile imaginable illuminated his face and with a laugh, a shout, his hands closed around her waist and he swung her off her feet. Whirling them around like a wild man, he grinned at her. "We, *Madame*-bride-to-be, are parents! Is it not the the most wonderful thing in the world?" His crazy dance slowed and his expression grew intent. Slowly he put Lisette down. Brushing her lips with his, he said thickly, "Actually, the second most wonderful thing in the world—the most wonderful thing is that you love me and that you are going to marry me—even if it is over twenty years later than it should have been."

He kissed her, his lips warm and caressing against hers. His mouth tasted of passion barely leashed, of desperate longing and tenderness and Lisette felt herself responding with all her heart, with all her love. As his lips moved on hers, the suffocating terror that she might have lost him forever gradually ebbed away. He loved her. Even after she had denied him his child. Tears of gratitude and joy suddenly flooded her eyes.

"Oh, John," she murmured brokenly, her arms tightening convulsively around him. "I was so afraid that you would hate me when you found out."

His lips tasted the tears on her lashes, and his face softened even more. "Hate you, my love? How could I? I have loved you all my life, and now I find that you have given me a gift that I never thought to receive—a child." A whimsical smile curved his chiseled mouth. "And after waiting this long to marry you, I am not going to let *anything* come between us."

His hand on her waist, he gently guided her to the wooden settee they had shared earlier in the day. Settling her in the crook of his arm, he said, "Now tell me everything. Everything about her, when she learned to walk, to speak. Everything."

They talked for a long time, their voices rising and falling rhythmically, the purple-and-rose twilight settling gently around them. Not even the buzzing mosquitoes seemed willing to intrude in their cozy little world. Lisette did her best to answer his eager questions, both of them laughing now and then when she related one of Micaela's more amusing antics over the years. When she finally had run out of anecdotes, John leaned his head back and gave a great sigh, a happy one.

Silence fell between them. Peace and tranquillity washed over them. There were still difficult moments ahead—not the least of them Micaela's reaction to the truth—but for the moment that problem was put aside. Micaela would have to be told, but not this very instant. Hugh would also need to know. They had already decided that for Micaela's sake, and to save her the embarrassment and scandal that would be sure to erupt, her true parentage did not have to become public fodder. Only those most immediately involved needed to know the truth. Not even François would be admitted to the secret. Micaela and Hugh were the only ones who needed to be told the truth, and very soon. But not right now.

Eventually John stirred and said in a tone of such deeply felt regret that it tore at Lisette's heart, "I wish I could have seen her grow up. I wish I just could have known that we had a child."

Lisette's hand tightened on his. "I am sorry," she said softly. "So very sorry for my part in denying you your child."

John glanced at her and shook his head. "You have nothing to be sorry for, my dear." His face hardened. "It is your father and Renault who have much to answer for—and fortunately for them, they are both already dead or I might have had to kill them with my bare hands."

"Do not!" Lisette cried. "Do not let us dwell on what

they cost us—it will only cost us more if we let their evil deeds cloud our happiness."

He kissed their entwined hands. "To please you, I shall not. Now tell me, who else besides Jean knows that Micaela is my daughter?"

"No one. I did not even know that Jean knew until last night, when he taxed me with my silence."

"For which," John admitted, "I am damned glad!" He slanted her a stern look. "I cannot believe that you were afraid of me—afraid to tell me. What did you think I would do—abandon you again?"

Lisette's eyes filled with tears again. She nodded, her woebegone expression so pitiful that John groaned and pulled her into his arms. Raining kisses on her cheeks, nose, and mouth, he muttered, "I do not think there is anything in the world that would cause me to leave you again—not when we have just found each other." He drew back and looked down at her, a crooked smile curving his lips. "Do you not know that you're my life, that life without you is unthinkable? Unendurable? For over twenty years, I have thought the love of my life was lost to me." His eyes darkened. "*Nothing* is ever going to come between us again. I swear it."

While Lisette and John basked in the discovery that sometimes love really could conquer all obstacles, Hugh was finding out that love did not exactly resolve every problem between a man and his wife. Since he and Micaela had finally confessed their love for each other, Hugh had been a happy man. A very, *very* happy man. There was only one blight on his unalloyed joy and that occurred, to his great and painful mystification, during their most intimate moments.

The afternoon that he had been wounded had been the

first and *only* time that he had known, truly known, that he had given his wife the ultimate physical satisfaction. For a few, fleeting moments, she had responded openly and generously to his caresses, her low moans and eager movements telling him clearer than words that he had pleased her. He had been thrilled, elated at her obvious pleasure in his lovemaking, feeling that at last he had broken through the iron control she kept on her emotions. He had, he admitted wryly, been smugly confident that he had finally solved *that* particular problem. The argument which had sprung up so swiftly between them had put them at odds once again and had made further exploration of Micaela's erotic nature out of the question. But with their differences settled and the knowledge that they loved each other openly declared between them, Hugh had assumed that all her inhibitions in the bedroom would have disappeared and that she would reveal again the passionate creature he had glimpsed the day he had been shot. To his chagrin, she had not.

His brow furrowed, he wandered around his sparsely furnished study, trying to understand what was not precisely *wrong*, but lacking between them in that one area. Without conceit, he knew that he was a skilled lover. He took his time making love to her, he did not hurry her, as much for his own pleasure as hers, and he wanted her to take as much delight in their lovemaking as he did. He was tender and wooed her gently when they made love, which since their mutual confessions had been indecently frequent. His wife's lush charms held a never-ending fascination for him.

Hugh knew that his wife loved him—she had said so and he believed her. Micaela was never cold or indifferent to him—nor had she ever refused him, except for obvious reasons. She always seemed to welcome his advances, and he could not say that she ever gave any sign that she found his lovemaking repulsive. And yet . . .

He scowled. And yet, when they lay together, except for the faintest of signs, Micaela was like a soft, warm, complaisant doll! He never knew for certain if she found their joinings as wonderful and exciting as he did or even if he had pleased her.

Hugh was well aware that Micaela had been gently reared and protected from the more elemental aspects of life. And he could safely assume that sex was not a topic of conversation among demure young Creole ladies. The Creoles sheltered and protected their daughters from the coarser aspects of men as fiercely as any puritanical father could have wished. His scowl deepened. But even considering all that, surely after all these weeks of marriage she would have begun to put aside some of her inhibitions? He loved his tart-tongued wife, and there was little he would have changed about her. But, he admitted glumly, for all her sweet charms, he did want something more than simply an accommodating body in his bed, no matter how warm and acquiescent! Making love was something one did *with* someone, not just *to* someone.

Hugh sighed heavily, wondering how he could introduce such a delicate subject without hurting Micaela's feelings or sounding like he was complaining. He felt greedy and almost guilty for wanting more from their marriage. His wife loved him and never denied him— surely he should be content with that? But he wasn't, and he was angry with himself for yearning for something that might never be his.

If only I understood why she is so oddly placid in bed, he mused unhappily, when in all other aspects of their life together she does not hesitate to make her feelings known. Was it just that she is merely shy about the intimacies that they shared and that in time she would grow more comfortable with his lovemaking? he wondered. Was just shyness the reason why she always seemed to hide under the sheets or insisted that the candles be blown out before he came to her? Had he never, he suddenly realized, actually seen his wife naked? Did their lovemaking embarrass her? Or was it something about him? His face grew grim. Could it be that though she loved him, she did not really enjoy his lovemaking? And was it just his lovemaking, or was it that she found the entire act distasteful?

Hugh could not believe that she found lovemaking not to her liking. She was too sweetly accommodating, too welcoming, to be repulsed by the act alone. His expression grew somber. It must be him, he thought heavily. Somehow he had to find a way to talk to her about it. Unfortunately for him, the unpleasant notion that there must be something about him that she found offensive would not go away and began to take on enormous significance in his mind. By the time several more minutes had passed, he was convinced that the fault lay with him—his wife, he feared, found something about his lovemaking so utterly offensive that she could only lie there beneath him and endure it.

Upstairs in her rooms, seeking relief from the humid heat of the afternoon, Micaela was luxuriating in a huge brass tub filled with lukewarm water. The water foamed with gardenia-scented bubbles, and as she settled back comfortably in the tub, her thoughts were on her husband, specifically on the delightful pleasures they had shared the previous night. She would have been horrified if she had known that Hugh believed she found him or his lovemaking not to her liking—especially since she adored everything about him and his lovemaking.

She was quite positive that she was the most fortunate of women and that she had the handsomest, kindest, most generous husband in the world. That he loved her and showed her so in a dozen different ways only made her own love for him grow. A dreamy smile on her lips, she washed languidly, the tepid water soothing against her heated skin, the rivulets running down her breasts and over her nipples bringing back the vivid memory of Hugh's lips traveling that same path last night. She sighed blissfully.

It had been torture, although of the sweetest kind, to lie so passively in his arms, to let him do as he willed with her, to keep her hands from caressing him, to stop herself from wantonly offering her body to him. It had nearly been impossible to tamp down the rampant urges of her own body, to smother the moans and wild responses to his touch that swamped her every time he made love to her, but ever mindful of *Tante* Marie's words of warning, she had managed to keep her passions in check. She was determined that Hugh would never find her behavior in bed anything to complain about—certainly he would never have reason to even consider divorcing her because he thought her licentious or lewd! Never suspecting that Hugh would have been overjoyed with a little licentious behavior on her part, Micaela continued her bath, already looking forward to the coming night and her husband's embraces.

The tub had been set up in her spacious dressing room and hearing the sound of steps crossing her bedroom, she assumed it was one of the servants bringing up more hot water. When the door opened and she saw that it was her husband, a little squeak of dismay came from her.

A flush on her cheeks, she immediately sank beneath the concealing foam, the flush increasing when she realized that the waning bubbles did not entirely hide her nakedness. "Hugh!" she exclaimed, greatly agitated. "Go away! You must not see me!"

Hugh stood in the doorway utterly transfixed by the delightful scene that met his gaze. Micaela's black, glossy hair was piled haphazardly on her head, unruly tendrils curling near her flushed cheeks, and her shoulders gleamed wetly above the translucent mantle of white foam, the tips of her breasts barely revealed. Desire seared through him, his manhood hard and throbbing in a second, his gaze locked on that teasing glimpse of her rosy nipples beneath the water.

"And why," he asked thickly, "should I not see you?" As one in a trance, he shut the door behind him and walked across the floor toward her. "You are my wife— there are no secrets between us."

His state of arousal was obvious. The impressive bulge in the front of his tight-fitting breeches made Micaela excitingly aware of precisely what was on his mind. She swallowed, then, ignoring the indecent rush of emotion that went through her, she said desperately, "I am naked—a good Creole wife never exposes her naked body to her husband. I do not want you to be ashamed of me."

"A good Creo—" Hugh looked at her, an incredible notion suddenly crossing his mind. Could it be? He had known that Creole women were raised to be submissive and passive to their husbands in all things. He had heard tales of Creole men, married for fifty years or more, never having seen their wives' bodies. Good God! Did Micaela think she was pleasing him by modestly wrapping herself in enveloping nightgowns and hiding behind a screen when she undressed? Did she honestly believe that he expected her simply to lie there while he took his pleasure? A gleam entered his eyes. If she did, she was about to be shocked. Very.

An alarming smile suddenly lit his face. Her eyes grew round when he sat down on a stool near the tub and proceeded to take off his boots.

"What are you doing?" she asked in growing astonishment and not a little excitement. When he stood up and shrugged out of his shirt, her mouth formed a perfect O of delight at the sight of his sleekly muscled chest.

"I am about to perform an experiment, one that I think you will enjoy, if you promise me something first."

Tearing her gaze away from his chest, a wary expression on her face, she asked cautiously, "What sort of promise?"

He bent over and pressed a warm kiss on her surprised mouth. "I want you," he said as he feathered small, teasing kisses over her face, "to promise me, to *swear* to me, that for the next several minutes, you will *not* be a good Creole wife! I want you to promise me that you will let your body guide you, that if I do something you like, you will let me know." Deftly he slid a hand down into the water to cup her breast lightly. Startled and unable to help herself, Micaela gasped with pleasure. "Yes!" Hugh said softly, "that is what I want. I want you to *show* me that you desire me, I need you to encourage me, to touch me as I touch you."

Every nerve in her body had come gloriously alive at the first touch of his mouth on hers, and the feel of his hand caressing her breast awoke a heavenly crescendo within her. Her nipples were already hard, and between her legs she could feel a damp, aching heat. But his words confused her. She angled her head back and regarded him with wide eyes. "Y-y-you want me to show you? B-b-but would you not find that repulsive? Distasteful? Would it not make you displeased with me?"

A decidedly carnal smile curved his lips. "No," he said simply. "It would, instead, make me the happiest of men."

He stood up and, in one swift motion, discarded his breeches. His manhood sprang free, the size and swollen state making Micaela's mouth go dry, her heart to beat thunderously.

Unable to tear her eyes away from him, she stared mesmerized. They had been married for over two months and yet she had never seen him naked, had never seen a naked man before in her life. The sight was absolutely breathtaking . . . and vastly arousing. He was wonderfully fashioned, Micaela thought admiringly, from his broad shoulders, lean hips, and shapely legs, right down to his long, elegant feet. And in between, oh, in between, he was everything a woman could have dreamed. Her eyes unknowingly caressed him, lingering helplessly on the stiff rod which jutted out from the black curly hair between his legs. As she stared, that marvelous object seemed to lengthen and enlarge right before her very eyes. Astonished, her gaze flew to his face.

He was smiling, an incredibly pleased yet oddly tender smile. "You see," he said gently, "just your gaze upon me can arouse me. By hiding our bodies from each other, we are also denying ourselves a great source of pleasure."

Micaela swallowed with difficulty and blurted out, "But *Tante* Marie says that no self-respecting Creole wife would let her husband see her unclothed." Her eyes locked painfully on his, she rushed on, hurrying to get the words out before she lost her nerve. "Or would act the part of a wanton in the marriage bed. She said that a Creole husband wants a wife who is self-effacing at all times, and that boldness has no place between a man and his wife. She told me that there was even once a Creole man who wanted to divorce his wife because he thought her too forward in the bedroom." Almost in a whisper she added, "I do not want you to divorce me."

Appalled at what must have been going through her head all this time, Hugh said softly, "*Tante* Marie is an old windbag who has not the faintest idea what she is talking about." He smiled tenderly. "I swear that no matter what you do, I have no intention of ever divorcing you, my sweet. And I shall tell you something else." He tipped her face up with one finger. Laughter dancing in the depths of his gray eyes, he murmured, "It may have escaped your notice, but I am not a Creole. I *am*, however, a man who loves you and wants you very much. And I do *not* want a Creole wife like the one this *Tante* Marie describes." He kissed her, a long, hungry kiss, and he was almost breathless when he added, "I want my own sweet little wife, and I want her to act as bold and as wanton as she likes in my arms."

Micaela sat there in the cooling water, blinking at him, her mind assimilating everything he said. A thought occurred to her and she bit her lip. "Have I displeased you?"

Hugh made a face. "*Displeased me? No.* Made me wonder if I displeased you? Oh, yes."

"*Non! Non!*" she cried, half-rising from the water in her distress. "Never have you displeased me. Never! You have been everything that is wonderful and kind."

His gaze fell to her generous bosom, and he said thickly, "I am not feeling very kind at the moment, my love. At the moment," he muttered, as he grasped her upper arms and pulled her naked, wet body up the length of his, "all I can think of is how very much I want you."

"And I w-w-want you," she said in a tremulous voice, equally delighted and terrified at her boldness.

"Do you really, my dear?" At Micaela's shy nod, he kissed her thoroughly and promised huskily, "Then I shall do my very best to see that you have me, all of me."

Heedless of anything else, he carried her into his bedroom. And there on his bed, in the seductive warmth of the golden afternoon, he proceeded to show Micaela precisely how very wrong *Tante* Marie had been.

Leaving the bed curtains open to admit the pale yellow sunlight, he stared openly and caressingly at his wife's many charms. "How could you think that I would find the sight of your very lovely and utterly enchanting body undesirable?" he asked softly. His eyes candidly explored her. "Do you not realize that seeing you, seeing your sweet and exciting charms and seeing the reaction my touch has upon you, is as important a part of lovemaking as anything else?" He kissed her nipples, his tongue curling teasingly around the rigid nubs. "You are lovely, here . . ." His lips slid down to her flat abdomen, sending a shocking tingle through her. "And here . . ."

His mouth was warm and provoking as he spread lazy little kisses across her stomach. Micaela was flooded with sensation and trembled, her fingers uncertainly touching his thick dark hair. He murmured, "Yes, touch me if you wish, anywhere . . . as I intend to touch you." With an endearing uncertainty, she followed his command, her fingers and hands growing more confident with every passing second. Hugh willed himself to remain still, to let her explore as she wished, the touch of her questing fingers a torment and a delight.

His own passions were fully roused, and it was all he could do not to sink into the sweet, welcoming warmth he knew would be his and instead hold himself in check and give her complete access to his body. The feel of her hands caressing his nipples, wandering over his broad back and taut buttocks, made him sigh aloud with pleasure. And when her hand moved to his throbbing, aching manhood, he was certain he was going to die of ecstasy. The rapt expression on her face was nearly his undoing, and, with a muffled groan, he caught her hands in his. Kissing them, he muttered, "Enough for now, dear heart . . ." He glanced up at her, his gray eyes bright with desire, and said thickly, "Now it is my turn."

Already excited and eager for his touch, with every probing kiss he bestowed, she became even more deeply aroused. His mouth seemed to be everywhere, and he made it clear that she pleased him immensely, his husky words of delight building the aching heat within her into a powerful inferno. He was seducing her, she thought giddily, with not only his touch, but his eyes and his words, making her aware of her body in a way that she had never known possible. Her breathing was labored, every inch of her skin on fire where his lips had touched. When his mouth suddenly slid even lower across her stomach, when his hands parted her thighs and his wickedly searching lips found her, his tongue seeking the most secret part of her, her reaction was everything that Hugh could have wished.

Micaela felt as if she had been seared by fire—a flame so sweet and so intense that she arched up uncontrollably, her fingers clutching his dark head, pulling him and his exquisite exploring mouth closer to her. What he was doing was unthinkable, surely depraved, but she found that she could not stop him, that she did not *want* to stop him. . . .

Her scent was in his nostrils, her taste upon his tongue and lifting her hips slightly, Hugh continued his leisurely, explicit explorations between the soft, delicate folds of flesh. A feral smile curved his lips when she let out a shaken moan, and his hands tightened on her hips when she jerked and trembled under his bold caresses.

Hardly aware of what she was doing, gripped by the most incredible sensations she had ever experienced, Micaela writhed beneath his caresses. She was feverish and trembling, frightened and thrilled by what he was doing, her nerves seeming to coil and bunch in the most exciting way possible. She felt on the brink of some new and terrifying discovery, and when it happened, when pleasure such as she had never even dreamed exploded through her, she jammed a fist in her mouth to muffle the scream which rose up inside of her.

Hugh felt her response, heard the hushed scream of delight, and a tight smile crossed his face. He kissed her throbbing flesh one last time and slowly eased up over her damp body. Taking her fist from her mouth, he said, "I want to hear you, my love. I want, I *need* to know that I have pleased you. There will be no more secrets between us." His warm glance traveled down her generous curves revealed in the pale glow of the sunlight which dappled the room. "You are incredibly lovely to me. And always remember that the sight of your body gives me great pleasure—never be ashamed of what nature gave you." He kissed her and murmured against her mouth, "And, remember, too, that I want your hands on me—that my body is yours to explore at will. I want you to drive me mad with your touch." Tenderly brushing back a tendril of hair that had fallen across her brow, he stared down into her stunned, sated eyes.

A wicked glint suddenly lit his gaze. "Of course, if you would rather follow *Tante* Marie's dictates . . ."

Almost too weak to move, loving him more than she

had thought possible, Micaela ran a caressing finger down his lean cheek. "I think," she said softly, "that *Tante Marie* has absolutely no idea what she is talking about."

"Excellent!" Hugh said as he smoothly angled himself between her legs. He kissed her hungrily, and, when her arms went around his neck and her body eagerly arched up to meet his, Hugh knew a sweet joy. His wife loved him—and just as important—wanted him as much as he wanted her.

Chapter Twenty-two

*I*f Hugh and Micaela thought that they had been happy before, that afternoon showed them the error of their thinking. Micaela discovered for the first time, truly discovered, the joys that could be found in the marriage bed with a loving, virile husband. And Hugh? To his ever-expanding delight, Hugh discovered again the passionate, sensual creature he had only glimpsed the day that he had been shot.

It was very late afternoon before they finally rose from Hugh's bed and Hugh proceeded to scandalize Micaela—but not to any great degree—by joining her in a freshly prepared tub. Bathing with her husband, she discovered, could be *most* invigorating. With more than a little regret, they finally dressed and descended the staircase to see how their guests had fared.

Of François and Alain there was no sign, but they found Lisette, John, and Jean sitting on the shady side of the house in several comfortable rocking chairs which, at Micaela's request, had been rescued from the pile of old furnishings left stacked in one of the barns and newly repainted a dark gleaming green. From the expressions on

the three faces, it was apparent that they had been discussing something fairly serious, but at the sight of their
hosts, they began to smile and talk rather animatedly
about the coming wedding. Hugh eyed them speculatively. If he did not know better, he would think that there
was a plot of some sort under way, at the very least a secret between the suspiciously bright and suddenly voluble trio.

But as the evening passed, Hugh completely forgot
about his earlier observations and set himself out to be an
exemplary host, considering that he had abandoned his
guests all afternoon to dally in bed with his wife—something he planned to do again at the first possible moment.
Down the long expanse of the table, he glanced at her, a
reminiscent gleam in his eyes. The sultry look she returned and the promise in that dark-eyed gaze almost
made him choke on his wine. Had he, he wondered with
a pleasurable ache in his loins, created an insatiable wanton? He certainly hoped so!

Too preoccupied with thoughts of what he would like
to do with Micaela as soon as they could decently bid
their guests good evening, Hugh only noticed in passing
that Alain's presence had not seemed to have lightened
François's mood. If anything François seemed more tense
and somber. But having other things on his mind, Hugh
promptly pushed further speculation away. There was
only one person who held his attention, and if she did not
stop throwing him those come-hither glances, he was
going to shock everyone by acting the part of the libertine
with his very own wife!

After dinner as luck would have it, Alain and François
had made plans to visit with some friends who lived on
the next plantation over. Their absence was welcomed by
everyone—Hugh and Micaela because it meant that they

could escape upstairs earlier and the other three because it gave them an unexpected opportunity to have a particularly sensitive conversation with their hosts.

The five of them, escaping the heat of the house, were sitting out under a pair of magnolia trees, the sweet scent of the blossoms lingering in the warm air. To keep the mosquitoes at bay, several small pots of brimstone had been lit, and it seemed to be an effective deterrent against the swarming pests. A lantern had been hung in each tree and they shed two flickering circles of light in the darkness. There was a welcome breeze from the river's direction, and the croak of frogs and the occasional roar of a bull alligator drifted through the night.

The conversation was desultory at first as they sat in the dancing shadows, watching the lightning bugs flit in the distance. But as the minutes passed Hugh became aware of a note of strain in Lisette's voice. John glanced at her. Covering her hand with his, he leaned over and whispered something in her ear. Lisette shook her head vehemently.

Jean was also looking at her with an encouraging expression on his face. Hugh's eyes narrowed. What the devil?

Her mother's growing strain had not gone unnoticed by Micaela, who asked, "*Maman*, are you all right? Do you have the headache?"

Lisette looked across the brief shadowy expanse which separated them, Micaela's face a pale, sweet cameo in the faint light from the lanterns. "No," she said slowly. "I feel fine." She glanced uneasily between John and Jean, and, at some unspoken signal between them, she took a deep breath and declared solemnly, "I have something to tell you—something that will shock you. It is something that has been a secret for over twenty years."

John's hand tightened on Lisette's. Staring at them, Hugh suddenly had an inkling of what Lisette was going to say—something he should have suspected the minute he had heard the tale of the long-ago love affair between the pair of them and saw that elusive dimple of Micaela's. Rising indolently to his feet, he went to stand near Micaela's chair, his hand lying protectively on her shoulder.

Unaware of the tension invading the others, Micaela glanced up at Hugh and smiled. Affectionately she rubbed her soft cheek against Hugh's warm hand before looking back at her mother and asking, "What is it, *Maman*? What could you possibly tell me that would shock me?" She laughed. "Especially something that happened before I was born." The instant the words left her mouth, Micaela felt a stab of unease. Lisette's affair with John Lancaster had happened before she was born . . . and it had ended an indecently short time before her mother had married Renault. . . . Her eyes suddenly fixed on the couple across from her, she demanded, "What? Tell me!"

Baldly, Lisette said, "Renault Dupree is not your father. I was pregnant when I married him. John Lancaster is your father."

Micaela gasped, and Hugh's hand closed around her shoulder. Unconsciously, her hand joined his, and she clung to him as if he were the only stable thing in her universe.

The silence which followed Lisette's confession was deafening as Micaela stared first at her mother and then at John Lancaster. With pain in her gaze, she finally looked at Jean. "You knew?" she asked huskily.

Jean nodded, his face grave.

She swallowed with difficulty as the real meaning of Lisette's words pounded in her brain. She had lived a lie her whole life. *Papa* was not *Papa*. Jean was not her uncle. The Dupree blood, the ancestors that she had thought were hers, were not. Had never been. She was a bastard child, only Lisette's providential marriage having saved her from disgrace and shame. Too stunned even to cry, Micaela simply sat there, staring dazedly into the darkness.

It was John Lancaster who broke the uncomfortable silence. "We do not intend for this to become public knowledge," he said gently. When Micaela stiffened and looked at him incredulously, he said hastily, "Not because I would not be proud and honored for everyone to know that I have such a lovely daughter, but because I would not want you to suffer the humiliation and pain that would arise if everyone knew the truth."

"It is no one's business," Jean murmured quickly, "but ours. We five are the only people who know the truth and will be the *only* ones who ever know the truth." When Micaela's features remained frozen, he added quietly, "We meant you no harm, *petite*, by telling you—we felt it was only fair for you and Hugh to know the identity of your real father." He smiled fondly at Micaela. "This really changes nothing, *ma chérie*. I trust that you will still consider me your uncle—I know that I will always think of you as my niece."

Micaela nodded numbly in his direction, her thoughts and emotions spiraling dizzily through her brain. Some of the first shock was leaving, and there was curiosity in her gaze when she looked at John Lancaster. He was her father, she thought stunned. This tall, likable *Américain* with the whimsical smile was her *father*.

"How long have you known about me?" she asked in a small voice.

A tender, eager smile crossed John's face. "Not as long

as I would have wished." He flashed a warm glance at Lisette's taut face. "Your mother, for obvious reasons, did not tell me until this afternoon. It was," he said softly, "the most wonderful news I could ever have received, next to your mother agreeing to marry me." He sighed. "I just wish that I had known sooner—we missed a great deal, you and I. But I am hoping that you will allow me privately to take up the duties and delights of fatherhood and that perhaps eventually you will look at me with affection." Their eyes met. "I do not intend to force myself upon you. We shall move slowly into our new relationship, you may set the pace. The last thing that I want is to make you uncomfortable or miserable. I, we, all want only your happiness."

Micaela smiled faintly. He was very charming, this father of hers, she admitted with a funny little spurt of pleasure. She felt so strange, not exactly excited, not precisely sad, certainly confused and perplexed, but not in a painful way any longer. In fact, with every passing moment, her initial dismay and hurt was fading. John Lancaster was her father! Somehow that knowledge did not displease her. Actually, the more she considered it, the more she began to like the idea. Her father was not dead—he was sitting right across from her! And he was going to marry her *maman* in just a few weeks.

"Are you very angry with me?" Lisette asked abruptly, her eyes filled with anxiety. "I-I-I never meant to lie to you—it was just that it seemed best for you, for all of us, if you believed Renault was your father." A tiny sob came from Lisette. "Oh, *petite*, please do not hate me! I did not mean to harm you."

Micaela's heart melted at her mother's distress. Slipping across the short distance that separated them, she sank to her knees by Lisette's chair. Smiling lovingly up at Lisette, she said simply, "*Maman!* How could I hate you or condemn what you did? It did not harm me. You did what you thought was right at the time." She looked over at John Lancaster and sent him a dazzling smile. "It is a good thing that you are marrying my *maman*—when I call you '*Papa*' no one will wonder at it!"

"Oh, *ma chérie!*" Lisette cried, hugging Micaela. "I have been so afraid. It has been a terrible burden."

"But one you no longer have to carry by yourself," Micaela murmured. "We will all share it now, *oui*?"

Misty-eyed, Lisette nodded, John's hand held tightly in one hand, Micaela's in the other.

With a twinkle in his eyes, Hugh walked over to the trio. Helping his wife to stand, he glanced at John. "I seem to remember," he said lightly, "saying something to the effect that I was glad you had not married Lisette, that if you had, my adorable wife would not have been born. It seems that I must rephrase that statement and thank you most sincerely for having had the foresight to have created the woman I love more than I can say."

Micaela beamed up at him. "What a handsome thing to say, *mon amour*."

Hugh grinned at her. "I am a very handsome fellow, remember?"

"*Bon!*" Jean said with a note of relief. "It seems that we have managed to cover the rough ground lightly enough, and I, for one, think some brandy would not come amiss right now." He smiled. "A celebratory partaking, of course."

Later that night, as they lay in bed together, Micaela asked softly, "You do not mind that your stepfather is my *papa*?"

Hugh chuckled and pulled her closer. "Mind? Sweetheart, when are you going to learn that I think you are perfect. That it doesn't matter a damn to me who your parents are. All I care about is that I have you. You are my wife and I love you and you love me. Nothing else matters."

Pleased and extremely gratified, Micaela kissed him. She started to speak and then, as if deciding against something, snuggled down next him. But Hugh had seen her expression, and, nudging her slightly, he murmured, "What? Is there something else on your mind?"

Micaela sat up and stared down into his beloved features. "We talk about many things," she began carefully, "and there are now few secrets between us, but the one thing you *never* talk about to me, is the very thing that brought us together—the troubles at our company."

Hugh looked uncomfortable. "I did not want to worry you," he offered lamely.

Micaela snorted. "You forget that it is my company, too, *mon cher*. That whatever happens to it affects me greatly. Should I not know what is going on—what you have found out, or have not? And how serious the problem is? Or how you intend to correct it? You tell me nothing, yet my future, our future, is linked to the affairs of Galland, Lancaster and Dupree. Do you not think that now that we have resolved our personal problems, it is time that *we* resolve the difficulties of the company?"

Hugh was quiet for a long time, turning her words over in his head. What Micaela had said was true. Everything. She was right—there should be no secrets between them . . . not if their marriage was to become a true partnership.

"Trust you to put your finger directly on the delicate issue!" he said ruefully. And having conceded the wisdom of her words, he proceeded to tell her everything that he had discovered; the method that had been used systematically to rob the company, and his suspicions that one of the owners might be behind it all.

"Even my *oncle* or François?" Micaela asked, clearly shocked at such a thought.

Hugh shrugged. "It is possible. I no longer think your uncle is involved, although I did in the beginning. And as for Jasper—I never did suspect him."

"But you still suspect *François?*"

"Unless I am mistaken, he still owes Husson a large sum of money. And one way to pay off his debts would be to help himself to the company's goods. It is not implausible."

"But unlikely!" Micaela said stoutly, unwilling to believe that François would stoop to stealing from his family.

"Not really," Hugh replied quietly. "He probably would not even consider it stealing—merely taking what is already his."

"You believe this?"

"I hope that I am wrong. I would like," he answered grimly, "for Husson to turn out to be our thief. It would make things so much tidier."

Micaela looked troubled. "I do not want to believe that François would do such a thing, but I cannot deny that there might be some truth in what you say. François is very spoiled—his wishes have been seldom thwarted—and unfortunately, I could see him justifying his actions. But I cannot see him committing cold-blooded murder, nor," she added frankly, "being brazen enough to steal the vast amounts that have been stolen lately. A little pilfering, *oui*, but not—" She glanced at Hugh. "Do you really think that Alain could be behind everything—the thefts and"—she shuddered slightly—"poor Etienne's murder?"

"You know him better than I—what do you think?"

Micaela's face became thoughtful. Uneasily, she remembered the look in Alain's eyes the night he had forced himself upon her. It had been a most unpleasant look, and there had been something, something extremely ugly and brutal about his actions that night. Slowly she nodded. "I think that in the right circumstances, Alain would make a bad enemy, that he might very well be capable of committing murder."

"So what do we do? Cast him out of our house? Accuse him?"

Micaela sent him a look. "Casting him out of our house or accusing him of being a thief and a murderer without proof would only provoke another duel, and I will not have you risking your life so foolishly." She kissed him soundly. "I do not intend to become a young widow."

"Such a lack of faith in my prowess on the dueling field! I think I shall be offended," Hugh murmured, grinning at her.

"You may be as offended as you like—at least you will be *alive!*"

"And that matters to you?" Hugh asked, confident of her answer.

"Oh, perhaps, a trifle," she replied airily, then ruined the effect by giggling. "You know that I adore you, you arrogant creature," she murmured as she slid down beside him, her arms around his neck. "And I shall not bolster your conceit by telling you how very much."

"Since we are not to talk about that particular fascinating subject, what do you think we should do about Alain?"

"We shall watch him," Micaela said sleepily. "He shall

not make a move that we do not see. While he is visiting us that will be simple enough, one of us can keep an eye on him—and when he leaves, you will hire someone to shadow his every step."

"That is a very good idea," Hugh said slowly. "A *very* good idea."

"I know," she muttered drowsily. "I thought of it."

Hugh lay awake a long time after Micaela had gone to sleep, thinking on the odd twists and turns of fate. It seemed, he thought with a smile, that he owed a great deal to Galland, Lancaster and Dupree. If John had not come south with the notion of starting up an import-export company and if he had not met with Christophe Galland and fallen in love with his beautiful daughter, Lisette . . . Even the cruel deceit practiced by Christophe and Renault had played a necessary part—without it, John would never have become his stepfather. And if someone had not been stealing from the company, he, himself might not have decided to relocate in New Orleans—might never have had the opportunity to fall in love with the bewitching little creature asleep at his side. Unthinkable!

Hugh was just about to follow Micaela into the arms of Morpheus when he heard footsteps coming down the hall. Despite the thickness of the walls, he heard the low undertone of two men talking and recognized the half-raised voices of Alain and François. He frowned, wishing to hell that François had had better taste in boon companions. Alain Husson was a born troublemaker, and the sooner he left for New Orleans, the sooner Hugh would like it. Actually, he thought with a decidedly carnal smile, the sooner *everybody* left him alone with his wife, the better he would like it.

François would have been more than happy to oblige

Hugh as guilt and fear made it increasingly uncomfortable for him to impose on Hugh's hospitality. But until Alain departed for the city, François was forced to remain at *Amour*. He did not quite trust his onetime friend, despite Alain's vow not to harm Hugh. He wanted Alain under his eye, where he could safely watch the other man for any moves against Hugh.

The two young men had spent a reasonably pleasant evening visiting with their friends and even during the ride back to the plantation, their conversation had been amiable. It was only after they had turned their horses over to the sleepy-eyed stableboy and begun to walk toward the main house and up the steps at the front of the house that the friendly state of affairs between them began to deteriorate.

Uneasy with Alain's presence at *Amour*, François asked him bluntly, "How long do you intend to remain here?"

Alain cocked a brow. "In such a hurry to get rid of me, *mon ami*?"

François's jaw clenched, but his voice was even. "Let us be frank. You did not come to see me—you came for another reason, and since that reason no longer exists—"

"Did I say it no longer existed?"

"You *swore* that you would not harm him. And I repeat, there is no longer any reason for you to remain here."

"Ah, but suppose I am enjoying myself? Suppose I do not wish to leave just yet?"

"But I want you to leave," François replied grimly, his voice rising slightly as they walked down the hall toward their rooms.

Alain looked at him, something ugly in his dark eyes. "Do you know that I find your company rather offensive just now? Do not push me, little man. I might be forced to deal with you, and trust me, you will not like my methods."

"Threats?" François asked dryly. "I should warn you—do not push *me* too hard. I might yet gather my pride and courage and tell Hugh everything."

They had reached Alain's door. Alain gave him a cool glance and said, "I see that there is no dealing with you in this mood. *Bonne nuit!* Perhaps tomorrow you will have recovered your senses."

François's state of mind did not change during the night and he spent another sleepless eternity in his bed before the soft light of dawn finally began creeping into his room. He continued to toss restlessly for another hour or two, before finally forcing himself to rise. Several minutes later, staring at the hollow-eyed apparition that stared back at him in his shaving mirror, he knew that he could not go on this way. His conscience lashed at him like a steel-tipped whip, and his pride would not let him forget that he was a coward and a thief.

But I do not have to remain a coward, he thought suddenly. To end this odious situation, all I have to do is confess all to Hugh. He stared for several endless minutes at his face in the mirror, feeling a powerful resolve build within him. Telling Hugh, he realized, was the only option before him. The truth was going to come out sooner or later. It would be far better if he were to speak first, rather than to wait like a craven coward for the blow to fall. And then there was the matter of Alain. Hugh would be warned. Hugh would know where the danger lurked.

Feeling better than he had in a very long time, François dressed swiftly. Not giving himself time to think, to crawl back into the black hole of despair where he had lingered these past days, he went in search of his brother-in-law.

There was a new purpose in his step, and a firm resolve dominated his young face as he walked down the stairs.

Knowing Hugh was an early riser, François headed directly to the sunny morning room, where they all habitually gathered first thing in the morning. To his relief, only John and Hugh were seated at the round table, enjoying a cup of coffee.

If either of the other men were surprised to see François this early, neither revealed it. They greeted him warmly, and Hugh indicated the pot of coffee on the long buffet, and said, "Sampson just brought that in—it's fresh and hot."

François shook his head, and said tautly, "Forgive me for my intrusion, but would it be possible for me to have a private word with you . . . now?" He glanced apologetically at John. "I hope that you will forgive me for interrupting your own conversation."

Hugh and John exchanged looks. Hugh shrugged and rose to his feet. "Certainly, it is no imposition. I was going to examine that new mare I bought last week from Jasper—you may accompany me to the stable." A smile crossed Hugh's face, and he said to John, "Micaela should be down shortly. When she comes, tell her where we have gone and that I would not object, after her coffee, if she joined me there." He glanced over at François. "You do not mind?"

François shook his head and muttered, "What I have to say will not take long."

A second later they set off, unaware that from the upper floor, Alain watched them go, his eyes hard, his lips curled in fury. It seemed that his hand was being forced. He would have to act swiftly.

Having gotten this far, François suddenly found that he was speechless. He did not know how to begin and for several minutes they walked in silence. They were almost to the stables before François said desperately, "Could we walk a bit farther? I do not want anyone to overhear what I have to say."

Hugh's brow rose, but silently he indicated a path that led eventually to the river. The stables had disappeared and the green, half-tamed wilderness had closed in on them before François, stumbling at first, and then finally in a rush, disclosed all. That he was consumed with guilt and deeply ashamed of what he had done was apparent, from not only the anguish in his voice, but the deep lines of pain on his face. He did not spare himself. He took the blame, his eyes fixed unflinchingly on Hugh's face as he told of the reckless gambling, the initial pilfering, and then the burgeoning network of thievery with Alain which had led ultimately to Etienne's murder. Lastly, he admitted his suspicion that Alain still meant to kill Hugh.

Hugh's expression did not change as François spoke, but his brain was working furiously. Alain he could handle, but what the devil was he going to do with François? Revealing his part in the thefts would destroy Lisette, not to mention how Micaela would feel. And then, he thought slowly, his gaze moving over François, there was this suffering young fool in front of him. The boy had obviously already punished himself a great deal, and the fact that François had come to him and confessed everything was distinctly promising. François, Hugh had decided sometime ago, was not inherently bad, just young, full of foolish pride, and very spoiled. Youth would pass, the spoiling could be corrected, and as for the foolish pride? Hugh smiled faintly. Pride was not a bad thing; they would just have to work on the foolish part.

One thing was certain, however. François could not get away without enduring some sort of punishment. He had stolen. And he had gone along with Alain, whatever the reasons behind that decision. Hugh looked thoughtful. It was possible that they could keep this between themselves. Micaela and John would have to know, and no doubt Jean, but there was no reason to distress Lisette. François would suffer enough just knowing that the men knew of his crimes. But what sort of punishment? Prison was not an answer. Banishment? Banishment, perhaps, to the offices of one of their English importers? Remove him from all that he had known and make him actually work for his living for a few years? It could even, Hugh thought, liking the notion, be given out that the decision to leave New Orleans was François's own, that he wanted to learn more of the business, strike out on his own for a while. That would create a reason for his departure. Perhaps.

Looking at François's hangdog expression, Hugh almost grinned. The poor young fool! It was time to put him out of his misery.

"I appreciate the fact that you came forward on your own," Hugh said quietly, his eyes fixed keenly on François's woebegone face. "It shows that beneath all that posturing and bluster, you have a strength of character that will give you good service in the future."

"What sort of future do I have?" François exclaimed despairingly. "I have shown myself to be a liar, a thief, and someone without any honor. My life is *ruined*."

"You are also young. You made mistakes, deplorable mistakes that you must pay for, but all the blame does not lie on your shoulders alone. Had you been left to your own devices, I am quite certain you would have stopped the petty thieving once your debts were paid. I would like to believe that you would have found a way eventually to repay what you had stolen. That is something we will never know, but you have made a good start by coming to me and admitting what you have done. I am relieved, I will confess, to learn that you had nothing to do with Etienne's death and did not know about it until too late. Murder is not something that can be overlooked." Hugh grimaced. "No doubt, in time, we shall be able to put this behind us. It is not," Hugh said softly, "the end of the world. In fact, it might just be a new beginning for you."

A faint spark of hope lit François's dark eyes. "A new beginning? You would trust me? You would give me another chance?"

Hugh nodded. "In time. After you have proven yourself—in England. I have decided that you should go away for a while. See another part of the world. And in particular be a safe distance away from the influence of Alain."

François looked aghast. "England?" he said in faltering tones. "I am to be banished to *England*?"

"Yes. It will be good for you, build that strength of character a little more," Hugh said dryly.

François swallowed, obviously dismayed, but it was clear that he was willing to do whatever Hugh decreed to redeem himself. "And Alain? What about him?"

Hugh's face grew grim. "You may safely leave Alain to me."

There was a crackle in the brush behind them as Alain stepped forward, a nasty smile on his lips, a pistol held in his hand. "And what precisely," he asked jeeringly, "do you intend to do about me, *Monsieur* Lancaster?"

Hugh stared at Alain and then at the pistol in his hand, the barrel pointed directly at his heart. "Do you plan on killing both of us?" Hugh inquired with only polite interest evident in his voice.

"Originally, no," Alain admitted candidly. "You were

the only one I wanted dead." He speared a venomous glance at François. "But that situation has changed since my onetime friend decided to come whining and crying to you. I am afraid that I will have to kill you both now."

"Hmm, and how do you propose to do that?" Hugh asked. He wore an expression almost of boredom on his handsome face as he rapidly calculated his chances of getting the pistol away from Alain—and not getting killed in the process.

Alain smiled nastily. "Why, I think that François will kill you and then the poor misguided boy will turn the pistol on himself. The explanation for this tragedy will be obvious when his systematic robbing of his family's own company is discovered. Of course," Alain added modestly, "I shall have to make arrangement that certain—ah—damning evidence against him is found. But that should not be too difficult for a man of my talents. It will be clear that you had found him out and that, in despair, he shot you, then killed himself." Alain's smile widened. "A rather tidy solution to a complicated business, *oui*?"

Startling all of them, François suddenly leaped in front of Hugh. "*Non!*" he shouted, shielding Hugh's broader form with his own body. "You will not kill him! You will have to kill me first!"

"Very well, if you wish," Alain said coldly, and took aim at François's forehead.

What happened next astonished all of them, the attack seeming to come out of nowhere. One minute Alain was on the point of firing, and the next a good-sized tree limb came crashing down viciously on his pistol arm. Micaela, looking like a fiery young Amazon with the heavy tree branch clutched in her hand, stepped out of the concealing brush and snarled, "*Non!* You dirty beast! You will not kill *my* husband or my brother!" Her bosom heaving, her eyes flashing, she was a magnificent sight. Her expression was so fierce that for a second even Hugh was taken aback.

Micaela's unexpected intervention had given them precious seconds, but Alain recovered almost instantaneously. His face contorted with fury, he swiftly swung the pistol up and fired in the direction of the other men. Hugh and François were already in motion as the pistol went off. The sound of the shot and François's scream were almost simultaneous, then Hugh was on Alain.

Oblivious to François's slumped, groaning form on the ground, Hugh fought for possession of the pistol, knowing that there was one more shot left in the weapon. Together he and Alain swayed, their hands grasping for a firm hold on the pistol, each man trying to turn it on the other.

Micaela spared an anguished glance at François's crumpled body, but her husband was her first concern. Holding the tree branch menacingly, she watched intently as the two men fought. Fearful of striking and inadvertently hitting Hugh, she held back, waiting impatiently for an opening to help her husband.

Alain and Hugh were locked together, the pistol between their two bodies, each man straining with all his might. They swayed almost like dancers, their faces contorted, their muscles bulging as they fought, and then, shockingly, the pistol went off. Micaela's heart stopped, only to begin to beat again when she saw Alain fall to the ground, a terrible parody of a smile on his face, a spreading stain of bright scarlet across his chest, dead.

Her club fell from her fingers, and she flew into Hugh's arms. *"Mon amour,"* she crooned. "I was so frightened. I did not know what to do when I heard him say he was going to kill you."

Hugh kissed her. "You did exactly the right thing," he said huskily. "How did you find us?"

"John told me you had gone to the stables, but you were not there—one of the stableboys had seen you and François go this way." She shuddered. "He had not mentioned Alain, but I caught a glimpse of him creeping up on you and after all you told me I was suspicious. When Alain pulled out his pistol, I knew he was up to no good, and I looked around for something to use as a weapon."

"Good for you," Hugh said warmly. Smiling down into her face, he murmured, "Have I told you how much I love you?"

She dimpled and started to reply when there was a sound behind them. Together they turned to look at François. He was sitting up, his hand held to his head, blood seeping slowly through his fingers. He glanced dazedly at them. "I am still alive," he said in a voice of wonder. His eyes fell on Alain's still form. "Is he dead?"

"Very," Hugh said dryly. "How badly are you hurt?"

Hugh and Micaela helped him to his feet. He swayed slightly, but gave them a ragged smile. "I shall live—perhaps with an interesting scar, but alive nonetheless."

"Do you think the story will hold together?" John asked thoughtfully, as he and Hugh and Jean were sitting in the study late that evening. François, weak from loss of blood but in no danger, was upstairs being fussed over by his mother and sister.

Hugh shrugged. "As far as we are concerned, Mr. Husson ordered his carriage and horses and left very early this morning for New Orleans. We were careful that no one saw me leave driving his vehicle. It was several miles from here before I left the carriage with his body in it and scattered his belongings along the road. When he is found, his death will, no doubt, be put down to bandits. We will be extremely shocked and saddened when we hear the news of his death, which should be sometime tomorrow. We know nothing, but that he left us in good health. As for François, he is under orders not to stir from *Amour* until his wound is completely healed." Hugh took a sip of his brandy. "And as for the shots anyone may have heard here this morning," he said quietly, "I was merely shooting at a water moccasin when François and I went on our walk." Hugh grinned slightly. "It was unfortunate that François had to fall and cut his head, but it was not serious."

Jean nodded. "It sounds plausible enough to me. But what about the thefts from the business?" His expression grew heavy. "And François's part in it?"

Hugh finished off his brandy. Rising to his feet, he walked across the room to replenish his snifter from the decanter on the table. After pouring the other two men some additional brandy, he reseated himself and murmured, "What thefts? Our fall in profits lately was only one of the usual cycles in business. We shall, I guarantee you, see a notable increase in revenue in the coming months. And as for François's part?" Hugh glanced steadily at Jean. "What *are* you talking about?"

Jean opened his mouth, then shut it and nodded. "Of course. You are right. It is the only way. It is best for everyone."

Hugh sent each man a long look. "Only we three and Micaela and François know the truth about the thefts and Etienne's death. Lisette has been told that Alain must have gone mad when he attempted to kill François and me—that is all she knows about the whole ugly affair and that is all that she needs to know. There is no reason to burden her with the sordid details of François's brief foray into crime. I think François has learned a hard lesson and that he will be a better man for it." Hugh's face grew somber. "I cannot forget that he risked his life for me this morning—that says much of his character. He is entitled to another chance, and I think the trip to England will give him time to face up to what he has done and give him a chance to grow up—without having to look over his shoulder all the time, to see if we are watching him, waiting for him to fall from grace. I have confidence that by the time he returns in a few years, he will have dealt with the situation and put it behind him—as we will have."

The two older men agreed. "It was a nasty business," John said. "I am glad that we can keep it amongst ourselves."

Jean shuddered. "The scandal would have been ruinous. It would have been terrible for the Husson family to have had Alain's crimes paraded before everyone. They would never have been able to hold up their heads again. It is better this way—for everyone."

Feeling rather satisfied with himself, a short while later Hugh entered his rooms and discovered his half-naked wife sitting in a decidedly seductive pose in the middle of his bed, her hair tumbling in a dark cloud around her shoulders. All thoughts of the day's events vanished from Hugh's mind as he approached her with a delighted smile on his handsome face. "I see that you have taken my words to heart," he said teasingly.

Micaela looked demure. "Why, *monsieur*, whatever do you mean?"

Hugh laughed. Scrambling out of his clothes, he

joined her in the bed. "I mean," he said huskily, as he dropped a kiss on one tempting breast, "that you obviously are not ashamed or reluctant to let me know your intentions."

"Is that what I am doing?" she asked, a sultry smile on her mouth.

"Oh, I sincerely hope so. . . ."

It was quite some time later before coherent thought returned to either one of them. Nestled next to each other, desire momentarily slaked, they talked about Alain's death. Lightly toying with the mat of hair on his chest, Micaela said admiringly, "I think it is a rather clever story that you so hastily concocted to explain everything."

"And I think it was rather clever of you, my sweet, to follow Alain and save my life and your brother's."

Micaela stretched like a cat, looking rather pleased with herself. "It was brave of me, was it not?" She glanced lovingly at him. "I told you I did not intend to become a young widow—I could hardly stand idly by while Alain murdered you, could I?" Her expression grew soft. "I love you, *mon amour*. Without you, my life would be nothing."

"Do you know," Hugh said thickly, "that I absolutely adore you?"

She kissed him warmly. Rubbing her nose against his, she murmured, "But not more than I adore you."

Contentedly they lay there together, their arms around each other. "It is strange, is it not," Micaela said after a while, "how things have ended. There were so many lies, so much deception and yet in the end, there is only love. When everything is taken into account, all the obstacles, all the pain and heartbreak and double-dealing, only love remains—ours for each other; *Maman*'s and John's for one another."

Hugh pulled her closer. "And that, sweetheart," he said fervently, "is just the way it should be and will always be for us. . . ."

*A Special Note
From
Shirlee Busbee
To You*

Dear Reader:

I hope that you have thoroughly enjoyed LOVE BE MINE. I have written several books that were situated in the New Orleans/Louisiana area around the time of the Louisiana Purchase, so LOVE BE MINE follows a long tradition.

As many of you may have noticed, I seem to alternate the settings of my books between the Louisiana/Texas area and England. And the time-frame I use most frequently, whether in America or England, is 1795-1815. Why those two places and that particular era? Who knows!

Seriously, my fascination with Louisiana started early: My Dad is from that area and though we were a military family and lived all over the world, many of Daddy's leaves were spent with his family in Baton Rouge, and of course, New Orleans. I remember Mardi Gras, sultry summer afternoons, soft, drawling voices, gumbo and pralines, the scent of magnolias and those huge, gnarled oaks, strew with ghostly gray-green Spanish moss. To an impressionable child it was an enchanting place. Spooky sometimes, too, which made it all the more appealing. I grew up hearing tales of going frogging in the swampy lowlands and catfishing in the bayous and of course, there were always warnings about of cottonmouths and alligators— wonderful stuff for a kid with a wild imagination.

As for England? Well, there you have me. I dunno. It's just a place that has mesmerized me for as long as I can remember. I joke about having lived a past life—in England, of course. As a wealthy, beautiful noblewoman, naturally! Does anybody *ever* dream they were a poor cobbler's wife in a previous life? I don't think so!

1

Explaining my love of the 1795-1815 time period is easy; so much was happening around the world then. There was the French Revolution; Napoleon's rise and the long wars with England that followed. It was the time of the Regency in England with all the fashion and foibles and memorable characters and mannerisms of the day. Closer to home, there was the Louisiana Purchase; the Lewis and Clark Expedition; the Barbary Pirates and the War of 1812 and that's just what I can think of off the top of my head! What writer *wouldn't* find the era teeming with possibilities for dozens of books?

The Napoleonic Wars alone provide great fodder for a writer and I have made shameless use of that period throughout my career. I mean when you need a wicked villain, who better than a spy for the French? Right? And when he is an Englishman . . . ooh, nasty, nasty.

If a little mystery and the desperate search for a murderous spy lurking in Regency Era London holds any appeal for you, you're gonna love FOR LOVE ALONE, which you can look for in the year 2000. FOR LOVE ALONE, isn't just about spies, of course, there is a strong element of romance, too. Gee, are you surprised? And while Ives and Sophy, the hero and heroine of FOR LOVE ALONE, are busy falling in love, they are also concerned with solving a murder or two, or three as the case may be, and trapping the dangerous spy *Le Renard*, The Fox.

I must warn you that Sophy Marlowe is *not* your usual Regency damsel. First she's a widow, who suffered an arranged marriage to an abusive husband, a much older husband, whose reputation was scandalous and whose only need from her was an heir. She quickly

2

learned to loathe the Marquise Marlowe and she eventually faced him down by coolly aiming a pistol at him with every intention of killing him—if necessary. When he dies unexpectedly, under suspicious circumstances, and she is free at last, she has no intention of *ever* marrying again. However, she is a practical young woman and if she were to change her mind, which is not likely but not impossible, she has sworn that the next time she marries it will be FOR LOVE ALONE. Doncha just love the way I snuck that in?

Ives, Viscount Harrington, was not born to the title. In fact, becoming Viscount Harrington was the farthest thing from his mind—he had been busy carving out an impressive military career fighting Napoleon's forces and had risen to the rank of Major. Becoming Viscount Harrington just never occurred to him—he was the son of a younger son and since his uncle had two strapping sons and his own father was in robust health, the likelihood of him inheriting the title seemed extremely doubtful. Of course. that was before *Le Renard* entered the picture. . . .

With his family wiped out in a tragic yachting accident, and having returned to England to take up the title and all that it entailed, the need for a wife and a heir became paramount in Ives's mind. The current crop of young ladies arouses no interest in his breast and he is utterly bored by London. Just when he is certain his quest is futile, a golden, laughing butterfly catches his eye. Now who do you think it was?

You're right, of course. The woman is Sophy, the notorious Lady Marlowe. She has brought her younger brother and sister to London for the season and just happened to be at the same function Ives had attended.

3

You'll find that Ives is a bold, audacious gentleman with devil-green eyes and a brigand's smile who brazenly pursues a lady who is perfectly capable of leveling a pistol at him—and does! Fascinated against his will by Sophy, he is impervious to insult. Not even the fact that there are rumors that Sophy may have murdered her husband, or the knowledge that her mother played a part in his adored older brother's death, impedes him. As for Sophy, she knows of Ives's search for a bride to bear him an heir and she wants nothing to do with him, thank you very much. Besides, he is absolutely *infuriating*

And that's just for starters. Don't forget about Le *Renard* and the murders—oh, and a kidnapping, too. If you want to learn how it all comes about you're just going to have to wait and read FOR LOVE ALONE.

all my very best —
Shirlee Busbee

4